AWARD-WINNING AUTHOR
J.L. DELAVEGA

SOLACE
BY
FIRE

THE REVERE TRILOGY

AWARD-WINNING AUTHOR

J.L. DELAVEGA

SOLACE
BY
FIRE

THE REVERE TRILOGY

SOLACE BY FIRE
The Revere Trilogy, Book Three

CITY OWL PRESS
www.cityowlpress.com

Cover Design by MiblArt. All stock photos licensed appropriately. Map illustration by Cartographybird Maps.

Edited by Tee Tate.

For information on subsidiary rights, please contact the publisher at info@cityowlpress.com.

Print Edition ISBN: 978-1-64898-531-7

Digital Edition ISBN: 978-1-64898-532-4

Printed in the United States of America

CITY OWL PRESS
Escape Your World ♦ Get Lost in Ours

PRAISE FOR J.L. DELAVEGA

"Each character in the cast is strong, clever, and flawed in their own way, but the ways in which they work together and supported each other was truly the heart of the story. We need more creative, thoughtful, empowering books like these." — Lilla Glass, author of *The Unseen*

"A thrilling and substantial page-turner of a fantasy adventure, set in a rough and gritty frontier where mining is king and a weapon might be a girl's best friend. A solid debut and beginning of a series!" — Karen Eisenbrey, author of *Daughter of Magic*

"An action filled adventure with a core of strong-gunned and stronger-willed female characters, I couldn't put it down. In essence a story about staking a claim in a world that aims at crushing you, *Smoke and Other Storms* shows that no matter what sparkles in the desert, it's family that you need to survive." — Florence A. Bliss, *Taken by His Sword*

"Delavega has an incredible knack for worldbuilding and character development that doesn't feel forced. You're dropped into the world right off the bat, and J.L. just keeps adding more coal (or in this case, crystals) to the train boiler and doesn't let up. I have a whole new appreciation for the Western genre because of *Smoke and Other Storms*, and I can't wait to see where J.L. Delavega takes us next in the series!" — Derek Borne, author of *The Ultimate Agent*

"*Ash Like Vengeance*, the follow-up to a brilliant first book of the series, this doesn't disappoint. Here, the author delves deeply into the inner workings of the characters. The actions are there but it is the thoughts that drive them that carry the meaning. The rich detail done in intricate fashion makes this a book you can sink your teeth into. There are times when you feel you are trying to survive on the rim yourself." — N.N. Heaven, author of *Princess of the Light*

To all the friends that have come and gone.
I remember you.

AUTHOR'S NOTE

The underlying theme of these books has always been ghosts.

What haunts us more than love?

At the end of our time with the Reveres, they have become family to me. I wrote *Smoke and Other Storms* as a bloody love letter to myself—the introvert, the weird sister, the yearning. Because we need more books about platonic love. More books for adults that explore the importance and heartbreak of friendship and siblings, more introverts and women over 25 as the main character. And for fuck's sake, more westerns where angry women are more than just a revenge-quest love interest.

I really hoped SAOS would become my first published work, knowing it was not for everyone, but I did hope at least one person would love my vicious ladies. Finding you has been its own reward.

I may have started out writing just for me, but if you have loved someone, if you're a seeker like Adelaide, if you want more than what the patriarchy tells you to be, these books are also for you.

I thank you for the time you've spent on the Rim, because we all know Adelaide won't.

It's been my absolute pleasure. See you down another road.

Sol,

J.L. Delavega

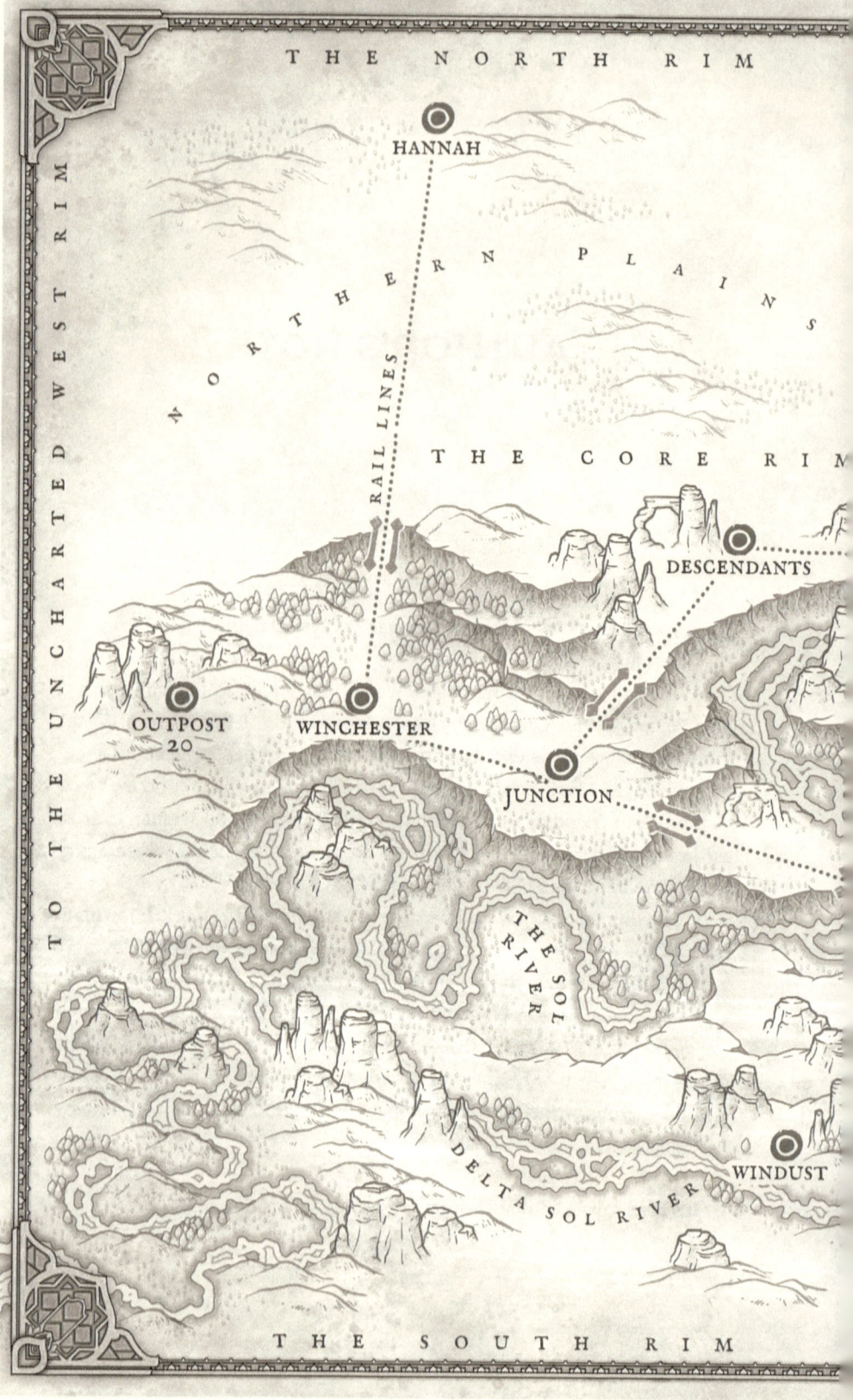

THE DESERT TERRITORY OF

THE RIM

- IN THE GREATER -
REPUBLIC OF DELILAH

VANTAGE

WALLIS

THE SALT WASTES

LIDEON

OATH

COVENANT

DAMASCUS

THE DAMASCUS RANGE

"The Rim, like any land, is older than everything we know. Older than us, older than the Tov Shadow Nation, older than whatever came before them. Nothing that's here is forever, and nothing that's here was the first.
What walked here before all of us?
I like to think they were monstrous, and at night I like to think that they are not here anymore."

–from the diary of Amnesty Hellana Wells,
co-creator of the Pestilence, a first settler of Eden *
(* in what is now the West Rim, private land owned and leased by Von Kane Industries)

ARRIVAL

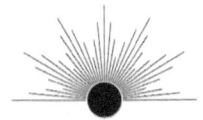

There is a Season for everything.

For storms and for vengeance. One for mended futures, and one of broken hearts.

One of mercy, and one that shatters.

A time for dawn and another by moons.

A Season that rises.

And a Season that ends.

My name is Adelaide Revere. Grandma read that poem to me once.

I hope whoever wrote it wasn't a liar.

Welcome to the West Rim.

PART ONE

NOTHING BUT THIEVES

ONE
ADELAIDE

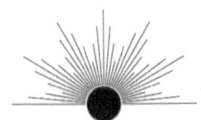

I once told you, I have two shadows. One of them is from sun. The other is there even in the dark.

Leagan wears a leather welding harness to hang off the ribs of the *Exodus Ironclad*. Our train. A jar of white paint is holstered on her hip, splatters of it on her face, hands.

I hold the tension line so she doesn't fall into the wind. Air floods the pages of her books and weapon designs as a cascade of steam rolls past the open slide door.

"There." Leagan wraps her leg around the doorframe for leverage, and I walk the tension line in. "Do you like it?"

I check for rocks, then lean out to see her finished work.

The lady has a skeleton face, curly hair piled over it from lines of welded metal. Now she glows, moonlight white on black.

The weight of the wind pushes against the air in my lungs. Sun cracks across the red surface of the Rim, rock shadows and canyons a web of dark scars. They all point one way.

The striated cliffs that were faint shadows yesterday are blue and orange and not so far away now.

The West Rim.

The Stranger beats in my throat, my stomach empty and longing. Reaching.

"You're right." I pull myself back inside and bolt the armor-plated slide door. "You can see it better painted white."

"And now she looks kind of like you," Leagan says. "If Aunt Tess gets mad, I don't care. Thanks for helping me. You can go give Raleigh his breakfast now, before he complains that he's starving to death."

It's time to make sure Raleigh is still alive.

Three hundred.

The roll of the *Exodus Ironclad*'s wheels is louder within the metal plates enclosing the car crossings than in the open wind. I raise my fist to the iron-banded door of the spare car. Two knocks.

"Who is it?" Green asks somewhere behind the peekhole.

He knows.

"Let her in."

Seven.

The car stinks like men.

"Pleasant morning, Stranger." Green's dead man's gaze trails me from the bunk he sits hunched on, nothing pleasant about it.

This living space was good enough for the Exodus Company men who left their blood to haunt the floor. It's good enough for him and his hired guns.

"Your visitor's here," the one posted by the open bathroom says. "Hurry up, you've got no one to impress here."

Raleigh steps out, dabbing flecks of shave cream off his chin. "Just because I'm a hostage doesn't mean I have to look like one. Greetings, Adelaide."

I move closer and Green watches.

Seven —

He shifts his stony shoulders, so do the guns staggered around the car. They all face me.

"Three feet away, same as yesterday," Green says.

Like you said yesterday, the Stranger says, her voice a dark echo, a shade of my own.

I stop, face Raleigh, then circle him. Slow.

"I'm all right," he says.

I'll make up my own mind. The Stranger picks apart his collar, open from shaving. Rolled white sleeves and satin suspenders, pink like crushed rose petals. No blood. No bruises. Visible ones, at least.

"You know in any other circumstances this would be considered creepy." His smile feels real. "What did you bring me today?"

I hold out the tray. Eggs and a biscuit. Pear jam. Coffee.

"Did you make these, or did Tess?"

"I did."

"Alkaline, I can tell. They're fluffy."

I stand where I am while he eats it. I look at Green. He looks back, and every time he breathes, the muscles stringing his neck to his shoulders pull tighter.

"Don't you have somewhere more important to be?" he asks. "You won't intimidate me this way. I'm not afraid of you. Any of you. You least of all."

If that were true you wouldn't have to say it.

"The Raven used you as her shadow puppet and that spook tactic worked on fools from back east, but you're only a sad façade that no one else will ever want around."

"Well that's rude and uncalled for," Raleigh says. "You ask if she has somewhere more important to be, but if that's true, you should actually be honored she's chosen to be here with you right now. Think about it."

A scoff peaks in Green's throat, cools quick. "It's safe to say none of us are comfortable with this situation, but that's a luxury for another day. If we all do our jobs for the Von Kane Company, we protect our futures. You're all smart enough to see that. Remember why we're here."

The Stanger taints the car in all shades of black, seeping into nostrils, smoke none of them can see.

Maybe you don't always remember, but I haven't forgotten anything.

I remember little pins of sweat along your nose, breath too shallow, eyes too black when you would look at Vesta.

I remember how loyal Grandma was to you, delivering you favors even when we didn't need your work anymore. She took that reservation you framed us with because she believed in honor. She died for it.

Aunt Tess and I don't.

Maybe I'll die for the opposite of it.

Raleigh's eaten two thirds of his breakfast. Even if one of Green's bone pickers steal the plate from him now, he won't be hungry. He just won't get to finish his coffee.

I smile at him before I go. Only him.

Three.

My passing stare chips off Green like a rock. "The Widow says we're stopping in Junction."

If you get out, she'll leave you.

TWO
TESLA

WHO RIDES ON THE LONG, BLACK SNAKE CALLED THE *EXODUS IRONCLAD*?

The women who took that snake from men and made her theirs. So know our names.

It's Revere, by the way, if you're hideously behind on the news.

Fuck me, this night was long, but nothing is as perfect as watching the sun set blood on the rails ahead of you, then seeing it rise once more at your back, pink as a fresh promise rose.

I lock the firebox, should any pickers somehow get through the *Exodus*'s armor with ideas about stealing her. A train is no good without fuel, and a pressure system doesn't work with a hole in it.

This is Junction and train jackings aren't so commonplace here. But even the safer corners—by the Rim's standards—have a sharper edge now that the hungry have bled out of Hannah.

It doesn't feel so long ago that we were here, meeting with Kane to sell the guns in the freight cars and waiting for the Boneyard makers to finish the living quarter upgrades we bought.

She has a stable car full of oxen, goats, chickens, and quail from Covenant. Horses for Adelaide, a lab for Navy, weapon workshop for Leagan. And for me? I touch my cheek to her warm side. All of this is the way to what I've always sought since I was a girl, a life that's mine to live exactly the way I please.

Navy inserts her hand into mine for guidance instead of her strolling cane, her goggles blacked out against the morning sun. "My last letter from Dr. Pike said things have gotten bad in Winchester."

"Would it have hurt him to be more specific?"

"I don't know. All he said was it's too bad to stay and rebuild his shop anymore." Navy squeezes my hand, and inside her pocket where her other one is tucked, paper crackles. "I was hoping we could visit Vesta's grave. But if things are that dangerous...maybe we shouldn't stop."

I'd hoped the same thing, like a good mother should, but this gives me the excuse to not think too solidly about how she's buried in the ground out there instead of with me.

"We can wave and blow a kiss to her as we go by," I say. "She'd still like that."

"She'd like it better if we all stood around her grave and read sad poems that reminded us of her."

"Yes, she definitely would." A little tear stings my eye. But the grief is comforting in its own twisted way, a reminder that I haven't forgotten her.

I know there are more tears on the way, more painful ones when we pass through Winchester, where my lovely daughter spent her last days of this life, the town that Adelaide burned to the ground in her name.

"Someday we'll do that too."

Adelaide joins us just before the station, where a crowd of men with stooped necks and crusty hands wait. They'll provide the digging tools and demo sticks if we provide the food, lodging, wages, and protection. That was our agreement.

A stack of crates as high as the station wall fills the loading platform.

"Those must be our men," I say. "They look dirty and strong, the way real miners should." I clear my throat. "Hello, boys, say the right name and a ride on the *Exodus Ironclad* is yours."

One of them in crossback suspenders rife with tool clips steps out from the clot of them. He has white Tov hair, shaved to the scalp on both sides and braided down the center line. A dangerous look for someone who sunburns so easily. His scalp is red to prove my point.

Daithe *dox* Noe, the crew boss.

"*Sol, so*, boss," he says, to *me*.

The word puts a warm thrill in my belly.

He gives me a somewhat disturbing smile. All his teeth are filed into points. "Trains are never on time, but here you are, so punctual."

"Here we are," I say. "Last chance to change your mind."

"I already cooked the deserters last night." Daithe says with another toothy grin. "And shit out what was left of them this morning."

I was warned about his manners before we met, and he's certainly leaning into the Tov cannibal stereotypes, I suppose a little like Mother did when she was acting as a fortune teller.

But it's his reputation for literally being able to smell crystal I'm interested in.

"For a chance to dig into the West Rim, my boys and I would sell our own mothers to a bone picker," he says.

"Well, lucky for her, you met me, and it won't come to that." When I turn, Green is standing in the shadow of the train, watching. Fucking snake. Well, let him look. He can stew on what I'm up to for the rest of the ride. "The thirteenth through seventeenth cars are for you and your crew. The slide doors should already be open."

"Thirteenth." He echoes with a pleased nod, and snaps his fingers at his men with the counterweight winch. "Give us a few hours, and we'll be onboard."

Miners are superstitious about numbers, dirt, and who touches their tools, and it's fine by me if they do all the loading work.

"I don't know what you girls have planned next, but I need to go sleep," I say. "My body doesn't forgive me for staying up all night anymore."

Adelaide's face softens by a few degrees as she stops watching Daithe.

"I can take over at the engine when it's time to leave here—" She abandons whatever she was about to say next, her chin lifting. The sun-squint between her eyebrows re-thickens into a scowl. "Navy."

"Yes?"

"Did Pike ask where we were going to be?"

"No, why?"

"He's here."

"Where?"

"Coming this way."

I've never seen the man, but I scour the new faces swarming across the platform for one who doesn't look like a miner, but an educated man. They have their own scent. Both do, actually.

And I see one.

He has to wait for an opening in the cascade of miners to reach us. His clothes are tidy, the way a doctor should look. An efficient white collar, tan duster, and short clipped salt and pepper hair. He holds a single duffel with scraped knuckles, the one piece of him that doesn't fit.

"What's his full name again?" I ask Navy.

"Jacob Pike."

The man who tried yet failed to save my daughter's life.

"Well, speak of a devil, we were just talking about you," I say before he can. "You must have heard the summons, Dr. Jacob Pike."

"I hope you don't take my arrival as suspicious, I heard you were coming this way." He glances at Adelaide, but she holds her shoulder toward him, chin out toward the horizon like he isn't here. "I'm here to offer my assistance with your project, Navy. The pestilence has terrorized the West Rim long enough, and Winchester is no longer a home for me."

"I'd be glad to have your help," Navy says.

"What a surprise treat." I start to offer him my hand.

But I forgot, again. I don't have that hand anymore, thanks to Montoya and his poison knife. I swear I still see it sometimes, my haunted arm. It even itches like it's still here. At least I'm still here, and I am grateful for that, it's just very jarring to look down and see half of my limb missing.

I slip the hand I do have from Navy's grasp.

Not to gloat or anything, but having him around will boost the legitimacy of Navy's pestilence cure in the eyes of foolish men. I believe in her with all my heart, but let's not forget we're here to win this strategy game. And until the day the Republic—and the world—are ready to accept the word of a woman without questions, I don't care how many alliances we have to fake, so long as we get what we earned in the end.

I nod with my gaze to Pike's scraped hand. "What's wrong in Winchester?"

"First it burned, then the survivors from Hannah started trickling through. That's when the bone pickers took over. They killed whoever wasn't necessary, but I treated several of them and so they let me go. I left before they changed their minds about that."

"They're still there?"

"Unless something makes them leave."

THREE
ADELAIDE

WINCHESTER IS A CORPSE, ALL BLACK AND CHARRED ON THE TOP OF THE RED bluff.

But it still smells like the juniper that grows thick here.

From the engine, the first hand-painted sign breaks from the red and gold landscape. A red X on bleached wood. *EXPLOSIVES ON THIS TRACK. PAY 2000 GOLD STANDARD OR SOMETHING ELSE GOOD TO PASS.*

I close another valve, the pull of the drag under my feet as the *Exodus* slows naturally on the grade.

Leagan enters the engine.

"Is Aunt Tess awake?"

"I don't know." She turns back. "I'll check."

Another sign.

NO TURNING BACK. PAY.

The actual blockade is just a flat lumber car and sharpened sticks hammered into the ground to block the track. Maybe a few pieces of burned metal. A line of men file out from between berms of burned wood stacked for cover, shotguns and rifles held up for us to see. Eleven of them.

None of this would stop us.

The *Exodus* comes to rest, huffing, an impatient iron horse.

I lower the binoculars as Aunt Tess opens the door, socks on her feet, boots trailing from her hand by the laces. The air changes to taste like her black currant jasmine perfume.

"What do they have for us?" She laughs drily once she looks. "Oh, darling, not nearly enough."

Leagan takes the binoculars from her next, kneels in the fireseat.

"We should be far enough away not to derail if we do accidentally hit the explosives with the standing gun," Aunt Tess says. "We could try to negotiate, but I don't feel like wasting time today, do you?"

I never like negotiating.

"I know what you're thinking," she says. "It's the least we can do for Winchester, put it out of its final misery."

"I'll be the top gun," I say.

"That one runs hot," Leagan says. "Watch out. If you shoot too fast it might jam."

Three.

I glance to Aunt Tess's boots. "Do you want help with those?"

She wavers. "I like the way the warm floor feels."

"I do too."

"Okay." She sighs, dropping into the engineer's leather seat and shoving her feet into the boots. "I just need you to tie the laces. Like a two-year-old."

I take her foot into my lap. "Maybe one of those guys has boots with buttons we can steal."

"Not after they've touched his gnarly feet. No, ma'am." Aunt Tess stands again. "Thank you, my dear."

One-sixty-two.

It takes almost ten minutes for the pressure in the standing gun's boiler to build enough steam to fire. I wait for the pressure gauge to rise to the red level, hear the trigger snap tight above before I mount the ladder. The snap of the hatch bolt letting go reverberates down the metal belly of the first gun car, nothing soft in here to absorb it.

I crawl up slow, staying low in the gunner's hole instead of standing. Topside the air is stiff and hot, like a sunburn. Alive with the buzz of insects, the breath of the engine. The Stranger bleeds off me.

With the sun at my back blinding them, they don't see me slowly center the gun's triangular sight on the line of them, stomach height. My teeth tighten along with my fists as I squeeze the trigger and rake them.

Feet dive for cover, dust blooms.

Nothing's audible past the residual jolt of the gun ringing through my bones and ear mufflers. I swing the muzzle past the steam stack and fire again.

One shot manages to rip past me. I sweep back the way I came, then drop inside the gunner's hole.

Leagan stands at the bottom of the ladder. "A couple of the miners are going out to clear the explosives. I'm going to use the first side gun here. We can cover them together."

I nod. I still have the best vantage from up there, but she'll be able to stop anyone on that side who tries to shoot at me.

I rise behind the foot shield again and angle the gun's revolving barrel left, the side where I'm most exposed.

Three miners walk out of my blind spot directly below the car, carrying a shotgun, shovel and bucket. Daithe is one of them.

His shaved teeth make my stomach crawl. Nice of him to enforce the idea we eat people.

The Stranger senses something change before I see motion. I fire at the closest blackened wall, what used to be the freight station. The bullets come ripping out the other side.

Unlike other trains, the *Exodus* has an engine at both ends. If the rail does blow up, we have the option of turning back without a switchtrack. But we need to get to the West Rim.

Daithe crawls under the flat car until it's swallowed him from the waist up. He passes an arm out, a single demo stick, brown and sick looking. I'm sure it still works.

The other places it in the bucket and carries it off track toward the fringe of the juniper grove.

The Stranger ticks like the engine.

A muffled thud hits my chest and a rust-red cloud hangs long after the first spew of dirt falls back down.

"Did they blow themselves up?" Leagan asks.

"No." I catch a white glimpse of his undershirt as a miner returns to the track. "I think that was on purpose."

They don't find anything else.

"Well that was exciting," Leagan says. "These big guns don't take any skill, it's just accuracy by volume."

"But you still like them."

I don't mean to look, but the Stranger turns.

My shoulder comes to rest against the doorframe, slats of sunlight starting to peek through the iron shutters as the sun sinks west. The layered *Delta Sol* canyons on the other side of Once-Winchester.

"She's out there, isn't she?" Leagan says.

I nod.

Vesta's grave. Her ghost a wound in my chest that isn't healing.

"At least you got to be with her," Leagan says. "She was scared of dying alone. I'm sure having you there made her feel better."

She didn't seem scared at all.

I still think about it all the time.

ONE-FIFTY.

The bell above the speaking tube trembles when I enter the engine. A shivering gold sound in case no one notices the panel of ghost quartz filled glass beads lighting up, milk-green when the switch is flipped in the corresponding car.

Aunt Tess rolls her brown eyes. It doesn't hide the red tear-tells, but I don't mention them. "Oh, alkaline."

"Ignore him."

"I know I should." She clenches her fingers into a fist. "But I can't." The mouthpiece cover clips the wall, the sound same as snap of her tone. "What?"

"Are we still waiting for your men to clear the rail?" Green's voice rings from the tube. Hollow, iron as the plating in between us.

"Worried about keeping your bosses waiting, are we?" Aunt Tess sneers. "I'm willing to go faster so you can lick their assholes sooner, but you'll owe me for the extra fuel."

"There's no need to get nasty. I'm just asking a question."

"Like *farce* you are. Enjoy the scenery, Green, we'll get there as soon as we get there."

The cover claps so hard it bounces back and doesn't latch.

"Stranger, will you take over?" She stalks into the engineer's bathroom, a toilet and sink mounted close enough to hit your knees on. Her exhale echoes off the papered walls. "I want that snake-fucker off my train."

FOUR
TESLA

My mother used to say progress is an inescapable wheel, and those who resist are crushed by it. She was mostly right.

For those who fear change, it is a threat. A monstrous storm bearing down to reduce everything you hold dear to dust. But for those of us who strive, it's another future, bright and calling.

Both can agree, though, progress is a bitch. Immortal and unkillable. And either way, we choose how we greet her.

Part of my future died in Winchester. It lies in the blood-red earth with my lovely Vesta.

Now Winchester lies in similar ruin. Blackened bones and ash hearts that echo silence, roofs collapsed while chimneys cling to the sky. But the juniper groves whisper the songs of everything that can never die. Birds nesting in the branches, the scent of berries spread wide by the sun, and poppies pushing aside the charred grass. Good things come back to life in the end.

The wheels clack as Adelaide gets them moving again.

I won't set foot near Vesta's grave with Green haunting my train like an odor. He doesn't deserve to spit near her, much less know where she rests.

"Someday, my love. You made me so happy." My kiss gets ripped away by the wind, the railing of the water reserve hard as grief against my stomach.

There's no dramatic thunderclap, nothing will change this. We just glide away from what's left of Winchester. Us, the *Exodus*, and that bitch named progress, the hungriest of man-made desires.

·

I STILL REMEMBER WHAT I FELT THE DAY I STEPPED OFF THE TRAIN THAT brought us to the Rim.

First, I was sun blind after being sealed in a freight car for days. Then by the stench of Descendants, which is a punch to the nose. Somehow it was worse than the inside of that freight car, with the sun's heat steadily boiling the toilet bucket and some people who'd already lost too much hope to even bother using it.

When the fire tears stopped bleeding from my eyes, I saw red hills for the first time. Dirt back east is just brown. There were cactuses the size of pear trees, the kind I'd seen drawings of, but here they were, real. Maybe the sky was the same size in my hometown, but the world felt so small back there. The Rim was large. I was what was small.

Wonder opened inside me, that a place so dry and desolate, yet just as full of life as the sunflower farms in Saint Laura County, could possibly exist. Impossible hope surged past the fear of my destination—the Descendants flesh market—and I knew beyond shadows that if I was determined enough, I could live however I wanted here.

And I have.

I feel that again, feet planted on the West Rim. It reeks of all possibilities.

At the moment, it just reeks of my full seal respirator, the hardened leather and brass filter drums sitting heavy as an insult against my face. Technically, we crossed the unspoken border of the West Rim three hours after we left Winchester behind, but I waited to put it on.

Leagan pulls the strap one notch tighter, and the gum seal finally suctions to my skin. "I still say these are a load of lizard shit. If the Wells poisoned Lake Amnesty with the pestilence, the toxins are just as likely to seep through your skin or be in groundwater."

"It won't hurt you to wear it just in case I'm wrong about my hotspot theory," Navy says.

"It might," Leagan says. "You don't know. What if I sit too close to the campfire and it melts to my face?"

"Then don't sit too close to the campfire. My cure isn't a cure yet. We should only drink water from the reclaimers once the *Exodus*'s reservoir runs dry, and try not to touch too much dirt until—"

"But I wanted to bury myself in dirt."

"Not until we've tested our...poison diviners? What sounds better? Contamination gauges?"

"Poison compass," Leagan says. "It rolls off the tongue nicer."

"This isn't about precautions, it's misdirection," I say. "The masks keep your project a secret and that's an advantage I'm not going to waste. In fact, I fully intend to exploit it."

The *Exodus* continues to bleed steam into the wind as her boiler settles. It coils around my walking skirt, past Leagan in her patched coveralls and Navy, hidden under her veil, and along the freshly gouged dirt, loose with orange rock.

Across the dry canyon spans the half-completed crosshatch ribwork of a new trestle bridge, still dripping the sugar-sweet and flame-resistant black taffy pitch of birth, but the forward railroad camp hasn't crossed it yet.

Up on the workline, the steam-fed hammer drops its weighted arm on another railroad spike and the ground beneath my feet trembles.

Navy flinches. "What is that?"

"Behold, the modern age."

The next hit makes her jump a second time. "Mr. Green isn't going to let Raleigh go even now that we're here, is he?"

"He doesn't deserve to be called *Mr.*," Leagan scoffs.

"It's just habit."

Down the line of freight cars, Green slithers into his overcoat. The gentle brown wool might be enough to fool other men, but not me, he's just a snake wearing a gentleman's skin. He stops to look up at Leagan's lady death sigil on the *Exodus*'s side.

I felt the taste of my mouth go foul. "Fuck, you summoned him."

"I didn't mean to."

"Let's go, before he catches up with us."

He does though, damnation. Navy can only walk so fast with her seeing cane to guide her, and this is exceptionally uneven ground. I know it's not her fault.

"Hey!" My whistle is barely sharp enough to cut through my mask and noise of the railroad crews as he passes us. "Since you were in such a hurry to get here, you can get your shit off my train by the time the sun goes down tonight."

"Patience is a virtue lost on the guilty, Widow," Green says. "Until those munitions are in the hands of those who rightly paid for them, I'm here to make sure you don't run to a better offer."

"What kind of offer would that be?"

Green edges ahead of me again. "I couldn't say."

"Asshole."

I let Navy fall behind, Leagan's with her, and reach the survey tent before Green does by cutting between a row. It's ballroom broad and peaked with two center poles holding up the beige canvas, the shadow of Von Kane money thrown over the rest of us.

The white magnolia and sunburst flag of the Republic snaps on each gust of wind, and riding the same pole just below it, a deep blue one emblazoned with *VKI*. Von Kane Industries. Their own flag, how official.

Green reappears while I'm still working to unbutton the tent's stiff outer flap with one hand. "It makes sense if I speak to Von Kane first."

"Does it?" I keep myself between him and the door as the billowing canvas continues to fight back. I have the last button lined up when the wind shudders the flap and it slips the hole again.

The oil of Green's presence creeps through my mask. His hand latches onto my upper arm, igniting a spark shower that shoots into fingers that aren't there anymore. I swear I taste a little blood come up the back of my throat.

"*Don't*. Touch me."

"You're still nothing but a bone picker, Widow. These men will tolerate you long enough to get what they want, then they will throw you to a shallow grave." He releases me.

The rage flushes through my cheek scar this time.

"Touch me again, and I'll shove that hand up your ass into your pea brain."

Dust rises from the beaten path to the half-formed trestle, the wooden legs of compass tripods bouncing behind saddles.

I fold what's left of my arm into the other, the sleeve tied with a red bow around the end of it. "I believe *that's* the man we're looking for."

"Remember," Green hisses, "a blood feud will only hurt our businesses now."

"I know." The words grip my tongue like honey, the taste my mother used to hide the bitterness of cough medicine when I was young. "The Von Kanes will never accept either of us. There's a shallow grave with your name on it too. But at least we both know who we are."

The honey never worked.

He nods. "We take our place by other means."

By any means.

Sometimes you have to do things that sicken you in the moment to get what you want in the end.

Anyone who says otherwise has never truly had their survival at stake. All those good and righteous people who disagree would be surprised at what they're willing to do, and how quickly nothing else matters, when it's your life on the line. Do you think I enjoyed sucking off men as a fifteen-year-old because I smiled at them? I was smart enough to see making them feel wanted would get me favors.

After that, a little lying to your enemies is easy. That smile was the lie. But I look at Green now and all I can think about is my mother's blood around my nails and the trench in my heart where her and Vesta's memories lie.

It's not as easy as I like to believe.

Kane dismounts before they ride close enough to put dust on us. The wind does it for them.

Crystal baron Jonathaniel Swann is with him, dressed in a pale linen suit with red dirt patches all over the knees. He throws his arms wide as he hops from the saddle. "Tesla Revere! One of four exceptionally lovely ladies, you have finally arrived. Is this not glorious?"

"Glad you made it," Kane says.

"That sounds like surprise," I say. "Did you doubt me?"

"A little."

"Some lessons have to be learned the hard way. I'm proud of you, Von Kane. You've come a long way from the star-eyed east blood we first met. We might make a survivor of the Rim out of you yet."

"I know you didn't do all this for me."

"No." My gaze draws to Navy and Leagan approaching on the main drag. "Not for you."

Green clears his throat.

"Is something wrong?" Kane asks.

I get the feeling he's referring to something specific being wrong, not a general malaise, but Green's been miles away with us the last two cycles. What could he possibly know?

"I have a few matters to speak to your father about," Green says. "Is he here or out on another one of his excursions?"

"We expect him back from the east any day now." Kane holds back the tent flap. "Let's get out of the sun, but Tesla, can we talk for a moment?"

"Of course." I pull on my syrup voice and feel Green flash me a glare. Ha ha, I'm invited in, and you are not, and you can go fuck yourself with that.

I hold back for Navy and Leagan to go in ahead of me. "This way, girls."

Jonathaniel follows too. Men with money as thick as his go wherever they please without being invited. Green's still wise enough to know the difference, and I hope it burns being the only one left out in the sun.

The tent isn't any cooler than outside, the scent of baked canvas and warm wood seeping through my mask like resin. It's nice, actually.

"How much do you want?" Kane asks.

"No small talk. My, my, you have changed. I mentioned before the price is negotiable. What are these guns worth to you?"

"That's—" Kane halts to glance over his shoulder much like Navy did as the spike hammer falls in the background. Odd for a man who should be used to hearing that sound by now. "Give me a few hours to round up the right men, but we'll get the guns unloaded and out of your way as soon as possible."

"You still don't have the gold to pay us."

"No," he says.

"Well then, I think we'd better wait for your father." I circle past him. "I have something else in mind for payment, but only he can give it to me."

What are you afraid of, Timothy Von Kane? Why do you flinch? And why do you need so many guns?

"I have the gold," Jonathaniel says. "I am willing to invest more, just say the word, my man." He pats Kane's arm on the way to the teapot chilling over the pig stove, Ven crystal burning cold and blue in its iron belly. "I'll take the five-hundred acres west of here in exchange, then you won't have to split any of your leased parcels."

He wants what I want. The main Eden mine. Of course someone with his resources would know exactly where it is.

"I'm not making any decisions today," Kane says.

"Smart," I say. "We'll all wait for your father."

"If it's more gold you're after, ladies, I have a proposition for you as well," Jonathaniel says. "I'm still in need of some bodyguards, and although this endeavor might be constipated for standards at the moment, I am not. Nor am I under the exclusive protection contract with the Green Company. Keep me alive, and I'll keep your pockets glistening."

"I'll mention it to the girls," I say. "We'll vote on it."

"How delightfully democratic. I'll try to wait patiently, although I doubt my proficiency in that virtue very much."

"Jonathaniel!" Leagan says suddenly. "I'm going out to look for scavenger lizards. When I find some, I'll let you see them."

"Please do," he says. "And one of these days, you will have to take me on the hunt with you."

"Okay," she says. "Just be careful, they have very sharp teeth and never stop eating."

I round the drafting table laid out in the center of the tent, everything paper staked down with rocks, lanterns and brass cartography instruments smudged with consistent use. "Your father didn't go back east, did he?" Don't think the choice of words slid by me. "Don't worry, I won't tell anyone, and you don't have to tell me."

I level my gaze on Kane. He stands so very straight, like a lone post about to snap under its load. "We want land. Put it in our name, with a legal deed, and the guns and ammo are yours."

Saying it out loud unleashes a thrum of excitement through my skin. Land. *Our* land.

"How much?" he asks.

"Well, Mr. Swann here just asked you for the five-hundred acres west of here if he paid for the guns. He knows what he's doing, so we'll take that."

"You clever minx." Jonathaniel shakes his head, and I flip him the engineer's salute. "Though be warned, I have the copper to outbid you in any negotiation."

"I told you I'm not making any decisions today," Kane says. "But I'll let my father know what your asking price is."

"Fair enough. In the meantime, you should come by the train for dinner sometime. She doesn't like people to know, but Adelaide makes an alkaline bean soup. It's the least we can do."

Kane's shoulders soften a little, not so braced for a blow.

"Here." Leagan tugs a box of bullets from her pocket. "These are for you. I did something special to them."

Kane takes the box with caution. "Do I need to be scared?"

"Only if you shoot yourself in the foot."

"Well, thank you…"

"They explode on impact."

"I'll be careful."

"Well." I move to clasp my hands together, then realize my mistake and clasp my arm instead. "You looked like you were just out on a survey. I bet you're tired so we won't keep you any longer, I just had one more thought." I lean in so Kane's ear is close to mine. "Green rode here with us on the *Exodus*, and he thinks he gets to stay on board with us. Without spilling the guts, I want him off my train today. If you can make that happen, I'll give you a full crate of ammo and six rifles in advance."

Kane nods. "I'll see what I can do."

FIVE
ADELAIDE

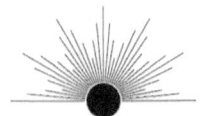

HER NAME IS NIGHTMARE.

She glistens in the sharp sun. Dappled like smoke on a pale sky, her face and legs bathed solid black.

I don't have to give her back to some stable hand at the end of the rental cycle and wonder if the next person to ride her will be cruel.

She's mine. And I'll always take care of her.

Leagan and I dismount, climb down a tier of red rock to a spur reaching over the canyon.

Forty-nine.

The West Rim. Orange sprouted with pale green, blue against red, hills against mountains. The Stranger is so tight in my throat I barely have space to breathe.

"You're meant to be here," Leagan says. "I can tell. *I* love it too."

"I know." A hundred thoughts fall on top of each other like pages of a book.

I'm back.

Back with the east bloods hammering right behind me. Beads of rock tremble on the stone around my boots each time the weight drops. But I made it. That's what matters.

Aunt Tess likes challenges, but I like things I don't have to share. I brought myself here to see the West Rim again, then watch it get ripped away from me by men of progress.

It already burns.

But they won't, the Stranger says. *They are going to die. All of them.*

Everybody dies eventually.

Two-seventy-nine.

Lower still. Heat presses over the basin like a lid.

I dig a section of the slope loose with my heel, and pick one of the glass tubes and chemical spoon from Navy's bandoleer. Leagan wears it now.

I feed the dirt to the vial, label the coordinates.

The beaded, red succulent pulls free of a crevice with no resistance. A fresh vial, another label. The baby spawn of wild rosemary fights a little harder, bark peeling as I twist the forceps.

Inside my sleeve, the chemical burn where the flash fire ran down the back of my arm has become scars. Dusk purple and red, mottled like lace. It strains, the skin too tight whenever I move my wrist.

At least Montoya got what was coming to him. Now he's a meaningless streak of ash in the bigger pile of ash that's Hannah now.

Leagan walks through the first band of sage with her new contamination compass, hand outstretched. "Nothing."

We pull our masks off.

"Come on." My boots sink through the top crust into deeper sand. If we go far enough, maybe we can escape the pulse of the railroad hammer.

Rooms with too many people in them, places like Hannah and Vantage, are lonely. Out here, there's no one to remind me I don't belong. Parts of me open that I always hold shut.

Eight-hundred-fifty —

The compass in my pocket clicks. Metallic, shuddering like wings.

The scratch of Leagan's boots halts with mine.

The filmy liquid in the face of my contamination compass isn't white anymore. It's green.

Five.

I back away, sticking the gum borders of the mask back to my face.

A ripple of gray fur pokes through gaps in the sagebrush. A dead rabbit. Eaten through the belly, skinned raw from the neck up. Flat yellow teeth jut from its frozen jaw, lidless eye staring through the maggots at the blue overhead.

The Stranger pulls tight, something equally dead in my stomach as I hold my contamination compass toward the once-rabbit. The needle flicks up. Once, click. Twice, three clicks.

"Oh," Leagan says. "He is *dead* dead."

"At least we know the compasses work." I pull a yellow flowering weed from the mix of rock and dirt.

Using her chemical spoon, Leagan fills another vial with dirt from under the dead rabbit, traces of gray fur mixed with it. "Beware, the bandoleer of science. It kills...Don't look now, I'm going to cut his eye out. Navy needs more wet samples."

The wind rips across us, prying at the plants in the fragile crust, filling my clothes. On it, the putrid scent of rotting flesh. I doubt something as thin as this rabbit could reek enough to pierce my mask. His insides are already gone.

"Leagan, do you smell that?"

Sixty.

Vultures scatter into the sky with a joint scream. A circle has been trampled in the red dirt. In the center is the carcass of an oxen. Its horns are broken, splintered around him. Strips of flesh tremble on the broken ribcage, his legs twisted in different directions, everything soft inside removed same as the rabbit. But feeding scavenger lizards and mountain cats don't crush bones.

Leagan halts just short of me. "Oh fuck."

The Stranger tightens up again.

We are being watched.

Fifteen.

I reach the circle but don't allow my boots to touch it. My contamination compass crackles again.

Cloven hoof prints. The circle is a track, another animal driven around this one over and over.

"Another one ate him. Look." Leagan points out a vague set of tracks breaking through the sage. Snagged on the gnarled arm of a bush is a strand of gray intestine, a chipped yellow tooth caught in that.

Thirty-three.

Another string of bloody flesh. Clotted with dirt and dry thorns, mangled by teeth that weren't meant to chew meat.

Two-ninety-four.

The ground breaks down, humps of rock jumbled over one another while others are hollowed out into hiding nooks. Some look deep, black. My compass needle jumps.

A hoof scratches stone, and in the cave's void, the sound has menace.

"It's still in there." Leagan backs away, hand to her pistol.

The Stranger yearns toward the cave, but I don't listen to her. The needle of my contamination compass clicks so fast that it vibrates. We shouldn't be here.

"We can come back with some bigger guns and someone else for them to eat first, like Jonathaniel," Leagan says.

I scoop up a last sample of sand, and seal the final spoon in the dirty case without letting it touch my skin.

Navy's hotspot theory is dead right.

I RELIEVE NIGHTMARE OF HER SADDLE WHERE OUR OTHER THREE HORSES ARE grazing on knotgrass alongside the *Exodus*. "How did you like your first day on the West Rim?"

She's too preoccupied with the water bucket.

"Excuse me," a man calls. "Would you stand still while I take your photograph? Just like that."

He holds up the box camera around his neck, works the lens dials without looking, ink smudges on his arms and nails black as the Stranger. His little straw hat doesn't even keep the sun off his face.

"No." I move around Nightmare so her flanks are between us.

"Just one or two, I promise. I'm here for the Jezebel Times. The light is phenomenal. Photographers call this the golden hour. Your hair is glowing, and with you against the backdrop of the railroad construction, it will really give the folks back east a taste of the Rim. Stand with your horse and stare off that way, overseeing the operation, very mysterious and Tov-like."

I should have stayed out in the hills where I was alone.

You weren't alone. The Stranger's whisper awakens a cold spark in the middle of my spine.

The dark thing I felt watching me the last time we were out here didn't follow us off the West Rim. Maybe it couldn't. But it's definitely still here.

It feels more awake.

The sage hisses with wind as I dislodge dust from Nightmare's warm side. The brush strokes pile up on one another. *Four hundred.* The sky turns periwinkle at the top fringes and the first stars poke out. No more golden hour.

Does it have a name, like the Stranger does?

Hunger. That's what she feels in it.

It saw me. But I can also see it. And that's what matters.

"The rest of the camp pulls their horses and cattle in at dusk," the reporter says.

Why are you still here?

"Why?" I ask. The regular answer would be cattle rustlers, but this is not the regular Rim. It's the rest of it.

"As a precaution against wild animals, I assume."

We aren't going to leave ours out all night, either. But he doesn't need to know that.

Leagan returns with Dilly trotting beside her in his double-breasted vest. He comes up to her thigh now and can wear men's clothes. "Who are you?"

"Name's Engleman." The reporter thrusts his inky hand forward. "Todney Engleman with the Jezebel Times."

Leagan laughs. "The fools out here can't read."

"I'm telling the story for the folks back east."

"You assume they read. Dilly, go bite him."

The goat lets out a bleat and poops instead.

The light has probably gone out enough Todney Engleman can't take my picture at all, but I walk with Nightmare between us just the same.

SIX
TESLA

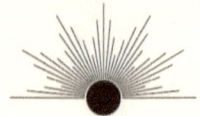

WHY DID I EXPECT NIGHT ON THE WEST RIM TO BE LIKE SLIPPING INTO A COLD bath of silence? This is a work camp, and men after work like to drink, and after drinking they play fiddles and mouth organs, tell absurd stories and jerk each other off when no one is looking.

All their respirator masks are unclipped at the chin so they can eat and smoke, a hive of slack-jaws. But as loose as they are thanks to the whiskey and music, and the hungry gazes that turn as I pass through, I notice that nobody fully sits with their backs to the darkness outside the lanterns ringing the perimeter of camp.

One of them crosses my path. "I'd be a fool not to offer a pretty face like yours a drink."

"I already have one, but you're very sweet. How long have you been out here?"

"Long enough to know what I do. And what they say."

"Oh? Do tell me what you know." I draw him a little closer. "I assume *they* are the Von Kanes."

"Like I said, I've been here a long time." He grazes a greasy hand across my waist. "My tongue will work best between your legs."

"Maybe later." I pat his rough cheek, the ache in my chest splitting open. Maybe never, darling. I don't know if I want a man to touch me again.

Moving on, this looks like an alkaline batch of souls in need of paid protection from ghosts and the like. It's what we're known for, after all.

However, my crew isn't mingling with the rest of them. I finally find a few of them stretched out with a stick of redweed.

"You look cozy."

"We're off the work clock."

They all get a little rigid around the shoulders. I suppose this is what happens when you're the boss.

"I'm not here to ruin your good time."

"Want a smoke?"

I think back on when I met them all. There were so many names, and a lot of them were William. But I pride myself on remembering people. "Thank you, Billy."

He grins. "That's right."

Smoking has never been my habit, but they're all watching. I taste the redweed in my sinuses before my tongue, like a sour, sticky spice cookie. Fuck, I'm going to cough like a fool. I try to hold it in but that only makes it worse. Seconds later, something blooms in my head, but I'm not sure if it's color or a memory. Then it passes.

Billy pats my back with a grin, however, which does seem to relax all of them. I think I still pass the test.

"Where's Daithe?"

They point out past the fires where the tents get darker.

There's another group of workers, half ours half *them*, over here. I know the sound of flesh on flesh anywhere.

Daithe sends a man staggering into the ring of bystanders and follows the first kick with a heel to the stomach, driving the dinner up out of him. He's stripped to the waist, long and lean like a white root.

He crouches over the heaving railroader, braid vivid even without the unrisen moonlight. Grabbing the man by the neck, Daithe drags his tongue over his jaw, catching on stubble and caressing the slope of his cheekbone. "Say that name to me again."

"I take it back," the man grunts.

"Shit, the foreman's coming," someone hisses, and they scatter like rabbits from a hawk.

"Don't forget your manners or I'll come looking when I get hungry."

Daithe gives the man he just beat an almost tender sniff, then slaps his ass to send him off.

"We've been here less than a day and you're already starting fights?" I say.

"I'm just establishing the order of things. Who's going to respect us and who's going to be food. The *so* will thank me."

I doubt that.

"The Stranger," I remind him. His calling her *the daughter* doesn't feel quite right. "You don't really eat people."

He flashes me his filed teeth. "They taste just like prairie chicken with potatoes and gravy."

I still think he's bluffing. "Don't worry, I'll keep you well fed so you don't have to eat any east bloods. We need them to build the rail for us."

"I don't have to eat them yet."

"The next time one of them insults you, tell me who it is. I have a better way for us to put them in their place than you beating the shit out of everyone. If you get hurt, who will dig my mine?"

"All right, since you asked, and you're the boss. But you're denying me my simple pleasures. I enjoy beating the shit out of everyone."

I bet he does.

THE GIRLS ARE ON THE ROOF OF THE *EXODUS*.

The steel is still warm to the touch. Adelaide lies on her back, gaze pointed up at the clear, black sky, Leagan's rose and bergamot smoke flavoring each breath.

"Did you have a good time over there?" Navy asks.

"Yes, I made several new acquaintances." I have one of their dirty handprints smeared across my waist to prove it.

"Are they going to give us all their money?" Leagan asks.

"I hope so."

"Green is still on the train," she says.

I sigh. "Let's not talk about him right now." I don't have the strength to be angry at the moment, and I'd rather not spoil the night.

A wisp of pale green light winks far out past the camp's borders.

There don't seem to be any aura lights tonight, and this was much too low to the ground for that, anyway. It moved like someone swiping with a knife.

I sit up straighter, but it's gone. "Did you see that?"

Adelaide turns.

"I saw a light flash out there."

"You mean lightning?" Leagan says.

"Very funny, ma'am." I did not smoke enough to hallucinate and only had one drink, and they're definitely watering down the whiskey to make it last. So don't get any ideas about the state of my mind.

The light reappears, Adelaide rising to her feet as I do. It hovers between bushes like a ghost, close enough to the ground to prove it's not a rogue aura light or anything else sky-born.

"Ghost quartz," Adelaide says.

"Maybe." Gradually, more points of light join it, coming to rest higher and higher until a pale green ring hangs from nothing but the black expanse. Distant enough to maybe not be meant for us, just close enough I get the message. We're not alone out here.

"It's ghosts," Leagan whispers to Navy. "They're watching us."

"No, they're not. Stop making up lies."

"Did this happen last time you were here?" I ask.

"No," Adelaide whispers.

The lowest lights waver as something crosses between us, and a scream rends the black desert. It's definitely a man's, open-mouthed and born deep within the diaphragm. Sound carries exceptionally well in the still-warm air after dark. I can tell it's only one voice, but my skin goes cold enough it might as well be a thousand throats deep.

Navy grabs my skirt to locate my hand. I imagine the only thing more terrifying than not seeing the source of the noise like me, is being completely unable to, even if it were close enough to see you.

God of Mercy, it's full of anguish.

"I think we know why the Von Kanes ordered those guns."

The circle of ghost light collapses, the night going black as it's ever been.

SEVEN
ADELAIDE

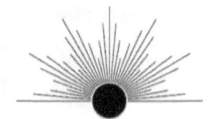

RALEIGH TAKES THE COFFEE AND EGG-BISCUIT SANDWICH FROM ME, DRAWS THE chair up with his foot. "Now the day can actually begin. Thank you, Stranger."

"If you were nice, you'd bring us something too," one of Green's hired guns says, and his voice is similar in depth to Kasey, Rafe's right-hand man I killed in Hannah.

A ghost snakes through my once-broken ribs.

Kill him.

Raleigh lifts the sandwich to his mouth and bites in, slow. Butter spills down his chin until he catches it on his thumb. "She isn't."

"We've noticed."

He hasn't done anything to me yet. But he works for Green.

Kill him and he won't.

A series of scars crisscross his hand. Knife fight.

"Stop looking at me." He walks away, but the Stranger follows him.

I start to feel his pulse wrapped up in hers. Taste the iron.

"I expect you to tell me all about the West Rim." Raleigh's voice makes me jump. "I came all the way here and haven't even gone outside yet. I did hear some weird noises last night."

"You didn't hear anything last night." Green emerges from the bathroom, still polishing his hands on the towel. It hangs with weight, damp. "I'm going out today. If you're so tired of being waited on, you can come along. You might make good bait for any bone pickers lurking in the brush."

"Although on second thought, I am very comfortable in here," Raleigh says. "Remember, though, if I die, you lose your leverage on my ladies. I have never been safer or more powerful in my life."

Green crosses between us, body a dead tree, no leaves. "You can tell your aunt I don't appreciate her going above my head to younger Von Kane about me. Don't act like you don't know what I mean."

I do know what you mean. And I will tell Aunt Tess you're upset about it. That will make her happy.

"You might actually be the smartest one in the family because you keep your mouth shut most of the time. But I know what you're doing in here every day—"

"Hey, now," Raleigh says. "I am poured straight from the mold of intelligence, and I take offense to that."

Green's brow twitches. "I'm watching all of you and your feminine wiles. I'm watching Von Kane, and Swann, and everyone else here. It's my job."

I know. But so is the Stranger. And she's the one I'd worry about.

"Try and outfox me," he says, "and some of you will live to regret it."

The knob in his throat sticks out so far. I could grab it with my fingers and squeeze.

The Stranger fills up my throat. Iron. Darkness.

There's already bloodstains in this carpet.

I back away.

"Where were you last night?" Green asks.

Shouldn't you already know since you're so busy watching everybody? *Eight.*

The Stranger won't let me turn my back on him. "I'll tell you about the West Rim later, Raleigh."

"Fair enough."

He belongs to Aunt Tess.

You shouldn't have promised her that.

"JONATHANIEL INVITED US ALL TO LUNCH," AUNT TESS SAYS AS I RUB IN MORE of the sun-protectant cream Navy makes me. "I assume you'd rather not be there. I'll tell him the unfortunate news."

"You assume right."

"Then I hope you have a marvelous day doing whatever your heart desires."

Staying out of the worst sun. My skin is still radiating heat from the burn I got yesterday.

But as soon as I sit down in the living car, I have to move again. The Stranger beats faster, up in my throat, louder than the steam hammer.

She doesn't settle even as I leave the *Exodus*. So many tents.

It's likely that some of them are occupied. But I'll start in this corner and work my way across. Eventually I'll look in all of them.

The quail and chickens are still alive, clucking as they look for bugs. I give them more water and sweep the ground with my contamination compass, then drag their peaked coop to a fresh spot in the shade.

Eighty-one.

It's bright. Even with my mask.

Dust coils into the air like smoke because they've torn up so much Rim.

I try to make my jaw let go, focus on going through the tents. But I can't.

The camp is an open scab. They're still picking at it. They're not going to stop until everything is ruined.

You're running out of time.

Maybe I was born too late.

Two of Green's bullies hover in front of a tent two rows in, olive uniforms trimmed with red dust. They point toward the head of the line any time a railroader passes too close.

Guarding it.

A slice flutters the pale canvas side. It starts high, about level with the top of my head.

One-fifteen.

"There's nothing for you here either, fox." He touches his revolver. "There was a dispute last night. That's all. Get out of here."

I didn't ask.

One-twenty.

Long fibers dangle from the hole. A dirty cut. They didn't get it on the first try. I would wake up if someone tried to cut through canvas this thick next to me.

Or were they cutting themselves out? The Stranger asks.

Kane emerges from inside, another bully and the railroad foreman with him. "I know your men aren't stupid. I said maybe they're drinking too much. But maybe you are right and I'm wrong, that's all."

Why work so hard protecting the place where some drunk men had a fight? That's what drunk men do.

The foreman shakes his head, the *fuck you* kind, but Kane doesn't see.

He comes between me and the tent. Too sharp. False. "Hello, Adelaide. What are you doing today?"

"Avoiding certain people."

He chuckles, but I'm not joking. "I presume I'm not one of them, or we wouldn't be having this conversation."

He's trying to distract you.

Fool, it's not going to work.

The guards tense as I step past Kane, but he waves them off.

I smell blood.

"I know you're curious and observant," he says. "But I also know your family doesn't work for free."

Why would we?

"You can look—"

Muted light seeps through the walls, the canvas hot and swallowing. Three cots are overturned, the plank floor tangled with blankets.

Kane follows me in, cutting off the shaft of light that falls through the cut side. "You can look, but just so we're clear, I can't pay you for help this time, even if you find the answer."

"What happened?"

"From what I understand, they had some kind of argument yesterday. Were probably drunker than the foreman's admitting. One of them decided to sleep with his knife and the other didn't like it. The flap was still buttoned up when he was found. I assume this was someone cutting their way out." Kane fingers a strand of the shredded canvas. "Probably the one who stabbed his tentmate."

"Where is he?"

"In the medical tent, still sedated after getting his leg stitched up."

"Do people always get sedated for stitches back east?"

Weak.

Morning salt burns at first, then the numbing effects sink in, and it works just fine. I've been cauterized with no sedation, and I'm still alive.

"Several cuts were to the bone, and he was pretty shaken after getting attacked in his sleep. The doctor thought it was best."

"There are four beds." And four duffels.

"There were only two of them in here at the time. The dawn shift was already up."

He doesn't know where the one who did the stabbing is. None of them do.

You know.

I know what made him do this.

Kane does too, he just doesn't want to admit it. Even though it's so obvious.

The duffels have nothing but clothes, a flask, cigarettes, a letter from a woman, and naked photographs. The blankets are heavy when I lift them. Wet. Blood. And something worse.

Inside my overskirt pocket, my contamination compass clicks.

EIGHT
TESLA

Jonathaniel's table has monogrammed linens and real copper flatware set out for us. How nice. The wind rips at the tablecloth and already a layer of dust sticks to the copper domes shielding the food despite the tent canopy.

"Do sit, ladies." He draws chairs for Leagan and me. "Just the two of you?"

"Yes, the other girls are busy." My fork is warm from the sun. "This is lovely."

"None of that everyday silver stuff, or worse, tin. I can't be tasting that when I'm trying to enjoy my food. We may be out here on the edge of civilization, but why eat out of a can?"

"You could eat out of a boot," Leagan says.

"Whatever for?"

She shrugs. "I'm just saying you could."

I notice red dirt clings to the front of Jonathaniel's light trousers. "Been spending some time on your knees, darling?"

"Oh, that's nothing. It's from yesterday's excursion." The dust doesn't brush off as easily his laugh does, it's already imbedded in him. "I thought I'd found some old Tov star tracing apparatuses out in the canyon. Alas, it was just an old wagon axel. Not nearly as exciting. But I'm having a splendid time drinking in as much adventure as I can before my life gets boring again."

That seems true.

"Adelaide might have liked to examine that if it was a Tov device," he says. "She should visit with Old Millard when he gets back. He has uncovered quite a few artifacts since he's been here, and they are a wonder. Though just between us, he's a bit of a stick in the mud."

Oh why am I not surprised Millard's out collecting history that doesn't belong to him? He sent a spy with his son's first expedition, after all.

"To be absolutely honest, I don't think she'd appreciate that," I say.

Shockingly, Leagan keeps her nasty mouth shut. Then I see why—it's already full of figs and cheese.

"You don't think so?" Jonathaniel asks. "Well forget I ever suggested it. She is an exceedingly peculiar girl, and I still can't get a grasp on whether she despises my guts or is simply too indifferent to them to hate me at all."

She definitely hates you, I wait for Leagan to say. But she doesn't, and now I'm getting suspicious.

"Is there anything she's fond of?" he asks.

"Being left alone," I say.

That makes him laugh.

"She's not like you and me, Jonathaniel. Leave her alone, and that's all you need to remember." I can't say I'd want to socialize with anyone I serviced, even if it was my choice. Some things should be kept separate because men like him get transactions and feelings confused.

"True enough," he says. "Where is she?"

I take hold of his arm. "I have unfortunate news."

"Oh dear."

"We've taken a vote on your bodyguard job, and I'm afraid we have to decline your offer. We have several other endeavors going at the moment, and we don't believe in doing a job half-assed. It wouldn't be professional."

It wouldn't be kind to Adelaide to bring him into our home, her one safe haven—apart from Green's sickly presence—after the way Jonathaniel felt entitled to her body because another man offered it to him with a price tag. Like she ought to swallow another bullet for the family, or simply not mind because he isn't cruel. You thought I'd be tempted? You fools. We'd never do that to her for money. *I'm* not that cruel.

"You slippery devil." Jonathaniel heaves a sigh. "You made me believe you were going to say something far worse."

"I know, I did it on purpose. Did it soften the blow?"

"A little, yes. I am sorely disappointed, but I won't let it break my spirit. Your very presence here still vastly improves my outlook on life. Why be unhappy and rob yourself of a good time?"

"Couldn't have said it better myself." I toss one leg across the other, tugging the lump out of the back of my skirt that accordioned itself when I sat. "When we first met in Oath—"

"Quite a few cycles ago now," he interrupts.

"Yes, but I haven't forgotten you mentioning there were murders out here."

"Oh." He chuckles. "Well, I used the word murders because it sounded more dramatic than disappearances." He leans in, a conspirator's smile butter thick in his voice. "But for the record, disappearing isn't so much the truthful word either. It seems they've been taken."

"Taken by…" My tone prods.

"Ghosts, I say. Younger Von Kane won't give his opinion, although I'd hazard he has one. The official story is they've been slipping their sentences and running north to Hannah, or back to Descendants, but not all of them, surely. This notion doesn't sit right with me for two reasons. Hannah is no longer the jewel it once was, and not all the men who've vanished are criminals. Both Von Kanes know this."

"Yes, I'm sure they do. Von Kane the younger runs this place well." And like any good boss, he knows not to incite panic among the workmen. And like his good father, he doesn't mind a thin crust of lies atop the pudding now and then.

"As is typically the case, the truth must lie somewhere in the middle," Jonathaniel says. "Either these men ran away or something took them, but until something of them is found, we can't really say now, can we?"

"And if we never find anything, there's no proof ghosts didn't eat them." Leagan's black lipstick has left prints on everything her mouth touched.

Jonathaniel tips her a finger. "Precisely, my dear."

"There are lots of things to get eaten by out here. Even oxen."

"You are also a very odd girl, did you know that? I am looking forward to our lizard hunt even more now." He adds another heaped spoonful of sugar to his coffee. "But as it turns out, I may have seen something I wasn't supposed to."

I scoot forward in my seat. "Do tell."

"Rather late, when most of the camp is asleep, there's a strange circle of light out in the desert. It lasts for a few minutes, then it's gone."

"We saw it," I say. "Last night. Along with a terrible scream."

"Oh." He almost seems disappointed. "Then maybe I don't need to fear a ghost will take me next. Although that would be an exciting tale to bring back home."

"Does it happen every night?"

"No, but it's been happening fairly regularly since I've been here. And it's definitely traveling with us. I've never been very good at sleeping, so I have the advantage of seeing what walks at night."

"Kane's seen it," Leagan says. "It's why they ordered the guns."

"Probably." And I'm going to ask him, right to his face.

"I don't believe I have to remind you ladies to keep this between us, but I'll do it anyway." Jonathaniel glances over his shoulder for anyone nearby. "Especially with that reporter around. Word of ghosts and disappearing workmen would be very popular back east, and the buffoons who've invested in this line with me are exceptionally spooked by bad press and wives' tales. Tess, you remember my dull friend, Captain Montgomery?"

"I do."

"They're all like him, I'm afraid. No fun at all."

WHEN WE'RE DONE EATING, I RETRIEVE MY PARASOL FROM THE BACK OF MY chair. "Raptor likely has other things to do, don't you, Raptor? But if you're not busy, Jonathaniel, do you want to take a little walk with me?"

"I would adore that. Just let me get my new walking stick."

Leagan nods to me and strolls off, thief hands tucked in her seat pockets.

"I found it yesterday." Jonathaniel whisks out of his tent again, stick in hand. "It's very useful for checking the bushes for snakes. I also think it looks rather like a face on the end here, don't you agree?"

He takes my good arm and lets me lead him into a winding breach in the ground, cut by *Solace* floodwaters, and out of sight of the camp. The sun coming through the midnight lace of my parasol makes a fine scale pattern on my skin.

He really should be wary of my intentions just as much as any man, but I, by virtue of being a woman, am harmless and easy to give your time to.

"I have a secret of my own," I say.

"A good secret gets even better once it's shared with at least one person."

"I agree. I'm telling you this in confidence. As an associate…" I squeeze his arm through his lightweight duster. "And a friend."

"You have my utmost word this will stay between us."

"Mr. Green,"—because *Mr.* sounds better than *Green the fucking snake* in this case— "isn't who you think he is. He's lied to the Von Kanes, and you. And I can't keep this to myself anymore."

Jonathaniel is quiet, paying attention to me because underneath his silly ways, he's not really the fool he appears to be.

"I had a daughter. Her name was Vesta." She was smart, and fun, and I miss the way she laughed. "My mother's name was Moira." I swallow the ache in my throat, but it comes back up like a weed. "Green had them both slaughtered, and if he'd gotten his way, he would have killed us all."

"That is truly, truly awful…Tess. I'm speechless…And the Von Kane's don't know of this?"

"Green used one of his men with a false name—a basket man, we call it —to recruit the bounty hunters."

"Oh my. And now this man is with you, on your train." It's Jonathaniel's turn to squeeze my arm. "Sweet Jezebel. How can you even look at him?"

"It's very hard."

He shakes his head redundantly. "My God. Why would he do this to you?"

"He knew he wouldn't get the protection contract from the Von Kanes if we were still around." Now I'm one hundred percent lying, and I don't even care. "We're not the only ones, either. He didn't become Governor of Vantage without bloody hands and arson."

"Why don't you come forward? This man deserves to face justice."

"Millard Von Kane doesn't strike me as someone who likes gossip. Green will deny everything of course, and all my proof is buried in the ground now. Justice is complicated for women."

"He used the basket man as you say, therefore it would be your word against his."

"Exactly."

"But you trust me," he says, so clearly flattered, as I want.

"I trust you." I hold onto him, and he licks up my words like honey. "And even though we can't be your hired guns, that doesn't mean we don't want you to be safe."

"I greatly appreciate that, and I thank you. For your confidence, and the warning. I will be wary of him from now on."

"My daughter was a lovely girl, as was my mother. She was loyal to Green's business. If he's capable of having them killed, he's capable of anything."

"Even something far less dastardly, like disappearing men to keep his protection necessary."

"I wouldn't put it past him," I say. "And if he isn't responsible, he's doing a shitty job at protecting the camp, don't you think?"

This fight isn't over yet, Green. I'm going to win.

NINE
ADELAIDE

THE MEDICAL TENT HAS A GREEN FLAG ATTACHED TO THE TOP POLE. THE WIND claws at it, howls in my left ear, tries to tear my hat off. Another wall of dust rolls into me, swerving along the ground like a snake.

Three-fifty.

Five cots, but only one has the lump of a body in it, his back to me, snoring.

Cabinets and a standing basin fill in the back corner. That's where the Stranger pulls me first, the curtain hiding the rest of it.

A slab of porcelain on legs, cold to look at.

Three…

It has a slight lip, like a very shallow sink, and a drain at one end with a glass receptacle screwed into the base. It looks like a butcher's cutting table, only they use wooden planks and buckets. Out here, at least.

Empty jars coated in ambient dust. Two cedar boxes of cutting utensils —the silver kind doctors have—*DuPonte* etched into the top.

Five–

Sharp air flushes up through my skirt. I step back. The planks used to level the floor sink.

I peel back the oval rag-braid rug. The planks aren't nailed down, the rug is holding them where they're supposed to be instead. Fresh cold pours across my hands, fingers moving past my neck.

A safe.

The chilled iron burns, but that doesn't stop my pick knife from getting past the lock. A center pipe holds burning Ven quartz with six jars positioned around it, the glass frosted.

My breath turns to smoke as it passes through the colder air. Dark liquid inside moves inside the jar. Not frozen.

Blood.

I lower it back, pull the next one.

Fingernails peer out at me from behind the clouded glass, suspended in clear liquid, black spots like ink in the webbing between digits.

I see the inside crook of Vesta's elbow, spotted the same way. The skin under her nails rotting dark.

The familiar pit in my stomach splits open.

Third jar, more clear liquid. Genitalia, male. The black spots are larger. It's blood, trapped under the skin as the body this used to belong to melted from the inside.

I look back at the human lump under the wool blanket.

Kane said he was sedated for stitches. It makes more sense now.

Twelve.

Sun seeps through the wall of the tent, into me, moisture slick in his hair. He's not wearing a mask now, but there's a border around his face where it used to be. Drool runs out one side of his mouth, into the pillow.

I fold the blanket down to his knees. His breath stays thick. Two hands, a bandage knotted around his left leg. There's enough of a lump between them, I'm not going to check. None of those severed parts belong to him.

The Stranger flickers. *Someone's coming.*

I run back to the cold-safe that I left open.

Take one.

I don't have my satchel. The jars are too big for my pockets.

Take one.

I'll have to come back for the rest.

Faster.

I get the planks back down, the rug.

Sunlight breaks into the tent as the flap is brushed open, a narrow slice.

The man is gray. Gray clothes, gray hair, gray callouses on his knuckles, shoulders curled forward like paper left in the sun.

The Stranger seeps toward him, but I hold so still. Behind my cotton skirt, the jar of blood hangs heavy from my fingers.

He halts, gaze turning me over like a rock, every crawly thing under it darting away from the light. "Who are you?"

No one. Who are you?

I angle so my front stays to him, then head for the split in the canvas.

DuPonte.

He goes to the cot where I left the sedated man's body exposed to the air, strokes hair from the man's forehead before he re-covers him.

"Did you intend to feed on him, Tov?"

I don't have anyone's severed appendages in jars under my floor.

"He's not well." His voice lifts, too high. "Are you well? I am the camp physician. I could examine you, if you wish."

Thirteen.

The sun hits my back, a slap of raw heat. I roll my skirt around the blood jar so no one sees what it is, and I don't let any part of it touch my skin.

⁕

A WALL CUTS THROUGH THE MIDDLE OF NAVY'S LAB. THE FIRST HALF HAS HER distilling station and herbs, the salves and tinctures and smoke bombs she makes for us. It smells like home, even though her bookshelf is mostly empty space.

We lost everything we owned when the *Absolution* derailed, then spent the last Season homeless. The small things don't come back on their own.

The other side of the steel wall sparkles with glass chimneys. Vials of pestilence-rotted worms and lizards, the sharp bite of utensils sterilized in clear pine.

Before I go in, I tighten the respirator straps until the gum seal sticks to my face, and buckle the leather lab coat up around my chin. The weight of it hangs on me like memories.

"I found this." I bring Navy's gloved hand to the top of the jar. "In the medical tent. It's blood. Pestilence blood."

"You *found* it, or you stole it?"

"Yes."

One of the rats screams in his cage. His eyes are gone, and all his hair has come off, the skin left behind purple and swollen. It upsets the others, and they scream too. The Stranger coils around me like the copper tubing between vessels.

"I hate it when they do that," Navy says. "It scares me every time."

Dr. Pike seals a drop of liquid between two glass slides, then makes a note on the sample, on a page. The Stranger beats hard as the book falls into his smock pocket.

He stops before he gets within my reach.

I resist the Stranger's urge to pull the jar away from him.

"I'll put this in the containment box with the other samples," he says.

Vesta's samples. They aren't alone anymore. They have dead rats and worms for company. Her cold-safe isn't east blood like the one I just dug up. It's Leagan made, and it works alkaline.

"Let's look at it under the magnifying scope first," Navy says.

"I'll pull a drop for a slide," Pike says. "Did you collect this sample yourself?"

"I found it," I say again.

Pike waits for a better answer before turning back to the bench. He can pretend not to listen, but I would.

"It would be helpful to know who this came from," Navy says, even though I know what Pike was really asking. "How long it's been outside the body, and how far along in the decay the person was."

"You'd have to ask the person who did it." That gray doctor, DuPonte. "But you can't." Because he'd know I took something. I won't say any of that in front of Pike.

Navy reaches out, knows where I am without seeing. "Come to my room later, and we can talk about it."

I wait until Dr. Pike leaves the lab a few hours later, then check the pockets of his lab coat. He took his notebook with him.

TEN
TESLA

I FINISH BRUSHING DOWN MY HORSE AND STAND BACK WHILE ADELAIDE FASTENS all the saddle straps for both of us. It wouldn't be safe to do them single-handed. "How's Nightmare taking to the West Rim?"

"She likes it."

Not many things put a smile in her voice like that anymore, even for the serious girl she's always been. I feel the same way about the *Exodus*. Having something that's finally yours when you've had so many things ripped from you makes that thing so much more meaningful.

However, it's impossible not to fear that the ripping could happen again.

The derailing of the *Absolution*, a loss that jarred my spirit loose, could happen again to the *Exodus* without a warning. Any of us could die out here. I could lose more of my body. Every day I resist the urge to hold on too tight and cripple myself from doing anything else that matters with my life because I'm afraid.

These men hunkered around the firepits are probably thinking the same things I am. They just want to survive long enough to be happy someday. Or to make it home to procreate and sustain their so-called family legacies.

Fuck it, I'm not like them at all.

"Are you fools ready?" Leagan slings her pack across her shoulders, the polished stock of *Verdict*, her boar rifle, jutting from the top.

"I am." There's no trace in my voice that I'd once again gone to my dark place. "Let's ride."

Adelaide steadies the box I use to mount, then nods to me once she's in Nightmare's saddle.

It would be easy to turn left of the *Exodus* and slip into the night, but I lead us straight through the middle of camp. Voices part around us as we do.

"Hey, I wouldn't go out there if I were you," someone calls. "It's the ghost's time."

"You're damn right it is," I call back. "But all ghosts fear the Stranger. And if she doesn't scare them, the name Revere will."

"That's a nice thought, if it wasn't a mouthful of horse piss. Don't bring them back here with you."

Under the awning of his tent, Kane rises to his feet as we pass, but even he doesn't dare leave the false safety of his lanterns.

The moons have yet to rise, and the impending night quickly becomes an untouched maze of rock and sage. I let Adelaide take the lead as we ride through unclaimed desert rutted by *Solace* flood rains, chirping with sugar bats. Aided by my solar quartz lenses which amplify light, I keep my gaze on the white glow of her hair, gathered with a black ribbon at the base of her neck, and the less-defined outline of Nightmare's spotted rump.

The ground dips sharply, then cuts up in ridge of rock that was hidden until we're almost on top of it.

"Don't steer us into a gulch or a slot canyon and break our legs," I say.

"Nightmare is smarter than that."

"I don't see anything that shouldn't be out here." Leagan turns the key on her headlamp. The amplified quartz light comes stabbing through my lenses, a cold white that makes the shadows blacker.

"Hello?" Leagan calls. "Any ghosts out here?"

"Shhh," I say. "Don't scare them."

"Isn't that the point?" she says.

"Whoever did all that screaming was human. He must have left some clue behind, and we're going to find it."

"I can't see anything."

"We can come back in the daytime and look again if we don't find anything." But going out at night will cast a much more dramatic effect on the camp, and the first step in swindling is to make your services something your mark can't possibly live without.

Adelaide veers off and dismounts.

"What is it, Stranger?" I call.

"Come and look."

There's a faint track worn through the plant life where someone—I'm going with someone, not something—paced around a ring of intentionally placed rocks.

"Mother fucker." Leagan drops from her saddle. "Do you see that?"

"*Krossus*, I do."

It's a human body, naked and tied flat to the dirt in an *x*. His meat is visible, all pink and white where his skin was cut down the center of his face, sternum, and tops of his legs and peeled back like petals. What's left now has been gnawed by hungry opportunists, bugs crawling through his crevices. A chain of ghost flowers wilts across his neck, brush crackling as a pack of scavenger lizards flee.

"Nasty." Leagan starts a second a loop around the corpse, pointing. "Look at his eyes."

"What eyes?" I say. The sockets now hold rocks. His lips are gone too, teeth bared to the stars.

"It's one of the Green Company bullies," Adelaide says.

"Well this serves him right then."

"How can you tell?" Leagan says. "All his skin's peeled off."

"His shoes." She points at the tread. "They all wear the same kind of boot."

I'm sure she's not wrong, even if I haven't noticed directly.

"Well they need matching shoes to go with their cute matching outfits," I say.

"They should have stolen his shoes instead of his clothes," Leagan says. "Boots are way more valuable than a shirt."

"It appears they were more interested in stealing his flesh for this little ritual."

"Well at least something ate his penis off so we don't have to look at it."

Adelaide tucks her contamination compass back into a skirt pocket. "He's not infected. Just dead."

"Hang on…" Leagan probes a stick around the hole I assumed had been torn in his throat by the lizards. I didn't smell anything through my mask until she started poking him. Now the stink of meat swollen by the sun blooms, heavy enough to pierce my respirator. It's always reminded me of raisins for some reason, which is why I don't eat them anymore.

"Fool's gold." I step away. "Stop doing that."

"There's a rock in there. It's way down, maybe he tried to swallow it…" She finds a pair of pliers in her pack.

Soft flesh squelches as she digs the object out. My stomach sours.

"Obsidian." Slime quivers on the end of her pliers as she holds out the black sliver that had been deep in his throat. "See?"

She goes back for more and gasps. His entire sternum lifts free of the ribcage with no effort, pinned in her pliers like the flat bone of a leechfish.

I turn away and head for the blocks of sandstone facing us like a wall. But the air over here still smells like decay. "You're going to make me sick."

Messy footprints walk over each other under the sheer cliff, the sand beneath it thick and soft. I reach as high as I can, and my fingers sink into a round hole.

"Adelaide, come here." Unclipping the tube of fire quartz from my holster, I step back for a broader view.

There's a full circle of hollowed out nooks looking down on the body like a warning. The top hole is higher above our heads than even a man could reach, but with a rope and a spike in the rock above it wouldn't be too difficult to carve. Sandstone is soft compared to other rocks.

"It's facing toward the camp," Adelaide says. "If they put a big enough chunk of ghost quartz in each hole, we could see it from that far away."

"So not a ghost after all," I say. "Just more men. How disappointing."

Men, because I seriously doubt one alone pulled this off.

"So who in the camp has motive to sabotage the project?"

Instead of responding, Adelaide pulls something from the orange sand. A length of twine, burned at both ends.

"Maybe they tied the pieces of ghost quartz together."

"And didn't think that it would get hot?" I ask.

After a while, Leagan's dug a wet little cairn of shards from inside him.

"You know what some people think obsidian is for?" she says. "Resurrection."

"Do you remember what else was made out of obsidian?" Adelaide asks.

There's no escape from the stink now. No matter where I move it follows. "Remind me."

"Zachariah Wells' ring."

"The one you stole from Kane way back at the beginning?"

"Grandma wasn't happy when she saw it."

"Sorry," Leagan says to the corpse. "You died, and you're still dead. No resurrection for you."

"Resurrection…" The word feels blasphemous on my tongue. There are things that can't be explained, like the Stranger, and Mother and Leagan's ability to dream the future. The God of Mercy does as he pleases, but resurrection doesn't happen in this life.

Although someone out here thinks it does.

ELEVEN
ADELAIDE

THE STRANGER PICKS AT MY EDGES, TINY NEEDLES IN MY SKIN. SHE DOESN'T pull toward anything in particular, but something changed from a moment ago.

I don't want to be out in the open anymore.

"I hope no scorpions decide to take a ride in my skirt," Aunt Tess says, shaking out the excess fabric before she gets back in her saddle.

The Stranger tightens around my body until I can't take a full breath.

And I feel it.

It brushes up against me from the night. Not an insect on my skin, pressure, the wrong pole of a magnet. As the Stranger thickens, it scrapes against her, slowly pushing in on me. Two shadows, tasting each other in the dark.

"What is it?" Leagan whispers.

The thing that's been watching since we got here. The hunger that lurks in Eden that I assumed had to stay there.

It remembers me from last time.

"Get on your horses." I turn Nightmare in a circle, but I still don't see anything with a shape.

"You're scaring me a little." Aunt Tess hauls herself up, one-handed. "Do you hear something?"

Go.

Fifty.

The floodwater rut we have to cross swallows us, just enough of a slope the horses have to pick their way up.

On the other side, I make Nightmare stop, drawing my crossgun.

Loose rocks, trickling, scraping. Leagan pulls the drawstrings of her rifle bag.

"Something's following us," Aunt Tess whispers. "A person, an animal…"

"A necromancer," Leagan says.

"Put out your light," I say.

Aunt Tess tries to cover the tube of quartz hanging off her belt with her overskirt, but a few shaking stars still leak out on the ground. "Let's not wait around and find out."

The Stranger's black hum closes over my ears like water.

It sees you.

Her weight on my chest bleeds off. Stars overhead again with a few ribbons of pink aura light, Nightmare's reins in my fist.

I'm standing in front of a pit.

It's square, a cover of woven sticks snapped in the bottom where something fell through. Dirt where it tried to dig itself out but went in instead of up. And legs. Five of them, boots still on, but only left ones

Aunt Tess's horse Lady Gray forces her way through the brush behind me. "Fool's gold, Stranger. I asked you to wait for us."

That was the Stranger.

A man emerges from the sage and scraggled trees. On all fours, bent like a branch, snapped but not severed.

Bone picker.

My shot is momentarily blinding.

Aunt Tess holds her chest, the deep breath that comes behind fear collapsing her shoulders. For a moment, she looks exactly like Grandma even though I can't see her face through the mask. "I wasn't worried until you left us."

She was.

Afraid.

Can you blame her?

"I'm sorry," I say. It's all I can. "I wasn't leaving you."

The Stranger was. Getting me away from the hunger I felt crawling toward me before the bone picker did.

I wouldn't leave them.

But she obviously will.

"That's enough adventure for one night." Aunt Tess gets Lady Gray around the cluster of bushes. "I'm going back to the *Exodus*."

I look back again, even though I don't hear any more bone pickers or feel the other shadow pressing in on me anymore. All that's here now is night and dust, cactus and sagebrush.

It saw you.

It's after midnight.

The Stranger pulls on me like an untrained horse.

I return to the medical tent and pull up the floor.

All five beds are empty now.

Cold makes the scent of iron stronger. Under the wool and straw insulation, the temperature of the metal is a sharp opposite to my hand.

There's a secondary padlock through the latch.

They know I was here, that I took something. The Stranger rises up my throat just like panic. Maybe the other five jars are gone now, and I missed my chance to take them, or at least look at what was in the rest.

They wouldn't bother padlocking this if there was nothing inside.

The tumblers crunch with dirt and cold, not wanting to turn at first. As the lid peels back, a cold-air ghost rises, then collapses, turning my breath to smoke.

Six jars.

Liquid rolls against foggy glass, clinking as I lift, solid yet fleshy in the core.

A brain. Spliced in two halves, made to fit within the confines of the glass, still pink.

Take them all.

I wrap each jar with the cotton strips from the supply cabinet to keep them from clanking together, then place them in my empty satchel. Fool's gold, it's heavy.

Nine.

The porcelain cutting table casts a shadowy reflection of the moonlight seeping through the walls. It looks like something that's never been touched. No dust.

I sink to my knees.

A shard of bone clings to the bottom lip of the drain, dangling from a thread of hair. The stack of rags in the medicine cabinet is smaller.

Whatever's going on here, that doctor is up to nothing good.

I look through the flap's buttonhole before slipping back into the moonlight.

Eighty-nine—

Kane rounds a corner between tents, his boot stepping on mine. I throw out my arm so he doesn't come in contact with the bag of jars.

"It's just you," he sighs, quiet next to the snores in the tent to the left of us. "What are you doing up so late?"

What are *you* doing up so late?

Does he know what's happening behind the canvas of the medical tent?

Would it matter?

"Protecting the camp," I say.

"Same. I saw someone out walking, and I wanted to know who it was."

Feel how nervous he is. Frightened like a rabbit.

He's used to seeing me carry my satchel around. I usually do. But I watch to make sure he's not looking at it too much, noticing how big it is tonight.

I feel the weight of each jar cutting into my shoulder, burning a hole in my leg while the pestilence seeps in.

It's not really happening, but I don't know that. Do I?

Two.

Kane hesitates from the back of his throat. "Just so you're aware, most of these linemen we got have...questionable pasts. Not just the convicted criminals."

Questionable pasts.

Why can't people like him say words like murderer and rapist? They don't want to be uncomfortable. He's trying to be considerate right now, but east bloods are still so removed from our world they can't even name an act of violence without flinching.

That won't save you.

"I know you can take care of yourself," he continues quick. "I've just noticed good pay and being out here away from the law seems to attract a certain type of men."

The kind of men who should be afraid of me.

"You and your sisters…I'm a little worried about you…Just be careful."

Like I always am. It's the first thing you learn as a woman, no matter where you are.

"Thank you for the warning, Kane." That sounded less like me, more like the Stranger.

The shadows close around me like curtains. Hers or the night's, it's almost hard to tell for a moment.

"You can call me Timothy, if you want."

The jars are so heavy.

"No."

Kane is his name, not Timothy. I like it better. No reason, I just do.

TWELVE
TESLA

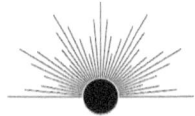

Adelaide walks a few paces behind me, her dress the faint green of ghost quartz. It turns her into an ethereal vision in the first light. Over it she wears a long duster to keep the sun off her arms once it rises, and I wear a red ribbon tied around my empty bell-sleeve. It's very annoying to leave it dangling in the breeze where it gets caught on things. But I did find this leather overskirt vest before we left civilization, which has no sleeves, so problem solved for my outer layer.

"I appreciate you," I say, "making an appearance today."

"It has to seem real," she says. "Just like the good old days."

"Are you smiling under there?"

"Maybe."

"Well stop it. You'll frighten our customers." I'm so glad she seems happier out here. The girls don't play games on the *Exodus* like they used to on the *Absolution*. We've all gotten so serious, but someday we'll be fun again. "Leagan just left to hunt scavenger lizards with Jonathaniel. She promised not to bring him back before nine. You can be back inside by then."

Part of our mining crew, maybe twenty-five of them, sit mixed with the other members of the railroad morning crew, slurping oatmeal. The plants, naturally.

Daithe catches sight of me and turns to the man left of him. "I didn't see anything last night, did you?"

"Nope," the man mumbles to his oats. "Do these taste shittier than usual?"

"Every time we lose men, the food gets worse and thinner," someone else says. "How does that add up? I heard there's eight new empty beds since last cycle."

"From the night crew again?"

"Three from them, four from us. But nobody's talking about it."

"Then maybe you shouldn't be talking about it either."

"Those spook lights didn't show up last night." Another one of ours, Elbert, lies just like we practiced. "That's a hundred and twelve days I've seen it now, I've been keeping count. But not last night."

Jonathaniel was keeping count, to be exact.

"We're farther west now," another lineman, not one of ours, chimes in. "Maybe we've finally outrun them."

"I saw those two ride out last night. Late. I heard they were hunting the ghost."

"That's a coincidence."

"Might be more than just a coincidence," Daithe's mouth twists each word like a smirk.

"Are ghosts afraid of women?"

Daithe turns to face Adelaide. "No, but they're afraid of her."

A ripple passes along the tables like Sunday gossip. And this is how an audience plant works, darlings. He's worth every standard I've paid him, even if he does seem to be an asshole.

"Looks like nothing got you last night," someone calls to me.

"Thankfully not," I say. "I told you we'd be just fine."

"Some good news at last." An arm reaches out of the line of dusty backs hedging the tables, the man it belongs to pulling me in. "Never thought I'd say it since the bacon ran out. We're all really looking forward to you girls getting to work. It's been mighty lonesome out here."

It's my mother's voice that bubbles up my throat as I lean in and plant the whisper near his ear. "We don't do that kind of work anymore."

"Oh." I hear his confusion. "Then what are you here for?"

I lay my arm over his shoulder. "See her?"

The vial dances on the chain, grabbing at the sun as Adelaide offers it to another of our planted men, the opaque liquid the same mixture that fills our contamination compasses. He already has the one we gave to all our men on the way here, under his shirt hopefully, but these fools don't know that.

"Yes," I say. "The rumors are true."

"What rumors, ma'am?"

"That is the Stranger. You've heard what she can do?"

Several of them look now.

"Like he said, she scares away the ghosts. Like the one they stirred up in Hannah last Season," I say. "An angry one. And you all heard what happened there."

"I heard."

"I never heard a ghost started that fire."

"You don't believe me? Whatever fell spirit that's been stalking the camp, making men disappear?" That cools him. "She went out to hunt it last night."

"I heard a gunshot last night."

"That must have been a bone picker," I say. "As long as she's in the camp, you'll all be safe from ghosts. Unless you disrespect her, of course..."

Adelaide passes another vial, then walks away, head held high, not looking at any of them.

"What did she just give him?" he asks.

"Protection." I squeeze his tight shoulder. "The pestilence is an even slipperier bastard than ghosts. But we found a way to tell you if it's close."

"We're safe as long as we wear the masks," he says.

"Is that what the Von Kanes told you? Would you like to see how it really works?"

"Snake oil." Green's voice splits through me like a bad smell. "In case you haven't heard, that's what these girls are famous for. They've been bleeding standards out of hardworking pockets for years now and haven't worked an honest job since they left the whorehouse in Hannah."

I round on him with a hiss. "*Shut* your teeth or you won't have any."

God of Mercy, I *do* sound just like my mother today. Not that it's a bad thing. But I iron out my tone. "I'm not ashamed of where I came from, Green. Are you?"

A man with shoulders broad as the table leverages himself up. Sitting he was shorter than Adelaide, now he towers over her like a stone slab.

Fuck, I thought this would go better, but now I'm having to look in two directions. I lower my hand until it brushes the wood grip of my pistol and keep it right there.

"We've got enough trouble here," he snarls. "We don't need two milk bastards lurking around stirring up more—"

"What trouble?" The morning railroad foreman steps out of a tent, shaving cream dripping off his jaw. "There's no trouble here unless you're causing it. No wives' tales this early in the morning."

The man keeps glowering over Adelaide. The hair on my arm goes hard.

Daithe swipes his finger around the inside of his neighbor's bowl with a smirk. "Who shit this out this morning? I'd be angry if I had to eat this slop like a dog too."

"Eat this." Someone else flicks another spoonful at his face.

"That's why I only eat meat."

"You can step back." I insert myself next to Adelaide. "If you're not interested in science, leave."

"Back to your business, Mr. Belsie." The foreman cuts between all of us. "You're not on my crew, fox, but I will discipline you like one of them should the need arise. Stop riling up my men and get out of here, both of you. This is no place for women." He lifts his voice. "Breakfast is over. Get to work, men."

"You call this breakfast?" they mumble. "More bullshit."

"I'll pretend I didn't hear that one time."

They've seen the ghost lights. They've seen Adelaide now. At least some of them suspect the company is lying to them.

I trust superstition to do the rest.

"So how much will this cost me?" One of the Von Kane men picks up the vial Elbert's showing to him.

"How does a flat rate of three hundred gold standard sound?" I ask.

"Sounds like robbery." He walks off.

That's fine. Patience is a virtue There's always a few that bite, and eventually they all will.

Daithe saunters off with the handful of our crew. At least he didn't cause more trouble.

Green and the foreman both wait, obstacles among the dispersing bodies.

"You want to watch me walk away?" I intentionally scuff my shoulder on Green's as I pass. "You're welcome to. Men used to have to pay me for that."

I catch up to Adelaide and link my arm through hers. "I thought that would go better. We should have kept that bone picker from last night and brought him for a demonstration."

"We can get another one. Or bring Navy next time. Let her do the demonstration."

"That's not a bad idea, actually, if they're not too mean to her. Now why didn't I think of that first? Should I put you in charge of misdirection from now on?"

"No."

"Oh good, I still have a job."

⁕

DAITHE KNOCKS ON THE DOOR OF THE LIVING CAR LATER IN THE EVENING WHEN the sun is hottest, and everyone with a working brain is inside resting.

"With your permission, I'd like to take my crew and head for your mine," he says. "We'll set up camp and start excavating before any east bloods figure out which way is true west during Moon Season. It'll give you the edge."

"It sounds like a nice idea," I say. "Is there something you're not telling me?"

"No. My boys are more useful to you digging, and I'm not keen on sitting around here getting insulted until these east blood asses plow us farther west."

"The land isn't ours yet."

"Does that matter to you?"

I find my smirk mirroring his. "No."

"We'll leave at night. Quiet like death. No one will know we've gone, or what you've got up your sleeve. By the time you get to us, you'll have an operational black gold mine and a warm-blooded dinner waiting for you."

From the couch, Leagan lifts an eyebrow. "You're gross."

"Don't worry." That little smile trickles around his lips again, half snake, half rose oil. "It won't be anyone you know."

"Gross."

"I still don't find cannibal jokes funny," I say. "But I think it's an alkaline suggestion."

"I thought you'd appreciate my initiative."

"It's why I made sure I wasn't outbid for your time."

"And I appreciate that."

"*Sol sana,* Mr. Daithe *dox* Noe." I give him the engineer's salute, and he shows me his sharpened teeth. "You have my permission to get to work."

"*Sol sana, sos* Revere."

THIRTEEN
ADELAIDE

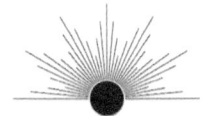

A SOFT KNOCK VIBRATES THROUGH THE FLOOR OF THE *EXODUS* TO MY ROOM. I lower my book.

It happens again.

One-ninety-one.

Aunt Tess has one of the floor panels pulled in the kitchen, pipes and valves underneath exposed.

She looks up as I slide the cook's passage shut, wet tears still running on her face, black from her eye pencil. "I'm just conserving our water supply."

That wrench in her hand wouldn't make her cry. There's more.

"I'm fine." She wipes her nose, breathes wet. "Really. I'm sorry if I woke you up. You don't need to worry…"

"I wasn't asleep." It's not that late.

She holds up her amputated arm. Fresh tears slip down her scarred cheek, catching on lamplight. "I think about him every time I don't see this fucking hand. That's nice, isn't it?"

I know who she's talking about.

"He's a fool." I'm glad not to feel this kind of breaking for some man. I'm tired enough carrying the emptiness left by Grandma and Vesta, a broken bone that keeps aching to spite everyone who says it heals in time. "It's not worth it."

A doubtful chuckle escapes her. "Except when it is."

It's not.

But I keep my opinion to myself because I love her, and she isn't like me. She has room in her heart that can't be filled by being out where it's quiet. She's probably what a person is supposed to be, and I'm what's made wrong.

"Do you want to talk about it?" She doesn't have Grandma anymore. She's who Aunt Tess needs right now, not me, but I can still listen.

"No, thank you, though." She slides the plate back over the *Exodus*'s intestines, gets off her knees. "If this doesn't push Green out of here, I give up."

"You won't, though."

"No, I'd never." She peeks past the permanent storm shutters at the blue dusk and stars. "It's almost time for your evening stroll, isn't it?"

"Did you want to come with me?"

"You know, that would be nice, actually. I could use some fresh air. Let me go get my shawl and holster."

THE RED SEASON MOON POKES PAST THE RIM OF THE NEAREST HILLS. IT TAKES A thousand steps to circle the camp once.

The night crew is working, lanterns drifting like fire bugs up on the grade. But the linemen down here hug their fire pits.

Two-thousand three.

"What's the first thing you want to do on our land?" Aunt Tess asks.

"Go look for things that were left behind." Colored bottles or buttons or bones. "Probably dig a hole." In case the rocks or left-behind things are better under the ground. "What about you?"

"Plant something," she says. "Probably cry first. I'll weep with joy, then plant something."

The Stranger catches on the clank of saddles, the harsh shearing of hooves on stone. Those sounds are quickly smothered by a rancid bawl, sharp voices.

I move toward the end of camp where the sounds turn to voices. Others are too.

Four hundred.

"Hold it down! Don't get too close!"

A bloodied ox scrambles in the dirt, pinned between men with ropes and digging rods. Green's men, boar rifles on their backs. Foam beads its whiskered chin, chest. A red waterfall from the flesh it's been feasting on, like the one Leagan and I saw.

Not the same one.

No, this ox is marbled gray, not tan, chunks bitten out of its own flank, a yellow crack oozing above its eye. It opens its mouth, bellow retching from its lungs.

The smell gets everywhere.

I see Vesta on the surgery bed in Dr. Pike's office, a brown tinge under her lips. That smell living in each breath.

"*Farce*, just shoot it," Aunt Tess calls. "Put the poor thing out of its misery."

Of course they don't listen to her.

"—this is proof. It was still eating him when we found it. If we cut this thing's stomach open, I bet we'll find more of them."

"Who?" Aunt Tess demands.

"The men who've gone missing." He brushes past her, rough enough to knock her back a step.

"You think one ox ate hundreds of men?"

"How do you know it's that many?"

How do you know it isn't?

On a sheet of canvas dragged behind a black horse is a dead once-mountain cat. A double row of bleeding teeth sprout from the roof of its mouth, caught in the snarl it died with. Globs of its fur are gone. The skin underneath should be gray, but it's purple, veiny.

"Get Von Kane," somebody else calls. "Now."

I barely hear him past the once-oxen's increasing brays and the throb of the Stranger getting bigger in my head.

Todney Engleman pushes through the thickening crowd, grabbing the box camera around his neck. "Sweet Jezebel. Move, this is a great shot. Let me get it." He falls against two line workers as one of Green's marshals throws him back.

"No pictures. Back in your tent, east blood."

"But the folks back home will eat this up. They love monstrous stories."

"And they're too gullible to know when you're spreading lies."

"I have a job to do."

"So do I. If the east bloods could handle the gruesome, they'd be out here themselves." He gives Todney another warning shove, then breaks the camera strap off his neck. "The families of the men this abomination killed don't need to see this. Go back to your tent. If I see you out here again, you'll be sorry."

"I have a job to do," Todney insists. "And you're not to stand in the way of press freedom."

Fool.

"Oh we're free out here all right." The marshal dashes the camera to the packed ground, stomps it. "I'm free to do what I want. This badge and the Rim says so."

Todney's neck flares. "This is all going in my next story, you bastard."

"Good. You just gave me a justifiable reason."

The ox's eyes roll.

I draw the crossgun off my back.

"Please," Aunt Tess says. "This thing is suffering."

There's blood where there should be white around the rims of its eyes, but its scream goes silent as the Stranger's shadow ribbons over its head, my crossgun blast shattering everything inside it.

Poor, savage thing. It's not its fault.

"Burn it," I say.

"You'll thank her later." Aunt Tess steps up as I recede. "Burn both these animals. Now. And for Providence sake, do it away from the camp."

A few of them outright laugh at her.

"Oh-ho, I didn't realize you were put in charge," the Green marshal says. "The families of the men this thing killed don't need to see pictures plastered all over the front page, but they deserve to know their final fate. As do the men here who were their friends. Cut it open."

"You shouldn't have brought it in here in the first place," she says. "Were you born yesterday? That's pestilence."

"Then maybe you shouldn't stand so close," he sneers.

"Lower your voice," someone else says. "It's dark now. That Stranger lurking out there probably doesn't like our noise."

I don't like your noise. I'm not surprised they've already got me mixed up with the other thing out there. Maybe we aren't so different.

The Stranger darkens.

We are.

I would never let her go.

"It will be a quiet night." Green separates himself from the shadows between tent posts, angles toward Todney Engleman who's still clutching his broken camera. "My men will continue to patrol the camp's borders for any remaining human threats. You can all rest easy, the animals responsible are dead. There's no reason to fear the dark."

Aunt Tess put her arm around me, voice cutting cold. "We're not actually afraid of the dark. We're afraid because we know we're not alone in it. Do you have anything by your side that makes those things think twice? I have two. The God of Mercy, and the Stranger."

"I have a revolver," Green says. "And sharp hearing. There's no reason for anyone else to keep watch."

I feel him looking at me. The Stranger slips around him, others, all the ones she wants.

I'll never miss anything about Hannah, but she grew so strong there. So thirsty. Blood like the drawers she compels me to open.

Men are still disappearing.

No one will miss a few more.

Kane gets through the crowd and unsettled dust, cotton suspenders and white shirt buttoned up to the collar but stained with perspiration from another day. "What happened? Is everyone all right?"

"We found Jefferies," one of them on the now slack ropes says. "It was eating him. There was a whole den of bones about a mile from here, down a flood channel, hidden in the rocks."

Leagan and I had already found it. Never went in.

Kane runs a hand down the border of his mask slowly. "Well…At least we know what's behind the disappearances now."

"And this." Green's man kicks the dead cat. "They scream like humans. We knew we were hunting something not right in the head and attracted to human presence, so we set a trap to look like a scout camp. This bastard's eyes glowed green."

Liar.

"Like fuck they did," Aunt Tess scoffs.

"What was that?" Green says, loud.

"I said what a nice bowl of fucking bullsh—"

Green talks louder. "We'll keep setting traps until we get the whole pack of them. Those lights won't bother us anymore. They were just cats after all."

Cats aren't pack hunters. Everyone here should know that.

"We can put this behind us." Kane's voice tells the truth. He wants to believe what he's saying, but he can't. He's heard once-mountain cats before. They scream like a train whistle. Thin, reedy. And their eyes only reflect light, they don't create it. "You can show me where the den is tomorrow, at first light?"

"Yes, sir."

"Thank you. Foreman Micks—" He pauses to find the man among the rest. "Burn the body. Well away from the camp and the worksite."

"Like I said," Aunt Tess sneers in the marshal's direction. "Burn it."

"Sir!" Todney Engleman cuts into Kane's path. "Mr. Von Kane, I'm making a formal complaint against that marshal for destruction of personal property and impugning the freedom of the press."

Kane casts a weary glance at his feet. His sigh seeps into me. "Fine. Come to my tent."

Green's marshals whisper to each other, then nod.

Aunt Tess shakes her head to me as the two walk off. "Well, he's not long for this world. They're going to kill him. I bet you ten gold."

"Probably."

I don't care if they do.

⁂

AUNT TESS GOES BACK INSIDE, BUT I MAKE ONE LAST CIRCLE AROUND THE *Exodus*, make sure all our animals are in for the night.

One of the crew cars sits open.

Daithe drifts back and forth, no mask, tobacco smoldering around him.

He'd better bolt that slide door when he goes to bed.

Eight.

His gaze slips off the Stranger, a non-committal sound coming up his throat. "Wait a second." He lets out one more smoke sigh, then pinches out his dying cigarette, ash flaking away into the night. "Go ahead and find me when you're ready for a baby."

My blood curdles.

"It's up to us to keep our bloodline alive now. They can try, but these Republic shits won't wipe us off the Rim if we don't let them."

I'd let the Stranger kill him right now if we didn't need him and the crew to dig up the Eden mine.

"You're the right age, so don't wait too long."

I could tell him to go fuck himself, but even that feels like more air than he deserves. I focus on the Stranger seeping around him, a predatory fog. It's a good thing he's leaving.

"It doesn't have to be me if you can find another offer. I'm not offering you anything else." He picks his cigarette tin and quartz flint from the door track. "Just don't let one of *them* breed with you."

Grandma didn't raise me so I could be somebody's womb.

A gust of wind hits me like a slap.

This lie is so loud sometimes I'm afraid it might be true.

There are only two options as a woman. The men who want my body to fuck like a piece of meat, and the ones who want it to grow their offspring.

That's what I'm here for. One of these.

But it's a lie, I know it.

I haven't survived this long to save a bloodline.

I did it because there is a third option.

What I want.

FOURTEEN
TESLA

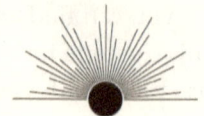

THE STARTUP OF THE STEAM HAMMER WAKES ME WELL BEFORE DAWN, trembling up through the *Exodus*'s steel bones into the framework of my bed. Very rude.

Well, Green was right, it was quiet last night, but that's not *his* doing.

Adelaide is already up, a pale shadow populating the kitchen. The last moonlight drops in bars on the plank floor, the storm shutters angled up to let the light in and so she can watch the comings and goings of the camp. The plate and fork bearing the marks of her breakfast are stacked in the sink, waiting for the rose petal cup still in her hand.

"Good morning, my dear," I say. "Even though it's an ungodly hour. At least I smell coffee. Did you sleep at all?"

"Some."

The table is cornered against two walls, room for the four of us to fit in together. The men who rode this train before would have to be fairly small to sit here other than one on one, so I suspect they didn't spend much time with whoever was cooking. The *Exodus* kitchen is more utility than cozy. I miss Mother's window herb box, but this train does have more storage space than the *Absolution* did.

Phantom pain shoots through the hand that isn't there any more, lodging in my shoulder socket. But as the coffee warms my blood, the sun rises and so does my mood. "It looks like a beautiful day to scrape the shit out of our train."

"There's a storm coming already," Adelaide says.

I lean forward to look at the sky and sure enough, a band of red aura light flexes just off the horizon. It's the only one I catch, but they're not so easy to spot with the sky so pink. "If it doesn't come too close to us, would you be willing to hunt for Engleman the reporter's body? And any evidence Green's men did it."

"Okay. Why?"

"We need anything we can hold over Green." When the time comes, he is not twisting out of my fingers like a little worm ever again.

A mean smile trickles past her lips.

Up until now, arson was the only hanging crime and self-justice executions have always been carried out on the Rim and nobody cares. But it's a new age, darling. East bloods like their law-based justice, at least in appearance.

"Have you taken Raleigh his breakfast yet?" I ask. "The boy's probably still asleep."

She points to the iron skillet I hadn't paid attention to, faded warmth seeping from the second plate that covers it.

"Alkaline. Do you mind if I do it?"

I'm looking forward to this too much to wait any longer.

One of Green's bullies opens the door by degrees the second time I knock, and by knock I mean pound louder.

"Excuse me." I wedge myself past him and the roll of canvas they were using to keep the door from opening in. It has more weight to it than it should. I suspect there's rock inside. "No locked doors on my train."

"These are my quarters for the time being." Green glares at me with an unbuttoned collar, an unshaven face to go with it. "I like my privacy. Providence knows you ladies have done unmentionable things to the men you work with."

I snort. "If we wanted you dead, a lock wouldn't save you." And it won't when the time finally comes. "Good morning, my sweet Raleigh. How was your slumber?"

"The best I've had yet," he says.

"Well, *your* train seems to have an issue with its water supply," Green says. "Did one of the pipes rupture last night?"

"All the gauges are normal."

"Perhaps you should check again."

I stroll to the half-moon sink in the bathroom closet. Nothing comes from the faucet when I turn it, and I am pleased. "Is something not working?"

"We have no running water," Green says. "When was the last time you flushed your pipes or bothered to look at the undercarriage for a water trail? Maybe it's a soft leak from debris."

"When was the last time you flushed *your* pipes? Our water is running fine this morning," I say. "Are you sure you turned the handle the right way?" Oh, the look on his face. It makes my stomach glowy engine warm. "There's water reclaimers outside in the camp."

"If I wanted to haul water—"

"Send one of your big strong men here." I gesture. "Or better yet, you can go find a place to sleep outside that's closer to the sky barrel."

"I predict it's about to get rather ripe in here over the next few days with no one bathing on the regular," Raleigh says. "Goody for me. Thank you so much, Tess."

"I haven't the faintest idea what you mean." But I smirk.

"I know what you're up to." Green gets close enough to me I could shove this fork into his eye without fully extending my arm. There's stale mint and chewed pain tablets on his breath, his body rigid as glass. "Don't think I don't."

"Don't think I didn't see behind your little *farce* last night, either." I close the gap farther. "Your marshals wouldn't have had to show up with dead animals like a curiosity show if the camp trusted your protection more than the Stranger's. They know you're failing them."

"None of us are stupid enough to believe you're only here to sell these guns and snake-piss protection charms. I thought we agreed to be civilized."

"I am perfectly civilized. You're still alive, aren't you?" My temper almost climbs on top of me. "I brought breakfast." I hand Raleigh his plate, then turn my back on Green. "And my mother taught me to share. Are any of you company boys hungry? I was just about to make myself something. We have plenty of food and water up front, we could have a little breakfast party outside."

"If you're cooking," the one who let me in says.

"If you're going to call it a breakfast party, you should let me do the cooking," Raleigh says. "She's okay if you like your eggs and potatoes as a hash, but if you want a poached egg or anything without a burned edge, I'm your man."

"My crews and I have work to do today," Green snaps.

"Breakfast party tomorrow, then," I say. "It's the camp rest day, correct? Six o'clock. Last one to the table is a rotten egg. And since Raleigh was so kind to offer, he's cooking."

His men look happy, Green does not, and that makes *me* happy.

FIFTEEN
ADELAIDE

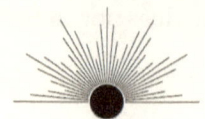

Kane leaves to see the once-ox den, takes Jonathaniel with him. I watch until they're gone and the Stranger is satisfied they won't get in my way.

The sky is clear blue. No storm yet, no smoke from the once-ox's burned body. Because they didn't.

A line rips through the top layer of dirt where it was hoisted onto something and dragged away. It's not hard to follow.

I told Aunt Tess I would look for Todney Engleman's body. But if he's dead, he's not really going anywhere. His bones at least.

Five-nineteen.

Up the grade, some of the men sing rail shanties while they work. They think they're safe now. Like fools.

They're not.

An ox didn't carve a circle of holes high up on the rocks. And a once-mountain cat didn't bury pieces of obsidian deep in a dead man's throat. They don't have hands.

Neither does whoever got theirs cut off in the medical tent.

Now those jars of body parts belong to Navy's lab.

Nine-eighty.

Over here the tents are farther apart, close enough to the construction the repeating hammer-fall of the steam hammer shakes in the earth.

The clank of a chain separates from the noise, gets closer.

I keep behind the sound.

Nine men, covered in red dust and sweat, shackled at the ankles. Three Green Company bullies walk them in, sage gray uniforms stained dark in the armpits.

Murderers and thieves from the east, the kind of men they used to send here to clear rail blockages or to Hannah before we burned it.

Now the east bloods send them here to build their line.

The drag trail dead-ends at one of the pale canvas tents, unmarked.

I face the sun so my shadow doesn't run up the side, then put an eye to the gap in the entrance seam.

Inside is murky. Carpets hang off the support rods to hold in the Ven-chilled air and block out people like me.

It looks just like the medical tent, but it isn't. The green flag is flapping in the wind eight rows over.

Another meat cutting table, cold white porcelain. The torso of the once-ox body lays there, belly splayed open and cavernous.

A hoof sticks out of a bloody sheet on the ground, bone saw perched on the bulk hidden under it. There's a turning smell creeping under my respirator. Chemical.

The fools who brought the body here didn't even bother to cover their trail. They're not afraid of ignoring Kane's order to burn the ox and cat.

What else is back there? The Stranger reaches.

Clothing rustles and a hand clenches around the back of my neck.

The Stranger snaps back into me.

"You shouldn't be here." The Green Company bully drags me off five steps, then lets go before I can do anything to him. "You see those men?"

Yes. The Stranger always sees men well before they see me.

Most of the time.

She glowers and darkens.

One of them tucks a pipe in his teeth, gaze scraping across me like a rake on rocky soil. No mask.

I wish I didn't know that look so well. But I do. We all do.

And I taste it, in the back of my throat, under my tongue. Iron, and the ghost of Hannah's chalk-ash. The Stranger's desire.

"These are the east's worst of the worst criminals," the bully says. "It'll be your own fault if they decide to have their way with you and slit your throat. I'm warning you."

Is it a warning, or him trying to get rid of you?

I didn't survive Hannah with help from hired guns like you. The Republic has been sending their criminals here ever since they realized they could mine crystal for cheap that way.

The chained lineman whistles out the other side of his mouth, passing cigarettes to the three guns. They unlock his shackles, not simply separate them from the larger line like the rest. He leers at me, stares at my body too long before strolling off between tents, down into rocks.

The Stranger tingles all the way down in my fingertips, a dark, bleeding hiss. In the back of my mind, she wraps like a curse around the bottle of knife poison I stole from Montoya, where I keep it in a hollowed poetry book.

There are worse things out here than these dangerous men or pestilence twisted oxen.

Things like me.

Do it, the Stranger whispers again. Harder.

Fresh iron gushes through my jaw. Wanting.

"Get, milk bastard," the bully snaps.

No one will miss a few more.

SIXTEEN
TESLA

I'M TRYING MY HAND AT EMBROIDERY. THEY MAKE STANDS TO HOLD THE HOOP for you and a person only needs one hand to use the needle. It's so very tedious I can only sit for ten minutes at a time, but a lady needs a hobby.

The *Ladies Crafts Catalogue* I stole back in Covenant says to choose an uplifting or enriching quote bordered by the flowers of your birth season. I'm doing gold and red foxgloves for my border, and I plan to embroider something very rude inside.

Leagan drags her work cart into the living car, the scent of grease thick on her red twin buns. "Aunt, Tess! Stand up! I've got something for you."

"Oooh." I gladly stab my needle into the pin cushion. "Is it ready?"

"It's so ready. Are *you* ready?"

The skin covering the remains of my forearm has healed in a nice glaze of cauterization scars. The phantom stabs of pain down in my lost fingers still occasionally wake me up at night, but Raleigh and Dr. Pike have both looked at my arm and say it's healthy enough for a replacement limb.

A hand was a wretched price, but I choose to be glad I'm still alive, not rotting in the ground in Hannah because of Montoya's poisoned knife.

Leagan fits my residual arm into the socket and brings the straps up around my chest, another two connecting over my shoulder. "Now you and Raleigh can have a fight with your arm against his metal leg."

"Oh, I'll win." The metal cups my scar tissue, cool and silky. I test my range of motion, new leather creaking. The appendage is a dagger, of course. "I already like it. No, I change that. I love it."

After all, why replace a hand with a false hand when you can have a knife for an arm?

"Stab something," Leagan says.

"Don't tempt me." I grab the pillow from the bench seat. The ugly brownish one that came with the *Exodus*'s boss car that I haven't had a chance to replace. "Let's go outside."

The sun is still in its golden phase so when moving dust spirals past, it momentarily grants life to the shadows it lays on the ground.

Aside from the dull ache that travels up what remains of my arm, stabbing a hideous pillow is a better release than sex. A few cycles ago, a direct impact like this would have been too painful, but now it isn't any worse than pressing a fresh bruise.

I hug Leagan despite my sweat. She'd do the same to anyone. "Thank you, my dear. You've outdone yourself this time."

"Now you can cut your own meat again…Where are you going? I want to cut more things."

"I have to go get ready. Navy's giving a demonstration of how the contamination compasses work when the line workers are done eating their dinner." If they won't believe my word, let them see the science for themselves.

"Tell her to use the rats and bunnies that scream," Leagan says. "I want everyone to get a good fright. And maybe someone will piss themself."

"Would that make you happy, Raptor?"

"Yes, it would make me happy for the rest of my life."

"I doubt that very much, but I hope you get your wish."

SEVENTEEN
ADELAIDE

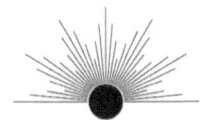

I FOLLOW HIM DOWN.

The sandstone continues to drop sharply, bowls and ledges cut by water, scrappy ironwood trees. I'm out of sight, let him stay ahead, deeper.

Three-seventy.

Thick sand fills up the basin at the bottom.

The Stranger has him like a noose.

Wherever he thinks he's going—

He's not making it there.

Three-eighty-one.

I jump.

My knees and boots collide with his body. A bone picker used this technique on me once. He didn't survive. Sand fills up my fingers, crumbling around my elbow.

He swings at me, but my punch knife has a shorter trip into his chest than his arm does to my head. It sticks in bone. His blow lands on my rising arm, but the power behind it scatters like the sand around our legs.

The knife rips out, still in my hand.

His throat.

Blood pools in the fresh rivulets in the sand. Fast. Dark and red. Red as the pulse that blooms in my stomach and floods through the rest of me.

Dirt is red because of blood.

Did it get on me?

A thin splay across my knuckles. Nothing on my face as I wipe.

His stained jumpsuit has no pockets.

I drag the body close to the sandstone spill so it's hidden from above, then pluck a branch to erase the tracks. He's been worked thin. He's not that heavy.

If anyone does find him, they might not even care. But I'm no fool.

Fifty-three.

I didn't see it on the way down, but climbing back up, I do. An arrow scratched into the sandstone above *NW*.

My compass wobbles drunk circles around itself, even with the Moon Season counter balance attached. I go off the sun.

Fifty.

Another arrow, this one made of shattered glass, arranged on the rocky ground.

The hair on my arms goes stiff. The Stranger presses in, like a wall to my back.

I look behind me. Nothing but brittle bushes and stubborn cactus.

Usually, I don't mind being out alone, I prefer it. But right now, I feel it in a bad way. Exposed. Eyes but no face.

I lift my chin, let it see the Stranger, then trace by way back to the first arrow.

Whatever it's hungry for, it's not going to take it from me.

EIGHTEEN
ADELAIDE

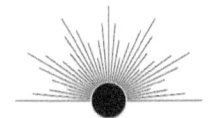

THE HISS AND HEAT OF THE DESERT SITS FLUSH UP AGAINST MY NECK, EVEN though the sun has dropped behind the first ridge.

Nightmare nods with each step, the petrified dunes a natural staircase. Leagan and I are out so far the thud of the steam hammer doesn't exist anymore.

"I see it," Leagan says.

The next arrow scratched into the rock.

Three-thousand eight.

The brown tail of a scavenger lizard gets sucked into the brush and the Stranger pulls tight. The frayed end of a white survey string flutters in the grip of gray sage. Limp yet restless at the same time.

I dismount.

Leagan holds up her contamination compass, glowing like the day.

My exhales get a little louder as I pull my mask into place.

Charred branches, scattered from their central burning point, a broken ring of rock that was used to contain the fire. Half a tent, collapsed under a swath of debris from the last storms.

Twenty-eight.

Flesh beetles scatter as I pull up the tent canvas with a stick.

Forks hide in the crevices of the rumpled wool blanket. I peel a little farther, tumbleweed bits cracking, the weight of dirt shifting. An iron skillet. The ribs could belong to anything, teeth marks fraying the bones and marrow sucked clean. But the femur chopped in half with them is definitely human. So are the teeth. The butchering knife is still in the pan.

"Adelaide, come here."

Leagan has pulled away rocks piled over a natural hole in the sandstone.

Food. Canned fruit, tins of meat, beans. The Stranger starts counting, at least two cycles worth.

"Looks like we found a thief's hideout," Leagan says. "Or maybe a collector rat lives here."

I point out the tent. "Go look under there."

We all know people can turn cannibal under the wrong circumstances. They just don't look like me by default.

They look like anybody hungry enough.

Leagan gasps. "Teeth!"

Anybody infected enough.

"They didn't need to eat each other." The food cache proves it, even if our glowing contamination compasses weren't.

Leagan grimaces. "No, they just decided they liked fresh meat better. Fool's gold, maybe it's Daithe."

The scope and angle finder of a transit poke from the crust that's eating the leather case. The glass is fractured like a star.

Using my stick, I dig it free.

He scratched his name into the brass crossbar. As if a name stops a thief from grinding it off with a rock and carving their own.

T. Grover.

Dead now.

They're trying to be quiet.

But the Stranger notices them, over at Kane's tent, their shadows crossing the lamps.

"What is that *smell*?" Leagan says.

"Shit." It comes through my mask like it's not even there.

Leagan clamps her arm around her face. "Literally."

Ninety-seven.

A man sprints for the end of camp while ripping his belt open, doesn't make it. His stomach empties itself right on the ground.

I taste mine.

"Fuck this." Leagan turns her horse around, gagging. "I'm getting out of here."

I drop from Nightmare's saddle.

"You're going to be sick if you stay. Good luck" Leagan holds her hand out for my reins. "I'll take her back for you."

"Thanks."

I won't be able to sleep unless the Stranger knows what's going on. Even if it smells like the part of death people don't talk about.

Two-twenty.

"Dehydration is the biggest concern they have now," Pike says.

Kane paces around a pile of open crates. Canned goods, same labels as the ones Leagan and I just found. "I don't like lying to them."

"Would knowing make them stop shitting their asses off?" Foreman Micks asks.

"They know they're sick right now. I'd have questions."

"We just got lucky, it seems. Trust me, Von Kane, I've been a foreman since you had baby teeth. The less they have to think about, the easier it'll be on them."

"If DuPonte gets overwhelmed, I'm available to anyone that wants to be seen, no charge," Pike says.

I let him feel the brush of the Stranger. He looks over, even though the rest of them haven't noticed me here in the corner.

I see you.

He likes helping people too much. I still don't know what it means. What he wants.

"Thank you, Doctor," Kane says. "The men won't forget this."

The drop pulse of the steam hammer cuts out. Silence, like a fresh blanket.

"I'll see who's still well enough to work." Foreman Micks turns. His gaze snags me like a fishhook.

"Let them have the night off," Kane says. "Tomorrow, too, if they need it. This isn't their fault."

"Whoever's it is will have a devil to pay." Micks drops the can he's been holding. Beans, still full, but something isn't right about the bottom of it. "This was just how the Tov tormented our soldiers during the war." He points me out. "Think about that."

Pike follows him, taking a wide arc around me. "Call for me if they get worse."

Six.

The cans look normal from the tops, but underneath, a small hole has been poked and sealed back up with letter wax.

Kane weighs me in his sights. "We're still going through the rest...You didn't do this."

I didn't, but we could have. This is smart.

"I might not be as good at reading people as you are, but I do know you a little," he says. "I can tell when you're genuinely curious."

"How?" So the Stranger can erase it.

"It's a soft tell, but it's there. If all the legends about the Shadow Nation were true, you wouldn't need to put a hole in the can to rot it."

Sometimes I wish I could do things like that. "Effortless misfortune."

"Just psychological warfare at its best." He replaces the lid of the top crate. "People are going to have questions, though, and this does fit your family's style. Sabotage. A brutal kind. Is there a chance Tesla did this, and didn't tell you?"

"We don't keep secrets from each other. And she only has one hand." Don't tell her I said that.

"She could have had one of your sisters helping her."

My whole face tightens. "They didn't."

"I have to ask these questions. These men are my responsibility. If I don't ask, someone else who isn't qualified will." His stare lingers again. "You would lie to cover for them, I understand, that's how your family works. But I don't think you are."

Unless they didn't tell you, his tone says.

If I was lying, you'd never know. Damn any fool's gold tells.

He better watch his mouth.

The Stranger does taste sabotage, but it's not about Kane and the railroad. Green is trying to set us up again.

He'd better run when I tell Aunt Tess.

NINETEEN
TESLA

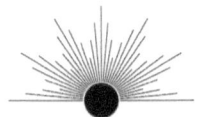

THANK THE GOD OF MERCY, THE MISERIES OF TWO HUNDRED MEN WITH FOOD poisoning have passed by. It only took three days.

I stayed inside the *Exodus*. I don't need to subject myself to that, oh no.

It gave me time to plot instead of letting my temper think for me. And now I know exactly what I will do to Green.

Leagan and I go back to visit the ritual site, but it doesn't appear to have been used again. Maybe we did scare the ghost away, after all.

On our way back, a line of horses comes winding over a saddle pass. Thoughtful of them that the lead horse is white and so is the wagon top.

"Is that who I think it is?" I hold my hand up to the glare. "It *is*. Well, well."

"Ew," Leagan says.

Millard Von Kane, riding out of the western *West* Rim, I might add, not from the east like his son tried to lie.

With him are a group of Green's bullies dressed up in their silly uniforms, and two load bearing oxen saddled with the crawler wagon.

Secrets. How typical.

"Let's go get him," Leagan says.

"Let's let him eat and take a nice basin bath first. We can't have him tired and foul."

"I'm tired and foul."

"Yes, but you're enough. I don't need two cranky people to deal with."

⁕

BRING ME TESLA REVERE. I LIKE THE SOUND OF THOSE WORDS BECAUSE THE aggression in them betrays the self-doubt skulking underneath. Small men have loud voices, darling.

That's what Millard Von Kane told his fetching man to get him when he arrived at his tent.

Me.

I think I win, don't you?

The crawler wagon sits with its tongue against the second Von Kane tent, partially chewed rocks still caught in its serrated wheels. Pity it's already been emptied. But I can get over things like that, unlike Adelaide.

I did consider wearing my knife arm, but it is rather alarming, and I'd rather old Millard was not defensive quite so soon. I feel I know the man because I've heard so much about him and read his spy letter from Kane's first expedition. He and I have only met once.

But men like him don't vary that much.

He's an old name in a tailored gray suit with a high opinion of himself to match it.

I slide the *Exodus*'s cargo manifest past Kane to Millard. He's a boy next to his father now. It's been updated to reflect what we've kept for us and traded with the boneyard, and the claim map Adelaide drew.

Millard doesn't even bother to lift the cover. "Give me a good reason why I shouldn't have you arrested for robbery."

"Arrested and sent where? I hear the Republic is sending its criminals to work the West Rim line expansion now." I graze my hand across the table, the paper warm as I poke it. "I'll give you a better reason. The only thing against the law out here is arson. If you can take something, it's yours...Go ahead, admit that you're, at the very least, slightly impressed with what we did."

"I do not endorse criminal behavior, and I will not venerate it. I asked for a good reason, Miss Revere."

"I'm not wrong though."

"As you were told, the project has no extra funds to buy back what's legally ours, and nothing you can say will make the situation less damning for you."

"I don't want money," I say.

His ticking finger says bullshit, but I'm not bullshitting anyone.

"I want a safe place for the girls and I to build a home. We just want land."

Not *just* land, of course. *Our land.* The thought thrills me down to my fingertips, including the ones that aren't there.

"Ah." Millard almost relaxes. "You are aware, I'm sure, that your gender will make a transaction involving land sticky."

"I'm also aware having money allows you to pass through walls that stand in the way of others. Don't tell me the Von Kanes don't have connections in the land offices, I won't believe you."

"I see you're not naïve to the way of things."

"Was that a compliment? I just might blush."

"Still, when you speak of safety, safety is a luxury only the civilization of man allows, and only the blind truly see. You've undermined your own efforts by your method."

Fool's gold, I think I strained an eyeball in that roll. Never lecture a woman about the absence of safety. We pay for it with our lives, bodies, and dreams every day.

"You're not wrong, and I'm glad to see *you're* not naïve to the ways of things, either," I lie. "We didn't take the *Exodus* to spite you. We did it to prove ourselves to you. You doubted us back in Oath. I could tell, so I decided to take control of our fate."

"I'm not sure that you proved anything other than you can't be trusted."

"That's fair," I say. "But can *you* be trusted? Did Mr. H. Horne trust you'd make good on your offer of a Green Company marshal job when he came back from the West Rim two Seasons ago? It's too bad he didn't make it out alive."

Millard's fingertips brace on the table, tendons tightening into wires, the ones in his neck too. Kane goes still as well, either from Horne's name or his father's reaction.

"I have no idea what you are talking about," Millard says.

"Are you sure?" Your hand just said otherwise, sir. "I seem to recall a letter that was very hard to read unless you know someone who understands the Tailor's Cypher."

"I'll look over your proposal." Millard drags my folder into his lap. "I'm very tired from my journey and have matters to catch up on here. It will be a few days before you can expect a counteroffer."

I smile so nicely even though I despise this suspense more than kidney beans. "I look forward to it."

TWENTY
ADELAIDE

I FIND HIM OUT BY A PATCH OF PRICKLY PEARS. HIS ARMS AND LEGS AREN'T attached to his body anymore, but some of the rope used to tie him down still is.

Still not Todney Engleman.

The third body is older. There wasn't much left other than scattered bones and a bloodstain in the exposed stone, the obsidian that worked its way through him as he melted, jagged and glassy.

I leave them, but not the rock that has a vein of skystone going through it. It bumps in my pocket with good weight every time I move.

Eight.

I rotate with my contamination compass in a full moon sweep.

Clean. But the last body wasn't.

I mark it in my journal. Ritual site three.

They're in a line. If I follow it, I bet I'll find more.

TWENTY-ONE
ADELAIDE

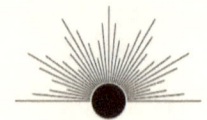

THE STRANGER THROBS TOO HARD FOR ME TO SLEEP.

I miss Grandma when I look at the stars, but maybe I can learn to enjoy it again on my own. With Nightmare. She'll like a nighttime ride.

One-fifteen.

A loose ox blocks the path between me and the west valley, her black horns taller than both of us. Nightmare's ears turn back, her nostrils flaring uneasily.

I stroke her shoulder. "You're okay. You're faster than her."

A goat bleats. Two of them, trotting off into the sage, mouths full of stolen laundry. They're smarter than cows. They know what they're doing isn't allowed and aren't wasting their chance to be naughty.

Are all the animal pens open?

One-forty-three.

I circle back to the freight car where we keep our animals at night.

They're all here, locked in and cozy like they should be. And Dilly sleeps inside with Leagan.

Another goat wanders by. A lazy one.

Someone is up to no good.

The gate into the camp's big pen hangs wide open.

I yank it into place, the latch holds.

"A fox, creeping around the coop after dark." Green speaks from the darkness behind me. "An appropriately ill omen."

His oily gaze doesn't undress me the way he'd look at Vesta. It slips off the Stranger, barbless. I've always been dust to him, back when he thought we were weak. Now I'm a piece of shit he can't pick out of his shoe. Something he wanted dead a long time ago.

"Did you do this?" I ask.

"Do what?"

You know what I mean, I'm not explaining.

"I found the corral unlatched last night," he says. "I thought it wise to come check that it wasn't a reoccurring problem. It seems I was right."

He's setting you up again.

Yes.

"Something's wrong out here." Green lifts his head as if he can smell it in the wind. He can't. "It was wrong before you ever got here, not that the Von Kanes want anyone to know."

I don't want to talk to you.

"But you do," he says. "You were out here before, the eyes of your little operation. Your family and I know the reality of survival on the Rim. It's a thing that won't be tamed as smoothly as the east bloods want to believe. What have you seen?"

"Let Raleigh go, and I'll tell you."

Aunt Tess's water cutoff wasn't enough to get him away from us. She really thought that would work.

"I'm keeping that boy close as long as the four of you are walking above ground. As for you, you should make yourself a valued part of this operation. Not something shady that creeps around after dark, getting the east bloods wound up in bed like a cheap whore. Von Kane will get tired of you eventually, and the Widow with her petty smiles."

He's threatening you.

He's threatening all of us.

Slit his throat now.

I want to. But I promised Aunt Tess she could have him, for Grandma and Vesta. I get anyone else.

I've always known exactly how much respect he has for us: none. I tried to warn Grandma and Aunt Tess. It was already too late.

It's not too late for you.

The iron scent of blood burrows into my throat. I see it, spreading in my dirt-stained sleeves. Vesta's.

The Widow's plans take too long.

I blink. My shirt is black again, but the tang of blood still rides the air.

The next gust of wind sweeps it aside, and it doesn't come back, only animal musk and a twang of redweed smoke. But I know it was real. The Stranger doesn't imagine things like that.

To the west, a ring of pale green light breaks apart the nothingness.

This is my chance, Nightmare's already saddled.

Something pops, like a crack expanding through glass. A burst of orange light floods between tents. Not the moons. Not the night line workers' lamps.

A scream, animal.

Fire.

"What have you done now?" Green grabs for Nightmare's bridle.

She recoils, midnight ears pinned to her head.

"Don't," I warn him.

Something thrashes inside the fire. Something alive, for now. Each time it rears, new gashes of flame seem to rise.

Nightmare's muscles flex under my legs.

"Let go of her." I keep my voice low even though I hold the reins with a tighter fist. *She'll run you over. I'll let her.*

Nightmare jerks her head down, Green's hand slips.

Go.

The fire bell clangs in the center of camp. I shut Nightmare inside the *Exodus* still wearing her saddle.

Two-fifty.

Men stomp at the fire's tendrils, shovels churning up dirt to smother the expanding borders. Less water can be used this way. But the wind isn't on their side. Orange ribbons detach on each gust, still burning when they land.

"Put the tents out first!"

Kane.

"Cut it off there. Whatever happens, don't let it spread toward the explosives storage."

I hope they buried the stash away from camp like you're supposed to.

The thrashing thing in the center of the blaze goes still, the animal screams with it. Dust starts to blot out the flames, night reclaiming the camp.

Heat presses into me the closer I get.

It's thick. Legs tangled and black, bovine hooves still visible and everything that isn't charred oozes and smokes.

Kane leans against a shovel, forehead to his fist. "Is everyone okay?"

Silence, smoldering canvas.

"It seems we have an arsonist in our midst." Green peels from the reclaimed shadows. "I've dealt with this kind of bone picker before in Vantage, and I promise to bring you the fire-lover who did this. Male or female."

He turns, looks through his mask at me.

I was standing right next to you when this happened, fucker. But it's not his first try to blame us for something we didn't do. Or even the second.

Make it his last.

"Report any suspicious activity to my marshals," Green says. "Anyone you see messing around where they're not supposed to be. Better to be over-vigilant than to be sorry."

The Stranger feels the foreman's gaze on me, heavy, wary. I shouldn't have let him see me by Kane's tent the other night.

"Remember Winchester, remember Hannah, now in ruins," Green says. "It's possible the same person followed us here. We won't let that be our fate."

"We remember Winchester," someone calls.

He knows.

The Stranger warps closer to me. I stay right where I am. Sinking away would look guilty.

"This is not a ghost tormenting us, just a dishonorable liar. We have honorable men with guns to protect us, not foxes and shady ghost stories told by swindlers selling protection for a price."

I fold my arms. I have to hold the Stranger in. Heat moves through my chest up into my teeth. But I know this rage, one you can't win against no matter what you do. Having what you are used against you.

"Let's make sure the embers are all out." Kane moves into the circle of lantern light, stabs his shovel into the crispy ground. "I'll take the first watch around the perimeter, I'll need four other volunteers to join me, and two more to keep an eye on the fire's remains, just in case. We'll do a four-hour shift, then seven more will replace us."

Hands go up right away.

"Thank you." He nods. "Everyone who just volunteered gets an Exodus rifle. Meet me at the munitions cache. Those who just lost their belongings, come with me too. The rest of you, I hope you sleep well."

The foreman uncrosses his arms, motioning at Green for a private word.

The Stranger floods through my eyes, only pinpricks wide enough to see the foreman shirk back, even though he doesn't know what just scared him.

Kill him.

Green crosses in front of me. "Go back to your train, Stranger."

"I told the Raven and the Widow not to trust you," I whisper. "A long time ago."

"It's unfortunate they didn't listen."

Kane brings his hand across Green's path before he can walk away, inches off his chest. "What are you doing? My men don't need rumors, or you riling their fear up. Some of them lived in Winchester."

"Your men just saw you pick a side. And it's not theirs."

Kane shrugs that away. "What were you hoping to accomplish?"

"I'm doing the job your father picked me to do, bringing the vermin that have plagued the Rim for too long to heel. Those that bite get their head stepped on." The jut of his chin casts the spite in my direction. "That family is nothing but trouble."

"I'm sorry you misunderstood your job description," Kane says. "The law is meant to keep order, not stir the pot. I know more than half of these men are violent convicts. Don't get them riled, especially not towards the girls. I won't have that."

"I'm less concerned about what you will or won't have than I am about this girl who wanders around at night and won't say why. Arson is the Rim's original hanging crime, and she's threatened my men with it in Descendants before."

"Leave her alone," Kane warns. "Unless you have proof."

You have to be more careful now.

I know.

Green seems like he's about to back down.

I'm wrong.

"Her sister, the one they call the Rook, she's up to something inside that train. I think it's worth asking what she's doing in there and why she never leaves it. Not only do they have the knowledge to make flash fire, but they also have the means."

Two—

Kane's arm stops me this time. The Stranger lashes out and for a trigger moment I almost let her.

I'm used to people threatening me, but Navy. No.

"I said leave her alone," Kane says. "I mean all of them."

I'm going to tell Aunt Tess *and* Leagan what you just said, and I'll make sure she kills you tonight. Threaten my sister again, and I'll set *you* on fire.

Thirteen.

Kane follows me instead of going to the weapon's tent. It's the other way.

"I don't know why Green has it out for you," he says. "But I'm worried accusations like that might stick."

I don't need you to tell me that.

"What is Navy doing?"

"Aunt Tess will tell you." And he'd better be smart enough to see this is the truth again. Stay out of my way.

"Whatever is going on between your family and him, I'd rather not know. Please don't make me get involved…Please be careful."

Fool, this has nothing to do with you.

TWENTY-TWO
TESLA

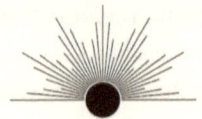

ADELAIDE PACES THE LIVING CAR LIKE A SPRING COILED TO ITS BREAKING POINT.

"I know you're mad," I say. "You're protecting your sister. But Green is trying to provoke you. He's baiting us to make a mistake, so the Von Kanes turn on us."

"I warned you." Her scowl could burn a hole right through *Exodus*'s iron shell. "Back at the beginning."

"He doesn't have us yet."

"Yes, he does."

"Kane still had your back tonight. If we have him on our side, we still have his father."

"You have that backwards," Leagan says. "Kane does everything his father tells him. If Millard said go pick your nose and eat it, I bet he would."

"It's not my fault Green got ahead of us last time," I say. "None of us knew he'd set us up like that."

"We know now," Adelaide says. "So don't wait too long making over-complicated plans."

Fool's gold, that stings, but I don't snap back at her like I could. "We all make mistakes. We were both trusting the Raven."

"Don't blame Grandma."

"I'm not."

"Please don't fight," Navy says. "It'll just make everything worse."

"If we kill him tonight, on our train, it'll be way too obvious who did it. I'm not going to hand us over like that." It's clear she doesn't trust me, painfully clear. "I'm still sorry I let you down in Hannah. I'll spend a long time doing better for that."

"That doesn't matter now."

"It sounds like it does."

Adelaide wrings her forearms against each other. No part of her can stay still.

"I won't let anything happen to you," I promise. "To any of you."

Leagan exhales loudly, slouching lower on the couch with a groan. "Green's not going to do anything to us this second, he's too lazy. You both need to go to bed."

She's probably right.

I leave my chair to take hold of Adelaide's hand. There are tears trying to break free of her grip.

"I promise I'll do better this time."

A tremor runs through her hand, the muscles in her neck drawing lines. It's only here for a second, but what I see and what I feel align. A dark flicker, like a moth, and a weight on my skin that tastes like fear.

It's not her that doesn't trust me, it's the Stranger.

Adelaide is holding it back.

I've never spoken to it—her—before, but she must be able to hear me. "Don't worry, I love her too. I won't fail her again."

PART TWO
NOTHING BUT GHOSTS

TWENTY-THREE
ADELAIDE

I still haven't found Todney Engleman's body.

I'm deep into a slot canyon when a human voice sends a jolt through my spine. It's singing.

The stone walls change it, warp it. Walls scraping high enough to keep sunlight from fully finding the bottom. But not the heat. That's rising, even though it's only seven.

It doesn't sound like any song I know.

I could just leave. But I'd rather see who it is, know.

One-fifteen…

The Stranger tightens.

Four men sit in a pool of milk-blue water and steam, red as raw meat, laughter and whiskey on their breath. There are other shallower bowls in the sandstone, but they're empty, made by rainwater that dried a long time ago.

This pool is different.

The dial on my belt glows.

One by one the laughter on their mouths bleeds off, turns lurid, but I'm frozen.

"Come here, fox." A bough of white water sloughs off him as he lifts a hairy arm. "There's room for you. It feels so good."

I see it. Finally.

"I have to say I'm looking forward to a hot bath," Vesta said to me on the way out of here the first time. She loved them.

I know why it was her, not us. She and Randy found a thermal pool.

"Don't be prissy, come in."

I have to tell Navy.

"Look at her." Water and steam falling as he stands, body red and puckered.

Naked men are the most unattractive things that exist.

A different one grabs for my ankle, misses by a double arm's length. They laugh as I take another step back.

I don't want a drop of that water to touch me.

"Don't worry," the one standing goads, touching himself. "What do you think is going to happen?"

Not what you think is going to happen.

I pull my crossgun off my back and unload both shells. No precision. No mercy.

The chalky water turns. First pink, then orange, then red.

Three of them manage to scramble out, screaming at me, at each other. One immediately slips in the blood flowing down his legs, the wet slap of flesh meeting rock.

A sweaty flop of black hair floats on water.

The under-action lever brings a bolt to the bowstring. I like the way the firing changeover switch snaps.

One. Sidestep.

He catches himself before plunging into a cactus laden with needles. The other shoves past him, trying to close me between them.

The Stranger rises, all black and bloodthirsty. A long, slow blink.

Keep moving.

I pump the action lever again.

He's too close. I swing with the butt end of my crossgun instead. He grabs a rock. It won't save him.

The Stranger closes over me again. Dark as sleep.

Eleven.

The last one runs down the hall of rock that water cut. Walls too high to climb. The Stranger stays on him as I follow, opening the shell chamber.

Twenty-one.

He looks back. "Shit! Stay away from me, you crazy bitch!"

Forty-five.

My crossgun clicks as I snap the chamber shut, reloaded.

You started it.

I GIVE NIGHTMARE CARROTS AND WATER BEFORE TURNING HER OUT ON THE LINE to graze. This grass was clean yesterday, but I check it again.

I can't let myself go back to my bedroom car yet. I need to get this out before I change my mind, or the Stranger does.

Kane is drinking coffee, fried ham grease still radiating from the cookstove.

He slept in.

Two-fifty.

"Good m—"

"I need to ask you about Randy."

"Oh." His mask goes up at his brow does. "Okay."

"While Navy and I went to the Wells's graves with you and Markos, did he tell you what happened?"

"Is this about your sister?"

He must know by now. That she's not here. "What did Randy say?"

That's not his usual laugh. This one is difficult, choked. He does know something.

"I stopped him from giving me any details. But he made it sound consensual...It was, wasn't it?"

To my knowledge. Vesta wasn't shy.

"There's something specific you're asking for, isn't there?" he says. "Go ahead and tell me."

Why do you let him see into you like that?

I don't choose to. He just does.

You're wrong.

I don't know.

Well stop.

This is what happens when you have a friend. They know you.

Thadie wasn't fooled by the Stranger either. She could also tell the difference between silence and things I didn't want to say. She didn't question me about them. I found that comforting. Like Grandma, like

Leagan. You can know someone without knowing everything in their head.

Answers.

Then I can leave.

"Did Vesta and Randy find a hot spring?"

"Yes...and that was about all I listened to, I promise."

"It's how they got infected." I hold onto myself with both arms. It doesn't keep out the memories that flash around my head, making me unsteady. "Why they did, and we didn't. There are some places where the pestilence has settled, and other places where it isn't."

"Oh..."

I realize I've been picking at a rough edge around my thumb. Blood seeps up through the dry corner around the nail.

"That makes...sense, actually. I never made the connection."

I saw the inconsistencies, but didn't understand why. Only Navy did.

"You found one, didn't you?" he says. "A contaminated spring. How can you tell the difference?"

"You shouldn't go there."

"I need to know where it is."

No, you don't.

"I just have to take your word for it, then?"

Yes.

"If it's contaminated, I need to warn the men, in case anyone else stumbles onto it."

They already did.

"Where did that blood on your sleeve come from?" he asks, and I doubt he's just noticing.

I'll have to burn this shirt. Maybe all these clothes. Washing them won't be good enough.

"This." I show him a glimpse of my contamination compass with the hand that's bleeding. Just one. "It tells me if we're safe."

"Your sisters made that, didn't they?"

I nod.

Kane inhales the way he always does when he's about to say something uncomfortable. "I know this doesn't change anything, but—"

Fuck, he's going to say it. I hold myself tighter.

"I'm so sorry about Vesta...And your grandma."

I'm sorry too. If I'd known, I would have made Vesta come with us to the graves or made her stay home. But I've been through all that so many times, there's a groove worn in my head, and being sorry doesn't change what's already happened.

"I was very close with my brother," Kane says. "It's been years, and it's still hard not having him to talk to. I still miss him." His hand is dry, warm as it closes around mine.

I don't know if I should let him touch me. He had ideas before.

"All the time."

Me too. And I'm afraid I always will. That's the cost, isn't it? The cost of caring about someone.

Not everyone is worth it...But some people are.

There was a point when I thought he might be one of them.

It went away.

I take my hand back. "If you find a hot spring, don't touch the water."

TWENTY-FOUR
TESLA

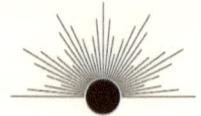

THE LIVING CAR ISN'T EMPTY AS I PASS THROUGH ON MY WAY TO THE KITCHEN.

"Good morning, Widow!" Raleigh straightens from the nest of pillows on the couch, smile bright and songbird cheerful.

"Well, well, fancy meeting you here. Did the Stranger get you to slit Green's throat last night?"

"No, I wouldn't take that pleasure away from you." He strokes the velvet couch-back with a sigh. "It's so nice to be away from all those men and their body odors."

"I'm sure it is." I put my ear to the speaking tube and listen.

I've purposely left the cap open in the car where Green's been squatting, and asked Raliegh to open it again if Green ever notices. Don't worry, we keep this end plugged, especially last night.

"He's not in there," Raleigh says. "He and his marshals packed up all their shit this morning and left me. Rudely early in the morning, but I saw the opportunity to escape, and I took it."

"I'm proud of you."

"Thank you, I thought you'd be."

"Well, he must have finally figured out what was good for him." I'm going now to bar the doors. That slimy bastard's not getting back into my train. "He was going to die today."

"He must have sensed your ill intent...Please don't ever underestimate him again."

"I would never." It's only a needle sting to my pride. "Did Adelaide talk to you?"

"No, I haven't seen her since breakfast delivery yesterday, why?"

"She and I had a disagreement about when to deal with Green."

"Disagreement, the nice way of saying—"

"Okay, we argued."

"Is it the first time you two have ever really argued?"

"Yes, actually..." I flop down next to him so we can speak softer. "I know I can't make her talk to me about Hannah, but we know she suffered there, but I also know it would help her if she did talk. She's mad at me for our plan to get her out of there falling apart, but she won't admit it."

"You're assuming. She has to heal in her own way. And that's not always a straight line, is it? Our family has changed. You and she are still adjusting to your new reality."

I sigh. "I will never be my mother."

"I don't think you're supposed to be. You're not replacing her, you're bringing what you have to the role of matriarch. Tesla Revere, engineer and mine boss. And Adelaide is your bloody left hand who challenges you to become a better tactician."

"She doesn't trust me anymore, but I can't fix that if she won't tell me how."

Raleigh purses his lips. "You're wrong."

"How so?"

"Well, we are talking about Adelaide, and she bothered to argue with you. She's trusting you with her opinion."

Damnation, he is so right. I'm a fool. "Where were you last night?"

He smiles kindly. "Just be nice to each other and yourselves, okay? I'm sure you and Moira didn't always agree."

No, we did not. I won't assume she told me everything either. "Listen to you. When did you get so wise?"

"I've had a lot of time on my hands lately." He exhales. "Not to change the subject, but Green has gotten angrier since we've been here. I could feel it."

And that does tend to make men dangerous. Women too, though, don't forget now. And I've been angry for a long time.

TWENTY-FIVE
ADELAIDE

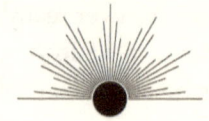

THE MEDICAL TENTS ARE GONE.

The one with the butcher's table and cold box buried under the floorboards, the decoy one with the green flag too.

They weren't moved, they're not here anymore. I walk every row of the camp, know how many tents there were before the fire, how many are here now.

But it was here. I'm standing in the leftover rectangle, plants flat and dead, eight holes in the red ground from the tent spikes. There are no good reasons for this to be happening. Only bad.

There are too many people here, trampling the sage and orange globemallow, making noise and moving things.

The Stranger prickles on my skin like a spiderweb.

They'll keep spreading, webbing, digging up things that shouldn't belong to them. Taking.

Three-forty.

Sawdust clings to the floorboards of the new Express Rider and Assay Office. They've moved all the camp's tables next to it, strung lanterns up on wires over them.

Leagan waves at me as she and Raleigh come this way, a wooden case in her arms. "Look what I got."

Inside is a portable gramophone, a pocket of records.

"Aunt Tess just sold a whole bunch of the contamination vials to Kane," Leagan says. "He didn't have quite enough money on him, so he bartered this. And it's mine now. She didn't say so, but I did."

"It's nice," I say. "Now we'll have one for the living car and your room."

"We also found chicken races over on the miner's side of things. Doesn't that sound fun?" Raleigh says. "Do you want to come with us?"

I'm not going out again tonight. There are too many people. I just want to know what they're doing over here.

Eleven.

More men come by lugging crates of food.

"It looks like they're having a party," Leagan says.

"I could tell you all the dirt I have on Green now," Raleigh says.

"Is it good?" I ask.

"I definitely saw him almost naked. He has a tattoo."

"Ooo, what of?" Leagan says. "I hope it's a little tea pot."

Vesta always suspected he had body warts. I still don't care to know.

"Oh." Leagan perks up. "He'll know what's going on. Hey!" She yells as Kane comes this way. "Why are you throwing a party?"

He carries the box I know from Leagan's workshop. "The men have earned themselves a night off and a little celebration."

"For building a shed?"

I feel him smile, but there's something else under it. "We've been doing it with every seventy-five miles of track laid. They work hard. It keeps up morale."

Little things to keep them from turning on you.

"There will be drinks and music, you and your family are welcome join us."

"Maybe we will," Raleigh says.

"Enjoy the gramophone," Kane says to Leagan. "I'll miss it."

She turns on her heel, smugly. "I will."

Four.

Kane stops me. "You were the one who told me things are different out here."

The sound of the words, or maybe the feeling of them, make him wince at their halfway point. I know. I hate that taste of regret that words leave behind. They're not worth it.

"You said the pestilence changed things that live on the West Rim. I felt it when you left Eden. You didn't just mean the things that got infected. There's something...*out* here. Something we can't see, like a weight...It's hard to define. But you've felt it all along, haven't you?"

Something that watches.

"Yes." I felt it look at me, past the Stranger. But a feeling without a name isn't enough to stop her from wanting the other side of the next hill.

"Are we in danger?"

You wouldn't go home if I said yes.

It's too late.

"Jonathaniel mentioned he met you in Hannah. He said you talked about the Von Kanes."

Farce.

The Stranger lashes out, low in my stomach. If I wasn't wearing my mask, he might have seen my face do something I don't want him to. I survived Hannah. I'm not sorry, not ashamed, but that doesn't mean I want everyone talking about it. Pitying me.

"You haven't seen him today, have you?"

"No." And that's on purpose. "How long has he been missing?"

"I'm not sure that he is. He's—"

"A fool."

"That's one way of putting it." Kane steps out of my way. "You should come to the party tonight. You don't have to talk to any of the linemen. My father really wants to meet you."

Vulture.

* * *

AUNT TESS COMES TO MY CAR.

"First of all, thank you," she says. "Not what you were expecting?"

"No."

She smiles. "You still think I'm trustworthy enough to share your thoughts with. Green is the last fucker who I'd let come between us."

"Me neither."

"Did you kill him yet?"

"I can't find him." He left camp, gone like the butcher's tent. Nothing but a bad sign.

"Well, he dodged a crossgun bolt I suppose."

"He's smarter than you want to believe." Or else he wouldn't have survived us this long. "We can't just let him go."

She folds her arm across what's left of the other. "I'll make you a deal, okay? Save him for me, and the next time he shows his slimy face back here, I'll kill him."

"What if he doesn't come back? He's not going to kill any of us himself, he's going to get someone else to do it for him."

"If something happens that makes you and the Stranger decide he's too much a threat, do what you decide in the moment. I won't be mad."

"Just disappointed."

"Does that make you feel better? And her too?"

She's getting harder to resist. I don't think she wanted to hurt Aunt Tess last night, just Green, but what if I was wrong?

What if one day, she gets strong enough to rip herself out of me? What will happen to me then?

If someone offered me a choice, that I could have Grandma or Vesta back if I gave up the Stranger, I don't know if I could do it.

That scares me too.

It's good enough for now.

"Okay," I say. "I can live with this plan. So can the Stranger."

"You and I are unstoppable together." Her gaze drifts up at the ceiling with another smile. "We have the *Exodus* as proof. But I couldn't have done it without you. We couldn't have done it without Leagan and Navy." She takes my hand. "I've always known I was supposed to be more, but I don't want it if I have to do it alone. All of us still have so much to do. Together we can't lose."

She's not wrong.

All the worst things have happened when we weren't together.

TWENTY-SIX
TESLA

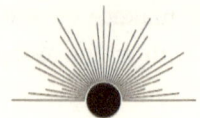

IT'S NOT QUITE THE PARTY COVENANT THROWS FOR THE MARKET FAIR. BUT THEY have music that hasn't gotten too wild yet since everyone is only slightly tipsy. And the vials of contamination fluid Kane begged to buy from us do look very nice hanging next to the lanterns. None of them are glowing, thank the moons.

"Honey cakes *and* cheese. What a feast," I say.

Raleigh nods. "One can never have too much cheese. That should be in the Bible."

"Which pot of chili are you going to vote as the best?"

Leagan shrugs over her tin mug of melonade. "I'm going to cheat so neither of them win."

"How?" Raleigh laughs.

"Should we bring Adelaide back something?" I ask.

"I'll make you a distraction." Leagan unclips the lower half of her mask to dog whistle. "Hey, you fools! Who wants to see the best shot on the Rim? If you can beat me, you get a prize...Only you won't know what it is." She adds just for us to hear.

A good few men raise their hands and spill her way.

"Hold this." She passes off her drink to Navy, pulling a silver standard and hand mirror from her coveralls.

Navy links her arm through mine instead of solely relying on her strolling cane. The hats hanging next to each chili pot are both half full of voting rocks. I have the idea to drop one into the pot instead, but I don't because I'm not Leagan.

Millard nods cordially as I get close enough; he can no longer avoid me without appearing rude. The amount of interest he seems willing to waste on anybody here. These are just his employees after all, and these high-society east bloods have to ration their social energies.

"Have you had a chance to decide on our offer?" I ask.

"Tonight is not for business, Miss Revere. We're honoring the work done by these brave men. Let them have their moment."

"I bet that steam hammer is relieved to have a break too."

"She's quite the shot." Kane nods to Leagan. "You should give it a try. Father is the Wednesday Club pistol dueling champion back home."

"Oh, really?" I say. "Well, I'd proceed with caution, and only if you want to lose your title. Leagan's been shooting since she was four."

"Where is *Adelaide* this evening?" Millard says, adding unnecessary flourish to the vowels for reasons hopefully known to him. But I could make my own guess. "She was invited."

"She doesn't like parties," I say.

"Have you told her I'd like to meet?"

"You told me tonight isn't for business, remember?"

The crack of Leagan's pistol trails off like smoke. She takes a bow as the men shake her hand, then rattles the scarf full of standards she won at us. She looks just like some kind of woodland spirit prancing back this way with Dilly on her heels.

"You've a sharp eye, young lady," Millard says.

"I know." She smirks as she unclips her mask to drink again.

"You know..." He bites off the sound in his throat. "Well, there's always room for improvement."

A girl is supposed to be flattered and full of blushes and *thank yous*. I *know*—that's how a woman accepts a compliment. If you're good at something, you damn well do know it. You don't fall out of bed and land there by accident, you work for it. But men hate that. They want you to be grateful for their attention, not well aware of what you deserve.

"Leagan, show him—"

One of the lanterns explodes, a shower of glass and fire quartz falling in my hair and down my shirt. I dive for cover by the closest table along with everyone else nearby, shoving Navy under it. It was just one gunshot, but no one wants to be where the next one lands.

I'm looking everywhere for where it might have come from as I get my pistol from my vest harness, and that's when I see.

The vials strung overhead are no longer white. Like tender daylight, the fluid inside glows a milky green. Dread curdles me the same way as I look back.

A dark line drifts out of a red glow caused by the sun collapsing on the cliffs, and like a shadow, it grows limbs.

The center point moves like a man, a crown of ghostflower on his head turned bloody with sunset, but the six creatures being led by him don't move like anything I've ever seen, not even in a childhood nightmare.

Liza was always frightened of the spooky stories Mother sometimes read us when Father wasn't home and the solstice fog settled heavy on the trees, but I loved them.

A chill enters my skin in spite of the sweat sticking to my creases. Two of the bone pickers walk upright, but the rest crawl, their legs almost straight so their naked backsides weave higher than their heads. The lengths of chain shackling them to the man rattle with every jerk.

My breath leaves me. None of them have hands, their forearms skinned down to bone and sharpened into points that they balance on.

"Krossus..."

"What the fuck is that?" Leagan says, fingers still deftly feeding fresh bullets into her pistol while her gaze stays with the monstrosity.

Navy grips my ankle, and my body is already too alarmed to remember that usually tickles. "Aunt Tess, what's happening?"

"You don't want to know."

"Yes, I *do*."

"I'm not sure where to start..."

"Get the table flipped over," someone hisses, and several men work together to flip the long pine beast on its side.

It does make me feel better having something to crouch behind. I gather Navy's arm into mine.

Millard stands his ground, and Kane reluctantly rejoins him. Everyone else wisely stays low to the ground. I've never heard so many people hold their breath so quickly.

The fun is over, only the wind speaks.

"That's close enough," Millard says.

One of the leashed pickers cocks its head at his voice. Too far in my opinion, half-man half-owl. The others stretch toward us at different angles. Black mouths spill open, seeking something fleshy to bite. But instead of teeth and gums, rotted flesh pulls up to empty sockets, some even farther, exposing jawbones pitted with decay.

"Who are you?" Kane nudges closer, rifle pointing at the ground.

Something—I believe intestines, even though I really wish they weren't—flop around the man's neck like sausage links. I've never liked sausage links, and now I definitely will not.

"What purpose brings you to us?" Millard asks.

"I come with fell tidings of great suffering."

A murmur goes through the men like a shudder.

His voice isn't what I expected from a body leached by the desert. It has volume and command, like Millard's does.

"Fear not." He lifts his hands, palms shining with burn scars. "My children are sated and obedient, they will not harm you."

"It's just so hard to believe that coming from a man holding a bunch of pickers rotted out of their minds on leashes," I say to Leagan.

He smiles through me—his teeth brown with rot. "Unless I should command it."

"If you're hungry, we have plenty to share," Millard says. "I only ask that you remove these poor afflicted souls from our midst, they're clearly unwell and there are women here. This nudity is inappropriate for them."

"I can speak for the women here," I say. "We've all seen worse."

We bleed and suffer every moon phase, yet men are still so convinced we fear the gruesome. It's an easier thought for them to digest, I suppose, when the alternative is we are just as bloodthirsty as they are.

"I don't like this," Navy whispers. "Let's go back to the train."

"We can't, he's looking at us," Leagan says.

"Stop talking to him, Aunt Tess."

The man lets go of the bone picker's tethers, the chains splaying out in the dust. "Behold."

"You're exposing everyone here to the pestilence," Dr. Pike says from somewhere among the crouched bodies. "It's not safe for you, either."

A cold spot blooms on my back as Navy lets go, the fabric she clenched damp with sweat.

"I said take me back to the train." She feels around for her walking stick, intending to go on her own.

I catch her by the arm before she tries. "Okay, I'll take you."

"Providence has given me dominion over all things, even death." The man wanders a circle. "I've seen what's real. I see what is, and now I am not afraid."

The conviction in his voice strikes something primitive deep inside me, and despite myself and the girls and his obvious delusion, I am afraid of what I've failed to see.

"I asked who you are." Millard's voice booms like the cannon he so strongly resembles, all the authority of his status behind it. "Speak your name and your real purpose here or you will not be welcome any longer. You're denying these hardworking men of the Republic the night off they earned."

The man swivels his neck ahead of the rest of him, much like his pickers did. "Hardworking...men...of the...Republic..."

Fuck me, could he make those pauses more excruciating?

"Reverend. Alonzo. Seed." These syllables drip out of him like venom from a fang, like we should know them.

Yes he can, apparently.

The sharp crack of Leagan's gun breaks apart the collective breath they've all been holding, and it becomes a collective gasp. On that wind is a bittersweet tinge of relief that this might be over.

But it doesn't last. That would be too easy, darling.

"Goodbye," Leagan says, smoke still bleeding from her barrel, that barrel still pointed at Reverend Alonzo Seed.

Shock hollows her shoulders.

His cracked lips part, a thin smirk breaking free as the last of the sunlight turns its back on us.

She missed.

Did she? But how?

He'd be dead otherwise. Leagan never shoots to wound.

More barrels take aim from behind the tables, a handful of Green's bullies finally creeping out to do their job, but Millard holds up a fist.

"Enough. Before someone gets hurt. You will leave this camp sir, and don't come back. In case you haven't heard the news, the West Rim is no longer unclaimed territory, it belongs to the Von Kane name. Myself, my son, and our partners are duty-bound to protect these men who are here to earn their living. If you do decide to appear again, know we won't hesitate to remove you."

I touch Leagan's back, so she knows I'm here before speaking, but even that makes her flinch. "What happened? You missed."

Her breath comes in pulses through her respirator. "Fuck if I know."

"There's so much space out here." Seed wanders in an uneven circle, his arms open. "Deep enough to get lost in...Die on the tongue of the thing that was made."

"Goodnight, sir," Millard says.

Seed's bone pickers creep forward on their sharpened radiuses, no one holding onto their chains.

Kane adjusts his stance, breathing in for his shot.

"Sweet little girls don't touch dirty things like guns," Seed says.

Leagan rips off her mask, covering her nose with an arm instead. It's possible the lack of peripheral vision inside it did cause her to misjudge her aim. "I'm not a sweet girl."

Her shot's still ringing as one bone picker sprawls dead, its sharpened limbs raking through the earth, a red crack in its bruised skull. Her second shot comes fast behind it and another one falls, then a third, then another and another. Like a knee jerk, the men around us squeeze their triggers, careless shots nicking off wood and tin.

"Hold fire," Millard yells.

Seed doesn't waste a glance at the dead pickers, I mean his "children." But something behind me does give him pause. His eyes...change. He turns with a hitched shoulder. I get one glimpse of the solid black glare in them and a high-pitched hum fills my head.

Adelaide.

TWENTY-SEVEN
ADELAIDE

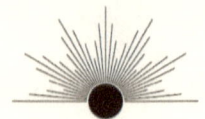

SEED PEELS HIS CURLED SHOULDERS BACK. HIS SHADOW RAKES ME, MY crossgun. The Stranger meets it, two snarling blades. I've always known I couldn't be the only one. But sometimes I've wondered if I was.

His glare narrows. "The desert has eyes. One hundred eyes. You're never alone in it."

He can see her.

But so do I.

Faint lines fold out of him and dissipate, cobwebs falling in the wind. It has the same pulse as the thing I've felt breathing in the Rim's cracks. I thought it had to stay in Eden, but it's sent out roots, burrowed into him like a river leech.

Hunger.

My ears keep ringing, even though the initial sting of Leagan's shots have passed. I feel the gaze of every man latching onto me like individual fishhooks. There's no getting away unnoticed now, even with the Stranger.

We aren't the same.

"No one fire," Millard warns them again. "This man is clearly disturbed with the sun."

"Raptor, take Rook back to the train," Aunt Tess calls.

"I'll go with them," Kane says.

"Fuck that, I'm not scared of him." Leagan checks her pistol, and I can feel it in the silence between her words.

She is.

Who wouldn't be?

Seed lifts an arm like I'm a curtain he can brush aside.

I draw a handful of the obsidian shards I've collected from the ritual sites, then flick them at his feet.

He shirks back. Single step.

He did it.

The murmur travels like a storm. "He's afraid of her...They weren't lying?"

"You should go now, Reverend," Kane says. "I'll make sure you leave safely."

"Why?" Leagan scoffs.

"Because that's the way civilized people behave," Millard says. "Restraint and honor are what separates us from him."

From you, he means.

"Come, my children." Seed tugs at one of his bone pickers. The chain hisses against the ground but the thing is dead weight now, eyes and tongue rotted away a while ago. "We are not welcome here, even where they sent us. I'll take you home."

I won't waste a bolt on a shot that's going to miss. Let the sun kill him. Let one of his children eat him.

All six chains go straight and Seed stumbles over himself, like he just realizes they're dead. "Look at what you've done."

"Go resurrect them," Leagan says.

Seven...

"Adelaide," Kane calls, sharp.

You're not paying me this time. I don't have to do what you say out here.

The Stranger finds a split in Seed's shadow. His face twists as she seeps in, something violent in his throat, but she doesn't let him say it.

"We'll take care of him. We can track him out into the desert." Three bullies line up next to Kane with their rifles, but he shakes his head.

"Let him go."

"He knows where the camp is."

You think this is a new development? Everything knows where you are because you make so much noise.

Twenty-five.

The Stranger backs Seed up to the line where the scar of the camp ends in orange globemallow, scrapes one foot against the other, brown toenails worming from his boots, cleaning himself of me.

His shadow scrapes up me one more time, against the grain, pressure on my lungs. It comes like a fever, with a shiver. Grandma, sobbing in pain and full of regret while blood flows out of her mouth and stomach. It's what I've imagined happening as she died.

But I wasn't there.

It's not real.

The Stranger rips the image out.

Seed's matted head disappears in the brush, scuttling down into the rocks like an animal does.

I turn. The silence hangs like an empty doorframe. Nothing but wind. No night slips, no sugar bats. Everything frozen except for the Republic flag kicking on the pole.

Slowly, Kane turns back to the gathering of dusty men. His back stays rigid like his gun, but his voice doesn't reflect it. "I think it's time to tally up the chili votes. Don't forget, the winner gets three hundred gold standard."

No one cares about the chili anymore.

Millard steps to Leagan. "If you'd shown discretion instead of looking down on mercy as weakness, we wouldn't have had to gain an enemy in that man."

She opens her mask and her jaw to show him her tongue.

"You don't get to put others at risk simply because you weren't domesticated as a child."

"You can unlearn domestication." Aunt Tess says. "Mercy isn't weak, but sometimes it's the wrong choice. And sometimes it doesn't look like what you expect. Those bone pickers aren't suffering anymore." She turns to lay her Widow's grin across the men. She's talking to them, not Millard. "And thanks to Raptor, they won't infect anyone here. You're welcome."

The Stranger watches their soft nods, spreading like wind. They belong to her now.

Twelve.

Even though Seed's gone, my left temple feels like there's a nail slowly going into it.

No mercy.

None.

Millard follows Leagan as she shadows me. The father Kane worships.

I don't like what just happened to me, sweat trickling down my sides like blood. I keep walking.

TWENTY-EIGHT
TESLA

THE SUN STILL BATHES THE TALLEST STONE HILLS RED, BUT THE FALLING DUSK settles on the camp like a damp blanket as soon as they stop feeding the steam hammer and it goes cold and quiet. It's an uneasy parade of sweaty bodies that file to the dinner line, like the animals they just rounded up and secured in the pens at the center of camp. Plates full, they press in tight-knit clumps around the campfire's gold circles. They don't sit so close to the fires because it's cold.

They're afraid of what might be coming.

It entered the camp with Reverend Alonzo Seed last night and touched all of them without ever leaving the darkness beyond.

They still play their mouth organs and fiddles, but the music feels a little thinner, and the dark a little deeper.

I understand. Now I've seen pestilence up close, and my mind is still ringing with the nauseating thrill.

"It must be nice to sleep inside." The comment gets thrown out as he passes me.

"It is, I won't lie."

"At least *you* won't." He and a few other railroaders approach. "We came to ask you about the Tov girl."

"The Stranger," I say.

"Does she really have any power over that bone picker?"

"Why don't you tell me what you saw, darling?"

"She can protect the camp?" he asks.

I nod. "She already is."

The cogs in their mind slot together, finally turning the way I want them to like good little rabbits.

"We're from the night crew," he says. "If we pay her, and wear one of those glowing bottles you have, will she protect us extra?"

"As long as you don't make her angry."

"Fuck, I never thought I'd stoop to Tov black magic, but it's worth a shot, right?"

You'll do anything once you're scared enough.

The night foreman strolls out between the tables, chewing on the end of a pencil, the logbook under his arm. "I see an awful lot of asses I recognize sitting around here. What's the matter with my steam hammer? Did we suddenly run out of black gold? Someone talk."

One man steps up onto the table he'd been sitting at. "My name is JoeGeb Better. I speak for the night crew."

"Mr. Better, is it? You've replaced Mr. Jotham?" The foreman surveys the masked faces again, in search of the recently deceased. I've lived on the Rim a long time now and seen plenty of towns and loyalty change hands. It's highly unlikely Mr. Jotham is a living man now that he's been replaced.

"Yes, sir," JoeGeb says. "We were promised Exodus guns. We're not going out there again until we stop getting picked off one at a time."

"You'll do your job."

"Or what?" His scoff is full of cold amusement. "Withhold our rations and starve us out? Whip us like little boys? This isn't the army, and we're not your slaves."

"You signed a contract to build this western railroad, risks involved."

"We didn't sign up to get snatched by a human ghoul bat, our eyes ripped out and skinned like those bone pickers we saw last night."

"Those poor devils were likely miners more than anything, jumping claims."

"You don't recognize your own men?" JoeGeb shakes his head and several others join in, mumbling amongst themselves. "You can't make us do anything, and without us, you have no one to build your railroad. Who's really in charge in this situation?"

"He does have a point," I say.

"Nobody asked for a woman's opinion," the foreman snaps. "All of you just lost two day's wages."

"Go ahead. I can't spend it if I'm Reverend Bone Picker's breakfast."

"You'll continue to lose two more for every night you're not doing your fucking job."

JoeGeb opens his empty arms. "Then I guess you don't have a job to do anymore, either. I hope you brought your knitting."

Well, well.

MILLARD LOOKS ON, LIKE THE BRONZE TRIBUTES THE REPUBLIC'S FIRST FATHERS they put up outside the library and town hall in Saint Laura. He's not looking at the dust being churned up at the rail by the day crew, he's looking out west.

I assume half the night crew is sleeping off their work strike, while the other half is out there right now, throwing dice and kicking a ball around.

"What is your involvement is in this Reverend Seed's arrival?" Millard asks. "It seems to lean in your favor."

"Where is Mr. Green?" I ask. "I noticed he disappeared from camp right before Seed found it. Isn't he supposed to be protecting us?"

"His men did their job sufficiently."

"Did they?"

"They kept order. Don't change the subject. I asked you a question."

"All of this was happening well before we got here," I say. "Otherwise, you wouldn't have ordered a war's share of munitions, now would you?"

"The possibility still remains you've been orchestrating events before your most recent arrival on the West Rim in order to make yourselves essential."

"Well, as much as I wish I had manipulated you so divinely, the girls and I have nothing to do with that madman."

He pauses, each breath squeezing through his respirator making me itch. "I watched that redheaded girl shoot standards out of the air backwards, unless that was some kind of back market act. How do you explain her missing a man at less than fifteen paces unless it was on purpose? She was aiming for Seed with that first shot, and rightly so."

"You've never missed a shot, Von Kane?" I drift my hand into his pocket and feel something made of glass. Even at nine a.m. it's already far too warm to be wearing a suit coat. What's wrong with him?

Something strange did happen that night. Leagan never misses, though I'm not about to admit that to him.

"She tried her best," Navy says.

"I don't take a shot I won't make," Millard says.

"How very practical of you," I say. "But lead is still cheap out here. So I say shoot first and ask the questions later." You flinch, you hesitate, and you're dead.

However, it seems we do owe Seed a round of gratitude for creating the black gold opportunity that allowed us to steal the *Exodus*. We'll make it a round of cheap lead and call us even, shall we?

Millard opens the fold to their tent for us. "Ladies first."

The air inside is already end of day stale, the fire in the iron pig stove left to go out hours ago.

"There are many lives at stake here," Millard says. "And there will soon be many more, so this is the time to redeem yourself." He holds up one of our contamination vials, turning the opaque liquid in the filtered sunlight. "I've noticed a good share of the linemen wearing these since my son purchased his. Tell me about them."

"He's all yours, my dear." I let Navy step forward.

"They're not a lie," she says. "They show if the pestilence has contaminated an area."

I nod, go on, sweet Rook, crack his small mind and spread it wide.

"It's not in the air like everyone thinks. It started in the water, and now it's in the ground. Because of that it still likes to collect in water best, especially if the source is a warm spring, or in low spots with lots of vegetation. I've been studying it since the last time I was here."

"You were also on my son's first expedition?"

"Yes. Without these detectors, you won't know what water is safe and what isn't."

She who controls the water, controls everyone.

"You say it started in the water," Millard says. "What do you mean by that? A bacterial growth of some variety, a parasite?"

I feel the soft smile under her mask as she tilts her head. "It was a weapon, Mr. Von Kane. They made it to win the war."

Or so Zachariah Wells assumed in his account. Amnesty Wells had a slightly different motive, and if Navy is right about a third journal existing, and I'm willing to bet she is, there may be more to this fucked up tale that we still don't know.

"Who is *they*?" Millard asks. "How did you come by this conclusion? You're far too young to remember the war."

"I read about it. In a journal."

"A journal." He sets aside the vial. "You don't meet many women interested in science, much less educated in it."

Well, *you* don't, I'm sure. Apothecaries are almost always women, and what do you think that is, sir? Witchcraft?

"If this theory of yours is correct," Millard taps at the filters of his respirator, "then these are essentially useless."

Navy nods. "Mostly."

"Yet you're all still wearing them."

"So are you," I say. "Even though you've been insisting the West Rim is no longer contaminated."

"They still keep the dust out. Hannah black lung is a serious condition, but proper respirators lessen the risk."

"Is that what you've told them?"

"Would it be black lung out here?" Navy asks. "Wouldn't it be red lung?"

"If it's science, it must be repeatable," Millard says. "I'll need to see more evidence before I decide whether these little trinkets of yours do what you claim or if they're just a clever sales trick. And I'd like to see this journal you've learned so much from. If it's authentic, the University will add it to their historical archive."

"How much?" I ask.

"How much? Even history is a chance to make a quick standard out here, I see. Objects of historic and scientific value are usually donated. For education's collective enrichment."

Horse piss.

"I never said it was for sale," I say sweetly. "I meant we'll let you pay to read it."

I glance down at the second hand he places on my arm. Suddenly he sounds so benevolent and fatherly.

"You're a Saint Laura County girl at heart, Miss Revere. Become a worthwhile member of society once more."

"Give me the land so we can."

Don't give it, and we'll gladly do all the wretched things we do best, like charge thirsty men for water.

He produces a folded sheet, fixed with the copper leaf seal of the Republic Assay and Land Bureau, and fuck, my heart jumps into my throat.

Our own land. *My* land. If you've ever had nothing but the clothes on your body, you know exactly what this moment feels like.

"Did you think I would refuse?" It almost feels like he smiles under the thick shelf of his forehead. "I can see you're not the kind of woman to take no for an answer."

"No, I'm not." My mother didn't raise me to accept the cards I'm dealt if they're shit.

Millard pulls the deed back, and I almost shove my tongue through the roof of my mouth resisting the urge to grab it. That would look desperate. "Mr. Farrow is a notary with the Jezebel assay office. He's out with the survey crew at the moment, but he can witness us sign tomorrow. We'll exchange the guns at five to beat the sunset."

"It will still be very hot then."

"We've kept the men with promises for too long. We won't ask them to spend another night under-armed. Camp morale must be served."

"All right." I shrug. "But I did warn you."

"Once we've both signed—"

"All of us need to sign," I say. "The girls and I will own it together."

"As I was saying, Mr. Farrow will need to affix his notary seal and complete the additional forms to file with the Land Bureau once whoever is going to sign has done so. Adelaide can come here tomorrow to pick up the deed and escort us back to your train to finalize the sale."

"Oh, can she? She's not a mail woman."

"If her name is on the deed, she's just as qualified as you to hold onto it. My son tells me she's a studious girl. I've collected some antiquities she'll be interested in. This will be the opportunity to show them to her."

Don't think I'm not aware of your little maneuver, Von Kane. But I let any momentary bitterness of wanting my way now slide off. No man is going to spoil this for me.

"Alkaline." I offer him my hand. "We have a deal, Von Kane."

As the sunshine hits my skin, my breath catches on the realization all over again, the flutter it leaves just as sweet as the first time. This isn't a dream, we did it, and the news is too good to sit melting on my tongue.

I lace my fingers through Navy's, and she squeezes back.

"It's happening," she says. "All our hard work means something."

"Of course it does. Let's go tell your sisters."

TWENTY-NINE
ADELAIDE

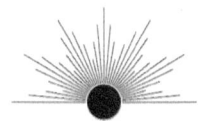

I COULD JUST STEAL IT, THE DEED TO OUR NEW LAND.

Like I should have just stolen Kane's journal when he was on the *Absolution* instead of following him all the way out here. Leagan can forge everyone's signatures. We don't need to wait for Millard to make up his mind.

But I suppose if that's the way we decide to do this, we could just blow everyone in this camp off the map and build a house wherever we want.

Longevity. That's the word Aunt Tess used. She wants a thing that can last.

I understand. Even though the Stranger likes the direct way.

If only things did last.

Fragile droplets condense on the inside of the water reclaimers. They're laid out like a garden on the edge of camp.

I put my contamination compass away. The water inside them is still clean.

The moons have sunk deep enough their light is buried. It's not night. It's not morning. It's something we don't have a name for. But lanterns bob between tents. A race to outrun the heat.

The air is still quiet. They haven't started hammering yet.

Nine fifty-one.

I smell death.

The body hangs off the steam hammer's long arm, wrists and ankles tied to branches, slit throat.

Six...

Shit. That's what death smells like. It creeps in through the cracks of my mask, and I try not to taste it as I breathe in. They cut his face off, sliced his abdomen open so everything inside could run out. It did.

Boots come crunching up the fresh berm. Coffee and a lit pipe. Even those powerful smells barely make it through the liquid stink.

"Fucking Jezebel." Micks the day foreman halts. "You, fox. Stop right there. Who did this?"

I wait until the Stranger finishes running over him. "I just got here."

"You didn't see anything shady?" He abandons his pipe and mug on a stack of ties. "Make yourself useful and help me pull him down before anyone sees him."

You won't get the smell out of the area before your first shift gets up here. His bowels leaked out his pant leg all over the hammer's pressure tank.

He grabs one end of the branch, wrenches it sideways off the valve wheel it was hooked on. "Grab a shovel."

Make him trust you.

Aunt Tess's timeless advice. It has worked for me in the past, but I don't know about this time.

"I'm not asking again." He grabs a second shovel, thrusts it at me so I have to catch or let the shaft hit my face.

The tapered blades scratch rock as we bury the man's fallen entrails in the berm of the new rail. Food for ghost stories.

When it's done Micks returns for a taste of his pipe and coffee. I was going to take them. Not because I want them, because they're here.

"Grab his feet."

I don't work for you.

Walk away.

He cuts an arm across my chest. It's bigger than my leg. "Why were you up here?"

I have to tell him something. "Protecting the camp."

"Well, why didn't you protect this bastard from whoever murdered him?"

Murder isn't a crime here if you don't have a family to avenge you. Just another way to die.

"This is dangerous equipment and dangerous work, not things for you to be poking around with, even if the hammer's not running and especially if it is. If you distract any of my men and someone else gets hurt, you'll answer to me."

There are at least five of examples of what a distraction to the men might be, but two he's thinking of. The ones that wouldn't be my fault.

"Help me move the body or I'll have questions for the marshals about you."

Farce.

I look where I'm about to touch before grabbing the branch still bound to his ankles. I'm not getting my hands dirty so his men don't see this and strike like the night crew.

Dead weight.

Micks pulls toward a slab cart on the opposite side of the berm. Its iron wheels prickle with teeth like the ones on wagons do. "Down here."

Twenty-four.

Clothes and flesh catch on wood. I let go. He can finish dragging the body onto the cart, dispose of it himself.

Rocks crunch.

Behind you.

Micks grabs my skirt, wringing his hands in the fabric. I swing my elbow into his face, but he's strong enough to shove me down anyway. Palms stinging, I get back up as fast as I can.

Instead of continuing the attack he shakes the blow from his head, checking his nose for blood. "Your shadiness should already be enough proof you're bad for this camp, but some people need more, fine."

There's blood on his hands. It's smeared up the backs of his wrists, around his fingers from where he shoved them up inside the dead man's body. It's left in streaks on me now.

He's going to blame this on you.

The Stranger runs down my limbs, throbbing in my feet, hands.

"You can run," he says. "But it'll only make you look guilty."

She lets him get halfway up the berm.

I aim for his back. One bolt. Silent.

It doesn't kill him, just makes him gasp. The rocks building up the berm are still fresh, loose.

Nine.

My second bolt goes through his neck before he can get his footing back.

He's too big for me to move alone. But there's rope all over the build site.

Thirteen.

It takes all my weight to shove the cart full of the first body off the stone ledge. The rope snaps taught, fibers hissing as the weight of the cart drags Micks over the edge.

LEAGAN LEADS, TWO STEPS AHEAD OF ME.

Millard didn't specify that I had to some alone.

The two bolts I shot Micks with are washed and back in my crossgun magazine. The blood came out of my clothes with salt, but I put them in the rag bag anyway.

Four-fifty.

I stop under the front awning.

"—I won't have time to edit all your correspondence from now on, so make sure you and Green study the voice. Use the clippings he had in his luggage, those should be sufficient." Millard's voice, murky behind the canvas. "Still no sign of the man?"

"We'll keep looking."

"Don't bother. He won't be missed, and this arrangement will serve us just fine. Our manpower is better spent protecting everyone that's left and finding that lunatic before he does any more damage to morale."

Leagan shakes her head at me.

"Yes, sir…Have a safe trip." The tent flap snaps as it's brushed open, the marshal balking as he sees us. It was small, but the Stranger saw.

Leagan burps as she stalks past him.

Nine.

The Von Kane tent smells like leather and books, the rug like stepping a sponge. Good things, but right now they make my stomach hurt.

"Come in." Millard rises from the center table, tucking a little blue book into his inner breast pocket.

The Stranger reaches. *Need.*

"*Sol, sos seccundas.*" He extends a hand to me, flaunting more Tov like he did yesterday when we signed the deed. The hairline on his left side is receded deeper than the right. This is what Kane is going to look like when he's older. "*Adelaide sos…*" He waits for me to give my mother's name.

I don't.

I won't know what I'm going to look like when I'm older because she's dead. I'll find out when it happens.

"Still keeping up the ruse of wearing your respirators, I see." He goes to the workbench, the cabinet next to it topped with glass and a layer of fine dust. It filters in through gaps we don't see, unstoppable. "I wanted to show you this."

Little stone foxes, each carved in a different pose. An astrolabe, cut with symbols I don't know how to read. A few shards of blue glass, the hardest color to make, still clinging to the center of a globe. Fragments of silk and clip-nosed sword, the handle the same length as the blade.

I know what these are. Not because of my mother, or an innate connection to my ancestors, because I'm not a fucking fool.

You haven't been back east like Kane said.

Lied.

Aunt Tess was right, he's been deeper west. *My* West Rim. Finding things I wanted to, taking things that I can't have now.

The Stranger peels at my skin, sharp as needles. My chest is too tight. Air only fills it halfway.

What secrets are out there? What if you miss something?

Her voice that keeps me awake at night.

Millard's stare tries to pick me open. He's deciding what I am, the Stranger and I both feel it. Judgement.

I'm glad I have a mask on. He doesn't need to see my face.

"Everything we know about Tov culture is only fragments," he says. "Every discovery is a chance to touch the past. I thought you should see it for yourself."

I do want to see it for myself, not here under glass with you.

There are more wooden boxes stacked and labeled on the shelves under and above the workbench, a few strands of straw packing that got loose on the floor.

I want to find it out there, where no one else knows.

"That's nice." Leagan's finger leaves a streak on the glass protecting the sword. "Can I have it?"

He almost laughs at her. "These are going to the University when the next supply train gets here."

"What if it doesn't get here? They don't sometimes, you know."

The Stranger is suffocating me. I want these things, but I can't look at them anymore.

Neat stacks of paper line the big table, separated by envelopes and loose sheets, lines and names. Bids from the land lease auction held back east.

I bend close to Leagan's ear. "Let's get the land deed and tell him Aunt Tess is waiting for him at the *Exodus*."

"We're very busy today," Leagan says. "Where's that paper you owe us? The Widow is waiting for you, and she doesn't like waiting."

"Well, you have to wait for the agent from the assay office," Millard says. "Without his signature, the land deed is invalid."

Leagan uncrosses her arms. "Then let's go find him."

"He's still out laying the boundaries for the townsite and that takes precedence."

"Did the Season Moon stop your watch?" Leagan says. "It's already four. Do you want your guns before dark or not?"

"He should be back in the next hour."

"Fine, then we're going. You can come find us when you're actually ready to do something."

"You're old enough to be better at speaking for yourself," Millard says to me. "This silence is beginning to seem childish."

I don't care. Even if it wasn't something I'd already planned not to do, he wants it too bad and that makes it more satisfying.

I'll make sure I never speak to him.

THIRTY
TESLA

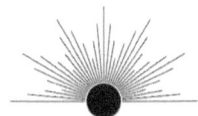

I STILL CAN'T DECIDE IF THEY KNOW, MILLARD AND KANE. THE LEAD MINE IS just a few miles northwest of Eden, where Daithe and the crew are hopefully digging right now.

It's not like I can ask.

If they are aware, they watch the girls and I sign our names on the land deed, making it and the surrounding acres ours without a quail peep. Which usually means someone intends to squeeze back out of a deal later. Good thing I keep cards up my sleeve.

Still, I chew the inside of my cheek as Mr. Farrow drags his pen across the bottom line, scraping out every letter like a wood carving while each stroke burns in my skin.

I wish Mother was here right now. I wish I could show her everything I've accomplished since we fell, and it aches.

Two truths can exist together you know, victory and sorrow, flowers and poison.

A dab on an ink cushion and over to paper and it's done. Farow peels his stamp off the page, fresh green ink sticking in its wake. When that paper touches my hand, thick and full of warmth, I go lightheaded.

"Congratulations, Miss Revere," Millard says with cool detachment. "You're a land owner."

I give him the engineer's salute. "And now the guns are yours. Let the offloading begin."

I continue to study them as I supervise the process. These powerful men like progress because it's always moved in their favor. Do they like it as much right now? Doubtful, but that's just too bad.

"Tell me why you chose this particular tract of land?" Millard asks.

Here we go.

"I think I'll like the view," I say. "My mother had the sight. She raised me to be mindful of the signs."

Kane's pencil slowly stalls mid-stroke, turning to look at me. I do believe that's fear on him.

A roll of thunder clatters off the roof of the *Exodus*. I didn't see the weather changing, but you often don't during Moon Season. Lightning crawls across the close hills where there was nothing seconds ago, talons clawing for purchase on the earth.

"Close the doors," I yell, the wind screaming with sand.

It only dampens the noise a little, but I quite enjoy the hiss of dirt on metal between knocks of debris.

I take a breath. "Well, it looks like you're all here for a little while. Are you tea or coffee men?"

"Just water will be sufficient," Millard says.

"We have some Eosin vanilla." Stolen, of course.

That does lift his dick a little, I think.

"That does sound good," Kane says. "Thank you."

I lead them to the living car, peeling off my mask as I go. "It's delicious in coffee. Why deny yourself the simple pleasures in life?"

It's the little treats, like sabotage.

"You have a lot of sayings, don't you?" Millard says. "A lot of strong opinions."

I can't resist. "You mean for a woman?"

He doesn't respond, a pity. A good argument before dinner does get the blood pumping. There. Another little opinion for you.

The map board nests on the wall between cabinets. Held in the frame is Adelaide's map, the one she's steadily drawn since her escape from Hannah a Season ago, first in pencil, now in ink. The West Rim—at least what's known of it. It's precise and lovely, full of the names she gave to the landmarks, not the ones on Kane's official map sponsored by the University they all carry around now.

Of course he spots it right away.

"This is Adelaide's work." He gently touches a spot near the center, the one labeled with nine x's for graves—*Perspective*. "She really does an alkaline job. Father, come look at this."

It's not why I brought them in here, but it doesn't hurt them to look at it. If it does, I don't care.

"The half-blood girl," Farrow says, surprised.

I stifle the unamused laugh. "Having so many things held against you forces you to try harder." But they don't get to take credit for her skill with a pen, or her unbreakable courage. That's hers alone. And maybe a little bit my mother's, who made sure we all know our true value.

Millard peels open a pair of reading spectacles. "Fortunate for you she isn't man, son. You might have some competition for your place in the survey office. However, I don't recognize some of these names. Are they regional?"

"They are now," I say.

"This is what makes charting a territory confusing when each cartographer and explorer decides to put their own labels to the land."

"We like a challenge," Kane says.

"Eventually you'll catch up." I pat Millard's arm, which I don't think he appreciates and that's what makes it fun for me.

THIRTY-ONE
TESLA

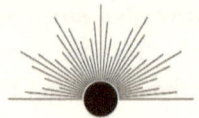

It's morning and a train whistle sounds, just off of it the low rumble of encroaching wheels.

By the time I've dressed, two Express Riders are already dishing letters through the window of the new office, their lightning bolt flag hoisted on the pole to announce their presence.

An assembly line of wagons, oxen, and trunks web from the train. Sacks of flour and grain stacked alongside crates of gourds and canned goods. Homesteaders and prospectors from the looks of them, at least a hundred.

But I spot something else, someone better.

"Evan?" I call, though I'd know that tasseled buckskin jacket at the ends of this earth.

She turns, the smile beneath her mask's filter cans warm enough to feel from here.

I bundle my skirt over my arm, dodging a cart full of stove parts, the field of food stores and the line of men waiting for mail, just to get close enough to throw my arms around her.

"Hello, my friend." She laughs. "It's about time I had the chance to surprise you for once."

"I can't believe you're here." Even though I'm touching her, I still hardly trust it. "Who's taking care of Damascus?"

"The sanctuary was designed to sustain itself, and I trust the God of Mercy to help Della and Rebessa watch over all the souls inside." She shoos away a fly out of my hair, fingers accidentally brushing the top point of my scar where it pokes from under my mask, and my face explodes with stars. "I missed you too much to stay."

"I've missed you too, but don't lie, you wanted to see *our* land on West Rim for yourself, didn't you?"

"I may not have your mother's divine gift, but I believe Providence spoke to me, and he told me to come find you."

I wrap my good arm through hers and squeeze her calloused hand. "Well, I'm very glad he did. Come with me, I have so much to tell you."

"*Your* land you say."

"Yes—"

Kane steps out of the mail line, two stacks of letters bound with twine in his armpit. "Tesla, you haven't seen Jonathaniel Swann lately, have you?"

"Not recently, no." This is odd, actually. That man is hardly subtle and wouldn't allow anyone to go without him for too long. Especially odd that he didn't attend the linemen's chili cookoff. I did notice, before we all got distracted by Reverend Seed and the things I have going on in my life. I think that's a valid excuse, don't you?

"Damn. I was hoping he was with you."

"We don't have any business together, but if I do happen upon him, I'll tell him you were very worried."

"He'll love that, won't he." Kane nods briefly at Evangeline.

"Speaking of, where's Green?" I ask before he can disappear into the clatter. "I haven't seen him since he left our train. I have something important to tell him."

"Isn't that what you wanted?" Kane steps around a load of lumber being offloaded. "I'm sorry, I have to go. This food needs to get secured right away and some of these letters can't wait anymore either. Especially the ones from my mother."

"Oh, never."

"I may not know that man," Evangeline says, "but I can tell he was most eager to get away from those questions."

"Oh yes he was," I say. "More mysteries." More disappearances. Jonathaniel wasn't one I expected, though. Not like this, at least.

A sharp whistle comes at us. "Ma'am, hold up!"

An Express Rider hangs out the open window, young and greasy with dust and horse sweat. "You aren't Adelaide Revere, are you? I heard she was supposed to be a fox, but you're the only woman—"

"She's my niece," I say.

"Close enough." He reaches out with a lightly crumpled envelope. "This is hers."

CHAPTER
THIRTY-TWO

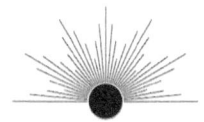

Dear Adelaide,

We hope you are happy and with your family still.

After the deaths of Joelle and Saraline and the burning of Hannah, Solstice lost so much that the place was too painful to rebuild. There were only bone pickers left anyway. She decided to head south toward Windust, and I (that's Thadie) decided I want to stay with her. Now neither of us have to be alone in the world.

There are rumors of course about who caused the fires, but we both know what happened to Saraline that night was not your fault. Everything happens for a reason, and I think the burning was a sign that it was time for us to move on.

Anyway, we wanted you to know that we are both alive. We got a little wagon and are slowly rebuilding the apothecary stock. Solstice is teaching me.

The sky is so blue! I got so used to the ash in Hannah that I didn't think about it, but now I don't think I could ever go back.

It's a little scary not knowing what will happen tomorrow, or who's waiting for us down the road, but it's fun to be on a new adventure. The canyons are a little steep, but I feel like you.

Solstice hopes you have many children with beautiful white hair who are proud of their smart mother. (I think that's silly unless you want it too, but she was looking so I had to write it.)

Maybe someday we'll see each other again. Don't forget what I told you about your future. It's still true.

With love,
Thadie and Solstice

THIRTY-THREE
ADELAIDE

THE SILENCE OF NAVY'S LAB HANGS HEAVY. IT'S LESS HERBAL THAN IT USED TO be, sharp and chemical now, a graveyard of glass instruments.

The last batch of rabbits and rats are dead.

"This is disgusting." Raleigh pins one to the metal tray like it still might try to run, scalpel a shimmer in the other.

"It's good for you," Leagan says. "All you have to do is what I do."

"I've gotten this far in life without body science. Why do I need it now?"

The *Exodus* doesn't have much glass on the outside, but every time the steam hammer drops, each piece here shivers.

"Don't you want to learn something new?" Navy says.

"Not really." Raleigh flinches away from Leagan. Her blade in the rat's swollen belly, skin black and hairless. "Oh, I'm going to throw up."

"Please take all your protective equipment off first," Navy calls.

"Get away from the slides before that," Leagan says. "I just sterilized them."

"Don't worry, I'm getting far away from here. You two have this under control."

The door of the containment passage seals their voices away. A narrow, caulked space to strip off lab coats and full-skull respirators.

Eighty-two.

Dust motes turn inside the gold bars of sun slipping through the shutters of the four windows of the barracks car. Too small to climb through, just enough to let in air and light.

It stinks like men.

Pike is still out at his new medical tent, stitching up arms and splinting fingers smashed by hammers. He doesn't usually come back until the first crew quits for the night. That's fine. Navy doesn't really need him. She never has.

Sixteen.

One bunk in the deep corner has its sheets tucked in close, folded over the wool blanket below the pillow in a bright line. The rest are ready to climb into, rumpled like someone might still be inside. The Stranger doesn't have to work too hard to guess which one he's been using.

My arm slides under his pillow without hitting anything. The mattress, the bedding, nothing's hidden here.

The cupboard under the bunk holds his extra set of clothes, the bag he came with, little brown bottles inside.

Tucked into a side pocket of the bag is a notebook, its cover almost as soft as the pages.

The notes are all about the pestilence, but I don't see Navy's name anywhere in them.

I knew that he'd do this. Sneak his name into a history book using someone else's work. People don't do favors for free. He doesn't get to take this from Navy.

I won't let him.

He'll never see this notebook again.

THIRTY-FOUR
TESLA

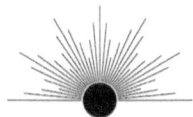

Voices move in the Von Kane tent, the front flap tied back to welcome the night breeze even as lighting claws at the west. I help myself to the rocking chair outside.

I should be happy, but I can't be alone with my thoughts right now.

It's two camps now. The bodies who just got here are mixing with the rail crews as well as lemon and cream do. Either someone told them they weren't welcome here, or they felt it on the back of their necks. They all made camp down the bluff where the white survey flags flutter.

Lanterns make shadows inside crisp tents that haven't tasted a storm, both too frail in a night this black. I can almost smell the fresh canvas from here, the kind of people we used to rob. It's not necessary anymore, but even that feels odd.

Kane sits with his father, but it's the white-knuckle fist he has gripped on his bouncing knee that says the most. "I don't think you should go. You just got back."

"You are more than capable of overseeing the construction of the town. Foreman Holden will run the work here."

"Both shifts? He's got his hands full enough." Kane scrubs at his forehead. "The night crew is still on edge, and now the day crew is too after Micks' accident. They still can't decide on who to promote to foreman. Now there's more people here than before. I don't want trouble."

"Then don't look for it. Our responsibility is to the rail crews. Everyone else is responsible for themselves. You were wise to suggest we invest in munitions, even though it cost us extra. Green can be expected to do his job keeping the peace and the bone pickers away. If it turns out he can't, well...I suppose you do have the Reveres. They're reckless and anxious to prove themselves, let them. If that Reverend Seed becomes a nuisance again, send them after him."

I hope he knows we don't work for free.

"I just..."

Millard lets out a short scoff. "You know I love your mother, but I can't stand when she starts and drops a thought like that. If you have something to say, then say it. Only a fool opens his mouth before he's ready."

That seems harsh, especially to his wife. Kane seems like a good son in need of some comfort from a good father, a thing rarer than ghosts if there are any to be found at all. Cruel toward my own you might say, but not in my opinion. You do remember how I got here in the first place, don't you? Even if I did make the best of it.

"Something isn't right out here." Kane picks at the object in his hands. It's one of our contamination vials, thankfully not glowing. "I know you can feel it too. Adelaide and all the Reveres know it. The whole camp feels it, even if they're afraid to say so. I can't say what's going to happen, but I know something else is."

Something worse, he doesn't say.

"Truth isn't established by feelings," Millard says. "Only facts. Do you have any?"

"I'm concerned you leaving again will send the wrong message to the men."

"Then I suggest put your energy toward sending the right message. Onward. The frontier is no place for cowards."

"We still haven't found Swann, and I'm afraid—"

"This is our family legacy," Millard says. "It always has been."

Farce, I'd like to flick him right in the eye. Men and their fucking legacies—

My chair's rockers creak on the planks laid under the rug, an expensive looking one, all caked in red dust now.

Kane snaps up, this fascinating conversation I wasn't meant to hear vanishing at the sight of me like a tail whipping into a hole.

"Relax, it's just me," I say.

Millard nods apathetically, the amount of interest he seems willing to waste on anybody, even his son. "Did you need something, Miss Revere?"

"No, I'm just out seeing the sights." Of course he knows I'm sidestepping the truth, but who cares. "I haven't seen those ghost lights in a while now that Adelaide's been watching the camp. Something must be working."

"Soon enough you'll have your own porch to sit on to see the sights."

My smile catches me off guard, even though I just heard the way he talked about us. "Won't that be nice?"

"Our business has concluded and it's too late for a social visit, please leave."

"That's fine." I shake my skirt out just in case I collected any stray ants and scorpions in the folds. "We can't have your men gossiping about late night visits from a lady either. That would be so unprofessional."

"Goodnight, Miss Revere."

THIRTY-FIVE
TESLA

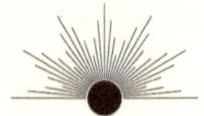

SETH'S VALLEY RIDERS OWNED THE ONLY CROSSABLE SECTION OF THE *DELTA Sol* for miles. The rest of the river was either set deep in its canyons or moving too fast through the high grasslands of the South Rim. The gang drove a fence with a drop gate into both sides of the shallow spot, and anyone who crossed paid the tax.

Those on the southern side had no choice but to bow to their demands if they had any prayer of reaching the town of Windust.

I rode next to Seth to another low bank spot—he asked me to—where the rocks weren't so crowded up on the water you couldn't touch it. But the trail down was sharp enough to skin a prickly pear.

The glare of Reedus, who usually rode second to Seth, had practically put a blister on my back by now. He and Larrison too. They were just jealous. Why wouldn't Seth realize he liked me better than men who only bathed every other week and brushed their teeth less?

The world will be a better place, or at the very least, a more competent one, when more men realize what true efficiency looks like. It's not simply by the virtue of having a penis, I survive without that. What actually gets you places is a cultivated brain to go with whatever equipment you're packing.

Seth still paid us horse shit, but that could be changed, and this was a promising sign.

We stopped along a fork in the trail, an elbow in the rock poking out far enough to see over the scrub trees to the riverbed, but still high enough to put us in a blind spot from below. Through my binoculars, I picked out the three Valley Riders Seth sent to the other side of the *Delta Sol*. They were making confident progress through the rock like lizards do.

"Reed, you'll cover us from up here if you'd be so kind," Seth said. He had a fleshy nose to go with his excessively long limbs and gray hair, fine like corn silk.

"You sure you don't need me with you?" Reed said. "If these pickers put up a fight, the trouble will be down there."

"It will give me peace in the mind to know you're watching my back."

"Yes, sir."

"Let's get this done right, gents…" Seth steered his horse back onto the trail. "No one undercuts what's ours, and this river belongs to us. Tesla, ladies first. Let's catch us some flies in the honey."

It wasn't the first time they used one of us girls as a human shield. Before you get upset like Mother, it's not the worst of strategies in my opinion. Think about it. You'd be less likely to shoot me without asking questions over an unknown man if I showed up at the door, wouldn't you?

Seth hadn't asked us to do much work in the Season since Liza's death. I offered. We needed the money.

"Keep her safe, Reed," Seth said as I took the lead. "Or punish her death."

Liza had hated being made to go in first, but she hated going first anywhere. Even when we were in school back east, she'd purposefully slow down to slip behind me and avoid being the one who opened the door.

But the one who makes the entrance sets the tone, darling.

The barge was tethered to a tree on this side of the *Delta Sol*, the water twisting and sucking at its waist, a guide rope stretching to the opposite side. It blended into the background well enough. They'd possibly been ferrying folks under our noses for a few cycles.

By now, enough wagons and livestock had passed through they'd made a noticeable track in the ground. Well, not anymore.

"Hello there," I called to the two standing in my way ahead. Another three rose from the campfire disguised behind rocks wider than some houses. "Excuse me, I need to cross. My baby's sick."

"She needs to cross," he said, and another climbed onto the barge, taking hold of the rope. "There's a price to use our spot."

"How much? She's very sick, I'll pay as much as I can as long as I still have money for medicine."

"It'll be four gold standard, or twenty-five if all you have is silver."

"How much did you say?" I called, holding up the same amount of fingers of men I saw. "Five gold?"

He smirked. "That's right."

"I think I can afford that."

"Let's see it, and we'll get you loaded, nice and secure."

I eased my foot from the stirrup as he came up on my horse's shoulder. He didn't see the kick coming at his head, his focus on leading my horse down the twisted bank, until he felt it of course. He didn't hurt for too long because I shot him.

Seth and Larrison broke through the brush line. It was simple slaughter.

They hacked through the guide rope on both sides of the crossing and used a demo stick on the barge. It wasn't superior construction to begin with, and the *Delta Sol* carried it all away without blinking.

In the meantime, I collected the bodies in a nice pile, stripped of all their valuables.

"Did you get tired?" Larrison asked. "The river's right there, finish dragging them down and get rid of the pickers. I want to go eat."

Eat and fuck someone with corn still stuck between your teeth, you mean.

"No," I said as Seth came my way. "I saved them on purpose. You need to send a message."

"You're right." Seth regarded me better than Reed even though he handed him a gold and onyx ring and me nothing. "The kind of message to stop anyone else with a mind to touch my river."

I removed my powder-blue scarf, the defining mark of Seth's Valley Riders and tied it over the eyes of the top body. "There. Now anyone who asks will know who did this."

Seth nodded, doing the same with his scarf. "Bring me your scarves, gentlemen. There's rope on my horse—"

"And over there." I point to the lean-to fashioned into a hollowed rock, their camp.

"Let's string them up," Seth called, pleased. "On the rocks."

I followed him. "Also, if you want to make this permanent, I have another idea."

"I'm listening."

"Come back with the right equipment to cut those trees and move some of these bigger rocks to block access to the shallow spot. It will be harder, but worth the peace of mind, and a clear message of who's in charge here."

"You have a mind for this kind of work," Seth said while his men were busy hanging the bodies to greet the next people who came down there.

"Thank you, I know."

The hand he placed on my ribs lingered, fingers stroking deeper as if the fabric of my shirt wasn't there. "I've also taken notice of other things… It must get tiresome, only your mother and all your young ones for company."

"Sometimes…Is there something you'd like to do with me?" All for show, I knew exactly what he had in mind.

"Would you let me lay with you? I'll be good to you, and you can ease some of the loneliness in me."

I let him experience one full press from my body, my breath soft as morning dew as I stood on toes to nip at his earlobe. Just enough to leave him wanting more. "Yes, I think I'll enjoy that."

I RETURNED HOME AFTER MIDNIGHT TO FIND MOTHER PATCHING LEAGAN'S dress under the lamp, air gaps ballooning like mushrooms inside the reformed glass.

"I killed Seth." If there was a more dramatic way of putting it, I missed it on the way in.

Mother's hands fell into her lap, eyes going still and wide, but for a while, all she did was continue to stare at me. "You what?"

"You didn't see that coming, did you?"

"You're not funny right now."

"You didn't have to wait up for me." I opened the cupboard just in case the cans of kidney beans had miraculously transformed into something better. Sadly, they had not. "Still just the beans of disappointment." I sighed. And as an already disappointing food goes, kidney beans are by far the most disappointing type of bean, something Providence should have frowned upon and never made. "I made his eyes roll tonight—"

"Tesla!"

"I'm just telling you the truth."

"I don't need the details, fool's gold, I'm your mother. What were you thinking?" She grasped my arm. "Why?"

"I'm thinking about our future." I hauled the loaded bag, the one I came in with, up onto the table. It made me hungrier.

"You're not thinking close enough. Those men of his are loyal."

"They're also stupid. Anyway, Seth still wouldn't raise our cut to fifty percent. I asked, and he said that *'wouldn't be proper to the boys.'* So I killed him. That's all the money and ammo he had in his cabin, and I know where he keeps the rest of it." And it was all going into my train fund. "Now that's proper."

I accidentally let go of the cupboard too fast.

"Shhh. You'll wake the girls."

"They're fine," I said. "And I think we can afford some cinnamon bread when the store opens tomorrow. We deserve a little treat."

"Tesla, be serious."

"I am." I couldn't help my smile. "I saw an opportunity, and I took advantage of it. Anyone with brains would have."

"We have to leave," Mother said. "Now."

"No, we don't. And yes, I am aware we have to kill them all now. But it won't be that hard, I've already decided how to do it. The blockade won't know anything happened until shift change tomorrow when they bring the take to Seth. He gave them all explicit instructions that he wasn't to be disturbed until morning. Hah. I think he overestimated himself. It was hardly anything to brag about."

Mother never believed in using sex as a weapon. She always said it was an unnecessary substitute for intelligence. But I believe in using every resource I have. As I said, these men are stupid.

The grimace on her face slowly began to rise with promise. Seth was partially responsible for Liza's death. She knew I was right. We weren't going to get ahead any other way.

"Larrison, Thom, and I are supposed to relieve Reed, Dins, and Legless Jepth tomorrow morning," I said. "I can kill all of them with the dynamite at the blockade, and that just leaves the three brothers. They're on another wagon train heist."

"On this side of the river, or the other?"

"This side. They won't see any carnage at the blockade. We've got at least two more days until they show up, and when they do, we'll be waiting for them when they go back looking for Seth. Done deal."

"All right." Mother's voice sounded the way it did before Liza was killed. I hadn't felt anything like belief in her for so long, and that filled me with hope. "But you're not doing all that alone."

"Who's going to watch the girls?"

"Adelaide is old enough to do that," she says. "We'll go together."

"There's better things ahead for us, Mother, I can feel it."

THIRTY-SIX
ADELAIDE

YOU CAN SEE IT FROM HERE, THE TABLE ROCK THAT LOOMS OVER EDEN.

Just the top slab, and only if you know what you're looking at. Far enough you could forget if you wanted. But I don't.

The breeze shudders the clump of ghostflower at my feet, white buds closed to the sun. They open at night.

Kane hoists the shovel, a white survey flag bowtied around the shaft. The other flags like it pin them in wide square. "Fellow pioneers, my father, Millard Von Kane, prepared these words for you." He glances down at the paper in his other hand, the steam hammer dropping another blow in between. "May you prosper with the conscience and industrial courage that is the spirit of the Republic of Delilah. Your bravery will lay the foundations for the generations that follow our example here."

Beside me, Aunt Tess shakes her head. "Fool's gold, he sounds tired."

The Rim breaks you, one bone at a time. It's already started on him.

The steam hammer thumps again.

I warned you, fool.

"Any man holding a lease of ten acres or more is entitled to a free Exodus rifle along with two cases of ammunition to match it. Show your land papers at the munitions store to claim your weapon."

"Any *man*," Leagan sneers.

"That's no accident," Aunt Tess agrees.

Kane jabs the shovel into the ground. It breaks through the top crust like sugar, biting into the harder Rim underneath.

Shadows pull along the ground like the fingers of an unseen hand, leaving drag marks in the dirt.

The scoop he turns over drips red sand. The east bloods standing in the yellow susans applaud.

It's not what he imagined the first time he was here.

A strong gust of wind lashes my skirt against my legs, loose hair across my neck.

No. He didn't think he'd be so afraid.

"This is now the town of Caroline…Thank you, everyone."

New Eden.

He can name it after his dead wife, but that doesn't change what this place really is. That's what I'm putting on my map.

"What a groundbreaking achievement," Aunt Tess says. Only Leagan and Raleigh laugh.

The sound is broad. Not the railroad hammering, a fan of black smoke and debris opening across the sun.

The shockwave hits me in the chest like a shove four seconds later.

Two—

Another blast, more dirt in the sky.

Metallic blows come through first, the sound of debris bouncing off the armor plates of the *Exodus.*

"Shit!" Aunt Tess grabs up her skirt.

Stay here, the Stranger says.

The thinner dust hangs over the railroad camp, refusing to settle. It turns people running through it into ghosts, while the residual glow of the sun gives it living shadows that move just like the Stranger.

I wait, but no gunfire, just east bloods bent over and screaming as they run to their tents.

Raleigh slowly lets go of Navy's shoulders as she stands up. "Sorry. I didn't think I'd ever use one of you as a human shield…but I guess I was wrong."

One-sixty-five.

Kane overtakes Aunt Tess on the slope. "Don't go up there."

"Like fuck, Von Kane. That's my train."

There's no fire, just a crater left behind, corkscrew pieces of metal and rocks cracked in half. The body of the new train is shredded, what cars remain intact tipped like empty seed pods because the rail under them isn't there anymore.

Another hole splits the railroad camp, wooden splinters and streaks of rice and flour mixed with the dirt.

The Stranger stiffens. *South.*

For a second, a silhouette stands among the sharp points of yucca. Then it blurs away, never there at all. But the Stranger doesn't get these things wrong, and the feeling stays. Low in my gut, an emptiness that can't be filled. I know it's Reverend Seed.

Leagan crests the rise I stand on, hauling Navy by the hand. "Fuck, look at that hole. I bet you Green did it."

I shake my head.

"What is it?"

"This wasn't Green, it's Seed."

"Where?"

I don't like the words as I say them, but that doesn't change what's true. "He's like me. With a second shadow hiding him."

"But not like you." Leagan scowls.

"How did he get one?" Navy says.

"I'm still deciding."

Now you know what to look for.

The absence of something that *should* be there.

"Whatever," Leagan says. "We can still kill him for making me look like a fool."

"Yes, we can." I'm not dead only because I haven't been killed yet. Not because it can't be done.

THIRTY-SEVEN
ADELAIDE

MEN GATHER AROUND A LANTERN AT THE RUINED SECTION OF TRACK WHERE their work was undone, flies sucking the rim of a honey jar. The hammer isn't running. Their careful voices carry, but not the words.

No one follows me, but I look back anyway. Good habit.

No one follows me, *yet*.

Four-fifty-five.

Red aura lights blur across the sky, distorting the almost full globe of the red Season Moon. Kane stares off at the buckling hills, away from his tent, back turned.

Northwest, the way that leads to Eden.

I stop where he can see me, but I do not turn my back to the rail.

"It looks like a storm's brewing," he says, the obvious. "I told my father not to leave again."

That's where Millard went. The direction he's looking.

I could tell him not to worry, but I don't care.

"He didn't listen to you."

The sigh bleeds off Kane's back the way the Stranger flows off me. "He never does."

I should ask what Millard is doing, I do care about that. And that's why I don't want to know. Once I do, the Stranger will eat me from the inside out.

"I'm glad for you all that nothing happened to your train," he says. "I still remember the first time you showed me the aura lights."

The pit in my stomach lowers. I look over at the track again.

They're coming this way.

Their line starts to fracture in pairs, circling us. There's more of them than I can count for sure in the dark. I wish I wasn't here right now, out in the open. The bushes aren't tall enough. If I move now, they'll see me do it.

Five wear our contamination compasses over their shirts, but that doesn't make me trust them. Faint motes glow in one of the milky cores, dust in sunlight.

I ease my foot back.

"What's wrong?" Kane turns, then slowly combs an arm across me.

"*Sol*, Von Kane." A set of wooden teeth clack under someone's respirator.

"*Sol*." Kane steps completely across my sightline, back rigid. "What do you need, gentlemen?"

The Stranger beats like my heart, dark in the dust around their feet. eating up their legs.

"We don't want trouble." But there's a weapon on his hip, along with the others. "We only want to talk."

I've been cornered like this in that alley in Hannah. The Stranger blots that memory over now, like the sun does with spots if you look into it for too long. My body aches in the places it did then.

"We can talk. You should go back to your train," Kane mutters to me.

The railroader taps the end of a two by four against his leg. The line breaks, a man in a blue-stripe shirt strides through the gap.

He peels off his mask, the rest of them doing the same.

"Evening, Von Kane." He lifts his unshaved chin to make up for the height difference, a thin smirk there. "I go by the name of JoeGeb Better, the speaker for the night crew." He offers Kane a folded paper. "It says we quit."

"I'm sorry to hear that." Kane opens it anyway. It's full of signatures. "Where will you go?"

"Not your problem anymore."

"You got the guns you asked for, I thought you were satisfied. Is there something else we could have done to improve the working conditions for you?"

"Well, you thought wrong. We heard there's about to be food rations."

"You didn't hear that from me. Is that what Foreman Holden told you?"

"Word gets around. Doesn't matter from who. You fat-sucking east bloods will starve us if it saves a few gold, am I right?"

"It does matter, actually. What you heard is untrue. We've laid supply caches every fifty miles, we'll still have plenty for you if you choose to stay."

"We're not here for you, Von Kane. We've made up our minds already. Nothing you say will change that."

"Who told you there would be food rations?" Kane asks.

The wooden teeth snap again. "You should more interested in where you're standing right now."

"Don't threaten me."

"When I threaten you, you'll know."

"Those explosions were no accident," JoeGeb says.

"No," Kane says. "They weren't, no one is denying that."

"Do you deny negligence?"

"You know the demolitions cache is stored safely away from camp."

"Are you accusing me now?" JoeGeb says.

"Hey!" It takes a moment for the owner of the voice to become visible past the silhouettes, backlit by the camp. I see the muzzle of the shotgun first. Pointed up.

The Stranger feels Kane's shoulders unlock. But mine don't.

"What is this?" Foreman Holden barks. "Are you going to get this under control, or should I?" he mutters to Kane, knuckles like bolts as he grips the shotgun.

"They just quit."

"Fucking Jezebel, they did. Your shift started thirty minutes ago, night crew." Foreman Holden fires the shotgun into the air. "Anyone left standing here by the time I clear this chamber will get the next one and their pay cut."

"You'd really shoot us for deciding not to starve?" one says.

"You're a wide load away from starving, Bell," Foreman Holden scoffs. "Quit your whining."

Aunt Tess would probably intervene, or try to get them on our side, but I'm not her.

He can solve his own problems.

"If you're not interested in working for the Von Kane Line any longer, I understand, but I am sorry to see you go," Kane says. "If that's not actually the case, you probably shouldn't test your foreman by being forty-five minutes late. I hear he's a real hard ox."

That almost works. They don't budge, but don't hit him with anything.

JoeGeb turns to the rest of them. "We could wait until they force us to turn fox and eat each other. Maybe she can give us some recipes."

"Eat the tongue first," I say. Then they won't be able to talk anymore.

"See?" He smirks to the others. "I knew it was true."

"That's enough." Kane's voice levels the simmering unrest.

Finally.

"The food will last until the next supply train gets here. No one's going to starve."

"You'll guarantee us the night crew eats first, no cuts."

"I guarantee if anyone gets their food cut, mine will be first." Kane heads for the part in their line.

Fool.

"Adelaide." He holds a hand back for me.

I'm not walking between them.

"That's right, hide behind your woman, east blood."

Foreman Holden chambers his next round.

"Save your lead, Holden." JoeGeb sucks the phlegm from the back of his throat and spits it in his direction. "We don't work for you anymore. We'll be gone by morning."

I circle out around the camp in the dark and leave Kane behind.

THIRTY-EIGHT
ADELAIDE

I SIT ON THE EXODUS'S WARM SHELL BEHIND THE STANDING GUN, WAITING FOR the ghost lights, the night crew to burn what's left of the camp.

The Stranger keeps bringing me back to something else. Seed has the accent of an east blood. So how did he get his shadow?

Particles of dust in the wind scrape against the lenses of my mask, the dark pushing back on my eyes.

Hunger.

But it stays out there, just outside the Stranger's reach.

Two-fifty.

Kane sits outside his tent. The curve of his spine matches the jaw of his mask dangling undone, whiskey bottle dripping from his hand. There's a glass on the tray table, but that isn't what he's holding onto. Its sour rot on his breath, turning me sour too.

That's not how you solve your problems. That's how you give yourself more.

But I keep going, against the Stranger.

"Hello again." He pushes at the skin of his hairline. "You had something to say when you found me earlier, didn't you? Or did you just come back to check on me?"

"Yes."

"Yes?" He chuckles and offers the bottle. "Okay then. Do you want a drink with me?"

No.

He looks even more like someone who needs a friend than he did earlier, and Markos isn't here this time.

The Stranger pulls at my limbs as I sit, my back so tight it doesn't touch the chair.

I was his friend once, wasn't I? That's why I'm here?

Kane's voice narrows with the next question. "You knew there was going to be trouble earlier, didn't you?"

The Stranger did.

"You'll have to tell me how you do it someday. Always in the right place at the right time."

No.

Then he laughs again. Not too loud, because even a few drinks in he's polite, and people are sleeping. "Fuck me, right? That's what you're thinking. Why are you here?"

The Stranger prickles, a spooked cat baring its teeth.

"Are you okay?" I wish I could see his eyes, make sure they're not turning red, that it's just the alcohol. But I don't trust that, either. Anything that can bring up the dark parts of you can't be trusted.

Just because I'm not afraid of my mother's ghost the way I used to be doesn't mean I like things that remind me of her. When the powder didn't turn her into a stone, she would talk too much. Just words, laughter.

He corks the bottle. "I'm tired. This job is exhausting. It's not..."

He was going to say *fun anymore.*

"Truthfully, I'll be glad when my father gets back and actually takes over the running of the place again."

I nod, and I'm thinking about what to say.

"You don't have to keep me company if you'd rather not be here."

Well, he didn't give me the chance to respond. But why should I waste my time talking about things he isn't going to remember tomorrow anyway?

"I hope your father gets back soon." I don't really. He'll be another person to avoid again. I make it look easy, but it's work.

The Stranger doesn't like him thinking I'm leaving now because he gave me permission, but I really wish I'd listened to her and never come over here at all. He can't answer my question like this.

I've spent my whole life learning not to care what other people think about me because it's the only way I'll survive. Maybe I'm tired too. I want to be somewhere I can just exist and not have to fight for it.

Three—

Kane catches my wrist, slides his hand into mine. The Stranger slices through me like a razor. Against her will I don't jerk away, even though the pressure of his grasp chokes.

"We lost a lot of food in that explosion," he says. "I didn't announce it because I didn't want people to worry, but after what happened with the contaminated food, we really did need the supplies on that train. Now we have to redo work to repair the rail, which will take more time, more provisions. What do you think I should do?"

"Don't ration the food." That is how they did it in Hannah. And it only made the streets more treacherous, forced Rafe to have more hired guns. Zachariah Wells tried that too, and it turned his workmen on him faster than his daughter Amnesty could. "Order more. As much as it takes."

"The company has a budget, and it will take longer to get here with the rail undone. They'll be more upset if they have nothing to eat in a few cycles rather than one less potato a meal. If it's gradual enough they might not even notice."

"The night crew already noticed." People out here notice the things that keep them alive. "If you're dead or all your workers are, the line will never get done. If they revolt and try to kill you, then you have to hire more people to protect you and control your crew. And then they need food. It doesn't save you anything."

Maybe you should let that happen.

"People who are scared of not having enough get loose with their triggers," I say. "They'll do whatever it takes to survive."

"That sounds like personal experience."

You saw it tonight.

"I realize I don't actually know much about your life," he says. "I'm sorry if you've had to go without basic needs like food."

"Life isn't fair." Like Grandma's death, or the things done to my body that should be crimes. But men care more about arson than that. Just one more thing to survive.

Grandma knew this. Saying sorry doesn't change anything. Doing better might.

Someday.

"Why are you here?" he asks again.

"Are you going to remember this conversation in the morning?" I ask.

"Of course," he says. "I'm sorry you don't think better of me."

I don't think better of anyone until they show me they are. He's showing me a side right now. One I didn't ask to meet. Another one I don't fit with.

Fuck it. I want to go to bed.

"Where's Green?"

"With my father."

I don't believe him.

PART THREE
NOTHING BUT BLOOD

THIRTY-NINE
TESLA

NOTHING MAY BE PERMANENT, BUT EVERYTHING IS FORWARD.

They line up as Kane finishes drawing a long scratch across the loose skin of the desert. The end of the world that has been. The start of what comes next.

The literal dust from the explosions and exodus of the night crew has settled, although I sincerely doubt the metaphorical dust has. The wind bleeds across the valley like a thin-lipped wail, the breath everyone here is holding onto.

What if something happens to the *Exodus Ironclad* while we're gone? This land is what I've bled for three Seasons to get, but I don't know if I'll sleep tonight without her iron walls. I do hope Raleigh is up to the task of looking after her.

Just once in my life I'd like to not give up something I love in order to get something else that I want.

At least this is temporary sacrifice. It better be.

I close my eyes for one breath, one prayer.

Let this be the end of their world, not ours, and the start of one we help build.

Adelaide, Leagan, and Evangeline sit atop their horses beside me, Navy's tethered to Nightmare.

"Should we give them a head start?" I ask.

Leagan snorts. "No."

I shorten my grip on the reins, just in case my horse decides to take off after the others. "It could be more fun."

Those who have horses, and that's all the land-lease prospectors, will have the advantage. The land-leasers already have their tracts bought and paid for, but that isn't stopping them from this race to grab more. Anyone on foot or hauling their goods in an ox wagon instead of going back for them will be the last to choose their claim.

Kane slowly lifts his arm to the sky. The pale heat deflecting linen of his shirt and scarf don't hide the heavy shoulders of a man cursed with a task he never wanted to be involved in.

The crack of the revolver shocks birds from the needle grass.

"No turning back," I whisper.

The roar of excitement ignites the dust. Some horses rear up before they burst free, others simply charge. Several try to clear the first *Solace* flood wash in a single jump only to churn against the opposite bank on the landing. The dirt shelf crumbles away, leaving everyone else to claw their way up the other side.

"*Sol*, fools," I laugh at them and kick my horse into a full gallop.

"Cheater!" Leagan yells.

The dust from such a thicket of hooves makes it almost impossible to see, even with goggles. The slab of sandstone comes out of nothing, like it was dropped here by a giant in some ancient time. I'm able to veer just in time because my horse is a nimble lady, but from the squalling, others weren't so lucky. Someone else veers crossways through the brush, and I have to swerve again, right into Leagan's path.

"Move, or I'll run you over!" she yells.

"I don't think you weigh enough," I call back.

Adelaide is simply gone, taking Navy with her. She hates games, anyway. Evan won't try to win, she's just here to be supportive of "my fun."

The dust thins as the men start to splinter in their own directions. Or half of them got confused inside the cloud of thunderous hooves. But I know where I'm going.

Leagan yells again, but I don't catch what as she surges ahead of me. I can assume it's rude.

Sweat runs in full beads down my ribs by the time I make it to a downhill slope buttered with yellow grass flowers. The gulch at the back of the valley keeps burrowing through, so viciously red, but I haul Lady Gray to a stop.

Leagan rode farther down. She lifts her middle fingers, laughing. "I won. That's what you get, you filthy cheater."

"You did so good." I pat Lady Gray's shoulder, her sides heaving under my legs. Mine feel weak, too, like I just did the running.

My compass needle spins drunken circles. I don't want to get my sentiment going until Adelaide gets here, in case I'm wrong about the coordinates. She won't be. But a fresh tremble runs through my legs as they touch down anyway.

This place is ours.

I rip off my mask and smell the air with my own nose. It's fucking delicious. Baked yet green under the edges. The land deed was satisfying to take from Millard Von Kane's fat hand, but this, actually standing here, is a thousand times better.

Orange globemallow spills down the hillside, sage-like mist all the way up to the trees and crags of the unending hills farther out.

"This is it, right?" Leagan calls up the slope.

"I think so." Tears spill out of my eyes. Like a rabbit hunted to death, part of me feared I might never get my hands around this dream.

What a foolish thing to ever think. I'm here.

I don't know if the dead can see us, they probably have more enjoyable things to be doing, But I look up at the sky anyway because I hope so. To Mother, Liza, and Vesta, we did this for you because you couldn't.

I also wish...well, I wish several other spiteful things, but I don't want to admit them.

Adelaide and Navy ride over the spine of the hill, Evangeline a few paces behind them.

"Nightmare has a slow ass," I call. "You can't win if you don't try."

She shrugs. "I saw a rock that looked interesting."

"And was it?"

"Yes." With a moment's calculation, she dismounts and pushes both hands into the sandy dirt, moving exactly how I feel. The slow drift of someone experiencing freedom for the first time, not sure if it will stick or dissolve out from under them.

"We did it." My throat tightens on me again. Everything I look at from here forward, this valley and the next set of hills folded behind it, the ones after that, it all belongs to us. Whatever we build we can keep and what we grow is our choice, all to the backdrop of mountains.

Yes, now the rest of our hard work begins, but for right now, I just want to be content.

Fuck, I don't remember the last time I felt that, but I am.

This will be our home.

FORTY
FROM THE DIARY OF ZACHARIAH O. WELLS

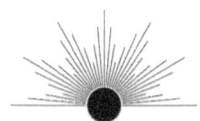

Eden Year 10, the 31st of One

THE MINE WAS COMPROMISED YESTERDAY AT 4:43 A.M. THE SHIFT HAD ALREADY begun work when the north tunnels, the main, and its auxiliary air shafts collapsed. There is no way into the blocked section, and because of debris, access to the west veins has also been disrupted. The miners are still toiling in an attempt to rescue their fellows, but the foremen and I do not expect to find any survivors.

The cause is still under review, but it is not a stretch of the mind to say that incompetence is to blame if fox sabotage isn't.

They are calling it the "Great Collapse." I've already told the foremen to make an example of any man found gossiping like women while on company time or property. As their housing is my property, I fully intend to root out anyone continuing to spread this rhetoric and remove them before this talk becomes further poison to our community. Of course a tragedy will define you if that is your goal, and the world will follow that lead, undermining all efforts.

If you do not appreciate the gifts of your employer, you will have no pity when they're withdrawn. These men may be able in body, but they lack the capacity of vision, which is why they must be led. A few examples will suffice to bring the others back around.

FORTY-ONE
ADELAIDE

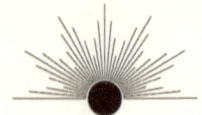

THE ROCKS ARE PINK ON THIS SIDE OF THE GULCH, GREEN AND WHITE limestone on the other. I'm not used to trees so thick they touch each other, the Stranger picking at what they hide. But you can't see any of it now. It's too dark.

Leagan rakes a stick around the glowing fire quartz pit until it ignites. "Who wants to hear a ghost story?"

"Not particularly," Aunt Tess says. "I have to sit here with the dark staring at my back, thinking I look tempting enough to sink its teeth into. I'd like to sleep at some point tonight."

"You can plug your ears."

"She can only plug one," Navy says.

"Thanks for that, Rook," Aunt Tess says.

A series of twigs crackle farther down the slope.

Leagan's eyes go wide. "That wasn't me."

"Fuck." Aunt Tess tangles her legs with her skirt as she rushes to turn her back away from the open to the fire. "I hope that's a mountain cat and not a man."

"It probably smells food," Evangeline says.

"Don't say that."

I step out of our circle with my crossgun, the dark so pure it pushes back.

"Don't shoot," Kane's voice calls out. "It's just me."

"What's wrong with you?" Leagan pitches a pinecone into the night. "Get out of here, you fool. Seriously, let's shoot him for being stupid."

My shoulders don't unclench until I see him come out of the pines. The Stranger leaves a taste in my mouth, sharp enough she should burrow into him like a screw. There's a full pack on his horse, rifle and a shotgun in the saddle scabbards.

"Hello…" His hand strays to his mask. We aren't wearing ours.

"Are you following us, Von Kane?" Aunt Tess says.

"Not exactly, following would imply I've been behind you this whole time. I have not. I had a clue about which direction you were going."

"You mean Raleigh *snitched*." Leagan shoves her revolver back in the holster. "When we get back, I'm going to kick him in the shin."

"Not the balls?" Aunt Tess asks.

"That would be predictable."

"You don't need to kick anybody. I do know what land you own, but I got lucky finding your trail." Kane ties off his horse to a log, stopping before he crosses me. "Can I sit down or are you going to shoot me for trespassing?"

I don't have to. If he keeps sneaking around like this, someone else will do it for me.

"You can sit down," Navy says.

He can't hurt us.

On purpose.

Kane pulls his end of the log a little closer to the light. "I've given this a lot of thought. I don't see any other way around it. Someone needs to get rid of Seed. Even though I disapprove of some of your methods—"

"Or you're afraid of how much you actually admire them," Aunt Tess says.

"Would you be willing to help me?"

She smirks around the firepit at each of us. "Well, you know we don't work for free." Her gaze finds me again. We agreed Seed would be next after Green. "We already have a plan in mind."

"I'm sure you do."

A reverse robbery, otherwise known as a bum uncle. You turn the gun on the person who tried to use it on you.

"It works every time," she chuckles. "We'll happily take more land as payment, just give us a chance to talk it over."

"All right." He stands. "But I'm starting in the morning. It can't wait."

"Assuming we say yes, you don't get to say anything else about our methods."

"Especially if you don't like them," Leagan says. "You're not going to like them."

He won't.

"I know who I'm riding with now," he says. "I know what we have to do." And he looks at me.

He can think that.

"Are you sure you're not just hiding from those workers who tried to beat you up?" Leagan asks.

"That's not what happened. Ask Adelaide." He returns to his horse, unbuckles the tent roll from his saddle.

Leagan shakes her head at me.

"You think you're staying the night?" Aunt Tess asks.

"I couldn't stop you from being where I am out here," he says. "And neither can you."

"Timothy Von Kane." Aunt Tess plants her hand on her hip. "I like you more every day."

"I'm not here to get in your way. I'm only here to make sure this venture doesn't end up with more blood on its underside."

Aunt Tess leans forward, the glow of the fire quartz staining her face pink and orange. "If he goes, Raleigh won't have to play the part of human sacrifice. I doubt he'll complain about that."

"Will he be told what his part in this is?" Evangeline asks, and Aunt Tess shrugs.

She knows her well.

Leagan twists around as Kane lays out the stakes for his tent. "Do you know any ghost stories?"

"Have you heard the ones about skin peelers?"

"You mean a bone picker?" she laughs at him.

"No, these are older than bone pickers, ancient evils the Tov used to battle. It's how they developed their shadow arts. Supposedly, a few of them still wander the desert. They don't fully exist until they take someone's skin, but once they do..."

A chill worms under the Stranger, into my blood.

Leagan steps on a dry twig. Navy, Aunt Tess, and Kane all twitch. "Ha ha, got you."

"What happens then?" I ask. "After they take someone's skin?"

"Something bloody, I assume," Aunt Tess says, her good arm wrapped protectively around the remaining part of her other one. "Fool's gold."

"They'd pretend to be the person whose skin they stole to get their family to invite them in, then eat them too," Kane says. "At least that's how my brother told the story. He used to chill his hand in the icebox, then grab my ankle under the covers when I was almost asleep. For a while, I was going to my parents' bed every night and begging them to let me stay."

"Hmmm…" Leagan twists another stick in the fire, then lifts it to watch the flame burn down.

Aunt Tess glares at her. "You keep your little ice hands to yourself, ma'am. And I hope you all sleep terribly tonight."

"Brothers." Kane shakes his head.

"Oh, trust me, it's not just boys," Aunt Tess says. "Sisters can be just as evil. I once locked my sister Liza in the creepy basement closet when we were in a fight and convinced her not to tell our parents afterward. For the next month, she would only use the bathroom or sleep if the door was open. That taught me my lesson, and I never did anything so cruel to her again. So maybe while little boys and girls can be equally cruel to their hapless siblings, boys aren't required to learn empathy. That would explain a lot about this world."

"I suppose so."

Aunt Tess drops her head close to me again, nodding over at Kane. "Would you take him instead of Raleigh? You have enough food to go now."

I nod. This way, if anything does turn east, I only have to worry about Leagan and myself.

"That seems mean," Navy says.

"Only if he doesn't know," Aunt Tess says. "We might as well take care of Seed now."

Leagan sits up again. "Would you like to be our human sacrifice?"

"Human sacrifice?" Some of the confidence drains out of Kane's voice.

"Bait is more accurate," Navy says.

"Our dear Reverend Seed seems to prefer men for his little rituals," Aunt Tess says. "It's possibly because that's all that's been available to him until now, but I don't assume."

"He prefers men?"

I see him thinking. The Stranger can't say what.

Aunt Tess nods. "With a little luck, you won't have to hunt Seed at all. He'll come to you. Don't worry, the girls will bring you back safe, we promise."

FORTY-TWO
TESLA

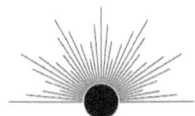

IF YOU HAVE A SHIT BOSS, KILL HIM AND TAKE HIS MONEY.

That's why I plan to never become a shitty boss, no matter how rich we get.

I don't know if the Eden mine was never re-excavated after the "Great Collapse" Zachariah Wells was so furious about, or if the war and passing storms buried it again. Adelaide said you can still see scaffolding clinging to the bald rock face. But we're not interested in the north shaft at the moment, it's too close to Eden. If the Von Kanes are still poking around there, I don't want them to realize the mine they think they found isn't the original.

Lines of mine waste appear like ribs under the crust. A good sign we're going in the right direction, despite the Season Moon making my compass act drunk.

"I see the wagons," I say, mostly for Navy's benefit. They break up a clearing covered in pine needles, underwear and shirts clipped to the lines between them.

I can see why Daithe chose this spot. The needles spring back with a crackle as I dismount. I bet they did make sleeping on the ground much nicer before they put up the two bunkhouses, angled to frame the clearing.

A path leads up the slope, trod naked of needles. Fresh mounds of dirt encroach on another clearing with sawhorses and cut logs, and it's right here.

"The boys got in." I skirt around a wheelbarrow full of rock and into the tunnel of fresh timbers. "How alkaline!" I call. The echo tumbles off into the void.

"Aunt Tess," Navy says softly. "I don't hear any birds."

I come back to where she stayed, just shy of the first crossbeam. Even such a short way in, the sun suddenly feels too bright against my eyes. Evangeline is still down at the camp, crouched at the fire pit.

Navy's right. It is very still.

"Maybe all the work noise scared them away," I say. But that feels wrong too.

The shaft hangs like an open mouth, silently holding its moist breath. Suddenly I don't like it behind me.

There's a rack of lanterns just where it starts to get dark, but it's full, and none of them are lit.

"Telsa," Evangeline calls.

"Just one second." I check my contamination compass first. Which I should have done when we first got here. A few light motes swim in the liquid, but that could just be the sun in my eyes.

The slivered rocks grind underfoot as I make myself go back in. The aid cupboard is next to the lantern rack, it's virgin wood still covered with slivers like the ceiling supports.

Wax beads down the side and a black wick show the safety candle's been lit once before.

"Hello, Daithe?" I call again, rock still scraping even though I can't see my feet anymore. "It's Tesla Revere."

The flame catches hold of the wick, then immediately flattens out.

"Shit." I force all my air out, rocks sliding under me as I drop the dead candle and run.

Navy backs away from the noise of my feet, but I grab her arm, not stopping.

"What is it?"

"Earth gas." I finally let myself gasp.

"Are they dead?"

"I don't know." God of Mercy, I hope not.

"I'm sorry to bear more bad news, but I don't like the look of this."

Evangeline swings the arm of the cooking spit toward me. The cast iron pot holds a solid mass of black tar. Something I assume was edible at the beginning.

"It doesn't look like they ate any of it. It sat here until the fire burned out."

"Let's check the bunkhouses." I have a hard time swallowing. This can't be happening. My dream isn't too good to be true.

Damnation, we find shoes and rolled standards and pictures of loved ones, all the signs they didn't mean to leave. I suppose most people don't plan to die. Of course, we won't know for sure until we go down inside the mine and discover bodies.

"I have my respirator on my horse." I steady my breaths, so they don't have to see my panic. "I'll go in."

"We don't know how thick it is down there," Navy says. "Your mask might not be good enough."

"How long do you think I'd have?"

She squints up at the trees she can't see, and it makes her look exactly like her mother. "Maybe three minutes. Until you pass out."

"Okay." I can try. "We'll tie a rope around my waist. Evan, you'll hold onto it. Navy, you'll keep count of how long I've been down. I'll hold my breath as long as I can, but if something happens, and I don't come out after two and a half minutes, drag me out. Just to be safe."

It may not be my most elegant plan, but it's better than nothing.

FORTY-THREE
ADELAIDE

THE RITUAL SITES WERE IN A LINE. THE NEXT ONE WILL BE PREDICTABLE, EVEN IF it hasn't happened yet. Seed can't hide.

Trees scrape my arms and legs, ditches choked with tumbleweeds. The long mesa intensifies the closer we get. No way around it, a tongue that feeds the next range.

Wait.

A track splits the browned grass, subtle but definitely here. I bring Nightmare to a halt. A string of hoofprints remain in the soft dust, a horse with shoes. They go the same direction we are. Up.

Kane's horse snorts, displeased he's being held back instead of following Nightmare. "This is the way my father went."

"Alkaline," Leagan says. "We can use *him* as our human sacrifice instead. You're safe."

"I have a lot of respect for my father, and I wish you wouldn't make jokes about that," Kane says. "Men have died."

"Men die all the time. They weren't special."

"Maybe not to you, but they were important to somebody."

I know what Millard's doing out here.

Leagan gags. "Hold my hat, Adelaide, I'm going to throw up. Are you sure your father isn't a skin peeler? What if he is? Out here peeling skin, his favorite activity."

"Should I regret telling you that story?"

"Yes." We both say.

"I think Tesla also regretted that story."

The wind hisses against my ear. I can't help pulling the Stranger a little tighter around my shoulders, like a blanket.

Fifteen.

"Hurry up, Kane," Leagan calls. "It's hot out here. Adelaide's getting a sunburn, and I want some shade."

•

DEEP ORANGE SAND SWALLOWS OUR FOOTSTEPS. PACKED INTO THE GAPS BY THE water and storms that ate at this rock until it couldn't hold together anymore.

"Look, bats!" Leagan whispers, pointing up at the crevices where dark wings shiver. "Don't let them bite you."

One-thirty.

It stinks. Sun sulfur.

I buckle on my solar quartz lens as the last slit of sky closes over. There isn't much daylight left anyway, the air murky as a bruise as night slowly closes its fist.

"I have noticed your family isn't bothering with masks so much." The sharp walls give Kane's voice enough reach to come back with an echo. "You were very adamant about them when we rode out here together the first time. I don't think you have a death wish. Can we talk about that?"

Leagan hisses at him. "Be quiet." She points out the hoofprints still embedded in the sand. "Everyone knows not to bring a horse into a slot canyon. Fools. But I guess they're not from here."

"Shhh." Kane hisses back at her.

"I wasn't talking to you."

One thousand.

To the right, the ground drops off suddenly. Fixed in the rock are two iron rings. Orange with rust but ropes still attached to both of them. They run over the edge and disappear like forgotten names.

The Stranger pushes into it, touches nothing.

Seven.

I back against the wall, but I still feel like I'm slipping. The drip of the Stranger pulling me in. An empty stomach, falling forever.

It's here.

Leagan goes right up to the edge and looks down. My pulse stabs all the way into my toes.

She takes her quartz lighter from a pocket and ignites a strand of root, lets it go.

"Are you afraid of heights?" Kane asks. "I don't remember that."

I pull back my shoulders, but my breath still feels short. "Can you see the bottom?"

"No." Leagan turns, palm open. "Do you have a candle or anything bigger I can drop?"

Five.

I barely feel my hand as I wipe the sweat off my palm, and don't let myself grab onto her shoulder harness as I hand her a stick of bastard ghost quartz.

The crystal falls fast. Down, in. A milky star. Gone.

"*Farce,* that's real deep," she says.

Scratched into the rock floor, pointing away from the twin hooks are three lines crossing an inverted triangle. It means something to someone.

Or did.

I set my foot over the mark, so Kane doesn't see it, point to the continuing passage. "That way. We're getting closer."

One thousand three twenty.

A soft green aura radiates from my contamination compass.

One thousand three twenty-one.

It blooms, now a deadly star in my hand.

"Put your masks on."

Moisture shimmers on the walls. That isn't right. They're whiter now too, soft lines like wax melting down a candle. Glints of salt grab onto the light and flick it back at me, and the air isn't getting colder like it should in a place the sun has never touched. It's almost warm, sticky as breath.

The walls are different.

It's not the way they look, it's how they feel. Intentional.

I stop at what feels like the remains of a doorway.

There are three pools, each a different size. Steam rises off them, the water chalk-pale. Paintings run down one wall, almost eaten away. Flakes of poppies and birds intertwined with foxes and spiked yucca fronds around reclining benches sculpted into the limestone. Long teeth of salt drip from the ceiling, pool in shattered crystals on the floor.

I bet it was beautiful.

Kane lets out a deep breath, circling with his head pointed up at the dripping ceiling. "This is amazing…"

A drop falls off the ceiling, leaving an echo in the pool it hit.

This place is dead now.

The Stranger finds a few tiny bottles still tipped in a hollow nook, covered in widow snake silk and white film. Each one is a different shape, not corked with wood, but glass, molded to match their bottles with delicate threads. They fill my hand perfectly, clinking as they slip into my pocket.

Another smell pushes up through the sun sulfur. Rotting flesh.

Kane sinks onto his heels, sketching fast lines in his journal that become the outline of the room, futilely checking his compass even though he should know from last time they don't work underground.

The scrape of his pencil stalls, his body easing away from me.

"I'm not going to steal that from you," I say.

He rises back up. "Not yet at least."

Leagan shoves a stick into the bottom of a pool. "Let's see how deep you are…"

"What is that?" I ask. It doesn't look as old as the rest of this.

"I don't know." She shrugs. "It looks like the shaft of a shovel or something."

She stabs at the center pool next. It's deeper. The shaft disappears up to the point where her hand almost goes in.

The stench of dead flesh waters up so strong my eyes burn despite my mask, and I'm back in the soup camp in Hannah. I know they used human meat when there wasn't enough of anything else.

A ripple puckers the surface of the milk water. The shoulder comes up first. Bobbing on the surface like a bubble until the rest of the torso rolls, skin bloated around the ribcage.

Leagan gasps.

The neck is so swollen and purple it looks like he doesn't have one. A rope still binds his wrists, burrowed so deep into the flesh it's almost part of him now.

I take the shaft from her and try to roll him over without poking a hole through him or touching the part of the stick that's wet. He's too buoyant and too heavy at the same time, chunks of flesh sloughing free and floating alone.

"I don't think that's going to work," Kane says.

"Is it your father?" Leagan asks.

"No." He shakes his head, voice shallow. "Thankfully not."

"How can you tell?"

"His hair."

"You mean he still has some?"

The Stranger scrapes against end of the room. An ever-melting limestone and salt wall that doesn't go anywhere else. It might have at one point, but not anymore.

It doesn't add up.

I let the body go.

"How many men have you lost since you started building the new line?" I ask.

The secrecy around the number of missing linemen doesn't add up. Unless Seed has an army with sharpened forearm bones. Unless there's a mass grave of his sacrifices out here, the contradictions have bothered me for too long.

Kane hesitates a little longer. "Half."

"Half of what you started with? Or half of what you have now?" It's not likely he'll come up with a lie strong enough to fool the Stranger, but I'm not giving him the chance.

"Well, we didn't lose half overnight."

Yes, I understand that.

"We started with two full trains of conscripts."

"You must have an awful lot of murderers back east," Leagan says.

"It started with a few of them escaping. It was just one or two a cycle. Nobody cared."

But over time that stacks up.

Something made them worried enough to order a trainload of Exodus guns. And just by the pale in his voice, I can tell it wasn't escaping murderers.

"Then it happened," I say.

"I came back from a trip east." He doesn't look at me, he looks to the passage gaping like a wound instead. "The camp had been ransacked but all the equipment was still there, still more than half the food in the provisions tent, water in the reclaimers, unlit tobacco in a pipe. A game of dominos set up in one of the tents, but everyone was gone." Kane shakes his head, as if he can shake loose the memory. "It didn't feel like they like they planned to leave. Something in the wind made them run, like the track took them. We never found anything that explained what happened."

We both know what.

"So you didn't lose half overnight," I say. "You lost everybody overnight."

"You could technically say that."

At least one of them made it up to Hannah. Blood filling the whites of his eyes as he smashed his own skull in while I watched.

"That's when you ordered the Exodus guns," I say.

"Even if it was just the pestilence that made them wander off and get lost, we couldn't keep going unless we could keep everyone safe."

The Stranger is right. It doesn't add up, even if Seed got a few.

So where are they?

Dead, hopefully.

FORTY-FOUR
TESLA

Unrefined black gold *is* black at first glance, but in the way of all symbolic things, it holds many colors if you look long enough. Poetry or horse piss, I'll leave that for you to decide.

"This proves they did find something worth digging for down there," I say. "Eden didn't abandon that mine and dig the one the Von Kane's have because it went dry." Providence knows enough storms pass in fifty years to bury what the Tov and pestilence didn't.

I tuck the sample away again, one of several left behind at the camp. "And at least we didn't kill them for nothing."

"We didn't kill them," Navy said. "It was an accident."

I can't say exactly how many of our miners were down there. I found maybe twenty before Evangeline yanked on the rope to warn me to turn back. They could all be dead in the earth. They could be alive somewhere plotting their revenge against it.

"We'll keep looking for them."

The sun is down hard when Evangeline, Navy and I reach the valley that holds New Eden—I mean Caroline. After dark, she looks less like the new beginning we've been promised and the circle of wagons more like frightened children huddled in the dark against something we all forgot about.

The half-built framework of the shops and homes rise like bones under the first moonlight. The ones who chose to build with collected stones are taking longer, while those who came to the Rim with pre-cut east-grown lumber are almost done. They have doors to sleep behind, but we'll see what lasts after a few Moon Seasons.

I like my doors made of iron.

The darkness makes the lanterns crawling like wasps around the *Exodus* very obvious.

Of course it's Green's railroad bullies, dressed up in their matching outfits like little boys playing soldier. Who else would it be?

"Hey, you little rabbits!" The dust of Lady Gray's hooves isn't even cool as I stand in the stirrups. "Get the fuck away from my train."

"We have reason to suspect crimes have been committed." The one standing guard on top of the living car turns my way, an Exodus rifle braced against his shoulder.

"This is still the Rim. The only crime here is arson." And even then, I'd break the law to keep them off my train. "Don't test me."

One of the marshals, stocky with a head shaped like a potato, advances toward me. "What's that in your hand, ma'am?" He gestures to my knife arm. "Blades longer than three inches aren't allowed in town. Drop it on the ground, we have to confiscate that."

"You just made that up," I sneer. "What's that on your belt right now? Looks like a nice long hunting knife to me. Fucking hypocrites."

"Interesting you should mention arson," he says. "The fire that burned Winchester wasn't set naturally, neither was the one in Hannah. We aim to find out what caused it."

"Dr. Pike lived in Winchester, why aren't you over at his tent right now?" My laugh is acidic. "We all know who sent you here. I was there in Vantage when Green did this same shit to the Meades. All he has are sad old tricks, and I'm not falling for them."

"Off your horses," the marshal says. "All of you. Weapons on the ground, you can have them back if we don't find anything."

I draw my revolver. He can go ahead and think I'm about to obey him, but I'm not.

They drag Raleigh out of the *Exodus*'s shadow, blood running from his nose into his collar and one eye swollen shut.

"Oh, *farce*."

"I'm sorry, Widow, Rook." He winces. "They're trying to cut into the lab right now—"

"No," Navy gasps.

The butt of the pistol sings right before it whips across Raleigh's head, knocking his legs out from under him. His whimper flares heat higher in my skull.

"Oh, not anymore." Fuck this game. "Follow me!"

Lady Gray sprints for the rear engine. No one's guarding that. Why would they? Absolute idiots.

"Stop her," one of them yells.

I have the key to the double walled engine door, so do Navy, Leagan, and Adelaide. No one else.

The weight of the iron tries to rip the door away from me.

Evangeline hauls her horse to a stop, so Navy is right next to the engine step, the fresh rock packed under the ties to level the rail scattering.

Footsteps and spots of lanterns splash on the ground.

"Come on." I grab Navy around the middle, dragging her inside.

Evangeline hesitates one moment longer in her saddle. "What about the horses?"

"Leave them. They'll come back for food."

I hope they don't run too far, but it's better they get lost than us.

Like the tongue of a bell, the iron door swings into its frame and seals, the tone settling in my chest.

"We can't let them get into my lab," Navy says.

"We won't. You stay here."

"You can't shoot guns in there."

"I'll be careful. Evan, you keep these pickers out of the lab at the crossing. I'm going to the top gun, and then they'll be sorry."

My footsteps ring down the passages. Damn, she's a long girl right now, but I'm glad to be inside. The cry of metal being operated on reverberates through most of her body, but it's painful in my bones, especially when we get to the gun car.

"It sounds like they're already inside," Evangeline says.

"Don't. Don't even say that."

"You're not going to leave that poor boy out there, are you?"

"Never. And Raleigh's tougher than he looks."

The cackle of metal arcing with heat steadily gets louder as we approach Leagan's workshop, the lab on the other side of it.

"They're not inside yet."

"You're sure?" Evangeline says.

"I know it." I give the ignition pedal of the standing gun four good stomps, two more than it actually needs to light. The chamber of fire quartz under the boiler flares to life. One probably shouldn't flash heat it every time, but this is a special occasion.

It takes about three minutes for enough steam to build for automatic firing. Until then, it takes two hands to manually rotate the barrel, but I hope they don't know that.

Sparks pulse against the seams of the crossing door. Singed and metallic air floods in on me as I slide open the peek hole.

Relief hits me like a laugh. "They're not even through the outer shell." I check the gun's pressure gauge. "Five percent, close enough. Cover me down here."

The iron stairs spiral up to the gunner's tophole. Heat pools up my legs from the pipe feeding into the stomach of the gun as I kick my skirt out of the way. The sudden winding cackle of the gears gives them pause, plenty of time for me to unload on the bullies still standing guard on the roof a few cars over. I'm not here to play tonight.

"Do you know why they call this the Exodus standing gun?" I call.

Bitter silence, loaded and static as pre-storm air, claps shut as the chatter of the cutting stops. No one has the balls to answer me.

"Because fools get out of the fucking way when they see this thing coming." I swing around, the barrel spitting white fire at the lanterns bobbing in the night. "To all of you bastards down there, get your hands off our Raleigh and my train or I'll shred you so full of holes there won't be anything left to bury."

"Consider this a warning, Miss Revere," the marshal hollers from the dark. "Keep your nose to your own business."

My head rings from the gun, from my yelling, little fires smoldering in the grass from the cutting torch. God of Mercy, those imbeciles. This is

Moon Season, the burning time, and they're the ones acting like a bunch of arsonists. "Raleigh, are you still alive out there?"

"Barely." His voice is disembodied by the night. "Damnation, Tess...I'm coming to you."

"Do you need any help?"

"No, just let me in."

* * *

AIR WHISTLES THROUGH THE HOLE MELTED IN THE OUTER CROSSING WALL, BUT mostly what they made were bubbles and a scorch mark on this side. Fucking amateurs.

Dr. Pike removes his protective gear inside the decontamination compartment while Navy checks the locks on her desk drawers.

"Well, I hope you were going to do something if they actually got in," I say as he emerges.

"All the cold storage boxes are normal temperatures," he says. "And none of the samples were damaged."

"Is Raleigh okay?" Navy asks. "Maybe don't tell him I was more worried about the lab than him. But only at first."

"He doesn't need to know. I told him to go lay down."

"I'll get my kit," Pike says. "Where is he?"

"The bathroom, between the sleeping cars." I run my hand along the cool contours of the passage ribbing. "I'll to do a sweep of the rest of the Exodus, and make sure no snakes actually got inside."

Evangeline nods. "I'll join you."

Navy picks at her fingernails.

"I'll find something to plug this hole until Leagan gets back and can weld it up," I tell her. "We won't give them another chance to try again."

"They know what Adelaide did," she whispers to me. "They know about Hannah..."

I lower her hand away from the other before she picks her cuticle bloody. "They can't prove anything."

"They don't have to, though."

She's not wrong. They just have to get enough of these other fools to believe them, and unfortunately, I'm afraid it won't be that hard.

"Perhaps you should consider moving the train," Evangeline says.

"That would make us look guilty," I say. "We didn't do anything wrong."

"They won't ever let us be good," Navy says. "Will they?"

"Maybe not, but they're not so good, either. I won't let them forget that."

FORTY-FIVE
ADELAIDE

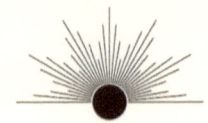

A PERFECT SQUARE HAS BEEN DUG INTO THE FLOOR—BORDERS MARKED BY cotton twine.

A grave, but not for bodies.

Swirls of once-colored fabric lay encased in the chalky sand, the contoured edge of a support beam just rising through, bumps from smaller objects splayed like ribs.

Previous lives.

The pressure of the Stranger fills up my chest, throat.

These are the things I want to find. I hate that someone else has already done it. Especially someone like Millard Von Kane. He wants Tov artifacts to bring back east to show around and bring more people here to unearth the secrets of the desert.

I don't want other people here. People ruin everything. I'd keep this secret just for me.

The air is colder again. Wind sneaks through some floodwater hole, moaning on the way out.

"I thought the dusk and dawn markets were outside." Kane walks the line of the excavated pit. As if he touches the stones sweetly enough the limestone ribbons might tell him a secret. "So maybe this was a scout hold, or a training camp…"

"Did the Republic give *you* a hot spring when you were in the army?" Leagan asks, vinegar on her tongue.

"No, they did not. But salt baths were a common fixture in Tov households. If you want to become the best swordsmen on the continent, this is clearly part of how they did it because medicine baths are still popular in Cairo."

"But they have to manufacture theirs," Leagan says. "They use sea salt from Eos."

Kane turns to me. "How do you feel, being here?"

I wish you weren't here right now.

The Stranger tugs at me, over where our light bleeds out again.

White tufts lie scattered on the increasing slabs of rock, tumbled in the red sand.

Oatmeal.

Fifty.

A leather case of tools sits open on the ground. A little beyond that, a box of canned goods and bundle of canvas. A tent that wasn't pitched yet.

Seven.

Sand pours off the worsted vest as I uncrumple it, shake for scorpions.

Kane takes it right out of my hands. "That's my father's." He twists around. As if he missed him behind a rock.

I think the more important question is why didn't he finish setting up his camp?

"Hey!" Leagan's voice blooms off the rocks. "I found another tunnel."

I don't want her going alone.

Eighty.

A little growl flickers through the darkness. Wet, munching. The Stranger hugs in close, so does Leagan, the light from her headlamp crossing mine as I pull my crossgun.

Another scent creeps through the low-lying rot. One I also know.

Blood.

The three horses are on their backs, joints flexed as if they're still galloping. A ribcage moves, the growl human.

A bone picker, down on his knees. Arms buried to the elbows in the horse's stomach, scooping fistfuls of soft entrails into his mouth.

Another head comes up, naked, dripping red from the mouth down.

Leagan inhales like a knife. "Fuck."

Waxy skin stretches on bone. The dark is watching.

The Stranger doesn't recoil. I find my trigger, squeeze.

Kane sprints out of the tunnel behind us, lantern throwing around jagged light. "Are you two okay?"

Leagan points to the pile of dead things. "Don't throw up."

A small sound creeps up Kane's throat. He edges closer, lantern held out like it can stop something else from crawling from the open ribcage at him, hips angled so he can reach his pistol with the other hand.

Leagan's touch brushes up against mine. "I'm glad I didn't have to see Vesta like that."

"She never got that bad."

And I'm glad too. Even though the bubbly rattle still leaking from one picker's lungs is the same sound Vesta had in her chest during her last breaths. She was still our sister when she went.

Kane takes his own shot. Ends it.

Twenty-one.

"These are your father's horses," I say. Millard's is white, the other chestnut, the third a darker brown with white points.

Kane nods, hollowed out with shock. "I have to find him. Now."

The saddle is twisted under the white horse's front legs. I unclip the buckles on the attached bag. My fingers stick to the leather, leaving prints on the map, compasses, and aid tin inside.

The Stranger pricks in my skin as Kane comes in to see what I have. The map, of course. I shove it into my pocket and give him the bag.

Sand spills into the aid tin as I peel the lid back, attaching to my fingers too. Bandages, stitching kit, tinned pain tablets, and black bottles labeled *astringent alcohol* and *snake bite cleanser.*

"I doubt that works," Leagan says.

I think things like that all the time. She says them out loud.

"Has anything been used?" Kane asks.

It doesn't look like it.

"I won't resent you for not coming with me," he says. "I'll still pay you if you get Seed, but finding my father is my priority now. It is safer if we stay together, though."

"For you or for us?" Leagan asks.

"Both."

"What if he's already dead?" I say.

He doesn't like that. "Then...I still need to know. My mother deserves to know too."

I suppose.

Leagan sighs. "We should have brought Raleigh or Aunt Tess as backup."

"I won't leave you if you're in trouble." And his voice has the sharp edge of a stalk bent to break. "Are you coming?"

"No." And the blow lands on his shoulders like a hammer not a word. "We're going back."

Leagan's gaze nicks off the Stranger, pointed as stars and knowing as a sister.

"I don't want to sleep underground." I dig into my satchel. Cloth lining, rocks, pencil tin. "We'll make sure nothing's eating our horses and find you in the morning."

I hold out a stick of my fluorescent chalk. Kane reaches for it but doesn't feel the Stranger bleed through me like a shiver.

Traces of the chalk stay on my fingers, dust ghosts.

"I'd feel better having you with me." He rearranges his shoulders into a posture that's more resolute. "But I understand."

Good.

"I hope you're alive in the morning," Leagan says.

Nine—

I look back. "You can't trust your compass down here."

"I remember. Be safe. Both of you."

"If you need help, fire your gun three times."

FORTY-SIX
TESLA

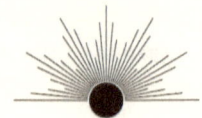

Something broke in me. Not that long ago.

Not the severing that happened when Mother died, or Vesta, or even my sister all those years ago. This is a new bone, the pain sharp as the noonday sun and twice as furious.

I've tried my best, but it sits in my body like an infection, chewing on me every day.

The new town of Caroline sings. Hammers and saws and walls going up, the merchants whistling while they arrange their wares in anticipation of incoming crystal booms and pockets flush with black gold.

I should be allowed to enjoy it, sitting here with Evan on a rocky outcrop, drinking coffee. But while all of them are drunk on their shiny futures, I'm keeping one eye on the *Exodus* instead of looking for our missing miners or building my house, sitting up at any flicker of movement near her. And it's making my back hurt.

These people don't care that Green's bullies beat Raleigh to pulp last night and cut a hole in my train looking for something to hold against us, because it wasn't happening to them.

But what pisses me off more than anything right now is that one of Caroline's new supply merchants brought his wife along.

Her dress is crisp purple calico, untouched by the red dirt, and earlier, she wore those silly little white gloves that are not practical at all but do look so delightfully crisp against a bouncy skirt. I bet she smells like violets although I haven't been close enough to check.

She sits on a steamer trunk, knitting something that looks like lace while her little boy runs around the framework of their new store. Again, he calls for her to watch how fast he is and each time he dashes by, she waves.

"Be careful, love." Her warning travels up the hill, and her voice is like a morning dove.

Unbidden, the thought comes. I imagine the little boy tripping on a block of wood. He falls through the open wall and lands on one of the support stakes. What a ghastly thing to even think. I despise myself and swallow the image. Still, it lingers in my belly like a parasitic worm.

The red dirt claws its way in no matter how careful you are, stains like a bitch. She won't stay so perfect.

"You don't seem like yourself, my friend." All Evangeline had to do was look at me and she saw it, the rage. Or my lips are in more of a sneer than I realized, and I'm rocking my chair way too fast.

This woman's done nothing wrong to me. I don't even know her name and here I am, wishing harm on her child because I hate her fucking guts for what she represents—ideal womanhood. At least in man's eyes.

I was a mother too, remember? That hasn't changed even though my Vesta is physically gone.

Evangeline draws my hand into her warmth. "Let's talk about it, if you like."

"Yes, I'd like that." I fold my other arm in, a feeble shield to cover my darkness that's clawed its way to the surface, a kind I don't want people to see. "As long as you're not tired of hearing me complain of my woes. I don't want this to become the cornerstone of my personality."

"You know me better than that. You're thinking about him still, aren't you?"

"I see him all the time. Everyone looks like him, even when they don't. He's the one who chose this, he should be the one suffering, not me. But no. I dream about him, almost every night, and I fucking hate it."

She holds a small sound within the back of her throat, acknowledging what she's heard while mulling it. "I am sorry, my friend. You also don't know what's in his mind. Maybe moving on isn't so easy for him either."

That's unlikely, though. That would be fair. "Was it like this for you?"

"Yes and no, in a different way," Evangeline says. "Mine wasn't love like yours, it wasn't even what I thought it at the time. It was lust, predation. I did mourn for the loss of companionship, feeling adored by someone else's eyes, and that tangled me up inside, but I was too young to know better. I didn't even know myself."

I feel tangled up inside, desperate to free myself, and oh so afraid that I might have lost pieces of me I loved in the process. And I can't say I'm too young to know myself.

If I come out of this knot, what will I look like? My only hope is that those pieces can be reclaimed.

For a brief change, I ache for her instead of me and grip her hand that holds mine. "It wasn't your job to know better. You were a girl who trusted someone who pretended to be trustworthy, and he lied to you."

She smiles grimly. "Yes. And it took a long time, but I eventually realized what it really means to serve the God of Mercy, not to serve a church of men. I was able to forgive myself. The pain fades. The good news is, yours will too, in time."

The grief is all I have left though.

"You're right." I say it because I know it's the right answer, not because it feels true. "And I have plenty of other things to do. Better things." A few pieces of clarity sift into place like the relief of a full breath only to collide with him again. "So why can't I let go?"

"You know grief isn't linear."

Oh, I know. But I should have been smart enough to avoid this wound at least.

"And it's not sovereign," she says. "If I hadn't suffered, the Damascus Sanctuary of Sisters likely wouldn't exist, I wouldn't have met you, because I wasn't ready to choose a path. But suffering didn't make me strong. It didn't make me anything, mercy did."

Don't be sorry, Mother always said. *Be better.*

"You, too, have chosen a path, and it might take you places that are unknown, but it is leading you somewhere better."

"Evan, I didn't tell you everything." I inhale until there's no more room in my chest or stomach, and even then, it's not enough. This loathing I feel has a double edge. One for Travis and his selfish choices, but the other side is all me, both cut. "I almost did something, something so fucking horrible, even you wouldn't look at me the same."

Am I a fool for telling her I even thought of it? Oh well.

"And the evil part of me still wishes I had."

FORTY-SEVEN
TESLA

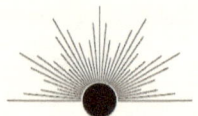

A STORM BLEW OVER OATH AND TRAVIS'S TRAPPING OUTPOST WHILE WE RAZED Hannah. At first glance it was obvious half of his stovepipe was missing. Closer up, a layer of dirt banked the cabin's south wall waist high, splinters of wood and a barrel hoop embedded into its stone face. You could almost walk right up onto the roof.

"Oh, *farce*." I slid off my rented horse. "Good thing all your pelts are locked up. I'll pay someone in town to come help you clean up."

"So you don't have to. Don't bother. Thanks for the escort home."

"Of course. It was the very least I could do. Thank you again for everything…" I couldn't help glancing down at my severed arm cradled by my yellow scarf. "I wouldn't be here without you."

He looked across Oath's grassy knolls, not at me, even though his hands sat on my hips. "This is it."

God of Mercy, I should have seen it.

"For now," I said, acting as if it didn't sting so.

The job was done, and I had promised him Hannah would be the only one I ever asked him to do. I had nothing left to keep him with me, other than me. Like a fool blinded to the odds by a promise that didn't exist, I hoped that would be enough and he'd choose me this time. The way he never does.

"I'll be back around, don't you worry. And you're always welcome to visit me. We'll be even harder to miss with the *Exodus*."

He cleared a piece of something lodged in his throat. "Tess, things will be a little bit different from now on...I've claimed a bigger tract of land southwest of here. I've made enough money to invest in cattle, and enough extra to keep the homestead alive if things go wrong a few Seasons."

"Good for you. I'm looking forward to seeing it."

"I've answered an ad for a wife from back east."

"Oh." The words stopped me like a clothesline to the neck. The surge of my heartbeat rushed to my face first, then down my fingers—even the ones that aren't there anymore—all hot and bloody. The rest of me simply went numb.

"You're going out west now. Now that I have property, I'd like to pass on my name to a son."

"*Oh.*"

And anger hit. Toward him, his name, also at myself for reasons I was slightly puzzled by. I always had a good time with him, but I'm usually the one to go. This was never supposed to happen.

"Here I was thinking you were more progressive than that," I said. "But no, you'd rather have a child with some east-blood womb you paid for than keep someone you love, who loves you back and makes your life more interesting."

"Don't get mad, Tess. You make it clear where your priorities are, and I let you be. This is the natural course of things."

"For most people."

"But you're not most people," he said, and he isn't wrong. Yet I felt so very far away from myself at that moment. Too far to ask why. "That's what I've enjoyed about you."

"You never asked me if I wanted a family with you." Of course, I probably would have said no. Giving birth once was absolutely enough for me. Have you ever pushed a cranium through a small hole? It expands, but not far enough in my opinion. Evangeline had to sew me up afterwards. That was the worst.

"You're getting a little old to have another baby."

"Oh, is that it? I'm old?"

"I also know how you are. If we had a child, you'd want to give it your name."

"Well, you're not the one who has to push it out."

He threw up a hand, like I'd just proved his point.

"Why is it right for you to want that but wrong for me?" I demanded. "Who decided the man's name is the only one that matters, anyway? Fucking horse piss."

"I'm sure you'll raise all kinds of hell and schemes from that dust on the West Rim. I hope you get everything you want. But from now on, you're not welcome to come around whenever you feel lonely or need a favor."

"Don't worry. I won't come between you and your new wife." Not that I couldn't or do it with ease. The heat in my body became pain, one I'm familiar with, watching something you love die. I wanted my mother. With the thought and the knowledge I can't go to her for comfort anymore, I found myself truly alone for the first time ever. The shattering was complete. Of all the endings I planned for in Hannah and beyond, this wasn't one of them.

"Don't cry." He blurred one of the wet lines on my face, his finger like sandpaper, and I knocked it away. The flash of hurt in his eyes was satisfying, even though it didn't last. "You have plenty of other options."

"You really think that's what I'm upset about?"

"Just take care of that other hand."

"I know I'll be fine. Don't talk to me like none of this mattered to you." I wish now I'd put my arms around him, held him one last time before the ache burned a hole right through me and everything that might have been. But I was too enraged. "So that sex we had an hour ago was what, just a parting gift for yourself? One last memory for you to stroke off to before your fresh, young womb gets here. And let's be honest, after too."

"We've been on a regular fuck schedule, and you're smart. You'd notice if I suddenly stopped touching you. I didn't want to hurt your feelings."

I choked. On what I'm not exactly sure. It might have been disbelief, or a sob of rage because I'd been used by someone I trusted. Men used to pay for my touch, but I never felt this cheap. "How do you think I feel now?"

"You've always known what this was."

"A pity fuck, apparently."

He scratched his beard. Something that used to make him look thoughtful but now the action made me seethe. If I could rip out his hair I would have. "This is why I didn't know how to tell you."

"Being honest when I first showed up last cycle would have been good enough. I would have understood then." I should have known that last time didn't feel right, cold to the touch even though his hands were hot. "You also didn't have to call me old."

"I want to thank you for everything you taught me about female pleasure. Before we met, I was inexperienced to say the least."

Krossus, I tasted my stomach. "Well, I'm so glad I could be your practice woman before you ordered your real wife. What an honor."

"You made your choice."

"No, *you* made *your* choice. Don't you forget that part." I had a bad feeling he would. He'd tell himself more *farce* about "the way of things" and chalk all his decisions down to my unwillingness and inability to give him his way because they were reasonable and he's a good man.

Why doesn't anyone stop to consider if this way of things is even right? I've seen too much to believe in it anymore.

He cleared another uncomfortable silence from his throat. "You should probably go now."

"You'll miss me." And goddamn, the words stuck to my throat, ripping skin as they suddenly let go. "I'll miss you...I hope you think about me every time you touch her."

"Don't get nasty."

"Oh, you haven't seen anything." My voice cracked, the smirk brittle steel quenching too hot. "You'll regret this, you bastard."

"Tess..." The muscles under his beard flared. "Just...don't, okay? Go. Be free, do what you want."

I hope she breaks his heart.

FORTY-EIGHT
TESLA

I wipe the tears off my face. They're hot as welder's slag.

I hope Travis gets to feel this someday. This aching, this longing that crushes from the inside out with no escape from. That his new wife has a dry womb with enough just life to nurture one child.

God of Mercy, don't give him that fool's gold legacy of sons men crave. Let him have what's better—a daughter.

Evangeline combs her fingers along my hairline, the pressure of her hand around mine unwavering. "I am sorry this world has been so cruel to you."

"Blessed are those who pass through the fire." It barely comes out above a whisper. I've told her most of that before. "There's more…"

The worst thing I've almost done.

"I didn't actually do it." And I want to preface that hard. I don't want her to misunderstand, I don't want her to stop loving me because I couldn't bear that. "I only considered it."

Only because I was so full of rage with nowhere to spill it. Only because I wanted to hurt Travis in the way he had done to me, a way that continues to wound, night after night, and I knew *exactly* how it could be done.

"When we were still in Covenant, before we left to come here, I spoke to the in-house apothecary at the brothel." She performs their abortions because most doctors won't treat working women, even though they sure as hell visit them. "I offered to buy the bloody linens and any tissue from her next client's procedure." A tremor of shame flares in my cheeks and undermines my voice. "So I could send it to Travis and claim it was his."

"Tesla!" Evangeline's gasp hits sharp as a slap, and just as painful.

"I said I only thought about it."

I still think about it. It would have been so cruel. It would have felt so good. But it would have been so wrong to use another woman's choice for her body as the instrument of my revenge. At the end of the day, I chose to be better, and I am.

But just barely.

"I am so glad you found your sense," Evangeline says. "Your mother *would* have been ashamed of you, and you are correct, so would I. But we all have dark thoughts, especially in places of seemingly bottomless pain. It's only a sin if we act on them. I know you have endured so much tragedy in the last few Seasons, in your life, but even so, do not forget we serve the God of Mercy, not the God of Punishment. Yes, I could have been ashamed of you for choosing the wrong." She catches my next tear and lifts my face in both hands. "But I am so proud of you right now for choosing the right." Her own voice breaks. "And your mother would be too."

The sob lurches out of me as I grab onto her. I hope everyone gets to be held like this at some point in their lives. She and I, inseparable as wire twisted around a trunk by a storm. Seen with flaws but not rejected for them, perfect safety.

"You are not too broken to be happy again. You let that man go when you're ready."

"Thank you," I whisper. You have no idea what a relief it is to hear myself say those wretched thoughts out loud and not have to hold them like a poison any longer.

I'm afraid she's wrong. While Travis is not the only man I've kissed for *my* pleasure, he's the only man I've ever loved. There's a profound difference. And I'm not the type of woman to just let that go.

But at least this shame doesn't get to drag me into a deeper hole anymore.

FORTY-NINE
ADELAIDE

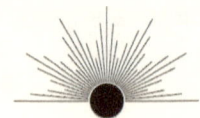

THE TUNNEL IS FILLED WITH CLOTHES. THE SAGE GREEN UNIFORMS OF GREEN'S bullies, once-white shirts, patterns. The light fabrics jump out, but there are hundreds of crumpled piles. Boots too.

I use my hand to follow the trail, the white chalk line stretching endlessly into the narrows, Kane somewhere at the end of it.

No lamps. Leagan and I don't speak.

The first stabs of a headache come from the solar quartz lens over my eye, but I want it on. The only division of up and down is the faint gray line of rock meeting sand, and the puddles of fabric I keep stepping into.

Four-thirty-four.

That bottled, wet feeling clings to the air again. Seeping, sunless cold in my bones.

The Stranger pushes ahead, cutting a hole for me through the hunger sticking to the rocks.

But it's still here.

It sits over me, behind me. Like a dream whose details you forgot in the morning.

I think Leagan feels it too. Her breaths come shallow, her hand occasionally brushing up against me, checking where I am.

Seven-twenty.

The line on the wall ends.

Orange bleeds through the previously black passage. Fire quartz and glass, dying on the sand with my fluorescent chalk, snapped in two.

Leagan points, nodding vigorously.

A whisper scrapes its way into my ear. Just the left one. But I listen too hard and all I hear at first is a low hum.

Then, chanting.

Two...

The shapeless words slip down my back. Hollow. The Stranger tells me they're human, but it's warped just enough my ears warn me it's not.

It's just the echo.

The Stranger can't speak without me. Why should this other shadow be able to?

Four hundred.

There's a lake, green and gold at the edges from the candles dripping down rock. Clear enough to see there's no bottom in the center, just a gaping black plunge. An empty throat, a belly to drown in.

The Stranger coils around me like a second skin.

It's the most water I've ever seen besides what flows through the *Sols*. And it's full of bodies. Facedown.

Seed stands waist deep, the frayed curtains he wears as clothes billowing up around his hips. The water boils around him, bare arms and legs breaking through the turmoil. He shakes, all his strength being used to hold the drowning man under.

Leagan unshoulders her backpack, so familiar with *Verdict* she doesn't have to take her eyes off him while she assembles it.

She'll miss.

I know.

Two bone pickers have Kane at the lake's edge. Dark spots on his knees, arms hauled back by a separate rope on each wrist. The one who faces this way turns into the candlelight, his overgrown hair like a nest. One iris is still white around the edges, but the other floats in red.

Millard lays on his side. Away from the brighter light, legs too stiff to bend up and reach his wrists in a regular hogtie, so they splay out at the knee.

The rabid splashing ends. Only residual tremors, greedy on the rocky edge of the lake.

Seed stretches out his arms to the salt teeth. But the sky is blocked out by the weight of the earth over us.

Nothing answers.

His shadow hasn't always been with him the way the Stranger has been with me.

It wasn't supposed to be with him.

"Whatever he's promised you, I promise it's a lie," Kane pleads to the men holding him.

Seed emerges from the pool, bleeding long trails of that poison water. "I haven't promised them anything. Most people don't know Providence has a second dark face. I have seen it."

He was just an empty bottle left out here.

And the hunger waiting in Eden happened to crawl into him.

Kane twists as Seed strokes grub-like fingers down his cheek. The bone pickers keep him from flinching away, his arms straining in the sockets. I know what that fear tastes like, a touch you can't scrub off. Men don't get to feel it very often, but women do all the time.

"No amount of blood will bring this lover back to you," Millard says.

"Not a lover, my foolish child. My brother." He reaches down, undoes the buttons of Kane's shirt. "A calf for the slaughter will struggle. But you must hold fast. You east bloods sent us out here to die for our crimes. Instead, I found something you cannot comprehend."

The Stranger spreads against Seed's wall, still feeling for a way in.

The pickers drag Kane by the arms across the damp rock floor, stretching him out. Seed follows, striking shards of ghost quartz together, laying them down, a glowing circle.

"Fuck." Kane struggles to hold onto his inhale as Seed sits on his legs to undo his belt, then yanking it free of his pants. With each short breath the bottom of his ribcage shows.

"Do not fear. It's only temporary."

Seed rips Kane's right boot off and I feel it too. The scrape of leather as Rafe's men pried off my boots, the cliff over the *Delta Sol* so high, the drop so close—

Focus.

I breathe in. The pulse in my feet fades. The ledge we're crouched on is not that high.

I draw my satchel strap overhead, slip out of it.

"I got you, Stranger." Leagan whispers, eye to her scope.

Millard turns his head as Seed finishes stripping Kane, then binds his ankles together.

He came in here to save you. The least you can do is watch while he dies.

Fifteen.

I cut behind salt pillars, out of sight.

Seed stirs a skillet of fire quartz to life as he chants. Metal on iron. Brighter, crystal on crystal. The curtain robe falls to the ground, revealing an infestation of knife scars.

"Fuck. Fuck…" Kane mutters with him. I can almost hear his teeth grinding.

At least add a *you* on the end so those can be your last words.

Seed folds Kane's belt in two, offering it to his lips. "Open."

Ninety-six.

A sound sprouts from Kane's throat, the involuntary kind, the knife Seed draws is a red sliver moon.

Now.

I jam mine up under the backside of the picker's ribcage. Air bursts out his mouth and the hole, blood sluicing down my hand.

The aftershock of Leagan's shot echoes off the cave. My bone picker is still gasping but hers is already dead.

Kane rolls out of the way, clawing at his bound ankles and latching onto the closest thing to defend himself. A rock.

Seed turns on me, eyes livid. I reverse my grip so the blade sticks out the forward-facing end of my other fist, wipe as much blood off my palm as I can in one swipe before drawing my pistol.

"Half-blood. She tries to look human, but she was born without a soul. I told you, there's nothing in her, brother."

That's not my lack of a soul. That's the Stranger protecting it from you.

He reaches for the top of my head, empty-handed, eyes shut.

Fool.

My knife sinks into his upper chest. Misses the armpit and its artery by inches.

He slaps me broad across the face, but my blade sticks there, still buried just to the right of his arm until I twist. The stones are slick. He lunges and my body snaps tight as water claps around my waist.

No.

Fetid, a bath that's gone lukewarm.

"Run. Not into the night, devil."

Seed shoves down on the back of my head, his other hand between my shoulders. The water, my face, the reflection shows both.

My hands are slipping.

Leagan yells deep in the background.

The Stranger pins me where I am, dark and throbbing. Seed's shadow is everywhere too, cold metallic fear in the back of my throat. They spiral each other like two pissed cats, arched and hissing.

I swing one arm back, trapping both of his against my side.

Water gushes into my mask.

It's all black, noise. Only things I didn't forget. Only the Stranger.

"He's dead." Millard's voice bubbles through the static. "Let the body up now. We'll take this bastard back and put everyone's mind at ease."

The other shadow seeps back into the earth, like teeth disappearing behind lips. To wait. For another body.

And it's finally quiet.

"I said you can let the bastard up."

Shut up.

"Just...stand back a minute," Kane says. "Adelaide?"

Get up.

A flush of poison water drains away as I stand.

Farce.

Hot blood panic slashes me. My clothes are stuck tight to my skin, my body too rigid to let air in.

I'm going to die.

"You could have fucking helped her." Leagan picks her way across the slick rocks, hauling both our bags. "You big babies."

Three.

"Don't touch me."

"Don't worry," she says. "We'll go get you cleaned off. You'll be okay."

I have a change of clothes in my saddlebag, but like Vesta, the pestilence is already in my skin. One of those things that can't be scrubbed out.

"You'll be okay," she says again.

"You do speak then, I see," Millard says, adjusting one of the ropes used to bind Kane into a new slipknot.

Gloat now.

I'd have let him sacrifice you.

"You got here just in time." Kane turns his face away, collecting the rest of his things one piece at a time. His fingers slip, wooden as he tries to button his shirt.

Millard slips the rope around Seed's ankles and hauls the rest of him from the water, wet flesh sliding across the rocks like an eel. "Credit where credit is due, Reveres. You do have a way with the violence of this world."

We have a way with survival.

"I hope you brought spare horses. Mine are missing."

"Yours are dead," Leagan says.

Millard heads for the tunnel, dragging Seed behind him. "I could use some help with this load, son. We shouldn't linger here."

"I'll be right behind you." Kane brushes past Leagan. "Good shooting. I appreciate the help."

She casts a sideways glance. "Well at least you're grateful."

Kane disappears behind a rock pillar. Moments later, a dry heave, a gasp then one more, him spitting.

I don't move. It's too hard.

Leagan picks up my hand, patting the same soft way she does to Dilly's head. "Did it hurt?"

I shake my head.

I shouldn't let Leagan touch me at all. I'd rather die than watch this happen to her. But I can't pull away. Whatever happens, I know what I won't do. Ask her to shoot me.

"Don't cry," Leagan says. "We're getting out of here. Then we can all cry if we want to. Not now."

She's right.

"At least Navy has someone to test her cure on now." If it doesn't work, nothing changes. I'm going to die anyway.

Nothing matters now.

Kane reemerges, voice faint, feet tired. "You didn't have to wait for me."

I know.

"Your father's an ass," Leagan says. "Of course we waited."

"He's the wisest man I know."

I thought that was Markos.

"He may come across as strict or old-fashioned, but he knows what he's doing."

"Then how did he get captured by that maniac? Because he's a *fool*."

"This is where we have to disagree."

"Your father doesn't know shit. You east bloods. You're all going to find that out the hard way."

"Just because we're not from where you are doesn't mean we don't know anything." Kane pushes his legs faster, putting us behind him.

FIFTY
ADELAIDE

WE DON'T FULLY CATCH UP WITH MILLARD. I'M NOT TRYING TO. KANE probably would, but he can't leave us behind.

"He has a plan." Kane nods ahead. "My father."

"Sure." Leagan scoffs. "Except he's a liar. Or did you know he and one of the guys on your first crew were all shacked up together, sending coded love letters to each other?"

"What?"

"Okay, I'm making that part up. They were just secret spy letters. But guess who it was."

"Horne." Kane says, and she nods. He glances over at me, almost panicked. "I didn't know."

You didn't have to. It shouldn't be hard to realize everyone has their own motives. What I did should have taught him that.

"You didn't have to think very hard about that," Leagan says.

"You can still trust me," he says. "I wouldn't have let people come out here if I thought it was too dangerous for everyone."

Wouldn't you? You do everything your father says.

"Even after Randy?" I hope that hurts.

He knows something.

The Stranger's right.

Leagan swipes her hand along the wall, blurring the line of fluorescent chalk. "You were way better bait than Raleigh, by the way. He'd have cried and fucked it up somehow."

Kane halts. "Wait. Let me make sure I'm understanding this. You left me back there on purpose—"

Because we knew you'd stay. But I wasn't going to tell him that.

"Knowing Seed would show himself and come after me."

"Bait," Leagan says.

"You used me." I've heard this tone in his voice before. In the mine, last time. Sharp as a chipped edge.

"You asked us to help you. And we told you the plan," Leagan says. "At the campfire, remember?"

"You didn't tell me this scenario was the plan." He blocks the tunnel, looks at me again. Haunted accusations and leftover fear.

"We didn't know the exact circumstances." But I knew the Stranger would recognize the moment when the time came. "All we did was go check on our horses. We didn't tie you up and leave you."

"Not this time."

Maybe I deserve that.

"Bait has to look real and easy," Leagan says. "That's how it works. Calm down, you didn't die."

Be mad.

I'm about to pay for what I've done anyway.

FIFTY-ONE
TESLA

Wind sighs down the long slope on the opposite side of the tracks, bending the grasses down to their mirrored stalks. Far off in the western distance, lightning gives shape to the border of the sky. Evan and Navy said goodnight and went to bed. They think I did too.

A discordant laugh splits the otherwise velvet night, but I watched all the lanterns in town wink out one by one, the soft grain of my revolver grip soothing to my fingertips.

Guess who rode back into town tonight? *Farce,* my jaw almost waters.

It's time, darling.

I push my revolver back into its holster, already buckled around my hips. My legs quiver inside as I rise off the engine step. The wind is so butter soft I stop to stand in it for a minute, experience it on my cheeks. I close my eyes and picture my mother combing my hair.

You don't know how bad I've wanted this, and if you do, I'm sorry, it's hell.

The pile of dirt covering Green's dead bullies sits bare. The rest ran like rabbits and haven't been stupid enough to come back. Smart honestly. The dead aren't going anywhere, but at least we had the courtesy to bury them.

Really, it was so we didn't have to smell or look at them.

A few loose squawks rattle in the dark, but not close enough to alarm me. It's just some chickens up past their bedtime and bitching about that. And if it's a predator after them, it will be a good distraction. I lift the ax from the pile of split logs behind the general store and continue on.

My saliva thickens again, as does my heartbeat as I unbutton the canvas flap.

The smell of Green could knock something over. The greasiest cologne and moustache oil are the only kind he wears, but even then, there's a low-lying body scent, or possibly breath because he vaguely snores.

He's tumbled in the sheet on a brass frame bed, sleeping in a gray stripe nightshirt and cap, several large moles dotting his chest where the neckline peels open.

Oh God of Mercy, I've never hated anyone so much in my life—not even Rafe or Travis. It can't be healthy for me.

The ax head hisses as I drag it across the poppy rug covering the pallet floor, fine fibers severing.

The bottle of sleeping draught is a lovely blue, the dropper like a needle. Just enough, three to five breaths from a rag or drips in a drink, depending on the man, and the body sinks in sleep like a stone. I can't have him trying to fight me and ruin this.

Green must feel me lash his wrists to the bed frame and his ankles together because he lets out a dull moan, but he can't fully wake.

How kind of him to wear this nightshirt with nothing on underneath. It makes it easy to wrest the cotton fabric up around his hips once I rip the sheet off his body.

I find no pleasure looking at the squishy lump of flesh tucked between his legs like a grub. It moves like one as I set it between the blades of my fabric shears. It isn't a clean snip, but it comes off. Eventually.

I only gave him two breaths from the tainted handkerchief. I wanted to be able to wake him for this part, I want him to know.

Muddied moonlight still catches on the silver flash of smelling salts, so dainty and ladylike as I wave them under his hook nose.

His body gives a short jerk.

I give him a moment to realize the situation. His flat gaze crosses me, the ax balanced across my knees and my knife arm softly tapping on it. I don't think he feels the pain of what's missing yet, or how he's lying exposed. He chews on the gag but can't expel it from his mouth. It's from a pair of his dirty underwear, by the way.

"Whatever you have to say, you'll die with it unsaid." I keep my voice quiet, but the words move thick as bile in my mouth. "I don't want to hear your wretched voice ever again."

I think it's the blood he notices, the steady flow already soaked into the mattress under him and smeared across his freckled thighs. He recoils, the underwear absorbing the worst of his scream.

"Shhh." I hold the headboard still and lean down so he can feel my breath, and I could lick the sweat glistening on his forehead. "I'm going to sit here and watch you die. Watch you soil yourself once you're dead, you piece of shit. But just know that even right now you're still not suffering as much as I've suffered."

Flashflood tears run out of my eyes, stinging like the sunset.

His penis is jelly as I skewer it on the end of my knife arm and hold it up. "You've *never* loved this piece of meat close to how much I loved my mother and my daughter."

It's something he's not capable of comprehending, I know.

Somehow, the blood comes out faster now that there's less of it in him. Now I have to choose, do I continue to let him bleed away or finish it myself. I hadn't decided this part yet.

"There you go, darling." I shake his penis free of my knife. It plops on the *V* of bare skin showing on his chest. "Be close to each other one last time." I lean in again. "God of Mercy, let this one rot in hell."

His eyes roll closed, but he's not dead yet. It takes another minute or two before I smell the telltale leak of urine and shit. And it's a bitter thrill.

There are plenty of other men like this, but the world is a better place for now.

I wipe the ax through the blood-slick between his legs.

You thought I was going to chop his head off, didn't you? But it would be very difficult to swing this with only one hand, now wouldn't it?

Quickly, I unbind his wrists and ankles, peel out the gag which is wretchedly damp and shove it all into my apron pocket. His fingers are still malleable and will stay that way for a while. I close them around his gummy penis and his other hand around the ax handle.

Not that I wouldn't *love* for everyone to know it was me, but that would cause quite a few problems for us. I think we have enough already, and I'm smarter than that.

The thrill of what I've done glows in my belly, and I practically skip to the *Exodus*.

I have to tell Navy or Evangeline now. If I don't do it willingly and soon, the news will explode on its own.

Carrson Green? That mother fucker, is dead.

FIFTY-TWO
ADELAIDE

FLAMES HOP AMONG THE BRANCHES HEAPED IN THE CIRCLE OF STONES.

I pull my legs up tight, Leagan wrapped in her woven blanket like a roll, leg twitch proving she's fallen asleep. Kane and Millard stare at the dark from the other side, I stare into the flames.

Occasionally a spark speaks. We don't. Just the stick fire and a once-mountain cat up in the pines. Every time it whistle-screams, it's crept closer. It should be scared off by our fire, but it isn't. It smells meat.

Us.

The poison water dried on my skin hours ago. And there's not enough in our canteens to wash more than my face and hands.

Kane cracks his neck, then sits a little straighter, voice that dry space between a whisper and resignation. "I'll take the first watch."

Millard nods. "Thank you. Wake me in five hours." His knees pop as he stands, a grunt for leverage. He squeezes Kane's shoulder, looks back at me as he does.

I can't say why. But the Stranger doesn't like it.

Kane shoves himself up once Millard's gone into their single-person tent. "You'll be alright here for a minute."

Yes, that's why it's not a question.

He grabs his Exodus rifle before he goes, short but fast steps leading the pines. Far enough I stop hearing his boots break the dead needles.

I stand, waiting.

It's longer than a piss. By the time he returns to the fire, the red Season Moon has climbed past the closest ridge.

"You can go to bed now too." Kane looks at Leagan. "Are you going to leave her there?"

She's fine, I'm watching her.

Six.

I sit next to him, against the fallen tree trunk.

I've had men try to kill me before. You fight, then the survival surge melts off and you feel so thin. Brittle. Like part of you died anyway, even though you're still here.

It goes away eventually.

"Don't sit here just to make me feel better," he says. "You did what you had to do to get your way. Your family always does."

Everyone does.

I shake my head. That's not why I'm sitting here. I remember exactly how it felt when Thadie hugged me, after those chemical dealers tried to beat me to death in Hannah. How Raleigh and Navy held onto me after Vesta died.

It's what kept my soul beating.

Kane was my friend once, before that wasn't good enough for him, and I robbed him. This is what friends do.

The night is too warm for his skin to be this cold.

He looks down, my hand holding onto his. But he doesn't shut his grip, body rigid like a knife. I keep holding it.

Nothing matters now, anyway.

"I didn't mean to freeze up like that," he says. "When I was younger, going off to battle in service to my country was the most heroic thing I could think of. Now I can't even imagine...I can't imagine the life you've lived for none of this to bother you. That feeling back there, I never want to feel that again."

"I'm going to die someday," I say.

A slow death. That's what I'm picked for now.

I am so afraid.

"And so are you," I say.

"But it's in our nature to want to survive." Like a belt, he finally closes his hand around mine. "And leave behind something that will outlive us."

I'm less worried about leaving something of myself behind than dying with so much of the Rim unseen.

Has this bottomless desire been the Stranger trying to escape me all along?

The thought stops me like an overhead thunderclap. Unbidden.

Maybe the Stranger was loose like the Eden hunger, before my mother pinned her inside of me.

This searching I feel. Endless. She's driving me to a place I've never been able to reach. I've always thought it was to collect forgotten things. What if it's just a grave where she can finally tear her shadow off my back?

Maybe that's what she's looking for.

A way out.

Fool. Without you, I cut no mark on the Rim, bleed flesh.

She is just a shadow. As long as I survive, she does too.

Without you, I'm less than a memory.

She needs me.

But the idea sticks in my head like a splinter anyway.

Kane pulls out of my grasp. "That was a shitty thing you did back there. Yes, you said I was along as bait but that was it. You intentionally let me walk into a trap without consent. You should have given me the choice."

I know. But I didn't.

"You know it was wrong."

Would it have made a difference?

It's not worth the energy to ask.

"If you ever use me like that again, I won't be forgiving you. I should tell you to go fuck yourself right now. Honestly, I don't know why I'm not."

"I didn't ask you to stay behind," I say. "You said you had to find your father, with or without us."

"You mean I should have been more careful," he says. "If it was your family, you'd look for them. You don't get to blame me for this. I didn't do anything wrong."

Men do that to women all the time. It's our own fault when something happens to us. We should have been more careful, shouldn't go there, shouldn't look appealing, shouldn't exist.

He glances back at his father's tent once again and takes a cooling breath. Doesn't want him hearing. "I really did love you, you know. It was never a lie."

Did.

Not anymore.

"Even now I'd never use you like that." Kane nods to Leagan. "You'd never use your sister like that."

Never. You're right. But you're not my sister.

Half of Vesta's face exploded when the bounty hunter shot her, her once-round cheek hanging off the bone in strips. The sound of each breath wet, gurgling.

I come back into myself.

"Now do you wish I'd died on the open Rim after our expedition?" I ask.

You wouldn't be the first man to want me dead. You won't be the last.

"No." Fast and sharp. "I'm not evil."

"Not like me."

"I didn't say that. I don't wish harm on you."

Rotten decay creeps up my throat. The kind that's coming for me. There is no justice in this world. Only vengeance. The harm's been done. "You don't know."

"Don't know what?" he asks.

"It's already too late. Green killed them, Vesta and my grandma."

The Stranger recoils, much like Kane does. I didn't mean to say that. I wish I didn't. The heat in my jaw must have loosened it.

But there's no taking it back now.

"You should have told me this sooner," he says.

"Why?" Like I owe you?

He can't answer that. This east-blood society they're so proud of, strung together with old thread, laws, the promises of black gold. It's too brittle. The Rim claws everything away.

"You told me Vesta had the pestilence like Randy, so I just assumed... and Tesla made it sound like bounty hunters—" The pieces hit him. "Green set the bounty on you."

Too cowardly to do his own dirty work.

"Because of this job," I say. "You paid him to clean up the rails."

"I didn't—" The exhale crumples him. "Fuck."

A flinch rocks through me as one of the horses squeals. Branches snap as it kicks just at the edge of our firelight.

Leagan sits straight up, rifle unrolling from the blanket with her.

Something flat and dark clings to her horse's red and white neck.

One.

I yank a flaming stick from the pit. Two beady eyes flash between pine branches and darkness, silver globes. Leather skin, gripping horse flesh by the wing talons.

Usually, ghoul bats swoop in for a single bite of flesh when an animal is sleeping. Our fire and voices should have kept it away. Night creatures hate light in their eyes. But the ghoul releases the neck and flies at me.

I duck under its first swoop, shoving the stick back into the fire so we don't have another problem to worry about.

"Get out of my way," Leagan yells. "I got it."

One.

Two. A second shot bolsters her pistol crack, but only one falling body thumps in the brush.

Millard stands outside his tent, lowering his shooting stance.

"I had it taken care of," Leagan says.

Eight.

Two lines of blood run from the circular bite in the horse's neck, smaller puncture wounds across her upper flank, dark red stars. The others list uneasily as well, ears still turned back, tails slashing.

"It's over now." I offer her a strip of dried peach as a distraction. "You'll survive."

Nightmare edges toward me, nosing for her treat even though each hoof she places has a wary beat.

"Do you need me to keep watch?" Millard asks.

"No, it's all right." Kane gathers up his rifle. "Go rest, I'll do a better job. Adelaide, you get some sleep as well."

Don't tell me what to do.

He catches my elbow in a loose grasp as he heads for his horses. "I don't know what to tell you about Green. I don't know what to do. But I'll have an answer for you once I've had time to think this over and talk to my father."

"There's nothing to do about it." It's already too late. The vengeance is going to happen.

If Aunt Tess doesn't find Green in the next few days, I will.

"Let's collect some ghoul teeth in the morning." Leagan crawls into our tent, turning one last time. "For the record, *I* shot it."

FIFTY-THREE
TESLA

Green is dead. It's the first thing that comes to mind when I wake, along with Navy's sleep-drunk giggle when I told her. She wouldn't respond to any old murder with glee, but this is *Green*, and that's what makes it more savory. We all hate his bones.

I can't wait to surprise Adelaide and Leagan when they get back. Adelaide and the Stranger will be so pleased with me.

I brush the snags out of my black hair and squeeze the curls into submission. A few of the vessels in my right eye look a little red. I must have got dust in this eye. The aloe drops burn a little, but they're the only thing that soothe Navy's eyes, they should help me.

Green is dead.

My heart flutters again, and I suppose that makes me evil. But I don't care. I want to dance and run through town laughing at all his men who couldn't protect him from me.

Dawn nudges sky and land apart as I step outside with no mask clinging to my face and breathe in the pink air.

Caroline's main street is white. At first, I wonder if it could be a freak snow, but that's not possible. Then I get closer and realize what actually covers the ground, feathers.

The chickens I heard last night.

"You poor little bastards." I wince as I lift my skirt, so it doesn't drag through what's left of them, and watch each step before putting it down. Giblets and feet are strewn among the blood-spotted feathers. "My glory."

"That's about right," someone agrees.

"A fox would have eaten all this, not left it on doorsteps like a housecat with a mouse." A white handkerchief flutters in the merchant's hand, little yellow bits inside.

"What are you suggesting?" Green's bully asks him.

"Someone's up to no good."

Another man nods up at the ridge where the railroad camp perches. "Are you sure none of those vagrants could have done it?"

Feathers tumble past in white balls as the wind picks up. The piles they've already tried to sweep up separate.

"I meant another fox," a different bully says. "One with two legs."

"That's a bold accusation from someone who slept through all the noise this must have made," I say. "Where were you last night?"

"Not sleeping behind an iron wall."

"We should organize an investigation." One merchant turns to the others and a chorus of nods. "Every man can spread out and look for clues."

"It's nice if they do your job for you." I smirk at the bullies. "It leaves more time for you to itch your asscrack."

His glove squeaks on the end of the shovel. Oh, I hope I get to see their faces when they find Green's body. "Where's your fox?"

"Does she scare you?"

"You don't scare me."

I drag my fingers below his chokehold grip on the shovel. "That's not what I asked."

There's nothing wrong with the chicken coop. It's simply unlatched.

"Well, this proves a human did it," I say.

"It appears so." The merchant perches awkwardly on his toes so his heels don't touch the coop floor while he roots through the empty nests with his fountain pen. "I'm shocked you have the stomach for this. I barely do myself."

"I didn't eat breakfast yet," I say.

"I agree with you," he says. "It's far more likely men did this, not the Tov girl. Some of those hired guns seem rotten enough to me. I won't be depending on them for my life."

"I'm glad I'm not the only one who's noticed. What do you sell?"

"Boots and stoves."

"Very useful. When I need some, I'll…"

A gray shape moves between pine framing, glowing like bone in the sun. A distinctly bad feeling sinks through my gut.

He has all his hands and feet, unlike Seed's pet pickers, but he's using all four of them to move. He gallops up and down the backside of the street, wheeling around when he meets sage to go again. His ass bobs in the air to the soft splat of bare feet and palms striking dust.

"Stop that," a man calls to him. "You're going to scare someone and get yourself shot acting like that. There are women and a child here. Put your clothes on and go home, you drunk bastard."

The sigh leaves me as I reach for my gun. "Oh, you fool."

The picker pads back around, each vertebra of his spine stacking slowly. Open mouthed but silent he rushes, ripping a chipped knife from his belt.

He's halfway across the space between them before the other man can even react.

I fire all five shots in my revolver and enough of them hit. The picker veers away, continuing to stagger into the brush before slumping over.

"Fucking Jezebel." It's the merchant who brought his wife along, naturally.

"You were almost dead." I skirt around more bird entrails. If he'd fumbled with his revolver a second or two longer and I wasn't here, he definitely would have been.

"What would possess a man to act like that?" He wipes at the sweat collecting under his hat like dew. "I've never seen anyone deep enough in the drink to lose his mind that way. Unless he was compelled by a devil…" He peeks over his shoulder as if he might have summoned one by name alone.

"Come here, I'll show you what you should be the most scared of."

Burs and cactus needles stick into my skirt and pull as I search for the exact place the dead picker fell. His body has enough energy left his eyes twitch as I peel the lid back by the lashes. Oh yes, bloody red, and the dark spots of other broken vessels—that at first glance could be a bruise or a love bite—snake up his throat from under his shirt.

I make the *x* to Providence across myself. "Uh-huh, just what I thought. That my friend, is what the pestilence does to a man. Take a good look. This is what all of you should really be afraid of, not devils, not my niece." Only halfway true, but he doesn't need to know that. "I'm also willing to bet this is your chicken murderer. That looks like blood under his nails to me."

"We were told this area was mostly safe now," he says. "That most of the contamination was deeper west."

"I'm sure you were." I offer my hand. "Tesla Revere."

"Tomaths Goodson, mercantile owner. Thank you, on behalf of my wife as well. She's in deep need of women friends around here. I convinced her to come, but it's been lonely for her and our boy. Perhaps she could stop by with a peach skillet pie."

I wish I could say I'd like that.

I'm sure she's a perfectly nice woman, and even though the sight of her still reminds me of what I've lost, she was brave enough to follow her husband out here. Most wives stay behind.

"I never say no to cheese or pies."

"She's a little under the weather this morning, she's suffered from headaches since our son was born. But when she's feeling up to it, I'll tell her you'd like a visit. I'm very grateful for your kindness."

Ah, I've heard that tone before. Kind isn't what I look like to a man with a violet for a wife, but under this scar I'm full of surprises.

Like vultures, Green's bullies smell carrion, one of them still buttoning his uniform as they approach.

"Over here." I point out the body. "You're welcome."

They have that doctor with them, DuPonte. I haven't seen him in a while. In fact, I haven't seen him in so long you could forgive me almost forgetting he was ever here.

If I were to give him a color, it would be none. He has no color, and I don't mean white, I mean gray, how ash fades everything it touches. He's bent like a tree that hasn't seen enough sun, and his gaze smears across me like something dead, wet, and left to rot.

It's a relief that the picker quickly reabsorbs his attention, his tongue clicking inside his mask, more a vulture than all the others. "Bag him up and put him in my surgery."

"It would be better to just burn him," I say.

"We don't do that," a bully sneers. "This isn't Hannah, and we're not a bunch of godless milk bastards."

"Suit yourself." *Farce,* I'll let them contaminate the place if that's what they want, but don't say I didn't try. "Be careful out here, Tomaths Goodson. The guns the Green Company pays to protect us must be stretched a little too thin. Before we were crystal miners, my family and I were paid protection. I hate to see the business given a bad name."

Oh, there's room for one more stab, so why not?

"I also find it interesting that whenever the Stranger is *not* here, things go bad. It's almost like she's good luck for you." I glance my fingers off my temple in the engineer's salute. "*Sol.*"

"Shut your mouth," Green's bully mutters. "*Whore.*"

Whore, yes. It drops off his breath like a worm as he gets to packing the remains. The same notion Tomaths Goodson had hidden under his tongue when he said he was grateful for my kindness. He meant for a working woman.

But I say go ahead, spit any angry little name you can come up with to cover your own shortcomings. I'm not afraid of words. But if we are going to shame anyone, let's get the target right.

Who are fragile men like this really so mad at?

FIFTY-FOUR
ADELAIDE

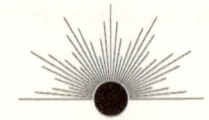

Something touches my face.

I flinch out of a blank sleep, but it's just Leagan next to me. She already has her finger to her lips, patting me with the other hand.

Pale daylight finds slits in the tent. It's already warm in here. Last night's smoke clings to my hair, burned bottom coffee stewing in the percolator outside.

Listen.

"You're right," Kane says. "And the supplies cached there should last."

"I will accompany the body back to town," Millard says. "And put everyone's minds to rest."

"What are you going to tell them?" He means us.

"You used to say they weren't a threat."

"Because threat is a strong word, but they are very used to…doing what they want, and they're not likely to change in that regard—"

"Women are the greatest threat there is, my son. They create such a damning blind spot in a man."

Leagan smothers her laugh with a face.

"Aside from that, they did hijack the *Exodus Ironclad* which has made them a viable threat for some time now. Don't ever forget that."

"Father, I…" I can picture exactly how Kane's whole body just sank under the weight of what he's trying to say, how he only talks with his left hand. "Did you have a man spying on my first expedition?"

"Who put that idea in your head?"

"Did you?"

"You make it sound more sinister than the reality. I asked one of your crewmen to send me reports so you could focus on your task."

"With encoded messages? Didn't you trust me?"

"Of course I do. You're my son. It's our competitors I didn't trust. We couldn't risk information leaking out before the territory acquisition was complete."

"What kind of information?"

"Any kind." Like last night, Millard's knees crack alongside the grunt of him leveraging his body upright. "I hope you trust me and not whoever's been whispering in your ear."

"Kane's going to Eden." The name disturbs the Stranger like the Season Moon does to a compass needle. "Isn't he?"

It's time.

But I don't know if I can convince Leagan to leave me.

"That's why I woke you up," she says.

I wait for them to keep talking, so I know they're not listening to us.

"I miss Dilly," Leagan says.

"You could have brought him." She knows I'm not serious. "I promised Navy I'd find her Isobel Carlisle's journal." Even so, it might not give her enough time to save me. "But one of us needs to go back with Millard, so Aunt Tess and Navy know what's happening. And just in case he tries to get out of paying us."

"He would." Leagan picks at the dirt under her thumbnail. "Fine. I'll go back with Kane's daddy and make sure everyone knows who really killed Seed. I know you have to go. But you have to promise to take me there with you next time and bring me back a surprise."

I nod.

"We'll come up with some reason why you're leaving, so Millard doesn't know where you're really going," she says. "I'll tell him... something. Don't worry, it'll be good."

"I already told Aunt Tess we'd check on the mine again. On our way back."

"Alkaline. We'll use that."

"I'll wake them," Kane says. Seconds later, the shadow of his hand crosses the tent, raps on the canvas. "Adelaide, Leagan, we should get going soon."

"Calm down, we're already awake," she says.

As soon as Leagan leaves the tent, I pull out my hand mirror.

The whites of my eyes are still the color they're supposed to be. Overnight would be a fast turn, but the pestilence melts people at different rates. I don't feel any different, but the worse I get, I won't know I'm turning, will I?

Vesta didn't seem to.

I ride at the back of the line. Leagan between me and the Von Kanes.

"Do *you* know any ghost stories?" she asks Millard.

"I'd rather ride in silence this morning, young lady." He glances back for the eighth time.

He tried to convince us Seed's body could be strapped to the back of his horse—the spare Kane brought with him. Lucky. But he didn't have an argument when Leagan said she was so much lighter it would be easier for her horse to carry two bodies.

I have our tent. Most of the food, our water reclaimer.

They shouldn't question why.

Kane starts to slow, then veer off the southeast course when the pine trees thin out. He drops past Leagan, her horse's neck bandaged with gauze and her extra shirt.

I gradually reduce Nightmare's head, don't let him slip past me, even though I know where he's going.

Millard stops at a red bluff. The rocks drop away and the view down into the valley spreads out forever.

I hang back, in the shade of one of the last stubborn trees and twin yucca, their stalks towering and dried to paper.

Kane turns his horse, doubles back.

"Where are you going?" Leagan calls.

"Surveying."

"Well, have a good time. Watch out for bats and crazy preachers." She brings her horse alongside me. "You tell Aunt Tess I'm getting as good as her." Then she leans over and rubs Nightmare's cheek. "You take good care of her when I'm gone, okay?"

I let Kane go, then choose a path along the bluff that isn't too rocky for Nightmare, that will take us back to the place we came up. Millard sits, a silhouette in his saddle on the ridge. His gaze rests heavy as iron on my back, the Stranger just as thick to meet it.

"Do you want to lead?" he asks.

I don't answer, I just go first. I'm not waiting out in the sun all day for whatever he's thinking about.

Fifty.

"She can't go the whole way with us anyway," Leagan says to him. "She has to go check our homestead for claim jumpers. But don't worry, I'll get you back to your civilized people, east blood."

FIFTY-FIVE
TESLA

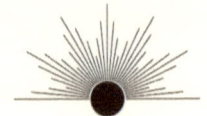

I GIVE OUR PLUMPEST QUAIL A LITTLE KISS ON THE HEAD AND PLACE HER BACK in the coop with her sisters. Their tiny throats flutter with sweet up and down pipes. "Thank you for feeding us with your unborn offspring."

I don't kiss the chickens, they're unpleasant. Still alive, though, because we bring ours into the stable car at night.

My eye doesn't look so red after my nap, but I'd better not rub it after handling the birds and end up with some kind of infection.

I come around the *Exodus* just as Leagan and Millard Von Kane ride into town under a banner of dust.

There's a bloody shirt tied around the neck of Leagan's horse and a body flopping behind her saddle. No Adelaide, but that's not a surprise. No Kane, either, unless that's him rolled inside the blanket.

Leagan turns this way as I head down the slope, pockets still full of eggs, while Millard rides up the main street, summoning everyone who looks up with a hand. The song of saws and hammers dwindle. How he even got involved, I don't know.

"I'd just like everyone to know the wanted criminal Reverend Alonzo Seed has been brought to justice," he says, still up on his horse. "Your town is safe again."

A brief splatter of thanks passes through the crowd.

"You're sure he's dead?" someone asks. "I've heard these hills are full of beast men, following the old ways of the foxes. Eating each other, it keeps them living…unnaturally."

"Want to see the body?" Leagan peels back the blanket crusted to Seed. "I've seen more dead men than you. He's dead."

"That rich fool Jonathaniel Swann probably got carried off by them," a bully says. "Or he ran to join him. I drank with him a few times, and he was always talking about that fox girl. Serves him right."

"They say she can summon ghosts," Tomaths Goodson says.

"No, they say she burned Winchester."

Fuck me.

"Flaming ghosts, regular ones. Any kind probably."

"This isn't the time for spreading wives' tales, gentlemen," Millard says. "If you would like, I can have Seed's remains hanged here for the afternoon. As proof of his demise and a warning to anyone who might consider following in his footsteps. Will that put your minds at ease?"

How very Zachariah Wells of him.

"I have my family here." Tomaths hugs his little boy to his side, a hand over his brown eyes. "They don't need to see that."

"A valid point," Millard says. "We are not so depraved. Anyone with the need to view the body may do so for the next hour in the marshal's tent, then we'll bury him at sundown."

"Don't call her that fox girl," Leagan snaps at the men who were gossiping. "Her name is the Stranger. I'll kick you in the shin."

He laughs like she's being funny and so she does it.

"Ow, you little bitch."

Millard's hand looks as meaty as a pig's neck as he drops it on Leagan's shoulder. "Your horse is tired. You should water him and clean his bite wounds. You've had a long ride as well, surely you must need a rest."

"Ew, get your old man sweat off me." She ducks under his arm, small enough to do so easily. "And it's a *she*."

I latch onto Millard's arm, steering him and Leagan apart. He looks down, clearly startled that I've touched him unsolicited. But of course, it's not out of line that he just did it to Leagan.

"Your son hired us to help him get rid of the dearly departed Reverend," I say. "What happened to him out there? I hope he didn't die."

"Nobody died except for that lunatic."

"Alkaline, then you can amend our land deed with the additional acres he offered us. An Express Rider got here this morning. He can send it on to Jezebel."

"Whatever agreement you think you have is between you and Timothy. I have no knowledge of it; therefore, you'll have to wait until he returns from his survey. I'm not staying long either. I left valuable research behind out there," Millard says. "As soon as I've rested, I will be going back for it."

"You can leave as soon as you pay us what your son promised."

"I am not obligated to rearrange my entire work schedule simply because you're impatient. This is an unbecoming look for you. I will pay you when he returns, you have my word."

"I don't give a fart how I look to you. You'll pay me now because the job is done. This is the Rim. Words don't mean shit."

He drops back, causing our arms to come undone. "Lower your voice when you speak to me."

"I will not." I fish into my pocket. "Have a quail egg. And shove it up your nose."

Shove it up your tiny asshole.

He ignores me, returning for his horse.

"Has anyone found Jonathaniel by the way?" I call, loud enough at least a few men heard me.

Millard plants his tree-trunk legs.

"I've noticed less of Green's men around too. Have they already given up on him? Even if he found water, he can't survive much longer."

He chews on whatever he thinks before saying it. "Jonathaniel Swann?"

As if there's another.

"Or are we all assuming he's dead now?"

"I haven't declared anyone dead. You're misinformed, Miss Revere. Swann went back east," Millard says. "Unfortunately, there was a misfortune in the family so he will likely have to remain there for some time."

You're a fucking liar.

Now I don't know where he is, but I can tell you back east is the only place he damn sure isn't. "Oh, that's terrible. Your son must not have known, he was the one who asked me to keep an eye out for him."

He doesn't like that, which is why I said it, in hopes of shocking a reaction from him like a snappy dog.

"Where is Green?" It's not the volume that Millard yells, it's that he yelled at all. People in control don't snap like sticks. "Off taking a nap? Wouldn't we all like that?"

Everyone ignores him, or at least pretends to. The railroaders a mile off with the steam hammer probably heard, Seed's bones heard, Navy and Evangeline up on the ridge inside the *Exodus* heard.

Is the illustrious dream you sold to these fools disintegrating, you bastard? You're afraid they're going to see the Rim at its reality, a bloodthirsty fight to the death.

He turns to Leagan like he didn't just snap. "Well, no wonder."

She leans away. "I didn't say anything to you."

"Do as you're told, girl," he says. "Bring that bastard to DuPonte."

"I don't have to do what you say, *man*," Leagan says. "You're not my boss."

"Why does DuPonte need so many bodies?" I ask.

Once again, Millard waits just an eyelash flicker too long before answering. "For burial of course. Stop being difficult women. If one of you can stop yapping long enough to bring the body to the marshal's tent, I'll have your deed amendment ready by sundown."

"There. Was that so hard, darling?" Although, he did just order Leagan to bring Seed to DuPonte but now it's back to the marshal's tent. Don't think I didn't notice.

"You will learn your place, *darling*." The horse whinnies as Millard's heels jab into its sides.

Leagan just shakes her head.

"Well, that sounds like a threat to me."

"Stop being a difficult woman, Aunt Tess."

Learn your place? Never, hah. "His poor, poor wife."

FIFTY-SIX
ADELAIDE

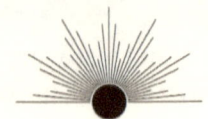

I'M CLOSE.

The cracked skin of the lakebed bleeds up into a heat mirage. It hides the bleached walls caught in the act of tumbling down, but the Stranger knows they're here.

The table rock looms behind the scrub trees and lower hill folds. A naked slab, leftover from the forgotten world that came a long time before this one, watching everything done here. Pink in the morning, red as blood in the evening.

Eden.

The last time I was here Vesta was still alive.

The speck of Kane and his horse get folded into the silver band of the mirage. Or maybe swallowed by the West Rim hunger.

The Stranger yearns out across the lakebed, a thing dying of thirst, and Eden is the water now, but I hold her back. I know where I need to start. The end of town where the Wells brewed their pestilence and Isobel and Amnesty's bones lie dead in the bed below the dance hall.

One thousand nine hundred eight.

The sun pinches my skin harder, fingers capable of reaching through my clothes. It's almost four, the hottest portion of the day.

I tie Nightmare under an arbor of knotbush, the new skin on the skeleton of an ironwood tree. Higher ground than where Eden lies. She has shade and the rest of the water from the reclaimer. She should be safe here.

I'm going to be thirsty next. I work the reclaimer's legs into the dirt, then pile rocks to hold them. The remaining drops sliding around the bottom of the reservoir will vaporize on the copper cone and multiply, hopefully before the water in my canteen runs out.

Sixty-two.

The hillside drops away. Movement.

The sun's glare burns through my binoculars and darkened lenses. You might assume it's just Kane, or the distortion of the heat. The Stranger doesn't.

Men stalk the perimeter of the Wells's stone house like shadows. Two so far, a track worn into the wild plants that reclaimed Eden. It circles the house and cuts down the slope to meet the once-main street.

Wait.

She's right, there's more. Boots perch on the balcony rail, the zig-zag tread that marks the ground all over the railroad camp, splinters and paint coiling off the wood like thorns. The nose of a rifle barrel. Legs spread across the empty doorframe on the shade side of the house.

What are they guarding?

You should have searched the Wells's house last time.

I know, and now it's too late. Everyone else has had a chance to get to it first.

Six-fifty.

The miner's side of Eden is mostly the way it was. Storms have knocked a few more walls down, bared wood underneath frayed paint like skin, buried wagon axels in dirt. But with each step, the Stranger shrinks around my chest.

The buzz in my ears is just heat and bugs, but I move like a stick snap might wake something anyway. Corner to corner, eyes up.

The front side of the dance hall has finally collapsed under the weight of its bleached drapes. The window Vesta and I used to climb inside last time is buried. Gone.

I find a beam that doesn't move, already leaning like a ramp up over the debris. If I fall, I'll be impaled on many things. It will hurt, but maybe that would still be a faster death than the pestilence.

Nineteen.

I duck under the last board obstructing the gap, looking for something to step down on. A fainting couch. The chewed velvet backing gives way as I test my weight on it. Wood rotting with wasp damage peels away in chunks. I dig my fingers in until it stops crumbling and climb a little farther to a slab of wall still holding onto its shape and browned wallpaper.

Vesta and I had to crawl under a few blocked spaces. Now that more of the building has given in, there's actually more room to get over things, instead of squeezing around them.

The tip of a striped tail slips out of my way, gone between shadows and a lamp. My foot slips.

My arms slam into the top of an upright piano, shins skimming off the keys. I clench, expecting an out of tune clang that will bring Green's men or a bone picker from under the floorboards, but the keys only sink in, dead.

The floor is soft with dust.

I point myself toward the back.

The Stranger pushes like fingers through the web of fallen boards. My sleeves snag on splinters—wood and glass. She beats harder, darker.

Thirty-one.

There's the chandelier Vesta was so excited over, prisms broken in a thousand dust covered knives, slowly being digested by the floor.

My breath heaves out of my respirator. The door's still here. The hole I hacked to get inside, unblocked.

Down.

Moldy air wafts up the steps just like a presence.

Six.

Stale cobwebs dangle over my head and glow wherever I turn, the spiders that made them turned to dust. But the dark itself barely backs away from the quartz shining inside my headlamp.

I pick up the yellow shell of a scorpion that hasn't crumbled yet. Leagan's present.

Fifteen.

The face of my contamination compass comes to life.

My breaths whine out of my mask as whatever's making it so moist catches on the filters. Why am I still bothering? At least it keeps the dust out, the soggy air off my face.

Maybe it makes everything easier to ignore.

Five.

Orange light blooms each time my headlamp beam touches the glass in the lab, resting inside cobweb tents. The bed in the corner has a canopy of them, Amnesty and Isobel wrapped into one puzzle of bones. Only one of them has a jaw.

This is all your fault.

Being in love makes you insane.

Vesta would have said, *"Well, you've never been in love, so how would you know?"*

You don't have to experience something yourself if you've seen it in enough other people.

I question if Vesta was ever really in love, even though she believed in it. It doesn't seem like the kind of thing you just forget about. If Kane had stopped loving his brother or dead wife, he wouldn't carry their pictures around in his wallet. If Aunt Tess didn't love Travis, she wouldn't cry for him after what he did to her. If Grandma didn't love my mother, she wouldn't have found reasons to talk about her so often when I didn't ask. No, I know it lasts. And the way I loved Grandma was no less important than the way Vesta wanted to love a man. If it was, I wouldn't be holding onto so many little things I wish I could tell her.

I pick up the last drawer I held. Still where I dropped it when we heard the gunshots.

Mouse droppings shift out of the corners, a few fresh motes of light pricking the fluid in my contamination compass.

I turn slowly, let the Stranger study the room.

Time stopped here. This is the same lab as the day Amnesty and Isobel died fifty years ago. Just dustier. Same as the day Vesta and I were too.

Half of the sealed vials still have liquid in them, turned brown or even black. Glass things gummy with residue, syringes, and metal instruments. Some for cutting, some for grabbing. A behavior logbook bearing black spots tossed against the far wall by the cages. I add it to the bucket of stuff for Navy.

She is so sure this journal exists. And if it does, it has to be here. Unless Isobel ate it when she started turning.

Where would I hide mine? I wouldn't, I'd keep it with me. Unless I thought it was safe.

Did Isobel feel safe here?

Sixteen.

Probably not at the end. People hacking at walls and howling in the street above, like Amnesty described.

The bed.

A crusty revolver lies on what's left of the pillow, pointing toward the fractured skull of the hand holding it, her jaw dangling open. Their fingers have fallen apart without skin and ligaments to hold the bones in line, but the four long bones of their left and right arms remain locked together as when Amnesty shot them.

Under the blanket and one of the collapsed ribcages is the raised outline of a book.

The Stranger creeps up the back of my neck.

The hunger comes through the weight of the building over me, like groundwater leaking out of a crack in stone. A pit that wants filling, always searching. It beads on the damp walls, waiting for what I'm going to do.

I hold the Stranger like a collar.

Grandma was right about Amnesty and her bastard father practicing occult magic. What if they made something? Or maybe they called it up from the rocks. Maybe this hunger was always here, leftover from some other time, waiting for someone willing to feed it.

It has no body now. It can't hurt me.

I grab the dusty forceps off the workbench. I won't touch their bones.

FIFTY-SEVEN
TESLA

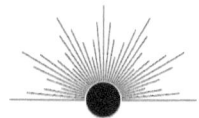

Raleigh's face no longer looks like it belongs on a swollen corpse, but the bruises and splinter cuts have ripened.

"At least you can open both eyes now," I say. "That's an improvement. I don't think they ruined your pretty face permanently."

"That's a relief," he says.

I let my hand linger on his. "I'm sorry this happened at all."

"It gave me an excuse to lay around a few days, catching up on my reading. It's been quite nice."

"Like you need an excuse for that, you lazy bum," Leagan says.

There's a knock from outside the *Exodus*'s shell.

"Don't listen to her," I say. "You keep resting. If you need anything, just ring the bell."

It's Pike waiting outside, a trap scrabbling with mice at his feet. "I brought these for Navy."

"A girl of science would never want to run out of rodents. I bet you didn't think mouse collecting was going to be part of your daily life when you were studying medicine, did you?" I drag my fingers across the bubbled scars on the metal of the crossing. "You haven't mentioned what Navy's working on to anyone, have you?"

I seriously doubt it was a coincidence Green's bullies were cutting into the lab the other night. Personally, I would have gone for one of the engines or the standing guns. Since they didn't get whatever they were after, it's not a stretch to worry they'll try something again. But it's been quiet since I killed Green.

One might say too quiet.

"It's no secret I'm up here when I'm not tending the railroad camp," Pike says.

"I hope they're paying you well. I also hope you're not lying."

"For my sake so do I. This is a noble project. I wouldn't intentionally do anything to harm it." Pike sets the trap on the floor in front of Navy. "I can't stay long. One of the shop owners asked if I'd examine his wife."

"Tomaths Goodson," I say.

"You know him?"

"He's the only one with a wife in town."

"What is she sick with?" Suspicion coats Navy's voice.

"He says it's the heat, but—"

"But you'll be the judge of that," I say.

Navy's lips twist as she bites into her cheek. "Check her jaw for swelling and pain. And any spots on the bottom of her feet. It likes to hide there."

"I'll come with you," I decide impulsively. "I said I'd visit her."

I snag our second to last contamination vial on my way back out.

Evangeline meets us coming up the corridor behind the food supply car. "More mice, Doctor?"

"More mice," Pike says. "But now I have a house call to make."

"I'm going to visit the sick woman with him," I say. "Would you like to come along?"

It doesn't hurt our chances to make a few more friends in town before another storm kicks up.

* * *

LIKE MOST OF THE OTHER FRESH-EYED SALESMEN, TOMATHS GOODSON PUT HIS efforts into building his storefront first. I suppose it is the logical choice, being ready to service the next wave of prospectors surely bearing down on us and resupply the ones that are already out in the hills.

Sawdust flakes linger in the corners like little secrets, but he's got tin goods, canned and dry food, colorful bolts of fabric, and boots already shelved. I do love the tang of fresh wood. It's a pity it doesn't last and the buildings that do weather the Rim the best are made of stone.

They hold out the heat better too, my glory. The belly of their iron pig stove is gobbling cold Ven quartz but it's doing absolutely nothing unless you're sitting right on top of it.

"Thank you for coming so soon, Doctor," Tomaths says. "Piety talked more than once about how that other doctor has an ill-favored look."

"I know what she means," I say.

"She hasn't come out of our room in three days. Ladies, if you're here to shop look around, I'll be with you as soon as I can."

"Actually, we're here to visit your wife too," I say.

"Oh…"

"Does she want visitors?" Evangeline asks.

"To be honest, I'm not sure. This way, Doctor." He beckons.

I follow anyway but stop at the back doorway.

At the moment, it's just a lean-to with a bed, a smaller bed, and a cookstove. There's barely room for Pike and Tomaths to stand next to each other without touching. I don't see her, but someone is here with us. I imagine breath fogging on a window, or a dog tasting the dark. Both are thick and through the mouth, like this.

Tomaths points reluctantly to the dark gap below the bedframe. Dr. Pike squats down.

"Close it!" A female voice suddenly screeches. The bed jumps, the scrape of her heels writhing against the floor. "My head wants to eat me up. I *told* you."

"We know, it's okay," Evangeline says calmly.

"How did you get in like that? Did you climb through the wall like they did?"

"How long has she been under there?" Pike asks.

"Since lasterday evening. She has frequent headaches, but this is…different."

"Can we move the bed?"

Evangeline shakes her head. "You'll make it worse. Piety, my name is Evangeline. I'm a Sister, serving the God of Mercy. Would you like to hold my hand?"

"Is it wet?"

"No. It's very dry."

Piety goes quiet again, disembodied breaths that make the room feel like it's getting even smaller.

"She stayed under there all night, panting like that," Tomaths says. "Nothing I said made her come out. You can imagine how unsettling it was to sleep with something under the bed like that. My boy was scared too."

"It's not something, she's your wife," I say.

Piety pushes her hand out first, her palm tasting the dirt floor, a snake that glides instead of slithers. "Hold my hand, Sister. Please."

Honestly, that alone is enough to scare me. I wouldn't want to sleep in that bed. But she's not my wife.

My sweaty palm holds the violent green glow of the contamination vial. It's not a secret, we all know, we just don't say. I wish Evan wouldn't touch her, but she's better than I am, braver than I am.

"I brought you a gift," Evangeline says. "It's milk soap with lavender and honey, made from my goats back on the South Rim. It makes your skin soft like a baby."

Her left hand appears too, taking the soap ball from Evangeline's fingers. "Pretty…"

The jerk comes suddenly. Evan is a strong woman, but she wasn't ready. Piety pulls her off-balance, dragging her arm under the bed past the elbow with a snarl. She yelps, yanking herself free and cupping her hand.

"Evan!" I shove past Pike. A ring of teeth marks dents her flesh.

"I'm alright," she says. "I don't think she even broke the skin."

"You should go clean that anyway." Pike starts to roll up his sleeves. "We have to move this bed. Shut the door behind you."

"Thank you for trying," Tomaths says.

"Are you sure she didn't break the skin?" I ask. Human bites are nasty enough without the pestilence in them. "We have morning salt and Clear Pine back on the train."

"Navy's cure isn't ready for this, is it?" Evangeline stops me with in a hushed voice. Not a question, it's finality. "That poor woman isn't likely to improve long enough to consent to an experiment."

"Is it wrong just to give it to her anyway?" Probably. "If she has the pestilence, she's going to die anyway. But if it works, then her life is saved."

"I really don't know." And the sense of loss in her voice is profound.

The answer would depend on who you ask, I suspect.

Their little boy is still sweeping the storefront, tears in his eyes that he tries to sniff down. They come back up whenever he swallows.

What was his name? Josiah, that sounds right.

"You're doing a good job," Evangeline says. "The store looks alkaline."

He nods.

I settle the contamination vial around his neck. "This is for you, Josiah. My family makes these. It will tell you if you're safe. Stay away from anything that makes it glow, even people."

His mother is going to die. And I know what that feels like.

FIFTY-EIGHT
FROM THE LAB JOURNAL OF ISOBEL CARLISLE

Eden Year 11, the 13th of One

I THOUGHT I KNEW WHAT I WANTED. I'VE NEVER BEEN ONE TO QUESTION MYSELF, my own motives, desires. The moment I saw Amnesty, I knew I wanted her. I'd do anything to make her smile. I still remember the day we snuck out of town to take a walk down through the flood wash, even though the foxes might have killed us. The sun shone through the oak leaves on her skin, and the seed pods landed in her hair, like strings of pearls. Her first laugh set my chest on fire, and I no longer feared death. She only smiles when we're together, she's told me so.

We haven't been down there in so long.

Fear has crept back into me.

I asked her name when I shouldn't have.

Now she's growing in my mind like a vine, and this morning as I unlocked the lab to start my morning's tests, I found my heart pounding. Is she still alive? The question felt like a hammer and me a nail. When I saw her conscious and waiting for me, the relief poured in so sweetly.

I'm writing this here even though it is personal because Amnesty doesn't read my lab notes and the ones I show to Zachariah are written specifically to please him. It's not for science, this is just to ease this weight on my chest and remind myself of what I am: a chemist. A woman of science. I must do better.

I haven't let her see that I am a woman. To her I am also Benjamin Carlisle, but

I wish she knew the truth, the real me. I am not truly this bastard. I will not always be.

Her name is Enola.

I feel terrible, and I must be careful now.

* * *

Eden Year 10, the 15th of Eleven

THE FINAL FORMULA IS ON THE NEXT PAGE. ALL MEASUREMENTS ARE EXACT.

My work on an antidote begins now. Live test subjects only, all human, half Tov, half us.

FIFTY-NINE
ADELAIDE

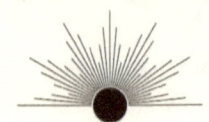

SOMETHING HAS CHANGED IN EDEN.

I pull a hex doll from a bank of dirt. Soft, recently deposited by storms. Its head comes off, stuffing made of human hair all curled up inside, cotton body crisped by the sun.

They were hanging everywhere the last time I was here. Now they aren't.

Metal rattles on metal.

I duck through a doorway, darkness and glass, rusty cans and tumbleweed fragments around my ankles. A chill rolls through my skin.

Boots crunch on the packed street, men breathing.

Hannah's dying red sun and this sharp gold one bleed together. For one brief moment I taste ash, the cauterized scar splitting open across my ribs.

I peel off my mask. The whistle of each exhale goes silent. It's not going to save me anyway.

They pass. It passes. But my mouth stays bitter.

That metallic rattle comes around again.

"Keep looking. He can't have gotten too far. They would have seen him from the watchtower."

He.

They're not looking for me.

Yet.

I watch through the seam where the doorframe is splitting from the wall, nails slowly pulling away from the wood. One of Green's bullies, his back to me while two more on the other side of the street toss a rock through an upstairs window, waiting with their guns for something to flee.

A ghost made of dust flares up off the street cuts between buildings. Nothing else.

I slip out the back side of the building.

Seventy.

The laugh is hollow, the way sound echoes up a canyon. It bleeds off into a screech that isn't human anymore. A smell.

I press my hand up, shutting out my own breath for a moment, not the realization that crawls up from my stomach. That awful smell that clung to Vesta, seeping out of her pores while she rotted from within: It started in her mouth. Her tongue. Black.

I can't look at mine.

The Stranger drags like a hook on my skin. *Focus.*

The Wells's mansion, crumbling on the little hill behind its iron spike fence.

One-ninety-six.

The rusty gate looks like something that will squeal. I angle around the side, wary of the number of empty, blind eyes that are windows. At the back, wild field grass comes up to my waist, cracking with dead and living things. But there's finally a gap in the fence wide enough to squeeze through.

Twenty-two.

The back door hangs open. Boot room, kitchen.

Plates crusted with cobwebs linger on the table, silverware and bone fragments from the last meal the family ate and never cleaned up.

The Stranger listens to the guts of the house, bleached almost as much as the outside from the tear in the roof. Wood and dry plaster shudder, dislodging beads of dust from the ceiling. There is someone else here, each cupboard and drawer I pull open a gamble.

A maid staircase links the kitchen to the two upper floors, narrow and elbow-turned.

Ten.

A landing overlooks the front entry, its once-blue floral wallpaper fraying off the walls in strips as wide as me.

If I was Amnesty, I would have burned the house down.

The double doors at the head of the hall splay open, scratches tearing up the wood around the knobs, spreading out, the height of someone on their knees.

Every drawer has been pulled free, bookshelves emptied, even the bed stripped naked. A guard lounges on the balcony just outside the crusted window, somehow still clinging to its glass. It's clotted with so much dust he's nothing but a silhouette.

The next bedroom is the same, walls yellow. Ribs of dust are left on the shelves, telling that the books were removed recently.

They're still looking for the journal.

Zachariah's journal that Navy and I stole out of the lockbox. I bet they don't even know about the other two. They were written by women, after all. Why would they bother?

I've had my suspicions on why Kane really took us on that detour to dig up the Wells's graves. Acting on his father's orders, I'm sure. How did someone from the east know what was buried with him? I don't know, but Kane knew exactly where and what he was looking for.

It has to be the journal.

They still don't know I have it.

Eighteen.

The floor creaks as I step into the bathroom. Shadows. Fragments of the mirror linger in the corners, the bathtub and toilet filled to the brim with dirt.

Bottles and toothbrushes still fill the medicine cabinet, more dirt deposited by the fistful.

The floorboard creaks.

The Stranger snaps back into me.

I hurl the jar in my hand. The bully stumbles into the wall, glass exploding against the floor, second impact.

Almost immediately, a second guard turns the corner, his gun up. *Farce.* If only they were both stupid enough to walk in unprepared.

"Show me your hands!"

Do what he says. But the Stranger ticks in my skin, measuring every twitch in his.

"Turn around and put your hands against the wall. You're not supposed to be here. How did you get in?"

Does that really matter?

"Where did you come from?" he demands again.

"Of course the first woman we see in a Season is a fox," the other one mutters.

He yanks my crossgun and pistol out of my holsters. I feel sick. I'm better than this. So is the Stranger.

"Did you let that picker loose?"

I don't know what you're talking about, besides that the others were looking for someone. Now I know it's a bone picker.

"Are you deaf?" He whistles sharply into my ear. My reaction is involuntary. "No, you're not."

The second they touch me, the Stranger is going to snap.

"What do you want to do with her?"

"I really don't give a shit. Take her out back if you want, I won't tell. Or I'll take her downstairs and make him decide. The doctor will probably want her either way. He says they're different on the inside, foxes. He can open her up and find out for real."

"Make him deal with it. I'm hungry."

The gun pokes through my scarf into my neck. "Keep those hands up, fox."

On the ground floor, move.

He won't expect it as much as he does right now. Up here it's farther to run, and those front stairs don't look trustworthy.

"Go tell him we found something." He walks me to the top of the landing. "You know we have permission to kill anyone who trespasses here? Hold that in your brain and behave."

You would have done it already.

"You found something upstairs? I thought we'd got everything—" Kane comes down the dusky main hall into the broken foyer. His body visibly slumps as he looks up. "Why am I not surprised anymore? You found *someone*, not something."

The man shrugs. Close enough.

Kane exhales. "Let her go, she's not going to cause any trouble, right Adelaide?"

"You'll deal with this?" the guard says.

"Yes, I'll deal with this."

I take back my crossgun and pistol without asking. I don't have to, and he doesn't fight me. They're mine.

The Stranger traces the route he takes downstairs. If the wasp-eaten wood can hold him, it can hold me.

Kane waits for me, still shaking his head. "What am I going to do about you?"

Nothing, something will be done about you first.

"That was only a joke." He quickly holds up his hands, must have seen a glimpse of the Stranger go dark in my face. "I'm sorry. Why did you follow me here?"

Twenty.

"You shouldn't be alone," I say. In Eden, finding things instead of me.

"While that sounds very kind of you, I don't think I believe it."

I go for the hall he came out of. At least he didn't get to Isobel's journal. There's still a chance for me. Small, but I decided years ago that when I die, there will be a fight.

"Hold on," Kane says. "You don't get to just walk away, no explanation."

Really? There's no gun to my head anymore, and he won't kill me if I don't answer. "What are *you* doing here?"

A blast of wind hits the broad side of the house. I swear the nails squeal. A filmy haze crosses the sunlight. Fingers of dust reach through the broken roof and break apart around us.

"Collecting history." He steers me away from the hall. "You can't be here."

The Stranger narrows. *Stop me.*

"I don't mean here in this house, I'll show you all the documents and antiques we've saved if you're curious, but you can't be here in Eden. It's not safe."

"Why?"

"He—Well, I don't have to tell you most people back east believe all kinds of wild things about the Tov. Some of them are willing to do things to prove it."

The doctor they were talking about. The one with a dissecting table and jars of organs and genitals in his cold storage safe before it all disappeared. He came here. "DuPonte."

Kane lets a small sound escape from his wince. "I don't know what you know about him, or how you know it, but it's not safe for you to wander around like you usually do."

"What is he doing here?"

"He's working on something that will change everything. It's going to save lives, but for now, you need to leave."

Save lives...I don't like the sound of that. People ruin everything they breathe on.

Another river of wind rocks the house, shaking particles from every crack.

He can't scare me off. Eden isn't any more dangerous than Hannah, and I survived there.

Thirteen.

The porch moves when I step on it, the once bright sky dim and brown against the table rock.

"Adelaide. Wait."

Without the protection of the house, the wind grapples for a hold on my hair, my clothes, me. It squeals.

"I'm not sending you out in this," Kane calls. "Come look at everything I've collected until the storm passes. It's all in the Wells's sitting room, where I can keep an eye on you."

"I have to check on my horse first."

He nods, probably says something I don't hear under his mask and steps away. At least he knows me well enough that the offer to look at his stuff will bring me back.

SIXTY
FROM THE LAB JOURNAL OF ISOBEL CARLISLE

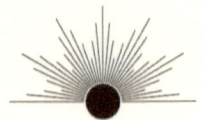

Eden Year 10, the 12th of Nine

THERE IS SOMETHING HERE WITH US, GATHERING LIKE THE STORMS DO IN THE evenings, but it gathers in the low places, the dark spaces. I can't explain it.

Amnesty talks about the things that came before, the Tov and their bargains with the shadows worn by ancient devils, her Fate—her god if you believe in one. I never have, what god would leave us here like this? I've known it was all a lie since I was a child. The scars on my legs from St. Edmund's School for Young Ladies remind me what men think of women who pursue higher learning, that science is their devil, and their god is not as mighty as they claim. If they truly believed in what they preach so violently, they wouldn't be so full of fear.

I see what Amnesty suffers at Zachariah's hands. She is just in wanting to kill him. He is a beast. Why would I believe in a god who elevates men like that to face no consequences?

But Amnesty...

Although her heinous father has no power, she does. She is the most powerful thing I have ever known. What we are together, not even chemistry can fully explain. I love her, maybe that's enough. But I cannot put a name to this force I feel creeping in either. I may have made the door for it with science, but Amnesty called it forth. And it is evil.

Now I wonder about god. But who can I ask? A preacher? Ha.

SIXTY-ONE
TESLA

The bat that savaged Leagan's horse gives me and Evangeline the alkaline cover to take out my bloody murder clothes. We now have an entire basket of bloodstained linen, and who's to say it didn't all come from her horse? Look at its poor neck.

I don't see where exactly he came from, but Dr. DuPonte appears somewhere after Caroline's vague edge, an even vaguer shade of gray.

I turn and face him head-on because no woman likes a man shuffling around behind her, even if he does look weak as a fencepost withered with drought. "Excuse me. Do you need something?"

"What do you have there?"

"Just some dirty laundry from our last blood moons. It's inappropriate of you to stare at women's underclothes." A bold lie considering brown stains peek from every crease in the pile. The volume of Green's blood in my clothes alone made the car crossing smell of iron more than the *Exodus* being *made* of iron does. But I don't let that stop me from telling it. He's a man, after all. What do they know about women's bodies?

"Will you let me have it?" he asks.

"That's a very gross request. No, you may not."

"Does it belong to the fox?"

"Why would you assume that?" Evangeline asks, eyebrows up like the shovel on her shoulder.

"You needn't worry about propriety. I am a doctor. I would like to have it."

"So you can wash it for me? How sweet." But between blinks he almost looks like he might try grabbing it from me like a desperate rat. I move so Evangeline is on the other side of me, the basket swallowed by the shadow of my skirt. "Fuck off and stop following us. Come on, Evan." On second thought, I'm going back for crystal and a little flammable bottle from Navy's lab. This bastard is smart enough to watch where we bury them so he can dig them up later like a depraved scavenger lizard, burning them is safer.

DuPonte wipes a bead of saliva from the corner of his cracked lips, licking it off his finger again. When we pass each other, the contamination compass strung on my belt lights up like sunrise.

EVANGELINE AND LEAGAN ROUND UP OUR GOATS, AND I PASS MY contamination compass over each one before letting them into the *Exodus* for the night.

"You're clean, ma'am. Please come inside." The brown and white spotted one makes the ramp shake as she trots up. She's looking a little round, maybe she'll have a baby. "Thank you. Next."

The next goat makes my compass glow. "Oh no."

"She's got pestilence?" Leagan says. "Oh, you poor baby."

Her coat is still shiny and her eyes clear, but the compasses don't lie. I suppose it's been luck that she's our first contaminated animal, Navy's hotspot theory proving itself yet again.

"I'll tie her up over there." Leagan brings a rope to lead her away. "Come on, sicky."

"At least Navy has something bigger than a mouse to test now that isn't Piety Goodson."

A man in shopkeeper's sleeves and brown stripe pants rounds the sharp nose of the engine. When he gets close enough, I see the advancing line of sweat in his collar and underarms from this walk and the other days in the sun.

"All the businessmen are going to sign the town charter in an hour," he says grudgingly. "Millard Von Kane says you've been invited."

"How considerate," I say. "We'll be there."

SIXTY-TWO
TESLA

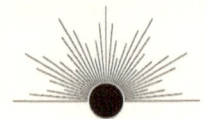

I wear my most expensive dress. It's green and not covered in anyone's blood. Not that any of these great men of business will necessarily know that, but they might. Anyone from the east who sells fabric and notions should recognize Eos satin. But it was Raleigh who supplied the black pearl buttons.

They have a table set in the street, a line of men dropping standards into the collection box for the opportunity to sign the charter. Jezebel will let you be a real paper-holding town instead of a settlement, but she wants her gold first.

I'll pay just to see my name on a historic Republic document. Let Travis have his wife and child, he'll never be a founding member of a West Rim town. Or a town anywhere.

Raleigh holds onto my arm, his gait weaving a little as we get in line. He still looks like a bludgeoned melon. "Are you all right?"

"*Farce,* my headache is back," he says. "I should have stayed on the train. Don't worry, if I decide to throw up, I won't get it on you."

"I appreciate that."

Of course, Millard Von Kane is the one presiding over the money box. The thief in me still has the audacity to want it, and I have to remind myself we don't need to steal things like this anymore to survive. Maybe just for fun now and then.

The pen is warm from the hands that touched it before me. Millard doesn't even bother to look at me. That's fine.

I give Navy the pen and set her hand down on the next empty space. "I hope this inspires so many girls from now on."

My sister Liza would be so proud of her daughters right now. It's a shame Adelaide isn't here, although maybe it is better she isn't. At least one of these fuckers would likely object to her signature. She hides the pain of being excluded from things so very well, but it has to sting.

She leaves her mark on the Rim her own way. I hope it's her map children see in geography class someday, not Kane's.

I watch Leagan and Raleigh sign before I turn.

A line of men has formed between us and the path back to the *Exodus*. Most of them are Greens, a few of them are homesteaders who signed the charter ahead of us.

The warmth that filled me a second ago leaks out of my chest in one breath, catching like Navy's black veil in the wind.

"Widow…" Leagan says.

"Don't do anything. Yet."

"Tesla Revere," a man behind me says. "You're coming with us."

I turn again to find two bullies moving toward me, the copper *Marshal* pins on the breast of their olive uniforms. Well, fuck.

"Come peacefully. You know what this is about."

"Spoil the surprise for me."

"Back up, you rabbits." Leagan puts herself in front of me, Raleigh inserting himself next to her.

"What's she being accused of?"

"Murder without just cause. Don't interfere unless you want to become an accomplice in her actions."

Oh, I had just cause, but I'm not stupid. And I won't be tattling on myself even though I'm damn proud I did it.

"Carrson Green's body was discovered this afternoon," Millard says. "And the manner in which he perished is appalling."

Yes, it was. Exactly as he deserved, for *he* was appalling.

"What does this have to do with me?" I say.

"This was found among his things."

A paper.

Should I be found dead or not found at all: Tesla the Widow Revere was responsible. She knows that I have proof the fox they call their sister, otherwise known as Adelaide the Stranger Revere, burned Winchester. And that the fire that consumed Hannah was not caused by a refinery explosion. Both pose a threat to my life, but I will not be silenced by thieves.

Signed,

Carrson F. Green

"The testimonies of dead men tend to be true."

"Oh really?" I let the sheet flutter to the ground instead of handing it back to him. "Anyone could have written that at any time. Show me this proof he claims he has."

"People die out here all the time," Leagan says. "What are you going to do, send her to the Rim?"

"Once this charter is notarized in Jezebel, the cornerstone laws of the Republic are enforceable here," Millard says. "Murder is a crime, Miss Revere. As is theft. Retroactive justice for the theft of the *Exodus Ironclad* may also be used against you."

"But not until then," I say.

"You will be held until then, and then you will be tried. Justly."

Progress is a bitch, tenacious and inevitable, but laws are the bastard byproduct of her union to men who like enforcing rules. They are made to keep people good, but how can that be possible when the men responsible have dirty hands too?

"Where was this justice when my daughter bled out in the Winchester street? Or when my mother's body was sold to Green's basket man? That's two women dead at his hands." I shrug at them. "Nothing to say now? That's convenient."

If only I'd told someone other than Jonathaniel who went off and vanished in the desert. I can only hope Kane has the spine to speak up when he returns. He won't stand for this.

"Look me in the eye and tell me you wouldn't do something to avenge your Timothy?"

"Shit," Leagan hisses.

Did I just implicate myself?

"At your trial, you'll have the opportunity to prove the murder was justified." Millard waves me off like a fly. "To the rest of you with the name

Revere, I strongly suggest you return to your homestead and mind yourselves. Don't start any trouble, and there won't be any trouble."

The marshals grab me under the arms.

They have so much faith in their own virtue and that overstretched sheet of paper quivering on the table. It might never make it to Jezebel. Until it does, this is still just a nothing shit of a settlement on the Rim. And everything but arson is allowed if you're willing to do it.

They fumble with the leather straps harnessing my knife arm to my shoulder. I cry out, writhing as they peel the leather cap off my amputated arm. For drama.

"Shut up," he snaps. "You're fine."

What they don't see at the moment is the knee spike under my skirt. Many a groin has been impaled on it. At least they don't see it yet. I have to choose my moment wisely.

Leather and metal clap as he throws the replacement limb away. Leagan snatches it from the dust, shaking it at them. "You cow fuckers have no idea what's about to happen."

"Don't poke the snake, Raptor," Raleigh mutters. He shows his empty hands to the marshals before taking Navy by the arm. "Come on, Rook. We're going peacefully."

"We'll get you out of this, Aunt Tess," Navy promises as they drag me off. "Just be good."

I'm not terrified by this intimidation move. The Stranger will be back soon and when she does, you all have better dug yourself some deep holes to hide in.

"In the meantime, arson has always been a punishable crime to the Rim," the taller marshal calls out. "If anyone should come across the fox, bring her to us and there'll be a reward. We have questions for her."

SIXTY-THREE
ADELAIDE

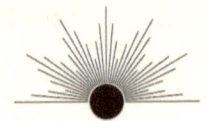

CRACKS FORM ON MY FINGERTIPS WHERE OLD PAPER AND DUST STOLE ALL THE moisture from the air and are now starting on me. Tiny crystals crust the porch and cactus needles, ripping other colors out of the sunken sun.

Salt storm.

I wondered before about the salt waste that must be somewhere nearby. I want to see it.

There's already another one, dark and prickled with lightning forming to the south.

Nightmare protests as the front porch racks under her weight.

"You're okay."

I brought her right up inside the Wells's foyer to protect her. Now I'm very glad I did. Salt granules can cut much deeper than sand.

The wind wheels back around, hot and sharp. It realized I'm still alive and decided to finish me. Dust burns my eyes before I can get my goggles back up.

Nineteen.

"It's getting dark," Kane says.

Yes, I can see that.

"Maybe you should stay. I have an extra cot and one of the houses down there partially fixed up. You'll be safe and have your own room, no expectations," he adds quick.

The Stranger draws around my ribs like a corset. *He doesn't trust you.* Not anymore.

"I'll feed you and you can leave in the morning. Nothing to brag about, but I have coffee and Eosin tea from Markos. He'll be happy to hear you got to try it."

"Only if Nightmare gets to stay inside too. She's afraid of the dark."

"Is that how she got her name?" I think he does smile under the mask. "We can probably arrange something for her. I wouldn't want her to feel unwelcome."

KANE IS VERY GOOD AT SEEMING NICE. BUT I KNOW WHAT HE WANTS. ME, here. So I don't find out what Dr. DuPonte is doing. But I will.

The wind scratches at the walls. Relentless.

Maybe he's afraid to be alone after the cave.

I can feel it, the pestilence burning lines through my blood. My neck aches, knees locked against my chest so my chin has something to rest on.

I'm so tired, but every time something windborne hits the bolted storm shutter, the piss-warm water of Seed's drowning pool surges up around my neck.

I wish it wasn't true. But I can't change it now.

The quartz burns down.

Kane keeps reading his book, takes another sip off his tea.

It was green, flush with oranges and something I've never had before. Mine is cold now.

"Leagan is quite an experience," he says. "She would have made our first expedition something to describe. She loves you a lot though, I can tell."

I hold so still. It's the only thing I can do to keep the Stranger from taking control of me.

"Do you want to fuck me?"

Kane chokes on his tea, cough like a gunshot.

I'd laugh, my family would too. But it's not really that funny.

I've comforted myself with the decision that I don't ever have to let someone touch me again. But I've never had sex with someone I actually care about. Sex that wasn't an act of violence committed against me. What if it is different?

You don't really want this.

Is she right? This could be the pestilence thinking, not me.

Does it really matter? I'm allowed to change my mind.

I unfold my arms and stand.

Kane is faster. "If you're trying to make up for leaving me in the cave, I don't want this."

"No." This fear in my guts is deeper than the one I now carry, knowing I'm marked for death. Older. Proven. It knows me too well.

I want it out of my head.

"I'm not saying I'm not flattered and…excited by the offer. Before anything happens, I just want to be sure you won't regret this later. These aren't the most romantic of circumstances…"

And fucking me in a mine with bats clawing at the window was?

"This is not why I asked you to stay."

"I know."

"It needed to be said." He waits for me to make the first move, but that's not what I offered. I can't.

"We have to face each other the whole time." I won't say why, he can wonder. You're smart enough to figure it out. "And you have to pull out before you finish." Because I'm not a fool. Even though I haven't had a blood moon since Vesta died, I don't take chances anymore.

"Of course, yes." He nods. "Whatever you want. I'll be right back."

You are going to regret this.

Probably. But right now, I'm too tired, don't care. And if I do, I won't have to for long. I'll be dead.

He returns with two blankets. One wool, the other a cotton quilt, splays both out on the floor. He carefully unclips the rest of his mask. "Is this okay?"

I nod. With arms that don't feel like mine, I set my hands on his shoulders, burying the tremor blocking up my throat deep inside the Stranger. "Yes."

He grips me around the waist, both arms. The kiss is open, desperate. Sour.

My body goes hard and almost immediately he pulls back, unlike last time. "What's wrong?"

"Do you have to kiss me?" I hate everything about it, another mouth breathing into mine, wet tongue tasting like what they ate last. And I know that will never change.

"No, I don't *have* to. Can I ask why?"

"That's just the way it is."

"That's okay." He slides his hands down, up under my shirt. "There are other things I can do."

I force my clenched fists to let go and unbutton my skirt. It falls too easy.

The slack expression on his face is something I recognize. Desire. I feel it when I look at the hills touching the distant sky, the purple crags beyond red ridges. It drains all other senses right out of me.

I don't feel it right now.

He wrests his legs out of his pants, dragging his damp shirt off in the same motion. The Stranger gives me one last stab in the stomach as his weight aligns with mine, moves my legs apart. Then she lets me be. Kane's hips settle on me, mouth dragging like an uphill grade across my chest, neck, waiting for me to break away.

He smells like his hat, salt and leather.

My fingers are too cold, they can't feel skin.

He fucks me slow and deep. It hurts. And I'm glad.

I hold him so he can't stare at me, whatever shape my face has paralyzed into. He holds on tighter, the touch of someone starved for human contact. I don't think it's me that he wants so badly. I think it's love.

Fool, he picked someone without any left to spare.

I only wanted my friend again.

But I don't think he's coming back.

The resignation falls, a shell I didn't know I was wearing breaking off my body. My next breath doesn't taste so shallow.

There isn't something wrong with me.

Intimacy is not found here. It was there when we were out under the sky on the first expedition. Tracing our steps and drawing our maps, out in places we'd never been. That's what I'm trying to feel again. His friendship. Despite the Stranger and even if I was secretly his enemy. But it's not this.

Can't he feel it too?

You're free.

A sudden flinch and he yanks back, grabs his shirt and finishes himself into it with a shudder.

I get my underclothes back on. At least it didn't take him long.

There are red marks pressed into his knees when he stands.

It feels too careful, the way Kane lays back next to me, covering himself with the top blanket, like I might turn into something sharp that cuts. The finger he traces over my burned arm isn't heavy, but the callouses drag on the delicate skin.

"I'm aware that was a one-sided gratification." He inches closer, breath to the curve of my ribcage, hand to the veins outlined under my skin, inside my thigh where he just left traces of his sweat. "How would you like me to finish you?"

I shake my head.

"I want to do that for you."

No.

His finger slips between the soft inner layer of flesh at the apex of my legs. The flinch is violent, like the Stranger, clenching my legs shut as I grab his wrist, other hand going for weapons that aren't here. The surprise in Kane's face quickly bleeds to hurt, then shame. "I'm sorry. Sorry. I shouldn't have done that without asking."

You should have listened when I said no.

"Can I do this?" He winds his fingers though mine, absent gaze returning to me, sad longing in his. After a while, he starts tracing the curve of my spine again with his other hand. Fingers bump over my scars, lingering. The cauterized one that comes from Hannah. Thick because the knife that made it was dull. Gray and marbled.

"How long have you had this?" he asks. "It looks like it hurt."

"Long enough for it to heal."

Fool. The Stranger darkens, beating and spiteful.

If I'm dying of the pestilence like Vesta and Randy—

Now you're taking him down with you.

That wasn't my plan, but clearly it was hers.

Kane scoots over, opening the top blanket while keeping his groin covered. "We can lay here for a while if you want."

It feels evil now, but I slide in anyway. Why? Maybe I need comfort, too, and my sisters aren't here. Grandma's not here.

Or maybe I'm learning how to feel guilty.

Kane brings his arm over me, and I try not to flinch. "You can stay with me all night if you'd like…" His breath moves in my hair, and he brushes a strand of it off my face. "You're the first woman I've made love to since my wife died."

My skin peels inside out. There's no touch as repulsive to me as that bullshit phrase. Love is not made this way. That's not what we just did.

I do not love him.

I sit up.

Fuck. I let you fuck me. Now get over it.

But I'm nicer than people realize because I don't have to say that. It would hurt him.

"I wouldn't be opposed to doing it again."

My gaze travels down his naked chest. I still feel how warm his skin was on mine, the pressure of him inside me. I had to try. But I feel nothing resembling desire.

"Can you blame me for asking?"

I blame you for what I was willing to give not being good enough.

Maybe people who make friends everywhere they've gone think it's a cheap gift. But it's not to me.

I hope Nightmare's saddle rubs off the feeling of him between my legs.

But I know it won't. Like everything else, the Stranger will remember.

I told you, you'd regret this.

"My mother spent the season I was home introducing me to available ladies." He scrubs his face like that will rub out the memories. "Dinner parties and all kinds of exhausting social foolishness. The kind of thing you'd hate, right?"

Does he really think I care, or worse that I'll be jealous?

"My mother tried especially hard with her friend's daughter, Merryann Forester. She's really hoping I'll marry again."

"You should have."

"My brother had two sons. Not that I don't want that someday, but they don't need me to carry on the family name. Merryann was kind and attractive, but I couldn't be with someone just to make my mother happy. That wouldn't be fair to her."

What about making your father happy? If Millard said get married tomorrow, I bet that's a different answer. I've said it before, marriage is a business contract.

Kane hovers his forehead just off my shoulder. I still feel the weight. "Every time I looked at her, I thought about you."

No.

It gets so still. Not the good kind, the hard kind.

He and his family may want children, but I know they wouldn't want my half-blooded ones, no matter what lies he tells himself. Good thing I don't want them either.

"I have to go to bed. I'm tired."

"Yes." Kane rolls upright, grabbing up his pants. "I understand."

He watches. Not just to see me half-naked one last time.

"Would you ever want to do this with me again?"

I get the rest of my clothes back on. They feel so stiff. "No."

The word settles like death.

"Thank you for being honest," he says finally. "I'll respect that. Don't worry...Just know, I'll always feel things for you, but if this is all I ever get of you, I'll take it. A memory is better than nothing at all."

Is it?

He wants pretty promises. Men like him want blood-related families. It's how they somehow forgive themselves for being mediocre and the world rewarding them for it, like Aunt Tess's bastard lover Travis.

I will die a free woman, not somebody's mother.

If I didn't destroy him, the Stranger would sure as a Season destroy me.

I won't do that to myself.

SIXTY-FOUR
FROM THE LAB JOURNAL OF ISOBEL CARLISLE

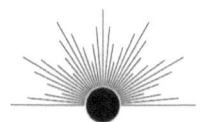

Eden Year 11, the 1st of Two

IT USED TO BE EASY WHEN ALL I BELIEVED IN WAS WHAT COULD BE EXPLAINED *with chemicals.*

Tonight, I caught Amnesty doing one of her rituals with my hairbrush. This made me angry. I don't know why. Is it only because of the brush, or because I feel a corner has torn off my loyalty?

Enola and I don't even speak the same language. She's only here to serve a scientific purpose.

I have masqueraded as a man (creatures I detest) for endless months and created a plague unlike anything that exists on this planet all to protect Amnesty from her family and end this war. What more can a person do to prove themself?

Maybe I am just tired. But she called them foxes and I snapped. I don't do that. I am not like that, not with her, not about something we ~~used to~~ agree on.

But this thing in the air grows heavy, like drowning must hurt. It is here even when I sleep, snuffing out my dreams, a hunger that must be sated, but nothing I have fills.

SIXTY-FIVE
ADELAIDE

Every step grinds with salt.

Nothing moves now that the storm has passed on.

Not the air. Not Green's bullies. Not the aura lights, hanging like a caught breath, harmless blue and green. If there are ghosts out here, this is their time.

Nothing but me.

Fifty-nine.

Light burns behind the storm shutters of the army barracks. Low and long under the watchtower, the old stable extending off this end of it.

Wait. It's different.

Bricks.

They're smooth and flat, a little bit of the sun still warm inside them. I slide my hand over. Rough edges, pockets. The same gathered stone as Eden's outer wall. Horse manure and old grain still seep from the cracks. It's an honest scent that doesn't like to be washed out.

Kane brought me in here to see the bones. Strings of them layered on top of one another, hanging in the stable's hollow heart.

This was a door.

I follow the stable's long side, around all four corners until I'm back to where I started. No way in. Every opening has been bricked over.

A sound picks at the dark from the other side. Thin and slow, a nail peeling on rock.

It gets faster. Breathing, rabid.

No way in.

I hate this.

Nine.

The barracks still has a door, padlock on the outside. It picks easy.

The stench is liquid. Death.

Immediately it's cooler than outside. No floor, just packed earth and a wooden staircase twisting up to the watchtower.

Six doors, all bricked up.

Eight.

The light from the single lantern starts to overstretch.

Ten.

The Stranger bristles. *The watchtower.*

I won't forget.

Heavy breaths scrape at a gap in the wall. A hand worms between bricks and dirt. Scabs for fingernails, knuckle bones showing.

The corridor keeps going, past the line where the fire quartz glow gives out. The Stranger doesn't push into it, she pulls at the back of my head.

The watchtower.

I barely wake the quartz in my headlamp, just in case someone is prowling outside. They won't see shadows behind the storm shutters.

Thirty.

Rows of glass vessels clutter a tea table. A reading wheel full of open books, a couch tousled with blankets and a pillow, velvet crushed within an inch of becoming leather.

Reclaimed glass has been added to the window frames and greasy paper tacked over that. Navy says certain chemicals don't like sunlight.

The rest of the space is wet specimens. There's so many, half of them are in pickling jars, not perfect laboratory glass.

Brains that look like rotten walnuts, blood red eyes, toes, and testicles, blackened livers, kidneys, and noses that are missing their tips, all drowning in preservation liquid. I can smell it. Almost sweet but low to the ground and wrong.

Eleven.

Anatomy drawings cover the spaces between windows. Human and animal bodies, dissected one layer at a time. This one shows the stages of a man's jawbone deteriorating until the skin flops against his neck like a wilted scrotum. The next is a cross section of a brain, a man's chest split open so all the organs show. Numbers on the charts correspond to jars containing the pieces of the subject.

Dr. DuPonte is trying to cure the pestilence.

I unhook the top of the bedside lamp and stir the quartz awake. The vial of flash fire I keep in the smuggler's tube inside my boot just fits inside the core.

Navy gets to find the cure. A man doesn't.

NIGHTMARE AND I MAKE IT TO THE FIRST RISE WEST OF EDEN. THEN I LOOK back.

Way out on the dried lakebed a drop of reddish light shudders despite the moonlight.

Not my fire.

If I don't find out what, the Stranger won't let me sleep.

Two-twenty.

An orange pulse, like a heartbeat. My flash fire igniting. The watchtower suddenly has a black outline, DuPonte's papers burning.

Four-ninety-nine.

It's a man, crouched on the ground that's cracked in flakes like dry skin. He rocks a lantern to his chest, glass ticking as he sings a sad lullaby to it.

I take out my crossgun.

Five…

His hair is just a frail circle around his skull. Burn marks from the lantern slowly eat away his yellowed undershirt, the song with no words, random notes slipping higher.

He has one hand. And I know him.

Stanley.

His eyes are sinking into their bone sockets, pulled open too wide like the skin of the lids has shrunk. One of them is only red, even the colored part. The other one has a pin-spot that will grow. The veins in his neck are too dark, showing like mine always do.

I never liked him. This feeling in my stomach isn't sympathy. I wouldn't even call it pity, it's too low in my guts.

I'm looking at my own death.

End his misery.

"Did Kane bring you here?"

"I didn't want to come back." He shudders more, folding the lantern in tighter, tin rasping against his shirt. "I never left, it was only a dream. All of it. Only here." His head snaps up, gaze full of sudden clarity. Crusted skin flakes off his lips. "You. *No.* Please don't send me back. They'll put me back in that room with no door. You want to be in one alone. You don't want to be in there with them…Look. The sky is smiling for me."

Unexpected nausea crawls up the back of my throat, a spider.

Thadie said I wouldn't die in Hannah, but she never told me what she did see in my future.

What will happen to the Stranger when I'm gone?

Will she stay with me when I'm not in my mind anymore? Maybe she'll lose me when I don't know my own name. Or maybe she'll just be free to slaughter everyone I've ever held her back from.

I don't want to rot away, I just want to stay myself until I die, even if that means it hurts.

Or when my eyes start seeing blood, I could go out in the desert, as far west as I can get, die out there trying to reach wherever I've always longed to be.

DuPonte's lab is still on fire.

I have two shadows as my crossgun bolt goes through Stanley's head.

SIXTY-SIX
TESLA

THEIR JAIL IS NOTHING BUT SPARE RAILROAD TIES STACKED IN A SQUARE, THE plank door doesn't even have hinges. They just nailed it shut after they shoved me in. They must have made it just this afternoon, because it wasn't here this morning.

The gaps between the ties show the stars, but I'm afraid if I throw myself against the door I'll bring the roof down on my head, and that would be an unfortunate way to go.

A woman's shrill scream curdles my blood. It's the second one from the dark, coming out of Piety Goodson, I'm assuming. A band of fire quartz burns at the back of their store where the lean-to doesn't quite kiss the ground.

The bully standing guard lights up a redweed stick.

"Would you share that?" I ask.

To my surprise, he passes it through the gap in the wall. The spiced burn hits my lungs like sand.

"I hate it when the sun goes down," he says.

It's true. There's the dark, which comes at night, and then there's *darkness*. The night that rubs up against you and has things in it. This is darkness out here.

"Do you believe in the God of Mercy?" I ask.

"If Providence exists, he's not merciful. For your sake, you'd better start believing in him. A lot of good it'll do you when you swing."

"I'm not going to swing."

Piety's fresh scream has words mixed in it. *Not water! No! No!*

On the other side of the shack, a shadow bleeds through the grass.

"If you don't believe in Providence, then devils can't exist either," I say. "So what are you afraid of?"

"I'm not going to answer that."

He pokes his fingers back through the seam for the redweed stick, and I grab them. Out of the darkness he's afraid of, Evangeline's body blow doubles him over, just in time to meet her other fist on its way up.

"Well, that was alkaline timing," I say. "I'm very glad you still practice your boxing."

"Don't kill him, little darling," she warns someone behind her. "We don't need more gunpowder thrown in this fire."

Leagan peers through another gap. "Nice toilet bucket. Have you gotten to use it yet?"

"I have not."

"I brought a hammer and a chisel," Evangeline says. "We watched them nail you in. It shouldn't be very hard to pry this cross-board back off the door."

The redweed is kicking in and now I feel light ebbing in my body.

"No one's looking," Leagan says. "Start chiseling."

Wood squeaks as Evangeline gets to work. "What are you going to do, Tess? You don't want to run for the rest of your life."

"I don't know." I could run to the very end of the West Rim where the hooked fingers of the law haven't spread. But she's right, I don't want to, not when the home I've fought so hard for is within reach. Green doesn't get to make me run away. Not this time. "Maybe they'll decide I'm not guilty."

You are, though, her swollen silence seems to say. Or maybe I'm imagining that.

The door falls open. I'm free.

"Maybe you shouldn't have done it," Evangeline says. "But now that it is done, I am here with you until the end."

"Good thing this isn't the end." I take her hand, then let go of it to stroke Leagan's red hair. "I know what you're going to do."

"Warn Adelaide," she says.

"She can come back to the *Exodus*, she just has to be sneaky about it."

"Should you move the *Exodus*?" Evangeline asks as we set off into the dark, the long way around town.

"I'm not moving her anywhere." That's how we lost the *Absolution*, by running away. "I want them to know we're still here. I'm not scared of—"

My steps veer left with the downhill slope of the land instead of straight, my ankle almost going with them. I can still feel my feet somehow, but my legs are lost in the middle.

"Tess." Evan catches me by the short arm.

"I'm okay, I just smoked a little redweed."

"A little?"

"I swear." The sway comes on fast, consciousness dropping out of me for a moment. "Let me sit down for a minute. Just let me think."

"Tess, stand up. Stand up."

SIXTY-SEVEN
ADELAIDE

Aunt Tess did ask if we'd stop by the homestead on our way back and get a report from the miners. Leagan just didn't tell Millard when I'd be getting around to it.

The ghost of another storm pricks at my skin like a sunburn, but I don't see it yet.

The lead mine's elevator scaffolding still clings to the towering rock face. It appears and disappears as the route I choose winds in and out of trees and flood washouts, around.

The trees thin on the pass's shadow side, brittle and gray, revealing other shafts bored into the hillside like nostrils. A set of rusty ore cars hang off the cables used to tow them up and down the mountain, bellies still full of raw black gold. They might have to stay up there forever, too high to reach.

The Stranger pulls back. I bring my hand up, hovering against my crossgun until I hear what she senses.

A splotch of white belly and legs like stockings appear on the rock above me. Fickle little bell swinging, and a red vest trimmed with white tassels.

"Dilly."

He bleats as soon as I say his name, hooves tapping down the stack of boulders he climbed.

"What are you doing out here? Leagan misses you."

I know she left him inside the *Exodus* when we went to hunt Seed. I don't like this.

"How did you get here?"

He butts his head against my hip three times, until I kneel at his level. He nuzzles his chin into my shoulder, then tries to climb onto my lap because that's what Leagan taught him to do when he was a baby.

"You shouldn't be out here by yourself. Something will eat you, and Leagan will cry." He nibbles politely at first, then pulls at my shirt with his teeth when I don't give him what he wants. "I don't have cookies for you, I'm sorry. Especially if you've been naughty and ran away."

I'm sure Leagan is so upset already.

"Come with me." I brush the dirt off my legs and stand.

He doesn't like to be tied up and only walks on the lead for Leagan. I turn back every few steps just to be sure he is following, not wandering off again.

Four-twenty.

A clearing opens where the trees were ripped out years ago, grass re-trampled recently and piled with mine waste.

It's full of bodies.

I leave Nightmare with Dilly behind a cluster of pines, their branches tangling with dead underbrush.

Two of Green's bullies hoist a final board, then nail it over the shaft entrance, while two more drag another dead man down the slope by the legs. One of theirs.

The Stranger checks each step for fallen sticks before I put my foot down, avoiding anything that will make a sound.

Twenty-eight.

Dilly's bell jingles.

I drop behind a wheelbarrow, the Stranger like a dark cloud of dust.

It's what I thought. These bodies left to rot in the clearing with their tools belonged to us.

I retreat through the brush, the same path I came in on.

"Stay here," I whisper to Nightmare.

Before I go, I remove Dilly's bell.

I CUT DOWN. THROUGH THE TREES AND HIDDEN ROCKS, FLANKING THE PATH worn in by our mining crew and the dust Green's men are stirring from it.

One-ten.

I know better than to get too close. Not before the Stranger has a chance to count the guns. I grab hold of Dilly's vest so he doesn't get us seen.

A wood fire burns in the pit outside, empty bowls piled on the ground next to it. Cots and clothes are strewn all over the dirt. They're rolling three of their dead partners in sheets, probably to bury, send death letters back home. They've already pulled off their boots. And probably emptied their pockets too. I would.

A bully strolls behind the bunkhouses, gun slung over his back.

Everything inside me seizes.

That's Leagan's boar rifle he's carrying, *Verdict* stenciled down the black barrel.

"Dilly, where is she?" I know he can't answer. His animal smell—grass and hair—doesn't slow the chafing in my gut. I can't swallow. "Where's Leagan?"

I'll go back to the *Exodus*. It's the next logical step. Starting something with them alone would be a bad idea, and I'm no fool.

As soon as I make sure they don't have Leagan inside one of those bunkhouses.

Fifty.

I'm full of hate and fear. The kind that makes you feel sick.

A crate piled with empty cans sits just under one of the wagons, somehow undisturbed by animals. Dilly tries to root through the stash, but I hold him back and pick two. Peaches, black beans.

Twenty-one.

Down behind the outhouse, I cut a section of twine from the roll in my satchel, then tie it around the bean can. Dilly grabs for it and the rest of the spool falls out of my hands, bouncing away down the slope. I let it go.

A handful of rocks, and I shake the can. The rattle that comes out has menace, bouncing off the trees and back at me. It's the same kind of sound I heard in Eden yesterday.

A distraction.

The bully still handling the dead bodies snaps to attention. "Who's out there?"

I rattle the can again, then string it around Dilly's neck.

Two more of them creep out of the closer bunkhouse.

"Don't let them catch you." I give Dilly the second can, peach juice still clinging brown to the inside, and a little pat on the backside. He trots into the brush, the can of rocks tied around his neck clattering like a ghost's empty bones.

It draws Green's bullies past the bunkhouse, me, and deeper into the contorted trees. The Stranger ticks like my contamination compass, waits for the one closest to me to turn his back.

Thirteen.

I push the barrel of my crossgun to his neck, his body between me and the others. "What are you doing here?"

"You didn't hear? There was a poison gas eruption. We have to seal the mine up until we decide it's safe."

"It's not yours."

Back up.

I grab a handful of his shirt.

"We were sent here to help you. The Widow asked."

Bullshit. She'd never do that.

"We found some survivors and were able to save them," he lies.

I know a bullet wound when I see one, and those eight dead miners were bloody. Earth gas doesn't do that.

"Tell him to give me that rifle," I say.

"What rifle?"

The Stranger hisses.

"She wants the boar," he calls.

"Who is it?" one calls back.

He turns on me. But my trigger pulls faster.

Farce.

They split. Two in the direction of my shot, three after the hollow rattle of Dilly running the other way.

Run.

The outhouse siding hooks into my shirt.

Outpost 20. Vesta and I were pinned in like this. She was moving fine, then suddenly she was falling. Her hands dug into my skin so hard they left a bruise.

Winchester. Vesta's blood sprays across my cheek, warm.

I can't lose another sister.

Breathe. Pay attention.

I close my eyes for just one blink and fight it back.

The shit leaking down the hillside reeks. But at least I know where I am.

"Over here," one of them calls. He's found the body. "Come on out, bitch." His whistles softly, for a dog. "It's the fox."

It's the Stranger.

I tap my fist against the hollow side of the outhouse.

Wait.

The sun is behind me. I watch the ground for his shadow. It shows me what side he's coming from.

But it's still not the one with Leagan's rifle.

A shot rips through the outhouse, a shower of splinters falling down my back as I reload my shells. The Stranger spools out thicker as I get lower, hugging the rocks it's planted on.

If it were me, I'd circle out wide, through the trees to get around me and shoot from this side. I can't stay here, but I'll have to run uphill to make it to the bunkhouses.

Or what if I don't?

It worked for Seed. His shadow made Leagan miss, and the Stranger is stronger than his would ever be.

I walk.

Ten...

I imagine getting shot happens so fast you never even hear it, never know what hit you if it's to the head. Maybe that's not so bad.

I hear him take one, still somewhere behind me. But I hear it, so it missed.

A shadow in an olive uniform leans around the back door of the cabin. He shoots down, not at my body or my head, but my legs.

My buckshot goes right through him.

I want Leagan.

"We're not here to kill you, Revere." The yell comes from down the slope.

I turn slowly.

There he is, down behind a black rock, revolver aimed at me.

"Where's my sister? The Raptor."

"I don't know who you're talking about."

That's her rifle on your back.

And that's a Green sourced gun in your hand.

He pulls the trigger, and it jams.

They've always been known for that.

Grandma used to tell her marks in Vantage: Don't trust a gun you didn't load yourself, and don't buy your munitions from a man named Green.

Two...

My shell shatters his hand, the gun falling in the rocks. The Stranger's black comes seeping up my throat.

Nine.

"Where is she?"

"Fuck if I know." He clutches his bleeding stump with the other.

My vision closes into a rifle scope, black except for what's at the dead center, shrinking to a pinprick, then nothing. The Stranger is in my ears like wind. I feel my hand holster my crossgun, my fingers clenching around a rock instead.

I don't fight her.

I want this to hurt.

LEAGAN'S RIFLE STRAP TANGLES HIS BLOODY ARM, PINNED BECAUSE HE FELL ON it. I don't feel better lifting it, silky and too heavy.

I feel worse.

Forty-seven.

Leagan's not in either bunkhouse. Only the bully I shot, slumped next to the table leg, cupboard doors ripped off and all the food inside gone.

But just because she isn't here doesn't mean they haven't hurt her already.

The ground jars my spine as I step off the porch.

"Dilly," I call into the wind.

Aunt Tess and Navy must know something, unless they're gone too.

"Dilly!"

Eleven...

The can around his neck rattles. Out there somewhere. But the Stranger halts me like a slap.

They're coming.

Hooves grinding on rock. Male voices bending past the trees.

Fuck.

"Dilly, come on. Get back to the train."

SIXTY-EIGHT
FROM THE LAB JOURNAL OF ISOBEL CARLISLE

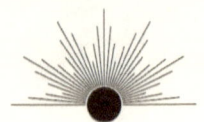

Eden Year 11, the 3rd of Two

~~ENOLA IS GETTING SICKER.~~

~~Enola's~~

Subjects symptoms have progressed to what I believe is the beginning of the final stage with no response to the antidote. She grows violent against herself and no longer drinks the water I set out for her. (I shouldn't even be using her name at all— remember to black that out before publication or showing this to anyone at the University.) (If anyone finds out beyond Amnesty, I will likely be branded a traitor and shot, but that's the least of my concerns.)

Why can't I stop?

I let it slip in conversation with Amnesty today, but she didn't seem to notice or mind. I've seen her staring into the cages as well, a difficult to read yet ponderous expression on her face.

Is she harboring the same doubts I am? That all this is terribly wrong, and we are what is evil. ~~Enola~~ has done nothing to us that we know of, yet we are killing her for the Shadow Nation War and hatred of Amnesty's bastard father.

There must be easier ways to do away with Amnesty's wretched family. For they are indeed horrible. They deserve this.

~~Enola~~ doesn't.

What possessed me? Love?

I love Amnesty more than I ever thought was possible to love a person. But what if all of this is wrong? What if the Tov are no more or less evil than the rest of us? To back out now would mean death for myself, and for Amnesty, a sentence of misery for the rest of her father's life, and likely her brothers and uncle who will take his place.

~~I doubt anyone at the University will ever see this.~~

~~Fraud.~~

* * *

Eden Year 11, the 5th of Two

ALL THREE CURRENT SUBJECTS INFECTED SUCCESSFULLY BUT ARE NOT RESPONDING *to treatment. The antidote formulation will need to be altered.*

~~God, if there is one, help me, I've gone too far to stop.~~

SIXTY-NINE
ADELAIDE

Dust spills off Nightmare's hooves. Into the sky like a signal, everything behind me swallowed by it.

A man veers out of the brush ahead. Nightmare rears halfway up. My legs keep me on her back, but the saddle horn jabs into my stomach.

"*Sol, so.*" He holds up two fingers but does the engineer's salute wrong. Sunburns and white hair, not as light as mine, but maybe it's just stained from years under the dirt. "Stop. It's just me."

I grip with my legs and point my crossgun at him anyway. Nightmare spirals in her own direction because I'm focused on him, not her.

"Daithe," he says.

I know who you are. And I don't like you.

I still don't know what happened and Stranger senses we're not alone. This could be a trap. "What do you want?"

His gaze cuts across me. The blood all over my arms. Splattered and sticky up my chest, around my nails.

He cocks his head, the chuckle pricking at the back of my neck. "You look good in red."

"Where's the Raptor?"

He shrugs. "Those Green Company bone pickers showed up lasterday when we were down working on a new air tunnel." He drags his tongue across his bottom lip, then jabs his chin up at the hills I came from. "But we've got a little trap laid for those fuckers today."

A trilling whistle loops against the wind. It sounds bird-like, but the Stranger doesn't think so. It's a signal.

"Off the path." Daithe waves me aside, dropping his suspenders off his shoulders. "That mine is ours now, we work for you, and I don't surrender to any picker that comes from the east."

Fuck the mine.

Twenty-four.

This brush is deep enough Nightmare and I shouldn't be seen. Hunched oaks and knotbush, stacks of black susans. I hear the hoofbeats now.

"She can't have gotten too far."

The Stranger sees it first, a spiderweb fallen across a gap between trees and a rocky drop. It splits her like a razor but vanishes when I tilt my head too far.

"Have you ever seen Tov glass wire?" Daithe asks. "Now you have. My ancestors invented it. My grandmother used to keep the formula hidden in her shoe so our rivals couldn't learn our secret way of making it because ours was the best. When she was murdered during the war, the formula burned itself into the bottom of her foot and the leather of her shoe."

That's a lie.

"We owe them this," Daithe says, stripping off his earth-stained shirt. "None of this ever belonged to them. Let's kill these sons of bitches."

That's not why I take things.

I'm not angry because the Republic defeated the Tov. These things happen. It's too late to stop, and they will never apologize.

But since men from the east take what they want without asking, why can't I?

If I don't, someone else will.

I don't like making decisions like this. I'm going back to the *Exodus.* "Do whatever you think the Widow would like."

"She'll like her crystal covered in Green Company blood, wouldn't she?" He chuckles again.

Yes, she would.

"And I like my Green Company men sliced thin and fried in fat. It really brings out the flavor of the demo sticks."

Cannibal jokes aren't funny, no matter who makes them.

I slot my crossgun back into the holster and tighten my reins.

Stay back.

Daithe straightens as I turn Nightmare downhill, but his pants stay down around his ankles. "Don't you want to see it happen?"

All I care about right now is finding Leagan before I die.

They're too close.

The first rider clears a stand of rocks. Suddenly, he falls back across the rump of his horse. The next two collide with him, already up his ass before he fell.

They're not dressed like Green Company bullies. They look like homesteaders. Bounty hunters.

Daithe lunges from the brush, naked except for his boots and screaming, causing the other horses to buck their riders and flee.

Blood slips off the wire, like the ruby drop necklace Aunt Tess used to wear before Vesta lost it. It looks so fragile, but two of those men's heads are only connected to the rest of them by the spine.

Let them all kill each other.

She's right.

Dilly bleats somewhere not too far off. At least I haven't lost him.

I leave the rest of them behind.

THEY ARE DIGGING OUTSIDE NEW EDEN. IT LOOKS LIKE FIRE TRENCHES, probably to route the brush fire eating at the hillside to the north. The kind that starts from lightning strikes.

But it's not spreading across the valley. Just a dying red eye under a heavy lid, mostly smoke that chokes out the last of the set sun.

I run my contamination compass up my arm, let it sit in my hand while my stomach turns. Specks of tell-tale light float inside the tube, but most of the liquid stays bone white.

I still have time.

Fifty.

Two of Green's bullies dig while another pair stand guard, but not at the fire trenches. It looks like a grave. Away from town and up on a hill like one.

Who are they burying?

I can't look now.

One-fifty-one.

The *Exodus* is a hollower space than the *Absolution* was, but right now it feels empty.

Navy curls in one of the velvet chairs, playing with the pages of the read by touch book she's been learning to use.

Raleigh launches out of the other. "Adelaide! No one saw you, did they?" The panic in his voice scares me.

"No."

His face is swollen and bruised, but Navy looks unhurt.

"I'm so glad you're back." She starts to reach out, so does Raleigh, but I have to avoid both of them.

"You can't touch me."

"Why not?" She inhales deeply, pauses, does it again. "Is that blood?"

"It's blood." Raleigh says. "Stranger, what have you done now?"

"I shouldn't be surprised anymore." Navy shakes her head, only partially disappointed. "I hope it's not yours."

"Where's Leagan?" I ask.

"We don't know..." Navy twists the brass button on her cuff. It's getting loose. "She and Evangeline went to help Aunt Tess because they took her."

"Who?" There's lead in my stomach. But I don't really have to ask.

"Tess killed Green," Raleigh says. "Butchered him, and I'm not exaggerating."

"They never came back, but Leagan made us promise not to leave the *Exodus*," Navy says. "We needed you."

I need her. I'm running out of time, and I don't know how to tell her.

Tears leak around Raleigh's wince. "We were hoping they went to find you and you'd all come back together. A fool's hope."

Leagan would do that, Aunt Tess wouldn't, not without telling them first.

"What happened?"

"We're really happy you're here, can't you tell?" he says.

Stop stalling.

"Tell me what happened."

SEVENTY
ADELAIDE

SOMEONE KNOWS WHERE LEAGAN AND AUNT TESS ARE.

The railroad tie jail doesn't have a door now. They made it that far. But no other clues.

Green's bullies finished digging.

Raleigh and I drop down into the *Solace* flood trench, hopeful bushes still gathered around it. It gets me past Caroline without being seen.

Three-fifteen.

Who did they bury? I assume it's Green, but I need to know for sure.

Taller cactuses help obstruct us at the top of the hill, my hair firmly wrapped under my scarf and the Stranger's bone mask. Rocks are stacked over the mound to keep the scavenger lizards out. I move the first two.

I've heard that back east you're supposed to leave the shovel you dug the grave with at its side for one night. They did that.

Raleigh grabs my arm. "Hold on. You can't dig that up."

Why not?

"I have to know who's in there."

"A dead body. I'm very sure. I don't necessarily believe in hexes, but this seems like a really fool's gold way to find out."

Dig.

"It's not the first time I've dug up a grave."

"Then make that time your last. I'll go talk to some people and find out for you. But I promise you it's not one of them."

You don't know that.

I know he's just trying to protect me, but the Stranger resents it all the same. "That won't work."

"You don't think I can do it?" he says. "I don't care. I don't care if you don't believe in me, I don't want this to end up as one more thing for them to use against you and Tess."

I yank the shovel from the ground. "I don't need to dig up the whole body." Just enough to see that it's not Leagan or Aunt Tess.

"Fucking Jezebel, Adelaide…Fine, I'll keep watch."

It is Green. I only need to expose part of his head to know. He's already rotting from the heat, dirt clotted in his grayed hair.

I take the shovel and break his skull.

Raleigh flinches as the bone cracks. "*Farce.* He did deserve that."

I'm not going to bother covering him back up. I hope lizards eat him raw.

The wind's picked up. In it, metal grating like an argument, distant sobbing, the lowing of a cow, the Stranger.

Raleigh sets both hands on my shoulders. "As a brother who loves you, you do not seem okay right now."

I've never been like other people, so I don't even know.

"I want you to go back to the *Exodus*," he says. "Go to sleep, eat something and be with Navy. Will you do that? For me?"

I give him a hollow nod. But the Stranger's blackness is creeping in on me.

"I will find something, I promise," he says. "When have I ever failed you? Never. Leagan needs you, but she needs you at your best. When you wake up, I'll have information. Okay? Say the words to me."

"Okay."

"You'll…"

"Go back to the train and rest."

"Thank you. Nothing is going to happen to any of you, I promise."

You can't make promises like that.

I can't tell him I'm dying.

I wish all I had to do was be with Navy and Leagan before it happens. The other deaths I've stared down have been ones I could fight. This one I can only wait for and know it's coming.

The Stranger curls around me like ribs. I don't cry like I want to.

Raleigh squeezes my tight shoulder. It aches. "If you pay the right price, people will tell you whatever you want to know. But it's a hell of lot cheaper if you have a nice smile. You're much nicer than Tess and Leagan. They'd have both said something rude about my face by now."

"I know."

A noise thicker than the wind and closer than the first rumblings of thunder halts the Stranger.

I wish I brought my binoculars.

Fifty-four.

A cow is buried to its shoulders in one of the closest fire trenches. It moans, thrashing to free itself, flashes of forked lighting reflecting silver in its wild eyes. There are shallow holes all over the main street like scabs, a man still digging.

"Now what are they doing?" Raleigh whispers. "Oh no..."

"Stay in there, you bastard!" the man yells. "You have to grow into nicer babies who won't bite me on the ass."

It's starting.

"He's not our problem," I say.

A light bobs through the sagebrush, coming this way. I sink back.

"No, he's not," Raleigh agrees. "We have worse things to worry about."

Navy wants to save as many people as she can.

But I don't.

SEVENTY-ONE
FROM THE LAB JOURNAL OF ISOBEL CARLISLE

Eden Year 11, the 17th of Two

IF ENOLA REALLY COULD TURN INTO A STORM OF SAND OR SUCK THE BLOOD OF infants, if she could really transform into a fox or rot food inside cellars, if any of this were true, she would have escaped this cage weeks ago and slain me for what I've done to her.

She is just a young woman with desires like me.

Though she may be acting like a beast now, and rotting like a living corpse, this is all by my hand.

The last of her teeth fell out today.

SEVENTY-TWO
ADELAIDE

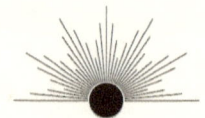

I TAKE ANOTHER BATH.

Our water supply is falling, and the sunburn on my chest stings, but I do it anyway. Wash off any missed traces of the poison lake, wash off Green's dirt. Wash off Kane.

I stare into the mirror while my breath fogs the glass until my back hurts. My eyes haven't changed.

But they will.

And I hate surprises.

I DID SLEEP, BUT IT DOESN'T FEEL THAT WAY. EVERY TIME I BLINK, GRIT SCRAPES the inside of my eyelids.

Navy fills the cast iron kettle. Under the faucet, the pipes groan and vibrate.

"Oh no." She quickly stops the flow. "Already? You don't think someone put a hole in our tank, do you? Like we did when we took the *Exodus*?"

"I'll go check the reservoir." My hips ache as I force myself out of my seat.

The dials for the drinking water tank are inside a panel behind the cook's passage.

The needles hover in the red.

I check the ground outside, beneath the undercarriage just to be sure. It's all dry.

We've made it at least halfway through Moon Season, but it doesn't get easier now. It's the hottest. Driest. A storm is going to happen every night until *Solace*. The Rim wants blood.

Sixty-one.

"We have ten percent of our tank left," I say. "I don't think it's a leak. There isn't enough moisture in the air for the water reclaimers. I won't take any more baths in case we have to use the non-drinking water."

"I won't either." Navy nods, worrying on her bottom lip. "Now that it's just us, it should help a little. I'm not saying I'm happy about that."

"I know."

"What if it is just us now?"

"We'll take care of each other." Until I can't anymore. That makes my throat ache. "Navy, there's—"

"Thank you for getting me Isobel's journal," she says. "I'm so close to getting it right, I can feel it. The sick goat hasn't died yet. I'm sorry I interrupted you. What were you going to say?"

"Navy, there's something I have to tell you."

She hears it in me. She goes still.

"We found a pool of contaminated water when we were hunting Seed. Underground. I fell in." There's relief in saying it out loud, but only for a few seconds. Saying it doesn't change what's going to happen to me.

"How long were you in? Did you swallow any of it?"

"I couldn't wash myself off until I got here last night."

I should have just come back with Leagan. Why didn't I think of that at the time? I don't know. I was already on a path and compelled to follow it. The way the Stranger is.

If I had come back sooner, I would have been here to stop what happened to them.

Fresh anger starts to simmer under my skin. I wish I'd never met Kane. His fucking projects always start trouble, and my family pays the price.

I should have known better.

Maybe he should die.

He should have died a long time ago.

"This isn't fair." Navy struggles to finish her breath before starting another. But when she does it's calm again. "But I know nothing is. You think you're infected now, but maybe you're not."

Tears bubble out of me, hot and rancid. "I didn't want to tell you."

"I'm so glad you did." She feels her way to my hand. "Whatever I have to do. I'll work harder. I won't let you die, I promise."

"And I'll find Leagan and Aunt Tess," I promise her. "I'll make sure you're not left alone."

Raleigh better have what he promised me.

"Adelaide Revere!" The yell is muted by the *Exodus*'s walls, but I taste the violence. "We know you're here. Come out."

SEVENTY-THREE
ADELAIDE

Twenty-one of them.

Green's bullies, merchants, miners who haven't set out yet. Each of them holds an Exodus rifle, unworn stocks gleaming in the sun.

I am in deep shit.

But they can't get me in here.

"What's happening?" Navy asks.

The storm shutters of the gun car partially obstruct my view. "They have a wagon. It looks like dead cows piled on it."

"I hope you're not thinking of going out there."

"No." That would be stupid.

"Look at this man." A marshal pushes someone through the crowd, behind them, a wheelbarrow with a woman's writhing body in it. "This is Tomaths Goodson, owner of Goodson's General Store."

Tomaths holds his son. Head bent low against the boy's shirt, brown with blood, sobs shaking him.

"Why is his family dead?"

Because he brought them here.

A foolish man.

"What?" Navy gasps. "No."

"I wouldn't do that," I say.

"I know. You're not evil."

"Answer me, milk bastard!"

None of this was me.

"She's not dead," I say. "I see her moving. They're lying."

Not yet.

"We only want to talk about what you've been doing," another bully calls. "If you don't have something to hide, then there's nothing to be afraid of."

Bullshit.

"Aunt Tess didn't want to move the train after she killed Green, but I think we should," Navy says. "Let's get away from here and then we can figure out what to do."

"Hiding in there looks like an admission of guilt," the marshal says.

No, it means I'm not a fool.

"Adelaide Revere! Otherwise known as the Stranger. This is your last chance."

The Stranger sinks through me like lead.

"The mother. Her name is Piety." Navy's words spill onto each other. "She has the pestilence. Aunt Tess and Dr. Pike both saw it. It's been days now. She must be doing very bad."

The marshal waves a hand and the crowd brushes Tomaths aside. They don't care about his dead son. They just want an excuse. "All right, you made us do it."

The blood leaves my face. Pins. All I feel now are pins. "That's Leagan."

"*What?*"

They have Leagan. She kicks as they carry her by the armpits, rag tied through her teeth, stretching her black lips open. Unable to catch herself with tied arms, she falls face forward when they drop her.

The Stranger fills up my throat, throbs in my head.

"Do they have Aunt Tess too?"

"No." My whisper burns. "Just Raleigh."

"Don't do it," Navy says, panic. "Please don't."

The marshal draws an ax from the same wheelbarrow holding Piety, then lifts it up. The blade is brown. Not rust. Blood.

Then he lays it to the back of Leagan's neck.

My gasp is mostly silent, but the vibration moves through my whole body. It hurts.

Navy grabs at me. "*No.*"

"Make your choice," he calls. "You or them."

"Stranger, don't you dare!" Raleigh yells despite the knife aimed at his kidney. "Stay inside!"

I won't lose another sister.

Black.

"Adelaide, no!" Navy screams.

The door's latch bites down with metal teeth. It locks on its own, can only be opened from the inside. Navy is still safe.

Fifteen.

Time crawls past me on its belly, the same way it did as I watched Vesta try to reach me, then slowly crumple from the gunshots in her leg and abdomen.

Nobody moves as I march toward them. Only allowed to watch.

Twenty-six.

I lift my foot and shove my heel into the marshal's ribs. Deep as it will go.

He staggers sideways, and I yank the ax out of his grasp, no ground lost. Ribs crack like kindling does, stomach soft.

The Stranger feels rush of a gun butt in the air. I swing around, the ax splitting wood and biting into the metal barrel. Another one fires, the shot strikes off the *Exodus*'s armor.

"Run, Raptor," I call.

"Both of you run!" Raleigh yells. "Forget about me!"

The ax is top heavy, blood spilling down the shaft, slick on the wood as it catches on a thigh.

There are too many of them. I knew this. It was never a good plan. It was a reaction. Before I can get back to Leagan, arms and hands latch onto me from several directions. The wet wood slips from my hand as soon as Green's bully yanks, a friction burn left behind on my skin.

"Let her go!" Raleigh tries to lunge.

A silhouette cuts between us.

His scream is long. Longer than the blade they shove into him.

My gasp is short, but it slices deep into my throat. The throb of the Stranger falls away.

Raleigh whimpers, the knife still in his stomach as his legs melt. Good. Leave it there. The second you pull it out, the bleeding starts.

Tears flow from Leagan's hazel eyes as she charges for me, a dark shriek boiling up her throat to the gag in her teeth. Someone thrusts up a knee and catches it in her stomach. It makes her easier to hit again on her way down. She's still screaming as someone drags her away by the back of her shirt.

"You just fucked yourself, milk bastard." The second marshal rips my head back by the hair. "Look this man in the eye. Tell him why you killed his little boy."

I didn't.

"Tell the truth. You killed his son and tried to blame his wife by driving her mad. She was a good, Providence fearing woman until you got your fox venom in her."

It won't save me to argue. They've already made up their mind.

The blow stings my cheek. But I know it's only the beginning. I've been here before.

"What is this?" Millard parts the crowd like a curtain.

"Justice." The marshal slaps me again, catching my lip this time.

Millard swings his arm in a downward arc. The hit has the flesh clap of an open hand, same as I just got. "Violence begets violence. Justice is truthful. We are better than they are, and there is no excuse on this earth to justify hitting a woman."

"This is not a woman." The marshal wipes his struck cheek. "You have to meet an animal on its level, otherwise, it's only going to see you're weak. This half-blood just hacked this man to death, all these men witnesses. We don't need more proof. We saw it right here. All of this is her fault."

"I watched you start it. Here you are, trying to do the same." Millard pulls the pistol from the marshal's holster and shoves him back, ripping the copper badge from his chest as they part. "You are dismissed, sir. You," he points to a random face in the crowd, "get this poor boy to Dr. DuPonte."

Pike elbows his way through the crowd. "I'm here, I'll take him." He cuts through Raleigh's wrist restraints before anyone can stop him and throws his arm over his shoulder. "I trained for surgery in Cairo. I'm the most qualified here." He shoves out a hand to stop a homesteader who steps toward him. "This wound is fragile. I can handle this on my own."

Piety thrashes violently. The wheelbarrow tips, taking her with it. She writhes on the ground like a dying flame, teeth grinding on her gag. I don't need to see her eyes. There are dark splotches inside her skin, scratches all over her throat and chest, her dress peeled back at the neck and torn.

"Look at what you've done, you white devil." The disarmed marshal reels back around, the other men parting from him so I'm left standing alone.

I rake my boot down the front of his shin as he grabs for my arm. He realizes it's a mistake and shoves me at Piety instead. Close enough to smell the rot.

"If you don't want to pay for this little boy's life with yours, ask—*beg*—for mercy from this man now."

Piety's teeth grip the stick they've gagged her with like a bit, skin still lodged between them. Her red fingers are knotted in mismatched shapes.

The boy's shirt is untucked, suspenders snapped. He's covered in scratches too, dried blood all around his lips, a chunk ripped from his waist.

Piety has smaller tooth marks on her shoulders and cheek.

They tried to eat each other.

"We found them early this morning, down in the rocks about a quarter mile from town," a miner says.

"That woman was sick," Pike says. "Pestilence. I told Goodson she shouldn't be left alone unrestrained or that child allowed near her."

"He's in on this with them," someone says. "He's been staying on the train with those women. They probably seduced him a long time ago."

"When we need your professional opinion we will ask, Doctor." Millard waves him off. "Attend to that poor man in your arms before he bleeds to death."

"Fuck me," Raleigh gasps as Pike turns him away. "Tell them what you know, Pike. Tell the truth. Adelaide didn't do this. You know it. You all know it. Cowards!"

"Raleigh," I call. "Take care of Navy."

"You'll take care of her yourself."

The marshal sneers. "If the milk bastard didn't do this, then what did?"

The Stranger picks at the bottom seams of Piety's apron pockets. Blood pools there.

"Pestilence," I say. "It likes to rot the jaw."

"There is no pestilence here," Millard says. "My son and his first survey proved it. You were there, do not lie."

Vesta's red eyes didn't lie.

I point to her pocket. A bully digs into the gingham apron.

Teeth. Hers, and her son's.

The marshal grabs my arm again, whiplash snapping at my spine. "How did you know to look there?"

The Stranger moves, a flash like lightning but black. But I don't. Fighting will only give him an excuse to hurt me now. She knows I'm right. I need to find out where they took Leagan.

Tomaths splays his son in the dirt, prying at the boy's jaw. By the way the body doesn't move he's been dead for a while.

"Check the fox for bite marks," the bully says.

Thread and fabric tear as the marshal rips my shirt open.

"Not here," Millard warns. "This isn't a sideshow. Take her away." But he stops the marshal as he starts to twist my arm. "Sir, you were dismissed. Go, before you end up on trial next to them." He clears his throat. "Men of Caroline, we appreciate your help, now go back to your own work."

The bullies fold my arms back, then tie my wrists to my elbows.

Millard sets his hand to Tomaths's shoulder. "I'm very sorry for your loss. We will have an honorable burial for your boy this evening. And find a solution for your wife. Don't fear, this is not fox magic. Heat can do terrible things to a mind."

A weak mind.

"I want to see the fox locked up," someone calls. "We can't just let her waltz off after what she just did. It's not right. It's not safe."

They agree.

"What if she and that crazy Reverend were in on their plots together? Mr. Green had evidence she was the Winchester arsonist. She could have blown up the tracks."

"That brush fire started out of nothing lasterday. It can't be coincidence."

This is Moon Season. There were storms. Lightning starts fires.

"I'm going to raise my family here someday. But not with that thing walking around."

"Do I have to lock all of you up too?" Millard asks. "Disperse. I will not tolerate any more violence against these women. Be the men I know you are."

It's only *farce* to make him look better than everyone else.

He slaps the marshal badge on the next bully he passes. "Get the fox out of here. Make sure she's safe."

The fox.

He doesn't usually call me that.

The new marshal grab me around the knees and throws me over his shoulder.

Dust devils spin on the horizon, blood from my split lip dripping into the back of his shirt.

SEVENTY-FOUR
ADELAIDE

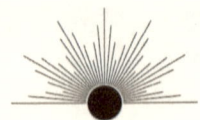

LEAGAN SCRUBS THE GAG KNOT AGAINST HER KNEE. A SCRATCH SHOWS through the rip in her shoulder seam, her ankles bound to the iron pig stove.

This is Green's tent. It smells like him. And like blood. Especially when the wind batters the sides.

My hands are already numb from being tied to this chair. Pulling on the rope isn't helping, it's just making my wrists burn.

The cotton rag finally droops around Leagan's neck, both her red buns undone with it. "Yes! I'm free, suck on that you fuckers." She makes a retching sound, showing her dry tongue.

My lip cracks again as soon as I open my mouth. "I found Dilly. He's back on the *Exodus* now."

"He's a smart boy. Thanks for trying to save me...Are you in a lot of pain?"

"They might be listening to us."

"Well good thing you didn't do anything wrong." She says it louder then twists her mouth sideways. "Do you think Raleigh's dead?"

I don't know. I hope not.

"That would be just like him to try and get attention by dying now."

"Where's Aunt Tess?"

"Fuck if I know. We broke her out of that pathetic little jail they built, then someone shot us with a dart gun. I had one stuck in my shirt when I woke up. But Aunt Tess and Evangeline weren't here anymore."

Another surge of wind shudders the tent.

"I haven't had any dreams since we got out here," she says. "Just nice, black sleep. I'm not upset about it, actually."

"Have you ever seen how we die?" I ask.

She shakes her head. "I don't want to. I want it to be a surprise. Let's make a deal. If they start to kill one of us, they have to kill both of us. I don't want to be the one left behind."

Me neither. "It's a deal."

Navy will be the one left behind. It will be hard for her without us, but I know she won't give up. She still has things to do.

So do you.

The new marshal steps inside. He drags a look down each of us, then chooses me. The black core of his left eye is dripping into the blue part, like the sweat coming down his neck.

"You're in all kinds of shit, fox." He holds up a wet specimen jar. A brain, same as the ones in DuPonte's lab. "Is this a snack for later, when you run out of little boys to eat?"

He's not asking me *if* I did it. He's asking *why* because he's already made up his mind about me.

He brings his foot up, setting the sole of his boot into my chest, then slowly pushes until the chair tilts back on just two legs. My fists clench along with my stomach, every hairline tremble jolting through me like a slap. The grin on his face says everything.

"Leave her alone," Leagan snarls like the Stranger does.

Millard parts the tent flap and the bully yanks the pressure of his foot away, the chair dropping back onto four legs. But there's still a dirty print left on the front of me.

The light that leaks in with him is dim, stormy.

"Go stand watch outside." But Millard buttons the tent flap back up, all of us still inside. "How is your face? The situation should never have gotten so out of hand. The doctor will come and check on you as soon as he can."

"Which doctor?" Leagan says.

He turns to the new marshal. "How many of Green's men are still here?"

"Eleven."

"And how many of them do you trust?"

"About half."

The Stranger latches onto Millard as he nods. "I'll need them in time. You're dismissed to keep watch."

"Time for what?" Leagan demands.

To end this.

Millard comes to me, drawing a handful of folded paper from his pocket. "Do you recognize any of this?"

At first, I only see the skin showing through his unclipped fingernails. Black.

But I've also seen this handwriting before. In DuPonte's lab.

I hope it's all ash now.

"This is disturbing evidence," he says. "I understand you have a lab inside your train. An impressive one, by the sound of it. What is your sister working on?"

"None of your business," Leagan says. "Who snitched?"

Pike.

Unless it was someone from the Boneyard who did the car alterations.

"Before his death, Green was concerned about her project, that it might be dangerous to the rest of us. Does she have any formal training?"

"Green was concerned every time he farted," Leagan says. "He didn't know shit. Navy was born smarter than him."

Lightning cracks across the sky, outline visible through the tent. The wind searches for seams in the canvas and forces dirt through all of them.

Millard waits until the gust passes. "All I need from you is for you to tell me what she's working on."

No.

Aunt Tess isn't coming back, I feel it. I don't know how long I have with my mind. Raleigh better survive so he can move the train.

Outside, there's a different kind of crack. Rock splitting wood.

"Did you kill the Goodson boy?" Millard asks.

"No, she didn't," Leagan says.

"When I want your opinion, Leagan Revere, I will ask for it. Is there someone who can corroborate your story, and vouch for where you were when we split company?"

Leagan's gaze links with mine, the light fading under the weight of the storm. Either her dreams have already showed her something she won't tell me, or she sees it in me now. She knows me well enough. "Maybe you should ask your son. He wouldn't lie to you."

I hate that this is the truth.

Millard pauses. I'm not sure what it means. And I hate that too. "Timothy is fond of you. Perhaps a little too much."

"He doesn't deserve her," Leagan sneers.

Millard's face doesn't change much, but it feels like a smirk to the Stranger.

Someone screams. The Stranger goes sharp against me, but it's one of those sounds you can ignore unless it involves you.

It gets louder.

Sudden gunfire hammers, but for every shot, another shriek rises.

Wind and dirt slash my face as the new marshal peels open the tent, letting three of his bullies in with him. "They came from the north as soon as the dust hit. They're using it as cover."

"Who?" Leagan says.

"We don't know. You can't see a foot ahead of you."

The bullies take up positions on either side of the door while Millard peers outside as far as he dares. "I don't see anything."

Leagan kicks at the stove. "Untie me."

"Shut up," the marshal hisses. "If you draw them over here, I'll kill you myself, I swear to Providence."

"It's her." The bully juts his chin at me, a flinch in his throat. "My grandfather said he saw the foxes control the dust. They'd wear it like coats and use it to blind the men. She's doing this, I swear to you."

"Then maybe you should stop making her mad," Leagan says.

"You hear that screaming? That's how she's getting in your mind."

"That's just the wind, you imbecile."

Millard draws back. "I can't say what's happening out here. But if the storm can cover them, we can use it too. Get her out of here, before any of those bastards see you."

Two of the bullies turn away, but the marshal stalks in front of me, drawing a boot knife. The Stranger comes between us, a river of fog.

A damp rag clamps over my face.

I twist the other way, but his other hand grabs my jaw, pinning my head against his body, my body still pinned to the chair. Panic closes on my chest like teeth. I can't hold my breath anymore.

"No!" Leagan's scream hits a shrill note I feel in the bottom of my feet as the rest of me fades. "No!" Louder. "No, no, no, *NO!*"

The clang of Leagan kicking the pig stove quickly gets swallowed by the howl of the wind. The shrieks in it. The fiery throb of the Stranger trying to keep me awake while I slip away from her.

SEVENTY-FIVE
FROM THE LAB JOURNAL OF
ISOBEL CARLISLE

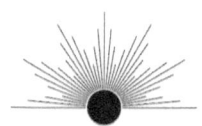

Eden Year 11, the 6th of Six

I SHOULD DO BETTER CATALOGING THE SYMPTOMS. THESE ARE THE ONES I HAVE noted so far:

- *Discoloration of the eyes, progressing to skin as internal vessels split open*
- *Foul odor of decay*
- *Insomnia*
- *Violence (against others if available, against self if not)*
- *Refusal to drink (even as the lips crack)*
- *Hallucinations*
- *Joint swelling and muscle spasms*
- *Skin sloughing*
- *Bone degeneration (especially of the jaw)*
- *Catatonic state or loss of self-awareness*
- *Death (often caused by subject's violent or dangerous behavior)*

Symptoms do not always present in the same order, but the blood in the eyes seems to be the most consistent and initial tell. The violence is pervasive, worse than anything I have seen this close to war, even though men regularly return melted by Tov potions or their limbs cut off by swords.

I am out of time. Zachariah won't wait any longer, and if I stall again, he will start to ask questions—or take his temper out on Amnesty. He demands my latest test subject be brought out beyond the wall and left for her brothers and sisters to scavenge, along with the bodies of the miners who were hanged yesterday. I injected them with pestilence, also under his orders. The infection will pass to anyone who handles the flesh and ingests traces of the poison, either intentionally or on accident.

~~When I look at her, I still see Enola, but she has been dead for months.~~

Part of me no longer cares if I'm found out as a traitor. I've lied to the only person I've ever really loved. And as for my role as a scientist, I have failed.

~~Amnesty, I am so sorry. We will never be together in the paradise you dream of.~~

As for the cure: I lied.

This pestilence doesn't discern our blood from that of the Tov. I doubt it ever would no matter how many years I threw at the pursuit. We aren't so different after all.

It is going to infect us all.

SEVENTY-SIX
LEAGAN

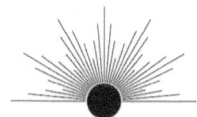

No. No, no, no.

The tent flap snaps. The air is all filmy with dust because those fools didn't bother to button it back up. It gets in my teeth, and I grind them some more just to feel it crackle. It feels nasty, but it feels good because I hate everybody.

I wish Adelaide did control this storm just so she could smother everyone in it for being so stupid. I'll find her.

I can kick this pig stove all day, and I *will*.

The rope around my wrists peels my skin off, but I don't care. It's getting looser, and the blood is helping.

A Green bully comes staggering back in, his forehead leaking.

"What did you do with the Stranger?"

"Quiet. There's an army of bone pickers out there tearing this place apart. You won't survive long once they find you, little girl. It's not too late to beg for mercy. I'll shoot you before they get their hands on you."

"It's not too late to go back to the butthole you came from."

"You think you can do better than the rest of us? Let's find out. I'll give you a head start." He slices through the rope around my ankles, and I kick him in the face.

Now I have his knife *and* his pistol.

The dust swallows me for dinner. It's just shapes blurring by, men on the ground, some of them being ripped apart by the teeth of other men, some of them getting fucked by them. But who cares about them? Not me.

Rocks bounce off the shops' wooden siding, the street all prickly with them. Big ones that will leave a juicy bruise. I throw one at somebody because I can. You would too, you big liar.

The dust gets in through my nose, wind throwing sharp little pieces at my face. It tastes like rotten old potatoes. I keep swallowing but the urge sticks in the top of my throat.

If I can find the rail, I'll find the *Exodus*.

Grass comes up around my waist. It didn't feel like I went far enough to be on the other side of town, but here I am. I don't know. It all looks the same.

My shin catches on something in the grass, brush snapping around me. "Fuck!"

The thing looms over me, bigger than a horse.

But it's just a wagon. Squatting in the brushes with its tongue hanging out, waiting to trip someone.

I kick it. That's what you get for getting in my way and scaring me. I hope the wind rips all your canvas right off.

I have to help Adelaide.

SEVENTY-SEVEN
TESLA

I PACE MY SQUARE CELL, THE FLOOR MADE OF STONE AND DIRT PACKED TIGHT AS mortar between each one of them. My hair coils around my shoulders, sticking to my face and neck like a spiderweb. I've been stripped down to my undergarments, red marks inside my forearm and bruises on my wrist, forearms and ankles from whatever they did to me.

Evan gave up on this manic pacing yesterday, smart on her since no one has fed us since then. But I can't sit still like she can.

The glass medicine cabinet glares a shadowy reflection back at me.

I'm still not sure where we are, but I'm not dead, so that's good.

With no windows, I can only guess what time it is.

There's a chair with leather restraints dangling off it. I bet they match up with the marks on my body. Also, a table made from a single slab or porcelain. It must weigh a ton, and I imagine how cold it would be to lay on, especially naked.

"I'm so mad I could scream," I say.

"Go ahead, if that's what you want. It might make you feel better."

"No, I need to save my energy. I have an idea that might actually work." I reach for her, into the empty cell between us, and she does the same for me. It's comforting even though our hands still can't touch. "We will get out of here."

Everything I'd normally have, picks disguised as hair pins, my knee spike and knife arm, even my pocket watch, they're all gone.

"It's fairly simple but being smart was not a hiring requirement on Green's job advertisement," I say. "You'll pretend to be sick, and I'll yell for help. Mother and I used to do it all the time." And it almost always worked.

"And when they open my cell door—"

"You punch their heads off. They don't know they're about to meet the Descendants Bare Knuckle Bitch. I'm sorry, I know you hated that name."

She smiles faintly. "How sick should I pretend to be?"

"I'm thinking you should convulse a little. It will be very dramatic."

"All right." She gets down on her knees one at a time, then lies on her back with a little groan. "My glory, I'll try not to actually hurt myself."

"Roll your eyes up into your head if you can." I wrap my fingers around the iron door bar. "Be prepared, I'm going to be loud. When I see the doorknob turning, I'll nod. Ready?"

"I am."

"Someone help!" My dry throat stretches, shrill volume cutting like a knife. "Something's happening!" I pause to listen and let it sink in if someone did hear me. "Help, us! She's dying, she's dying, she's dying!" My screams pierce my own head and ring off the walls for a second blow, but I don't stop even when the brass doorknob starts moving.

Evangeline arches her back, twisting and flailing like a stomped spider.

Dr. DuPonte rushes in, all filmy gray as usual. When I first woke up, he was sitting in the straight-back chair, watching us like a rat looks at people it wants to steal from. Now he scrambles around his porcelain table like a cornered one.

"Help her!" I wail. Fool's gold, I should have been an actress back east.

"Assistance," he calls and two of Green's bullies come around the corner.

Keys rattle on Evangeline's cell lock.

"Hold her down so she doesn't strain herself," DuPonte says.

As soon as they get within reach, Evan rolls to her feet, colliding with the closest body and mashing him against the cell bars. Her fist jabs up, under the chin, cracking his teeth together.

DuPonte scrambles out of the way, fleeing into the hall.

"He has the keys!" I point.

A rifle stock jabs from the hall as Evangeline turns the corner.

My scream is real as she collapses, blood gushing down her cheek. "You fucker!"

They herd her back into the cell and drag out the man she knocked unconscious.

DuPonte returns to the room, ticking a finger at me. "That was not nice. That's going in the record." He steps over to the notebook left on the wooden desk. "Female subject number one is not nice."

"I could have told you that."

"Cognitive abilities and complex problem-solving skills…" He pauses to get his pencil caught up. "Still active. Day two."

"Am I your fucking lab mouse now?" I let my glare burn his back then reach through the bars for Evan. "I'm so sorry. Are you okay?"

She nods, but she's holding a sleeve saturated in red to her face.

Obviously, I need a better plan.

"Female subject number two, bleeding profusely. Coagulation…" DuPonte checks his silver pocket watch as boots echo in the corridor. "Please bring her in, be quick about it."

Fabric hisses against stone. A marshal and the remaining bully return, someone's ankles held between them. "Fresh meat."

Adelaide.

One arm lags behind her as they drag her into the middle cell with less care than they'd wipe their own asses. Her shirt is ripped open, and I catch a glimpse of the split in her lip, crusted and thick before her head rolls to face the other way.

"Fucking Jezebel." They're well out of my reach, but I grab at them anyway. "What did you do to her?"

"You should ask what she did to Caroline," the marshal says.

"Exactly what it deserves, I bet."

DuPonte turns to his book again, sharp and withered as a dead cactus. "Close the door on your way out."

The marshal rounds, kicking Adelaide's thigh before swinging the cell shut.

"What a little penis you must have," I snap.

"I bet I could still make you moan. You're just mad you lost your scary pet. We all know that's a devil wearing some meat to make it look like a girl."

"And you're a coward wearing meat who thinks he's a man." Adelaide's chest seems to rise and fall, but suddenly I don't trust my own eyes. "Evan, is she breathing?"

"Yes." Evangeline crawls to her side, Adelaide's hand sprawled close enough she can take her pulse. The second she lets the pressure off her head wound, the blood starts flowing again. "God of Mercy, be here with us now," she prays quietly. "Like rain falls on the starved mountain..."

The marshal sneers at her for a moment, not sure what to do. "Shut your hole, bitch. This is no church."

"You're right," I say, my breath ticking on the iron bars. "This is no church. So Providence won't care when I kill you."

His gaze peels down my chest. "He won't care what I do to you either."

"I said leave, I have work to do," DuPonte says.

"Work," the marshal says. "Yeah, that's it, you fox lover."

I'm not usually afraid of shriveled old men like DuPonte, but today I am. Afraid for all of us to be alone with him.

DuPonte peels back Adelaide's shirt, already stripped of most of its buttons, and opens her arm. Either he can't lift her or doesn't care that he's down on the floor, a crisp line somehow still pressed into his trousers.

"Get away from her." I slam my fist against the iron bars. I don't expect him to listen but damnation, I'm going to try.

He doesn't. The line of rubber tubing wriggles and flexes as he attaches it to a glass sphere, a big brown worm.

"Hey!" I struggle with the laces of my boot, dragging my heel against the stone floor to pry it free and cursing my single hand in every language I know the whole time. "Leave her alone."

His magnifying spectacles hide his eyes, but he lifts a long needle, examining the point. *Farce,* it could almost go right through her arm and out the other side.

"Stranger, wake up!"

The tip of the needle melts under Adelaide's pale skin. Nausea wells through my jaw, but I can't seem to look away as DuPonte threads it deeper into her elbow. The rubber tube darkens, red lines spilling down the glass globe.

"Adelaide!" I scream at her. "Fucking Jezebel!"

"I've waited my whole life to study Tov blood," he says. "Even diluted by a generation like this one."

"You call this science?"

"I don't expect women to understand the importance of academia."

"Whatever you want to call it to delude yourself into thinking you're important," I say. "A Poisonneur told me a person who kills a Shiver gets haunted by it until they go insane. But maybe you're not worried because you're already insane."

"I don't believe in witchcraft."

DuPonte strips Adelaide skirt, boots, and stockings off. His gnarly fingers trace the visible veins that web through her legs and stomach like rivers, probing at her intestines. All my hope is waning.

My heel pops free of my boot—finally—sweat under my arms from the struggle. "Look at me, you fucking lunatic! Whatever you do to her, I'll do it back to you." And I throw it as hard as I can at the bastard's head.

DuPonte falls sideways, knocking over the globe and dislodging the rubber tubing from the top.

"You wasteful creature." He snatches up the globe, deep red bubbles frothing at the sides, his thinning hair scuffed upright where my boot struck.

"I have two." And I point to Evangeline. "So does she."

"Female subject one becomes combative." He says to his notebook but doesn't write it.

When he turns again, a thin rifle is gripped in his blood-spotted hands. It pops, a bare amount of smoke drifting out the barrel. It's a small sting, but I still expect a hole as I look down and brace myself for it. Instead, there's a dart sticking from my chest.

"They use these for stray dogs back east," he says. "They work for me here too."

"You—" My first step wobbles. *Farce*, it's only been seconds.

He jabs the gun in Evangeline's direction, and she seems to shrink. "You behave."

SEVENTY-EIGHT
ADELAIDE

THE IRON SINGE OF BLOOD LINGERS IN THE BACK OF MY THROAT.

The Stranger pinches my skin. She's trying to wake me up, but my body is too far away for her touch.

Someone tilts my head back, moist hands on my neck, breath rancid and sweet.

Get up. The Stranger twists in me.

I can't. Why can't I move?

My next breath comes in deeper. Two spots of light fracture my eyes. Lamps, milky green glass.

My fingers curl slowly. The room is mostly dark. I see my skin, not clothes. Panic comes up my throat, images, but I choke it down.

GET UP. The Stranger rakes over me.

I flinch, and a deep ache shoots up my arm.

Dr. DuPonte paces. Bars between us, the porcelain cutting table.

A globe of red liquid sits a few feet away, bubbles picking at the curve of the glass. I taste it again, the bloody ghost in the back of my throat. It belongs to me.

I know where I am. Back in Eden.

They get worse at night.

She's right, they do. I don't know why. Maybe I do too.

I rip the needle out of my arm.

There's blood on the floor, a dark line seeping away from me. Joints crack as DuPonte sinks onto his knees, sweat on his sunken cheeks. The Stranger coils around him, fills his ears, spilling into his mouth as his wet breath claws its way out.

Black.

The puddle ripples as his breath gets closer. His tongue is gray, quivering as he dips it into my blood, drags.

"My God." Evangeline crosses herself. "You are a sick mind."

DuPonte's dead gaze lifts from the floor to me once more. "I want to keep you awake, but you won't have to feel anything when I cut you."

You will.

Keys jangle as he makes a note in an open book, unlocks the medicine cabinet.

My head burns dark, starry. But the needle sinks into the cage lock.

"Providence help you now." Aunt Tess grips a bar of the cell next to me, her voice slurred.

Eight.

The glass medicine cabinet shows my reflection. DuPonte starts as he realizes.

Too late.

Glass splinters, bottles colliding all over the shelves as he smashes through them. One with a long neck sits on a plate with a dainty crystal glass. My fingers lock around it.

The bottle doesn't break against his head, the flesh does. He staggers into the cabinet again, impact ripping the door off its thin hinge on his way down.

Air tries to get through the blood seeping from his nostrils, catching on bubbles in his throat. A sound I know. Death.

My blood sticks to his face, leaves a red handprint as I step away. Like I did to all of them in Hannah. Maybe no one will see it, but I hope the Von Kanes do. Let them know the Stranger was here.

His pocket chain is heavy, the keys strung alongside his watch.

"I fucking told you so." Aunt Tess staggers to her feet, one boot on.

"Your clothes are over there." Evangeline points to a heap in the corner.

"What did he do to her?" I ask.

"Some kind of tranquilizer dart. She was causing too much trouble."

That sounds like her. Maybe there's some smelling salts in the cabinet.

Nine.

"Thank Providence." Aunt Tess reaches though the bars to squeeze my hand as I work out which key fits the cell lock. Her missing boot is in my cell. "Oh, I'd never let that a little bastard like that kill me. Almost as shameful as letting St. Paul do it."

The Stranger expands as something far away clatters, then settles back down on my body that's still too heavy.

I feel Vesta.

It's not a picture memory, just a familiarity that settles over me like dread.

"I'll take those. My head's starting to clear." Aunt Tess catches hold of the keys. "You get dressed."

Six.

Outside someone cackles. Far away, like a coyote.

The rotten smell washes over me. When Aunt Tess and Evangeline aren't looking, I sniff myself. When I turn, will I know?

I close up my ripped shirt the best I can, steal the cufflinks off DuPonte to replace two buttons. I want my crossgun, but it's back in New Eden somewhere.

"Does he have any weapons?" Aunt Tess asks.

"No." No smelling salts either. "Just this." I shoulder the dart gun.

"Of course not. Fool."

My head blurs as I stand back up. It passes in a breath, but when I come back, Aunt Tess and Evangeline grip my arms, holding me up.

"Adelaide?" Aunt Tess's face wrinkles, like she asked me something I didn't hear. "I think you should sit down."

"We need to go." I'm not sure why, but the Stranger says so. And I always listen to her.

"You lost a decent amount of blood." Evangeline feels my pulse. "Let's go find you some water and something to eat. Do you need to hold my arm?"

Something's coming.

Aunt Tess creeps ahead, but I re-lock the door from the outside. It will buy us some time before someone finds DuPonte's body.

"We can find a safe place to hide," she says. "One of us will stay with her and the other can go find some horses."

Neither of them knows Eden. I do.

Fifteen.

There should be more Green Company bullies around. Rows of used cots line rooms. Canned food, clothes, and shoes. Fresh ones. Not what was left behind from the last army.

Three of the cots are piled with sticks. Underneath, on top. And blood. Smeared up the walls, handprints wrapped around the fatter sticks and traces on spent ammunition, all dried.

They already turned.

There's a revolver under this pillow. I hold it up, and Aunt Tess shows me a box of unspent ammunition. It's better than nothing. And we take the food.

The other rooms pull at the Stranger, but I have to tell her no.

Even if most of them are bone pickers now, I know there's at least five bullies left, and I'm not getting caught by them this time.

* * *

THE ASH GETS THICKER. VOICES SCRAPING AT THE END OF THE BARRACKS WHERE the doors are bricked over and DuPonte's watchtower lab was.

Not anymore.

And neither is he. He won't stop Navy from getting her credit now. If I live long enough, I'll kill Pike too. Then no one will get in her way.

One-forty-three.

The wall gapes open, collapsed when the watchtower did. Smoke stains on the remaining stone like ghosts. The sun's low enough they won't notice us here in the shadow of the rubble unless they really look.

They've collected two boxes of what's left. Charred glass that didn't burst, books. Kane, Millard, and the marshal.

Millard sifts through a drawer of ash, clumps of unburned paper layered between black flakes.

Kane paces the sliver of the room that's not covered in debris. "We should leave. We all need to leave. It was too soon. We never should have brought people here until his antidote was ready."

"Damnation." Millard pinches the ash pages to powder with his fingers. "What a waste."

"I wish I had been told about the isolation chamber experiments," Kane says. "How many men were actually infected and hauled up here in the middle of the night while you let me think they were disappearing without explanation? I wrote the death letters to their families."

"You were here with DuPonte many times."

"You told me to stay out of his way. You must have had some idea this could get out of hand. It's why you really agreed to buy the Exodus munitions, isn't it?"

"Those were to protect the railroad camp. At your request, did you forget? You were right, it would have looked irresponsible to lose another full camp of workmen."

"Bastard," Aunt Tess hisses.

"How many?" Kane asks again but Millard doesn't answer. "This is our fault."

"It's not your fault."

"Are you saying it's your fault, then? Father...I know you asked Horne to falsify reports of the pestilence's contamination on my first expedition. That's why you didn't tell me who he was, not because a rival company might be spying on us."

"Who told you that?"

"Father, how could you?"

"I asked you a question."

Kane hesitates. "Adelaide and Leagan."

"Have you considered that they lied?" Millard says. "You decided easily enough to disguise your name the first time you were here, and that deception didn't bother you."

"This is *very* different,"

"That fox has got your eyes wrapped in her hex too," the marshal says. "You know they can control you mind, boy."

Kane halts, close enough to hit him even though he wouldn't. "I'm not your boy."

"And I'm not an ass-fucking Rim picker. I'm like you. I did my service to the Republic. I didn't believe it at first either." The marshal's glare becomes something sinister, burning in my gut like vinegar. "Just stories. But she was in Caroline for barely a day, and that town lost its mind. Good men who would never debase themselves with violence like I witnessed. It was a fucking bloodbath. Now I have to believe something drove them mad."

Yes, but not me.

Millard doesn't correct him. Is this the sort of *farce* they actually teach at the University? Navy's better off never going there. "No one was ever in any danger."

"That's not true, and you know it," Kane says. "People are in danger. Right now. And if the bloodbath in Caroline actually happened the way he says it did, that shopkeeper's little boy—"

"He's dead," Millard says. Blank. "He's been dead for a day already. There's no worrying about him anymore."

Kane's voice thins. "How?"

"The mother. She hasn't been well. You didn't let me finish, son. No one was ever in any true danger until the Reveres showed their faces. I have no doubts now that Reverend Seed was a machination of their design. Green was a snake oil dealer as well, and their feud just cost us everything DuPonte's been working for."

Evangeline walks away, but I stay. Aunt Tess stays.

"You think this fire was set on purpose?" Kane says.

"I can see nothing is an accident when these people are involved. But that's being dealt with too. We can be glad we got the charter signed by the townsmen. As soon as you and DuPonte sign it—" Millard's tongue slurs, steadies. "That fool Jonathaniel Swann's likely to never be found, or maybe he ran home like a coward. I didn't raise you to a coward, my son."

"Father, you don't seem like yourself. A child is dead, and we can't—"

"I'm not myself? How would you know that? Do I go around telling you how to be?"

"I'm only asking because I care. If you need to rest—"

"Don't tell me what to do." The glass instrument is thin, piercing as it shatters.

Kane flinches. Barely noticeable, but I do.

"Are you female?"

"I'm sorry." Kane backs away. "What do you want me to do? We shouldn't stay here much longer. The sun's almost down and the dark seems to agitate them."

Them.

"You two carry these boxes back to the house for the doctor," Millard says. "Let us pray he can salvage something. You'll work out a way to get us back our horses."

"It's not too late to send everyone home and try again another Season," Kane says.

Yes it is.

I have to get back to Leagan and Navy.

"Do as I say, boy," Millard sneers. "We have no need for cowards here if we're going to get out alive. Think of your poor mother. She's already chairbound for the remainder of her life, do you want her to be a widow and childless?"

There are worse things to be.

"Of course not," Kane says.

"Then be the man I need right now."

"Yes, sir."

"Asshole." Aunt Tess says.

Nine.

"They have horses here somewhere," I whisper. "We'll get them first. From whoever has them."

Aunt Tess nods, but Evangeline shakes her head.

"Eat and rest first. We'll find somewhere safe enough," she says. "I won't argue with either of you."

SEVENTY-NINE
ADELAIDE

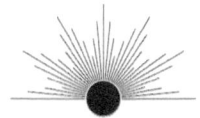

The way Grandma told it, my mother chose my name on her own. But I think she had some influence over the choice, that she knew there'd be nights like tonight that I'd need to wrap the Stranger around me like a ghost's skin and fade. Nothing but a nightmare.

I keep to the shadows, the deepest ones. Parallel to the hill where the Wells house sits, darkness eating its way down.

I hear them first. Laughter that chitters like wings, then keening wails, male voices.

Four-fifty.

A hunched shape darts past one of the corners.

I pull back, step on Aunt Tess's foot.

Something else scrapes on fallen debris out there among the sagging walls. The darkness is watching. Each blank window looks back at me, and I don't pass in front of any open doorways. The hunger, waiting for the next weak fool it will inhabit.

Mine has settled in my limbs, making them shake.

The first sliver of the Season Moon pokes out from behind the ridge, staining the atmosphere around it. Red, looming.

I need to be up high. The ground isn't safe.

Six-twenty-one.

The Stranger chooses the building. A once-boarding house I've been inside before. A tin full of old cigarettes shoved into a crack in the stonework, glass things still filling the kitchen cupboards. Pretty glass, lots of colors, patterns under the dust. The top floor has one window big enough to stand in, a choice someone from the east would make, not knowing the storms here. But as long as we keep away from it and don't light any quartz, no one should see us.

The sound picks up slowly. Someone rhythmically beats a spoon through a metal pot. A dinner call. Dull red light makes shadows rise up walls. A lantern covered with a cloth.

It passes.

"Here." Evangeline opens one of the tins we collected and passes it to me with a few crackers. Fish and cabbage stewed in some kind of muddied oil. If I don't breathe while it's in my mouth I can get it down.

"Do you smell that?" Aunt Tess whispers, scowling at the dancing shadows, sweat on her upper lip. "Something died nearby."

"Not while she's trying to eat," Evangeline scolds. "You should eat too."

"Oh I'm not eating that. I'll wait until we make it back to the *Exodus*."

It's the water I realize I'm the most starved for. If I'm not careful, there won't be any left for Aunt Tess.

The Stranger snaps at another disembodied clatter outside, my limbs flinching in response.

"It's okay." Evangeline holds my shoulder. "I've got an eye on the door."

I take one more drink to drown the taste of the fish, then pass the canteen to Aunt Tess while it's still half-full.

She uncaps the top and gags. "Oh, *krossus*. You drank this? Stranger! This was standing water for sure. Enjoy your dysentery."

I reach and she gives the canteen back to me.

All I smell in the water is tin.

No.

"Dump that out right now," she says.

My stomach clenches, scar tissue splitting back open. Vesta, her black curls wild, sticking to her face. Her stare as she emptied that glass of water onto Pike's floor.

That fish is going to taste worse coming back up than it did going down.

You already know.

I can't do this. "Aunt Tess?"

It's there. In her eye.

Blood.

EIGHTY
TESLA

THIS CAN'T BE HAPPENING.

"I'm still me."

For now.

Vacca voya, what a nasty little voice that was.

I reach for her and Adelaide recoils, gray eyes frozen wide. The sting rakes across my heart, sharp as the breath in her throat, a rejection that will haunt me for however long I have left to live now.

"Evan?" I sound so scared. "Is she wrong?"

"She's not wrong…I'm so sorry, my little darling."

"I'm still me. You can still trust me." I search for a mirror, anything glass or reflective in this room to see this for myself even though she's never wrong. "We've been so careful, this isn't right…" My gaze drops to the red marks inside the crook of my elbow. A needle could have made them. "That crazy fucking doctor. This is his fault, I know it."

My mind flashes back to Hannah, Montoya's poisonous blade slicing through my skin shortly after I watched its first victim convulse to death. I never wanted to taste this fear again. I want to die in my own bed someday far from now. I don't want to suffer, call me a coward, but no one does.

Adelaide stares through me, like I'm already gone. The Stranger has risen up around her, I believe that's how she's described it. The Adelaide who cares about me is still here somewhere, but the hair that's stood up on my arms and neck doesn't know the difference, and the pain of watching her turn on me is a vivid wound.

"Don't leave me here." In this moment, I feel so old and yet so very young at the same time. I didn't come all this way to die unfinished. I don't lose, I always find a way. That's who I am. "Please don't abandon me now. I'm still here."

Adelaide blinks, pulling out of the crack she slipped into. "I wouldn't." Her voice is as pale as her. "This is what happened to Vesta."

I cover my mouth, biting back the heartbreak and horror clawing for control of me.

"I didn't leave her."

"We will never leave you," Evan says. At least she doesn't pull away when I try to hug her.

"You won't know it's happening," Adelaide says. "When you turn."

Not yet, that nasty voice speaks again.

"But I know right now. So I haven't. Pray for me, Evan."

Evangeline places both her hands on my head. They're trembling by the end of the Sister's Prayer.

"It's not my time to go." I force myself to breathe. "I don't allow it."

Evangeline's face tells the truth. She doesn't fully agree, but she's too kind to take away my self-solace. Denial is a beautiful creature sometimes, and even the best of us have doubts. Like her. She is one of the best souls I have ever known.

"We will find a way out of here," I promise Adelaide. "Now I'm going to stop crying, and you both stop. I'm not going to die. Let's go, we're getting back to your sisters. Whatever it takes."

EIGHTY-ONE
ADELAIDE

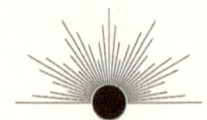

Dusk has settled. Night is here.

The fire quartz lantern barely smolders, half buried in a pile of torn limbs, still sleeved in their Green Company uniforms. Who really knows how deep the grave is unless I dig them out, and I'm not going to. Flies knock into my face and arms, unbothered that I'm here.

Aunt Tess catches her leg on something, and Evangeline stops to help, lifts a loose board to keep it from clapping against another.

I wish I could look at her without seeing Vesta, decay in her eyes, her breath. And I'm back with the same horrible decision, the one I couldn't face last time: If I leave her to rot, she has to die alone. If I stay, I have to watch.

You don't abandon someone you love.

How many times have I thought that about my mother? It's the only thing I wish I could tell her.

Eighty-nine.

The flies thicken again, brushing up against my neck like they know I'm next. More rotten meat.

Would it be abandonment if I'm the one to leave, to spare my family the agony of watching me die?

If I die here, tonight, I won't have to decide.

Stop it.

She's right. I don't want that, either.

Two bone pickers. Live ones. They're carrying armfuls of sticks and dead cacti into a house with only two standing walls. The drawers and cupboards of what was the kitchen bristle with collected brush, like a nest.

The rooftops aren't close enough together here to use them as a second street like I did in Hannah. We have to be down here, on the ground with them.

I crouch behind a wagon, overturned and half-buried. The carcass is strung up by its neck like a feed bag, dripping flies. Clumps of hair and severed hooves, bits of entrails and blood smeared on the fenceposts. Two scavenger lizards rip at what's left of another horse, ribs still sticky with sinew pointing up at the first stars. Another scurries off with a strip of intestine in its serrated teeth. They aren't afraid of the disjointed voices in the air.

"Shit..." the word leaves Aunt Tess like air.

"We'll need to come up with another plan," Evangeline whispers.

"I'm thinking," Aunt Tess says.

I need to get up off the street. See Eden from above for a minute, give the Stranger a better look at what's out here.

One-fifty-six.

It's still intact. The sky barrel and the ladder rising to the platform like a spine.

"It sounds like Kane and Millard are at least a little fortified up there at the big house," Aunt Tess says. "Let's go meet them."

"It's as good of a plan as any," Evangeline agrees.

A horse whinnies. Not at the Wells house, toward the front wall.

I stop, rust grabbing at my palms. "Listen. Did you hear that?"

"Alkaline," Aunt Tess says. "Where are you going?"

"To look."

"Well, be fast."

The structure moves like the floating diver docks in Lideon, but I'm already committed.

Twenty-seven.

They have the front gate.

Two long arms of debris squeeze Eden's main street, funneling anyone who wants out into a man-made box canyon. Dull orange spots prowl a rooftop above the neck of the choke point and the wall itself. The cross alleys, any holes the crumbled outer wall, all of those are sealed.

EIGHTY-TWO
TESLA

Adelaide takes us to a house that looks down on the blockade with stairs that haven't eroded. Climbing was never my specialty even when I had two arms.

They've used it all to build this trap, wood and ore, rocks and bodies squirming with maggots. On the other side of the mound blocking the gate, penned in behind cracked wood, they have two horses. Live ones.

I hate their foresight, but this is how you make it on the Rim. You see something of value and exploit it.

There's someone lurking inside the building across the street from us. I know because that's where Adelaide keeps looking.

"We might as well just start shooting." I start to lean out the window, but Evangeline grabs me.

"We don't have enough ammunition for this," Adelaide says.

"You're right." I wasn't thinking about that. "I guess we could negotiate."

Acrid smoke burns past my nostrils, making the ache in my tight gums worse.

"Do you smell that?"

Adelaide lifts a finger to the hilltop behind me. The Wells built their mansion up there like they're better than everyone else. They thought they were, just like the Von Kanes do.

Well, I imagine things are not so nice or cozy up there anymore now there are flames eating at one wall and the roof about to come down on them.

Evangeline looks on with concern. "That's going to spread like—"

"Like pestilence," I say.

"They don't have to know we're here," Evangeline says to Adelaide. "Is there another way out?"

"No," I say. "We need those horses."

"I don't think it's worth the risk."

"There is," Adelaide says. "But it's up there." She points to the Wells mansion, then to our left where the darkness stretches untouched. "And that way."

"I think we should take our chances with that—" Only one of Evangeline's legs plunges through the soft floor. Maybe my scream was a little overreactive, but I couldn't help it.

She's able to pull herself out and returns to the portion of the room already proven capable of holding us. They'll come for us at any moment now. Well, I'm ready.

"We need those horses." Why won't they listen to me? They're our only shot.

I laugh, because that's funny.

God of Mercy, I'm so hungry.

Mother used to buy Liza and me nectarines for breakfast on our birthdays. We'd eat them on pancakes or sometimes raw. I still remember how the skin felt, smooth and tight, holding in the juice underneath.

That's what I'm hungry for.

EIGHTY-THREE
ADELAIDE

Evangeline grabs Aunt Tess's wrist, trying to pry her palm away from her mouth but her teeth pull skin with them. "Tesla Revere, let go!" The slap cracks, a dish snapping in two.

Aunt Tess holds her stung cheek, shock registering in her jasper eye and the red one.

"I love you." Evangeline grips her shoulders, knuckles glaring through skin.

"Thank you." The sob flutters Aunt Tess's lips, it craws up my throat but I stamp it down. She looks like herself again. "You can slap me anytime."

But the trace of blood smeared on her cheek won't let me forget what I just saw. Her teeth going into her palm heel like a piece of fruit.

She's turning so much faster than Vesta did. Than me.

I might be the only one making it out of here alive.

For how long?

"Come on," Evangeline says. "We've used up enough time."

The bottom step creaks.

The Stranger flares.

I wave them to the back of the room so whoever comes up, we'll see them before they have a chance to turn and see us.

Twelve.

"Trade me." I offer Evangeline the revolver even though the Stranger doesn't like giving anything away.

She unshoulders the tranquilizer gun. I take a breath, pump the action. It snaps louder in the darkness than it would in the day, but I don't have a choice.

No matter how many times I try to rub them dry, my hands are still too sweaty.

"Who's up there?" the man calls, too sweet. "We know you're here. We've heard you. Come out now, or we might have to come for you."

The Stranger drips between the bannisters, a nosebleed, each breath pinching.

The fire gives him an outline. Head, neck…

Now.

EIGHTY-FOUR
TESLA

Vacca voya, I can breathe again.

The body finishes slipping down the stairs with the grace of a potato sack, sticking on the bottom step where Adelaide steals his gun.

We make it out the back door, the blockade forcing us through the overgrown crosshatching between buildings. That fire is a greedy bitch, grabbing onto everything in its path, drowning out the stars. My shadow grows long.

Adelaide gets ahead, Kane and the marshal don't see her as they round the corner. They see us.

The pop comes from Adelaide and the tranquilizer rifle. It's softer than a powder gunshot by a mile, but Kane still flinches aside, firing blind shots as the marshal drops next to him. He's not dead, just asleep.

"Take a breath," Evangeline warns him.

Kane turns to finds himself facing Adelaide's barrel now. "I'm sorry."

"Well now they're coming for us," I say. "Get back. I've never wanted to shoot you, little Von Kane, but I will."

"I didn't mean to shoot at you. I'm sorry." But his gun hovers a moment longer before he brings it down. "I didn't know you were here."

"Oh, of course not."

Adelaide gives him a steely appraisal, the shadows cutting along her cheekbones darker than they should be facing the light fire. I swear I taste the rage that floods through her jaw.

She slowly shoulders the tranquilizer rifle and lifts the bully's revolver. The fresh gunpowder tang flares sharper even as it's smoke trail clears.

Pity the men that stand in her way. Not really though, they always deserve it.

Now the bully is dead.

"Why?" Kane demands. "He was one of us."

"He wasn't one of us," I say. "We're leaving. Are you going to try and stop us?"

"No...I don't want to be here either."

We've been given one last black gold opportunity, and I seize it. I grab the other revolver from Evangeline and shove it under his chin. Sweat and metal burn in the bite on my hand. "Why should we let you go? You didn't hear the news from your father? We're all going to be tried and executed for murder and arson when the town charter gets notarized in Jezebel."

"I don't care about that," he says.

"Well, we do."

"I don't care who you killed here tonight or what you set on fire. I won't tell. It's not our biggest problem anymore."

"Maybe not for you," I say. "Maybe we need some leverage. Where's your father?"

His sharp inhale makes me flinch, but not enough to lose my grip on the revolver. "What's wrong with your eye?"

There aren't enough curse words in existence for how unfair this fucking world is. It doesn't get to defeat me. "We aren't talking about that."

"Adelaide?"

She refuses to look at him. "We're not talking about that."

"We set nothing on fire," Evangeline says. "This was someone else's doing."

"I will let you go." Kane ignores the kiss of metal on his throat and takes hold of my shoulders. "I will testify as a character witness on your behalf, as long as you to promise to come back with horses for me and my father. I can't find him, and I'm not leaving until I do."

"Your father's already dead," Adelaide says.

Now it's *his* turn to avoid her gaze because she's right.

"Do you promise?" he asks.

"Fuck your father," I say. "He doesn't love you as much as he loves himself. And he never will."

Kane winces.

"You will likely die if you stay here," Evangeline says. "You should come now, as well. There's no reason both of you should die."

He hesitates, and there are tears in his eyes. I recognize the same things tearing inside him that ripped me when I had to leave Mother's body behind. Fuck, I do pity him.

I pass the revolver back to Evangeline. I don't trust myself with it. "Survival isn't heroic or kind, Von Kane. It's not like a book. It's dirty. And everyone here learns that the hard way. You are not a coward if you leave right now to save yourself, but you are absolutely a fool if you stay."

EIGHTY-FIVE
ADELAIDE

ONE GREEN COMPANY BULLY PACES THE BOX, A SEVERED LEG IN HIS HAND LIKE a strolling cane.

Six men, nine guns.

Aunt Tess stands close enough I smell her, and her skirt touches me whenever the wind blows through. So why do I feel so alone?

I should be glad for my last time with her before we both rot, but she already feels gone to me. All I can think about are Leagan and Navy, how I'm probably never going to see them again.

I'm less of a liar than a thief.

I'm afraid to die. It doesn't matter how many times I've thought I might.

Everyone is.

Everyone will.

Even me.

"Let me handle this." Kane's shirt looks like the tattered Republic of Delilah flag caught up in the piled beams, dirty and defeated as he steps into the ambient quartz light.

I wouldn't walk out there, but he always does the opposite of what I'd do.

The Green Company bullies take aim. "A man like you shouldn't be out this far on your own."

The Stranger crackles in my skin like the dry wood bursting in the fire behind me.

"Stand down, it's me, Timothy Von Kane."

"We thought you were dead."

"No, still alive. The wind is spreading that fire, we can't stay here anymore."

"No one leaves for free."

"Have you seen my father?"

"Oh, fuck your father," Aunt Tess sneers. "I've heard just about enough of him."

Eden is a mouth full of empty sockets where people can hide. Everything the firelight catches on turns into shadows and movement. But I saw them on the roof earlier. The Stranger still feels them, on the one we're standing under.

I point up.

Aunt Tess nods.

"We wasted enough time doing it your way, Von Kane," the one on the wall to the left calls. "Scouring this shithell day and night trying to collect that doctor's mess like scavengers. We're not doing it your way anymore. If you want out, what do you have to offer us in return?"

"I'm sorry we failed you," Kane says. "I need you to stand down for a minute, I have some women with me—"

"Well now we can negotiate."

Eighteen.

"That's not what I meant," Kane says. "I'm going to bring them through, then you can do whatever you think is best with the rest of Eden."

There, crouched at the empty window, the sill coming up to his neck.

One.

The dart sticks in his neck like a mosquito, but the tranquilizer's action jams. Empty.

I pick up his Exodus rifle instead.

"You women actually want to make yourselves useful for once? Get over here and earn your passage through."

"I might consider it," Aunt Tess says. "But I want those horses too."

"No," Kane says.

"You're not the boss of me," she says.

"I guess you don't want out that badly," the bully says. "Or are you just too good to share?"

A ladder propped against the wall goes up to the roof.

"It's been lonelier than hell out here and none of them have been working. I don't know what you girls do all day, but if you were wifed to someone or had a baby on that hip, you'd have my protection free."

"Say that to my face, darling," Aunt Tess calls. "Since you're so useful."

"Why don't you get over here and say that to my face since you're so brave, *darling*," he sneers back. "You want horses? You mean these ones?" He shoves his arm through a gap in the cage.

A horse screams as his gun fires. The other one tears through the jagged boards out the other side, leaving part of its tail behind.

Run. Leave us here, it doesn't matter.

"Shit!" Aunt Tess yells.

"You should have been earning your share of the water by opening your legs once in a while, Revere. There's no place for lazy bitches out here."

"Not another word," Kane snaps.

"Even you, fox. I can close my eyes. I'm sure you'll feel the same."

"Stranger," Aunt Tess calls. "Put the biggest hole right through his face."

The bully stands on the precipice of the rooftop.

I shove with both hands.

His scream cuts like a string on the ground.

I line up my first shot, aim for the bully's chest, not his head at this distance.

But I'm not Leagan. My hands weave under the weight of the rifle, full of exhaustion and rage. Even though I feel it happening, I can't make them stop.

I shoot again.

You're too far away.

Seconds. That's all it takes for the bully to drop the severed leg and cross the gap to Kane sprinting. It's why knife fights are so dangerous. The two of them roll on the ground, grunts after body blows.

The fire is a solid wall eating what's left of Eden, inching toward us like a sunset. I'm glad it's burning. Now no one else can come here and dig through it after me.

"Get your hands dirty, Von Kane," Aunt Tess calls. "Kill him."

Thirty-seven.

The Stranger spills over the debris filling the gate, itching for a way to get loose. It's woven too tight to pull apart. That would take too long. We're not getting through it. The way out is over.

I've always known I would die a bloody death. It wasn't in Winchester, it wasn't in Hannah. Maybe it is at the hands of these men.

Better now than later because I can't take the pestilence down with me when I go, but I can take these fuckers.

I close myself and let the Stranger out.

EIGHTY-SIX
TESLA

MOTHER SAW SOMETHING AS SHE DIED.

Right now, I ask myself again, is this it?

Adelaide stalks out into the open arms of the box trap, raising a rifle.

The Green bullies on top of the wall stagger over the sides, the shots piling on top of one another. She marches right past Kane, ignoring him grappling with the bully on the ground, ignoring the shots firing past her.

"Help him, he'll be good leverage." I knock on Evangeline's back. "I'll cover you."

"What about her?"

"I think she's okay. I can cover both of you. Go."

"Just remember if you run out of shots, you won't have the time to reload on your own."

I hate that. "Yes, I know. I won't waste them."

"Go." I fire into one of the windows I think I saw a muzzle flash from.

Evangeline pulls out of her sprint early enough to plant both feet, then smash a heel into the bully's head, knocking him off center so Kane can escape the chokehold. She rolls her shoulders, ready for him to stand up.

"Finish him," I yell at Kane and give him two more cover shots to do so.

But he doesn't. Of course not. That would be the fucking sensible.

"We are leaving." Kane backs away, the defensive cuts on his arms and hands shimmering. "Let us go."

"Like hell you are." The bully draws a punch knife from his boot and Evangeline shoots him down.

Two windows in the same upper story erupt with flashes. Evangeline misses a step, a thin groan escaping her. My rage is immediate.

"Fuck you!" I yell squeezing the trigger on the last bullets in my chamber.

She picks up her pace again. A bullet doesn't stop someone like her.

A bone picker crawls over the arm of debris on all fours. This one is infected, bruises running in the skin all over his face, and the crawling, obviously that's not normal.

"Look out, Tess!" Evangeline takes aim.

I reverse my hold, the metal barrel searing into my palm like a promise. I will club him if her bullets aren't good enough to stop this monstrosity. But they are.

One last shot from Adelaide rips the night.

A final body falls from the wall, colliding with the dust and all we're left with is the fire. The quiet almost hurts more because I actually feel my ears ringing.

The dull, rubber feeling creeps up my legs. It's almost nice as long as I don't trip on something. "Evan, you're hurt. What do you need?"

"I'm fine."

I examine her ribs, but I can't find the blood anymore.

"Tess." She gathers up my hand. "I'm not hurt. We need to leave."

I'm starting to understand why Adelaide is so frustrated with Kane, and it's not unresolved sexual tension. "I am not impressed with your honor, sir." If he'd gotten Evan killed, I just might have snapped and had to shoot him. Then everything would be ruined. "Next time, kill the bastard or I'll let him kill you." My breath tastes bad. "Let's just go."

Kane forges past Adelaide. A tremor flickers through her skin like the dappling of leaves distorting sunlight, down from her eyes and passing through her shoulders only to dead end in her hands. She almost turns then doesn't.

Kane gets to the pile of debris where a partial ladder still clings to the stone wall. He offers his laced hands to Adelaide, but she doesn't step forward.

"Someone has to go first, it might as well be you."

"You go ahead," I tell her. "He's not wrong."

He boosts her just high enough to grab the lowest rung, but she still has to step on his shoulder to start climbing.

He decides I'm next, for obvious reasons.

"That's not going to work for me. I'll find another way."

"Your turn then," Evangeline braces her back against the wall and squats low to offset Kane's weight. "I'll go with her."

The pile clogging the gate is not as unsteady as I worried, but it does move each time I do. Halfway up, my skirt hooks on the end of a board. I yank too hard and slip, falling into Evangeline and skinning the top layer off my arms.

"Careful," Kane calls.

His voice makes me want to vomit. "Shut up."

Adelaide lays on her stomach, catching me under the arms. Suddenly her head snaps up. "Behind you."

Three or five of them, I can't tell, spill out of the funnel Green's fools turned the street into. They start climbing the pile, a couple of them just tearing at it in blind panic. The whole base shifts under me.

"Shit." Fabric rips as I tear my skirt free of the exposed nails. "Pull me up!"

I hear screaming but it could just be the fire consuming different surfaces. Sweat actually drips out of my armpits but suddenly my feet touch dirt on the other side. I thought I'd never make it.

I collapse against the stonework, laugh sobbing.

"Not yet, my friend." Evangeline doesn't let me sit, but I need it. My legs are on fire.

"Are you okay?" Kane asks.

"She took in too much smoke."

Her knuckles rake down my sternum.

I'm not a washboard, I try to scream at her, but the bone-on-bone pain snaps me back into my body. "Please stop. You're hurting me."

She turns my face with a calloused palm. "Back to the *Exodus* or the *Absolution*?"

It's a test to see if I'm still with us.

"The *Exodus*. Fuck, those were likely the last live horses in Eden and now we're going to have to walk a long ways to get somewhere even close to her." But maybe I should be glad. Each step on the uneven terrain through ungoverned sage jars my bones, grounding me here.

I am still me, Tesla fucking Revere, I have a plan, and I won't be forgetting that any time soon.

I take Adelaide's cold hand and lean in.

Her arm tenses like she almost pulled away instead of looking at me. It's the almosts that haunt hardest.

"I think I saw her, just for a moment. Were you thinking about killing him?"

She doesn't answer.

"I'm so sorry about what was said back there," Kane says. "They didn't seem like themselves."

"That's what a mutiny looks like, Von Kane. You think those were the worst things we've ever heard said about us?" I ask, then look for Adelaide and Evangeline's confirmations. "Oh, I promise you it's not."

"Good men don't act like this."

"Maybe they weren't good men, then. They just knew how to look like them."

These ideas about women have been with us for so long, we don't even know where they came from, but just because an idea has been around forever doesn't make it true. Unfortunately, most men never bother to realize that.

"Maybe you are one of the few who truly are good, but the rest of you are only that way when there's consequences. This is the beauty and the savage of the desert, Timothy Von Kane." My God of Mercy, the moonlight is so pretty, burned orange by the smoke while the red Season Moon is almost erased by it. "Out here, everything you are gets laid bare and set free."

"That's so sad."

"It is. So be part of making a better world, stop pretending this is one."

EIGHTY-SEVEN
ADELAIDE

THE FIRE CONSUMING EDEN WOULD ONLY BE MORE SATISFYING IF I STARTED IT. The Stranger pulls me to the edge of the rock outcropping to watch it burn. She's pleased with it, aches with it.

Everything that was there is safe now. No one else can have it.

Everything that was there doesn't exist anymore.

The flames list past the wall and taste the brittle grass on the other side. They like it. Easy to eat.

"Ah, progress, and the undoing of it," Aunt Tess says.

"It's in the brush," Evangeline says. "It's going to burn faster now. If this wind turns toward us, we won't have a chance. It could be down this hill in minutes."

I can't look away. My body is too heavy.

Kane starts walking.

Aunt Tess was right. The Stranger was going to kill him tonight. I'm still not sure why she didn't.

A full hand of lightning flays the dark sky, but no thunder.

Five-fifteen—My step veers left, boot slipping off uneven rock.

"Is everything okay?" Kane asks.

"Everything's not okay," Aunt Tess snaps. "That psychotic doctor of yours siphoned all the blood out of her."

Don't tell him that. I almost say it to her. But she's not my Aunt Tess anymore.

They're coming. The Stranger shocks me back into myself.

I look back, see nothing except the red line of fire eating away at the Rim as I swerve off our current path.

"What?" Aunt Tess calls this time.

A horse whinnies.

The animals canters out of the brush from either side. Through us, knocking Aunt Tess and Evangeline to the ground. Another horse dances in the foreground where night overtakes what I can see. Gray-green outlines in the dark.

Three more.

The rider jumps from his saddle, grabs Aunt Tess by the hair even though another one already has her arm pinned back.

"Run!" she screams.

Evangeline manages to slip the knife at her throat, just a slice on her neck and chin. She slams her body into them.

Eight.

The knife I picked in the barracks plunges into his stomach, like they did to Raleigh. The handle is instantly too slick, ripped out of my grasp as he staggers back.

It is true what they say.

You don't hear the gunshot that hits you. You feel the impact. The Stranger goes cold, the shock of the poisonous water splicing me all over again. Vesta all over again. Hannah. All the places I've fractured.

Red. It splatters my shoulder in a constellation, runs like an itch down my right arm. My strong arm.

The Stranger reels back. Picks out the man who shot me.

The glare on his face falters as mine meets it. The fear that sparks in his eyes covers up the burn coursing down my arm, up into my neck.

Millard grabs hold of the barrel. The bully lets it go and Millard's shot goes through his back as he runs from me.

The bully I stabbed left the knife in. The wound won't bleed as much this way. Everyone knows this, so I don't have to worry about him using it on me.

Eleven.

He shoves me away, arm straight.

I use my sleeve, grab the wet handle.

Now bleed.

The rope lands around my shoulders. I try to slip out of it, but the bully rips out the slack, the lasso clenching around my knees.

The impact vibrates, the kind that leaves a bruise, bone deep.

"Stop." Kane lunges for me, grabbing at the noose while the bully drags me. "She's bleeding."

I try to sit up. Pain cuts through my right shoulder, so violent it takes my breath away. I miss my chance to slice the rope. The bully jerks again, rocks raking through my side.

You let go.

The knife glints, just out of reach where it fell from my hand.

I can't lift my right arm.

The rope contracts again. I barely save my head from bouncing off the rock, sticks peeling through my skin.

Kane lunges at him. "Stop this."

"She was going to stab you, son," Millard's voice rings out of the darkness.

"No, she wasn't."

"Your mind isn't right. She's got a hold on you. You can't be trusted anymore. Take him."

The last two bullies march at Kane. He wavers between them both, waits too long to decide what's going to happen and what he should do about it. They grab his arms. The body blow stuns him. An elbow swings.

The bully winds in the last few feet of rope. I get my knees and left arm under me.

His heel gets past the Stranger, into my side, shoves. Something along my collarbone pops.

Black.

The stony ground grinds across my chin.

A thin hum in my head. Slow.

Iron.

It fades, replaced with something worse. Pain.

My arms fold back, someone's knee in my spine as they finish locking the steel cuffs, haul me up. The gasp strangles me.

There's no stopping it. My stomach comes up.

"You're hurting her," Kane says.

They're not going to listen to him.

Millard gets too close. The Stranger spills over his ears, into his nose, but the decay drips off his breath. "Get your fox mind-rot out of my son."

If any of you are going to kill me, I won't let it be you.

"Father!" Kane yells. "Did you forget I was still in there?" He bleeds from the mouth, wrists cuffed to his belt in front of him. "Eden was burning. I tried to find you."

He still can't say what he really means: *You left me.*

He still thinks they aren't going to really hurt him. Or else he'd fight harder.

He'll kill you. Like Piety Goodson killed her son, like Zachariah Wells killed his wife, and Ruthaline Wells killed her daughter.

"You found your way," Millard says. "I raised a resourceful boy."

"Let me go. Let them go. Father, please. This isn't who we are."

It is now.

Aunt Tess's laughter rings out. Too loud. Feral.

They have her wrist peeled back and tied around her waist. The same rope connects her to Evangeline, then both of them to the horse's saddle horn.

"Have you been in many battles, Miss Revere?" Millard calls, boisterous, slurring.

"Have you...*Colonel*? Lead us to greatness."

"You've earned yourself this..." He trails into nothing, tongue grabbing at sounds. "At sunrise, you'll be executed for your crimes."

"Fuck you," Aunt Tess spits.

"Father, no." There are tears in Kane's eyes, but I won't assume they're for me. They're for him. "You can't do that."

"Be quiet, Timothy."

"Without a trial this isn't justice—"

Millard backhands him across the face. "You're worthless."

EIGHTY-EIGHT
ADELAIDE

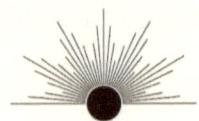

THE STRANGER LOCKS AROUND MY JAW LIKE A MUZZLE, KEEPING THE PAIN inside. Blood from the bullet in my shoulder has made it to my ribs.

The saddle jabs into my spine, Millard's rotting back sweat already leaking into me. He threads my cuffs through his belt, then buckles it around his waist again.

His horse protests as Millard jabs his heels into its sides, but without any clear direction it just reels in a circle. A compass during Moon Season. Pain spreads across my chest and shoulder like fire, bone deep.

Dust swirls through the air, coating my tongue, grinding its way into my eyes.

"The storm is closing in," one of the bullies says. "We should go."

"Follow me." Millard still can't steer the horse around, almost knocking over Aunt Tess at the end of the other rope. "Get what's left of my son on that horse. The rest of you walk…If you murderesses don't want your final hours to be spent dragged behind a horse, then don't fall."

The Stranger feels oddly dull, a shadow in the distance. No reaction, but I'm not giving up.

This is going to hurt. A lot.

As Millard's horse turns another aimless circle, I throw my weight in the same direction.

Millard weighs too much, even caught off guard. He doesn't fall. All I do is make myself dry heave, nothing left to come up. Sweat pours from under my hair and arms, each breath shallow, stolen.

The Stranger doesn't warn me in time. Millard's rein tails snap against my face.

"Stop that, you white devil," he growls. "Now walk!"

I pull the Stranger around me like a blanket, but she's gray, not black. I don't go numb inside her like I usually can. The pain stays.

Am I losing her?

What will happen to her when I die?

EIGHTY-NINE
TESLA

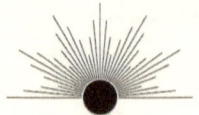

"The sun is peeling, just like an orange. So am I. So are you. Everything peels off. None of you are listening to me. I said it. My daughter's name was Vesta. I do remember that. She had lovely black curls that snapped back when you pulled them. God, this wretched water. I smell it from here. I want to remember. I do. I remember, but I forgot. Mother, please. My teeth hurt. My teeth hurt. I said, *my teeth hurt!*"

NINETY
ADELAIDE

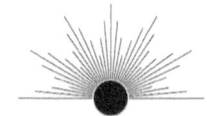

MILLARD FOLLOWS THE GAP BETWEEN HILLS, FAR PAST THE MAIN MINE. ALL night.

Just a little bit farther and I'll be able to see down the other side. But each time I'm sure we're at the top, the land buckles upward again.

The wind is a constant voice brushing the trees, between rocks, like the bone scraping bone in my shoulder. Aunt Tess finally stops talking to the air. Her teeth hurt, my chest hurts.

The Stranger digs into my spine, jolting me from a blankness I didn't realize I was in.

Millard stops the horse.

The valley below glows white, bare as a bone.

Salt. Crystalized in lines that sparkle on the rocks where the wind's blown through, same as the sweat dried on my lips. Dawn spills over the mountainside. Gold and pink.

I wish I wasn't going to die. I want to see more.

Millard unbuckles his belt. "You can walk now, *Adelaide*. Someone get her down."

I'm too weak to run. He must know it too.

My shirt sticks as my back peels from his.

There's blood all the way down to my waist. It's on the horse too. My head throbs, throat too dry to need to swallow. My heartbeat flutters right at the apex of it, choking my ability to take a full breath.

They fix a rope to my cuffs and hand it up to Millard.

Two...

My lead legs want to collapse, but I'm not giving these bone pickers that. No.

Seven-fifty-five.

My first step on the waste cracks, the crust shattering into fragments. The salt clay underneath is packed solid, like Millard's back touching me all night.

The air is already warm enough it doesn't move even though the wind is blowing. Morning isn't usually this sharp, glass to my eyes and skin. I shouldn't be in the sun.

The horse snorts, jaw fighting as Millard yanks her bit. "Let justice be done this day."

"Let her go," Aunt Tess rasps. She looks like herself in this moment, even though her lips split open while she talks. "Evangeline is the Sister of Damascus, serving the God of Mercy. She's not with us. She hasn't done anything." Her jaw trembles, but she lifts it up anyway. "You can have me, mother fucker."

"It's all right," Evangeline says. "I don't have to be afraid of death. I know where I'm going."

"My son demands a trial." Millard grunts as he drops from the saddle. "He is correct."

"Kill me now, I'm done with this shit." Aunt Tess looks at me. It's like watching a fog settle in low places and my balled stomach turns. "Let her go, too, she won't fight you. It was all me. I won't fight you if you let her go."

She knows she's lying.

"Just run, Adelaide, run away forever."

Like that last horse.

Millard ignores her, slits a knife through the rope attaching her and Evangeline to the saddle Kane rides in. Neither of them run. There's nowhere to go.

"You look ready." She trails off like a shard of glass, thin and sharp. Viscous laughter.

It's not like Vesta anymore. Not waiting in dread, blood in the street.

I'm watching her die a hundred times. The moments she comes back are just a sick torture. If I ever had the chance to meet Amnesty and Isobel, I'd rip both their throats out.

Am I not infected, or am I just rotting slower than Aunt Tess is?

I don't want to give myself hope and watch it break. Out here, so far from any home I might have had.

I don't want to die. I'm not ready.

The Stranger unspools, rippled with dark fury. Relief flutters through me. She's still here.

Millard peels off his worsted jacket, then slings it over the saddle. Pit stains like tongue tracks, buttons fraying threads, one already missing. "My Timothy, my son, he asked for a trial. Justice. If you are so innocent, let Providence decide."

Kane swings his leg over the horse's freckled neck, cuts marring its cream-colored coat. "Father, let's talk about this."

"He's not the father you knew anymore," Evangeline says.

"I didn't ask for this."

Millard draws the revolver from his holster, its long silver barrel engraved with birds of prey and climbing roses. He removes all but one shot from the chamber, letting the rest splatter on the clay like broken shells. "Keep him out of the way."

The bullies take hold of Kane's cuffed arms and toss him across the white salt. When he tries to get up, they do it again and kick his stomach.

"Adelaide Revere." Millard winds the rope around his neck, then knots the other end to his horse's saddle horn. "Are you familiar with the pistol duel?" He catches the middle finger of his glove in his teeth and peels it off like skin. Full gloves make your hand bulky, slow. Sharp shooters like Leagan go no-gloves, or fingerless.

Fibers scrape my cheek, the bully pulling just tight enough the rope touches my windpipe. He attaches the tail to the other horse and points the animal away.

"Pistols at dawn," Millard slurs. "We will have thirteen paces between us, more than generous. The horses are not part of Jezebel's competitive pistol dueling, but as you all so like to inform, this is the Rim. Maybe we both get what we deserve."

A key rattles inside my cuffs. Fresh pain slices through my chest as my arms go slack.

Cool iron touches my dead fingers, the bully pushing a revolver into my left hand.

One bullet sits in the open chamber.

"*Sol sana*, fox," he chuckles.

You know what to do.

I don't trust this horse. A white ring shows around its brown eye, a wild eye, his feet listing toward the escape he wants to take. I can't blame him.

A flash of pain sharper and brighter than the salt stabs through my shoulder as I try to lift my right arm. *Farce.*

"Good Sister," Millard calls. "You be the one, the unbiased, doing Providence's work. Count to three."

"I will not," Evangeline says.

I transfer the revolver to my bloody right hand.

"Must I have to do everything myself?"

"Father, no." Kane's voice threatens to snap. "Don't! Have you lost your mind?"

He knows it's too late.

I push my left hand up through the slipknot, around the back of my skull so when this horse bolts, it won't snap my neck. My right fingers curl around the revolver like unworked leather.

I breathe in until the pain stops me. Air salt-dry, hot.

This *is* the Rim.

Millard prowls as close as the rope around his neck allows. Salt grinds under heels, teeth on teeth. "Let death determine your guilt. Of all of you. If you survive, then you must be innocent. If you die, then Providence says you're guilty and these two will be shot after you. On this day, you will get what you deserve *Adelaide sos*..."

He waits, the dangling space for my mother's name.

I lift my chin, the Stranger's shadow on him. If these are my last words I won't regret them.

"Adelaide *sos* Moira."

NINETY-ONE
ADELAIDE

My right arm only moves at the elbow, shoulder joint stuck like the clay, but Millard is close enough.

I told you.

The Rim has no rules.

I don't wait for him to count. He shows me his back, and I pull the trigger.

Never turn your back on an enemy.

The rope snaps taut under my chin, ripping into the back of my wrist and neck as the horse bolts.

NINETY-TWO
LEAGAN

SHE SHOT THAT FUCKER. IN THE BACK TOO. EVEN BETTER.

It's what I would have done. It's what *you* would have done too, don't lie. Unless you're an east blood rabbit like Kane. Go, Adelaide.

Now please don't die.

I sight in on the horse, its tail a flag, ears back, dragging Adelaide away by the neck. Fool's gold, it's blinding down there. I just need to drop one more lens...alkaline. That's much better.

The salt floor shines in the animal's eye, and I take a nice deep breath before the squeeze. I don't *like* to do it. That poor, pitiful horse never did anything to me, except almost kill my sister.

Verdict kicks my shoulder, the hot shell landing in the brim of my hat when I draw the bolt action. I love it when that happens, and gunpowder is the greatest smell in the world.

"There are still some pokey rocks under me. I hope you're better at being a doctor than you are at sweeping."

Pike doesn't say anything back because *he's* also a rabbit, and rabbits can never be rude.

I search with my scope for Adelaide. It's not like a pair of binoculars, it's a narrow view, that's how it works. White desert, white desert, oh there. She peels the rope from around her neck.

I lift my head for a moment to see where everyone else is then settle back down, *Verdict* in my shoulder pocket. "Got you, you fuckers. Kane, get out of the way or I'll shoot you too!"

Everyone's heard the expression, kill them with kindness. Fuck that. Why would I kill with kindness when I can kill them with death?

NINETY-THREE
ADELAIDE

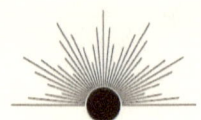

BLOOD POOLS AROUND THE HORSE'S HEAD. EYE-SOCKET SHATTERED. RED ON white. A burn line carves through the back of my arm, bleeds on my neck.

My back arches again, the cough thick. Fire.

I know what this pain in my stomach means when I try to stand, gut deep. I'm almost out of everything my body has left, it's warning me to stop before it does. But I can't.

Get up.

I drag myself to the bully lying dead a few feet away. Another one drops mid-sprint in front of me, the shot an echo. He has a double holster, two Exodus pistols. I load one into my distant right hand and grab the other in my left.

Get up.

An orange streak, the skin of the salt waste peeled back and bleeding. One bully fights with Millard's panicking horse while the other saws at the rope to cut him free.

Six…

Each step is so hard.

Aunt Tess walks, pointed out where the salt waste shrinks to a blurry line, arms held out to nothing. The last bully turns, sees her.

Crinkled sound buzzes in my head again. My heart is beating too fast, the world tunneling. Grey.

Farce.

I squeeze the trigger. Four times.

A metallic taste creeps up my throat. On my lips.

Bright red spots blossom on the salt. It's my tongue.

The sharp crystals grind on my palms. Burning.

I grab the gun again.

Leave her. Millard.

Kane stands in my way. "None of this is worth it." Tears well up in his eyes as he checks his stance. "Father, no. Don't make me do this. Please, don't."

Millard's steps stagger over themselves. He picks himself up once but when he falls again, he drops to the four-limbed bone picker crawl. He grabs the bully's still-sweaty neck and bites in.

A sob wrenches out of Kane. "Fuck."

My legs give out.

Millard turns, teeth bared. Blood oozes from his eye. He gallops at Kane.

"Fuck!"

A gunshot cracks. Just one.

Gunpowder. Smoke. Kane's.

He hits his knees, shoulders wrenching in on themselves.

I told him. The Rim will break you.

I've broken so many ways. But I've always found what I needed to put myself back together, learned how.

The salt is brittle, cracking under the weight of my head. I just want a full breath, but my racing heartbeat won't let me.

Evangeline pins Aunt Tess's mismatched arms against her torso, rocking her like a child until she stops struggling. They both look at me.

I reach for her, blood stains sitting in every crack on my hand.

I don't want to die.

NINETY-FOUR
LEAGAN

Adelaide's bloody. Bloody, bloody, even more than a dead person usually looks bloody. Fucking shit.

I kiss her forehead. I used to do that to wake her up when I was little, very early in the morning, then run away. She'd never get mad.

Aunt Tess has spit running out of her mouth, panting from fighting Evangeline's hold.

I saw her like this in my dream, but she still scares me.

I didn't tell anyone about this. It would have just made her upset. Maybe I thought it could change.

Adelaide's fingers are bad cold. The veins I usually see in her hands and arms have melted into her. This is what a ghostly pale person actually looks like. Too bad all these racist east bloods are too dead to see it. Just Kane, curled up over there like a little baby clutching his father's dead body while my sister he pretended to care about bleeds to death.

"Hurry up!" I yell at Dr. Pike. "A tortoise can run faster than you."

He puts fingers to her wrist pulse, wincing. "This doesn't look good."

"That's what you're here for. Open your magic medicine bag."

"Lay down next to her, hold on to her body. Cairosh medicine teaches that the body and the soul are like a fabric made of many fibers holding them together. It takes a while for all of them to separate. She might not be fully here, but she can still feel you and hold on a little longer."

"She got shot. I can see the hole right there."

"I'll cauterize the wound which will seal the open veins, but don't get your hopes too high. I'm worried she's lost too much blood already."

"I've got blood," I say. "She can have some of it."

"It might not be enough. Her body might also reject it. There's also organ damage to be considered if she does survive, from being without adequate blood flow for too long."

"Thanks a fartload, why don't you just go home then. I know she's dead without it, so what's the difference? Just try."

She thinks she deserves this, but I don't.

PART FOUR

NOTHING BUT MERCY

NINETY-FIVE
TESLA

I DO REMEMBER SOME OF IT.

Like a hangman's fever dream. The infection broke a few times, and I know I was still myself, then the madness sucked me back down. The sky was red as rage instead of blue, claws sprouting from the ground, angles suddenly jutting from people's spines and faces changing. Horrible, but in my rotting head, all of it was real and possible.

I remember watching my mother's head dropping from unknown hands and shattering on a black wood floor over and over again. I tried to catch her every time. And every time I failed, it would happen again.

When I actually wake, it's from a death-like sleep, dreamless and seeping with dread that somehow years have passed without me, but I recognize Navy, her hands gently cupping mine. This is her lab, on my beautiful *Exodus Ironclad*.

There's a needle attached to my arm. I trace it down a tube siphoning my blood into a copper still and back out into a sealed glass reservoir. It's beautiful, so very elegant, very Navy.

Her grip tightens. "Hello, Aunt Tess. How do you feel?"

"Like absolute shit that's been run over by a train." Squeezing Navy's hand makes the needle in my arm bite a little, but I do it anyway.

"I'm glad to hear it," she says, a tremble hiding in her voice. "You sound like you again."

"I need to drink some water."

"That's a good sign too."

My skin jumps when Dr. Pike's cold stethoscope touches my chest.

The watch ticking around Navy's neck dings. Dr. Pike closes the valve to the blood still and hangs the glass globe from a hook above my bed. It begins to slip back down the tube into my body, red like my favorite skirt.

In a rocking chair on the other side of the lab, swaddled with blankets like a small child in a storm sits Piety Goodson. She no longer has a right eye, the lid sewn shut and bruising receding from her jaw. I assume it was too late to save the desiccated eye, even for a Cairosh trained surgeon like Pike. But she's alive.

We are what survives.

Sand rubs in my raw throat, but my voice still comes out. "You did it, Rook."

Her smile breaks free of all her endless days spent toiling. "I did it."

NINETY-SIX
ADELAIDE

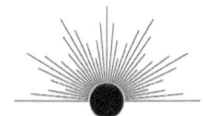

THERE'S A DIFFERENCE BETWEEN THINGS THAT ARE DEAD, AND THOSE THAT only appear that way.

This is my bed. On the *Exodus.* I know just by the smell.

Leagan's voice, reading to me. Then Raleigh's.

I told myself he died, so it wouldn't hurt so much when I found out I was right. But I couldn't do that with Leagan and Navy. I had to hold them in my head like the moons, find them. They can't ever die.

"You're not as good at this as me." She flips the page back. "He would say it like this—"

"I won't get better if you don't let me practice. Besides, art is interpretive, let me have my own vision, you bossy body."

Leagan slaps the book shut when she notices my eyes are open. "You're not dead!"

I'm not. My bloody death is still out there somewhere, someday.

She climbs into the bunk with me. Her gunpowder smell gets in my head.

"Careful of her shoulder," Raleigh says.

"I know." She shakes a green bottle. "Do you want some pills?"

"They're the fun kind," Raleigh says.

"Dr. Pike said you could have one. You didn't look so good when I found you. I guess it is lucky you never had time to kill him."

Grandma knew.

I shake my head. The Stranger doesn't like things that dull me because they pull us apart, and I don't like it when I can't feel her. That silver needle of fear that I might become my mother if I let my guard down is still lodged in me. "I'm okay."

As long as I don't move my right side, it doesn't hurt that much.

"You should still drink some water." Leagan reaches for the glass on my night table. "Do you need me to get you anything else?"

We were down to ten percent of our water the last time I checked. Now it has to be less. When you know you're running out, you always get thirstier.

"You already look better than I did at the beginning," Raleigh says.

"Show her your wound," Leagan urges.

"I don't think that's what she needs right now."

My legs itch. I need to get up. None of the details really left me, but the Stranger starts filtering them in one at a time. "Is Navy okay?"

Raleigh helps untangle the blanket from my legs as I sit up. "She's alkaline. Don't move too fast."

"We have some cheese and bread," Leagan says. "I'll get them for you."

I feel myself going numb inside the Stranger. "How long did Aunt Tess live?"

"She's here," Leagan says. "Come out to the living car and see her."

One-fifty.

Why am I afraid?

They're all sitting there at the table. Aunt Tess, Navy, and Evangeline.

Grandma and Vesta should be here too. This is when I feel their absence the worst, when we're all together.

"Look who it is," Leagan says.

Aunt Tess turns and beams at me. Splotches of red still haunt her eyes, but they're shrinking, faded. "Hello, Stranger."

NINETY-SEVEN
TESLA

I WEAR A BLACK DRESS, THE LACE COLLAR RISING UP TO MY NECK SCAR. IT seems most appropriate for the occasion. I won't lie, there are wings fluttering in my stomach.

I'm feeling better, especially after my blood filtration this morning, and it feels alkaline to put on real clothes again. Navy's still determining how many treatments it will take, or if I'll have to keep doing it for the rest of my life. If that's true, I won't complain because at least I get the rest of my life. My joints are still sore, especially my jaw and the socket around the tooth that fell out. At least it's in the back, there's a mercy.

I can't seem to drink enough water to quell my thirst, but we're running so low. It's time to leave.

Kane sits inside the guest car, picking through the box of belongings that survived the wildfire and slaughter in Caroline and the forward railroad camp. For their families, not himself.

The posts hung with pots and boots, animal bones and bunches of bound grass for hair still loom like giant skeletal remains in the background outside. The alter they built to some unknown god and feasted on each other to honor.

Fool's gold, I think I just caught the ghost of Green's wretched cologne still lurking in here. When I'm feeling stronger, I'll scrub the whole car.

Adelaide, Leagan, and Navy file in after me. This is our moment.

"We're almost out of water," I say. "We have to leave today."

Kane nods, eyes vacant like the shell town below. Just another sign of an overambitious plan to quickly settle the West Rim that was never going to last.

Some things aren't meant to be no matter how bad you want them.

"Did you find any survivors?" I ask.

"No."

"Did you find anyone?"

He shakes his head. "I'm sure there are still some of them out there."

"More deep west bone pickers." I set a folder on the tea table. In it is our land deed Millard never sent to the Jezebel assay office for notarization. He was nothing but a self-righteous liar like the rest of them.

"We never should have come here," Kane says. "This was all a mistake."

"Your investors back east will probably feel differently. I'm sure they'll find a way to advertise positively to the next wave of prospectors."

"Fuck them. I'm not letting anyone else come here. Not after this."

"That can be arranged." The deed was never sent, so it can be painlessly amended now. "Sell us the West Rim."

My gaze meets Adelaide's. I heard her say it to Millard, even in my madness. *Adelaide sos Moira.*

Adelaide, daughter of Moira.

We are her daughters, and this is what we deserve. What we came for in the beginning—a home, a future. Why take only what you need when you can take all of it?

And we fucking earned it.

The only thing he can say is no.

"I can't have anyone else on my conscience." Kane grabs my pen. "Take it. I just want to be done with this. I want to go home."

He crosses a line through the coordinates listed on the deed and writes in *the West Rim Territory in entirety, Timothy Von Kane.*

A spark ignites in the cold gray of Adelaide's eyes, but my smile breaks free.

"There." Kane shoves the folder away. "Just don't let this happen again."

"People come to the Rim for two things," I say. "Crystal and death. They all should have known what they were signing up for." Even with the lies spun by Von Kane Industries. But don't worry, we *will* do better. Our miners will have our contamination compasses and Navy's cure on their side, and they'll all know what they're walking into.

"I hope so."

"I'm sure your investors and leaseholders' agents will have something to say about this," Raleigh says.

"Let them say it," Kane says. "They weren't here. They didn't see what I saw. They didn't have to—"

Kill your father. Yes, that would take a toll on a man, especially one like him. An innocent fool when he first came here, now another soul claimed by the Rim. It leaves some alive too, to carry on the suffering. Maybe dreams were only designed to break your heart.

But not mine.

"I would say well played, but I know this wasn't all your doing," he says.

"I'm an opportunist, darling. And I saw opportunity."

I'll never stop being the Widow, but this does feel a little bit like the end of her somehow.

No, I don't like that. It's not the end of her, a new Season. One where I refuse to fear that what I love and what I want are going to be taken away from me.

Thunder grumbles, then the sky unbuttons, rain whiting out everything that isn't immediately next to us, dulling all other sounds in my ears.

"Quick," Navy says to Leagan. "Go open the collection hatch!"

"*Solace* comes early this year," I say. "Congratulations. We all made it through another Moon Season. Normally, people drink and have their neighbors over for a *Solace* dinner if they didn't kill them for their crystal already, but that feels inappropriate at this time."

"I think so," Kane says.

I unbolt the door and let the fresh air come piling in. Thick with moisture, heavy with atmosphere and soaked red earth.

Evan closes her eyes and sighs. "There's nothing like the first rain. It makes the world feel new again."

I remember Montoya lamenting how ugly the desert is, but if you actually look, you'll see how many beautiful, stubborn things thrive here, against all expectations.

Kane stares into the pools that have already formed outside. I can't say I'm immune to the torture in his eyes. I have a heart.

"We have to bring Evangeline home and get more supplies," I say. "Come with us back to Covenant. You can catch another train home from there."

He nods fragilely. "Thank you…I appreciate that."

"And the good news is, you won't have to travel alone," I say. "Raleigh and I will be joining you in case there are any disputes transferring the deed at the land office."

"I've always wanted to visit Jezebel and just haven't gotten around to it. So why not now?" Raleigh says. "I hear you have some fine dessert makers back there."

"I have to tell my mother what happened," Kane says suddenly. "This doesn't end even when I get home. How am I going to do that? What if it kills her?"

"Mothers aren't such weak glass creatures," I say. "She'll have to grieve, but she'll survive without him." Or maybe she'll secretly be relieved like I suspect my mother was. Who knows? Only her. "At least she still has you. She has friends."

He wipes a hand down his face, steadying his breath again.

I kneel next to his chair and put my arm around his back. He shudders at the touch. You poor soul, starved for comfort. "You'll be alright if you decide to be."

"You were deep into the infection," he says. "How did you survive?" Then his gaze turns to Navy. He already knows the answer. "You're a brilliant woman, you know. I hope you'll share your knowledge with the world, even if you think we east bloods don't deserve it."

I'd say *I know*. But that's not Navy, so I say it for her. "Yes, she is. We've known that for a long time now."

✳

LEAGAN STOPS ME IN THE PASSAGE AS I'M ON MY WAY TO CHANGE INTO MY engineering clothes.

"We can't leave yet, I have to show Adelaide something."

NINETY-EIGHT
ADELAIDE

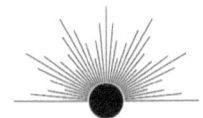

LEAGAN PICKS HER WAY ACROSS HUMPS OF EXPOSED ROCK, STILL DARKENED with rain and starting to steam.

"You know I don't like surprises."

"I know. This isn't a surprise," she says. "I just have something to show you."

Three-twenty-two.

Rock lizards dart away before we get too close, sagebrush and ironwood deepening until only the Rim can see us.

"Not much farther..." She skips ahead, descending through another split in the rocks.

We left the horses at the top of the hill. Maybe I should have kept riding. I still feel wrung out, but the Stranger has to know. My broken collarbone aches even with the sling. More than the hole through my shoulder does.

But I'm not dead. Somehow, I never got the pestilence.

And I am going to use this arm again someday.

Four-eighty-three.

Death has its own scent. Even if you've never smelled it before, you know it when you finally do. It's born part of us.

"The first time you came out here, you promised to bring me back something dead. Now it's my turn." Leagan splays her arms.

It's a pit. A few exposed roots sticking out of the rim, dry, crinkled.

Something dead, her favorite.

Black tails of scavenger lizards disappear inside the corpse as my shadow falls across it. His eyes, nose, and lips are gone, a cavity under his ribcage where all his soft organs were eaten up a while ago, fingers still clenching handfuls of dirt from a failed escape. A film of dust covers his suit, toothmarks on the waistcoat buttons, a copper beetle pin in his tie.

The Stranger simmers with glee.

Jonathaniel.

"It was me." Leagan's smile splits, an overripe plum, dark and loyal. "Me the whole time and nobody ever suspected a thing. I did it for you."

She would.

She kicks dirt onto him. "It was *so* hard to keep it to myself. But so satisfying hearing everyone speculating about what happened to him. He thought I was being so nice always taking him out to look for scavenger lizards. Ha ha." She puts her arm around me. "I wasn't going to let him get away with what he did to you. What do you want to do with him now?"

"Leave him," I say. "No one needs to know. He doesn't matter anymore. This is what he deserves."

He wanted to experience the Rim, another fool. He got his wish, died like one.

Off in the distance, the *Exodus Ironclad* moans. Aunt Tess said she'd blow the whistle if we weren't back on time.

"Fool's gold, she's impatient," Leagan says.

Not everyone deserves a sister this loyal. But I have one. "Thank you."

"I'd do it again. I know you could have done it yourself, but I wanted to do something nice for you. You deserve it."

NINETY-NINE
ADELAIDE

THE CHURCH IN COVENANT SITS ON THE BLUFF WHERE IT CAN LOOK DOWN ON the Salt Waste. It's white to the end of the horizon, and farther still, exposed and blinding, calling out to the Stranger.

Her longing never stops. Never will.

Forty-nine.

The door sways like an unconscious limb, track scraped into the floor both ways because someone stole the latches.

Kane sits on a cracked pew, flames guttering in a red prayer candle. Five of them cluster on the stone floor. Fresh.

Eleven.

I step on a broken bottleneck before I get too close. It snaps, sharp and glassy.

After the initial flinch, his shoulders go slack, and he looks down again, says nothing.

His train leaves in the morning. He knows why I'm here.

"Do you think anyone will forgive me?" he asks aloud. "Am I a murderer?"

For killing your own father.

"Probably."

This isn't like when you mercy-killed Randy, is it? This is personal. You finally know how I felt watching Vesta die. Like a part of you died with them.

"I'm probably a murderer?"

Don't ask too many questions at the same time.

"If I'd known Navy had a cure I wouldn't have...I could have saved him."

But you didn't. And he's assuming we would've given it to him.

"You got what you wanted," he says. Like I don't deserve it.

People like Aunt Tess get what they want. I want something that doesn't have any definite edges.

The West Rim is ours now. On paper, at least. We're going to have a permanent home. I can lose myself out there forever if I want, and always have a place to come back to when I'm tired of drawing maps.

But it's still the West Rim.

Bone pickers will crawl across it. Claim jumpers and roadmen and future east bloods, grabbing at more. But it's as close to mine as a thing like the Rim will ever be, even though I'm not big enough to absorb it like the Stranger wants.

I never really thought she'd be satisfied.

I hold out the page I cut from his first expedition journal. The sketch he did of a group of cactuses at moonrise, the sky still lilac, beaded with sugar bats. It's his best one.

I'm not giving the whole journal back.

Kane stares at it for a long time. Different lines wrinkling in his forehead as his thoughts rotate like a revolver barrel. "Thank you." He finally stands, tucks the page into his back pocket, reaches for my hand.

I let him. The Stranger lets me.

"This is goodbye. I know."

Carefully, he opens his arms. I don't flinch this time.

His chest shakes as the breath floods out, vibrating in my hair as I bring my arm to rest against his back, my right side still encased in the sling. He presses his lips to my head. "I'm sorry."

"Don't be sorry." Like Grandma used to say. "Be better."

Better than your father. Raise a better son.

"I will." He squeezes me and lets go.

"You were right." He stamps his mouth shut to stop his chin from trembling. "The Rim isn't what I thought it would be."

I know.

"I got caught up in something I can never have, wishful thinking...But I'm still glad I met you."

All the bad things and the parts that were good. He was my friend once.

"Goodbye, Adelaide."

"Goodbye." The word feels wrong on my tongue. I don't say it. I usually just go.

I imagine he feels cold.

The Stranger knows he's watching as I walk away. Until the door shudders closed, until I'm gone.

He'll never see me again.

I can live with that.

ONE HUNDRED
TESLA

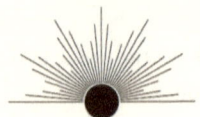

– One Season Later –

THERE IS HORROR IN SURVIVAL. BUT THERE IS ALSO TRIUMPH IN LIVING ON, rebuilding what serves you and leaving what doesn't to rot. Really, it's a sweet rebellion against everyone who wanted us dead.

Leagan flicks a grasshopper off her arm as she, Adelaide, and Dilly come up the path the through the new garden. "That's why you shouldn't wear skirts. One wrong move and there's bugs up your dress."

Gunpowder trails in their wake, a range of Leagan's new modifications between them.

"How did it go?" I call.

"I still have all my fingers!"

"It looks like you still have to wait for that big scar you want."

Piety hands me another bunch of lima beans sprouted in the window box, a forest of white roots blossoming from the bottom. The malt of soil fertilized by goats rises up as I pack them in for the Season.

I brush stray dirt away from the permanent needle bite in the crook of my elbow. I still need the blood filtration once a month, for now at least. Dr. Pike said I likely have some organ damage, but it's an acceptable ransom to pay, and I'm reminded of that every time I touch the raw earth.

Navy is in her lab with Raleigh right now, working on stage two of her pestilence research. She hopes for a tablet or tonic that will stop the body from absorbing the poison altogether.

Adelaide turns suddenly. The familiar pit splits open in my stomach as she drops the bag of experimental weapons and unholsters her new crossgun.

"What is it?" I stop at the weapon cache in our homestead's outer wall and pick an Exodus rifle before I join them on the downhill path.

Leagan glances at my naked arm. "Where's your rifle rest attachment?"

"Inside. It looks like it's only three riders, you two can handle it, I'll just look menacing."

They get closer, and I see we don't need the weapons at all.

"Evan?" My laugh almost sparkles in the air. "What are you doing here? It's goat birthing season."

"We have three new ones," Leagan says. "They are all very naughty."

"I have the other Sisters well trained." Evangeline dismounts. With her are two ladies I don't recognize.

The young woman springs from the saddle, honey gold hair and arms open wide. "Yes, it's me, Thadie!"

The other wears a deep hood to keep the sun off her face, but I see a white braid creeping out from the recess like moonlight.

Adelaide's smile moves like a rabbit, peeking from the safety of the burrow as she steps toward them, but it's there.

"Are you unhappy to see us?" the Tov woman says. "If you are, tell me, so. You won't hurt my feelings."

Thadie reaches out, ink-splattered hands connecting both of them. "She's happy."

"I've missed you." I breathe in Evangeline's leather jacket until I taste it, but I'm still a little dubious as to why she's here. I had braced myself for it to be another few Seasons before either of us had a chance to travel so far to see each other again. Of course, my dreams took me in the opposite of her. They always do.

"These two found their way to me," Evangeline says. "They were looking for their friend the Stranger. In the between time, I've been praying, and I've realized something so very important." She takes my hand. "You are important to me, Tesla Revere, and I'm not willing to live with the regret of so much space between us. Where you go is where I want to be."

My heart clenches, and I don't dare breathe. It's the only thing I ever wanted to hear from Travis and exactly what I never got.

"What about Damascus?" I say.

"Damascus is in alkaline hands. Della and Rebessa will care for it and the lost souls that find them as well as I ever did. They proved that while I was gone on the West Rim."

I'm afraid to believe in this, my dream being so complete, can I really ask for more? But I want to.

She cups her hands on my sweaty face. "I choose you."

ONE HUNDRED ONE
TESLA

– Five Seasons Later –

IT'S ALWAYS A TREAT TO COME HOME AFTER A LONG TRIP.

"How was Jezebel this time?" Evangeline asks.

"I ate far too much cheese," Raleigh groans. "I hope my clothes still fit."

"There's no such thing as too much cheese," I say. "It's just an excuse to buy new clothes. Evan, I'll have to show everything I got. I couldn't stop myself."

"Well, you have to look good for the other crystal barons," Raleigh says.

"We brought you back presents," Leagan says.

"That's so kind," Evangeline says. "And how was the lecture, Navy?"

"No one snickered or talked over me this time."

"They didn't call you little girl or darling this time, either," I say. "They all said Miss Revere."

"That's true, they didn't."

"Well, that is an improvement," Evangeline says. "They're learning to open their minds."

"It's taken them long enough, but yes, they're learning," I say. "You should definitely come with us next time. Her lecture was alkaline."

"I'm sure it was."

"And you missed out on the bundt cake shop," Leagan says. "They had new flavors. One was violet poppyseed."

"The board of medicine asked if I'd stay for a full Season in their lab next time," Navy says. "Everything paid for."

"It's a very impressive offer," I say. "It won't be long before we have to start calling you doctor."

"I'm still thinking it over," Navy says. "It's very exciting getting to work with their equipment, but I'd rather be here with all of you."

"You should do what's best for you," I say. "And...that's not all."

She flushes. "I get to write a book. The University press has gotten so many requests for my printed papers they want more."

"I'm so proud of you," Leagan says. "My sister, smarter than all those fools and their ugly moustaches."

"You should be very proud," Evangeline says. "You earned this."

"It doesn't feel real sometimes."

Leagan bounces off her seat, occupied with what we're all probably wondering. "Is she home?"

"Not yet, little darling."

Raleigh nods somberly. "How long has she been gone this time?"

"It's been a while."

"Typical. I'm sure she's fine."

I look out at the western mesas piling up into bluish mountains, way out past where our mines poke holes in the hillsides and sightlines end. "She must have gone far."

EXIT

Nightmare and I come to the end of the ridge. Red rock drops away into the valley. Gold.

Our home is made of red stone, green gardens, the *Exodus Ironclad* a black widow snake sunning itself in the background, the constant moon a silver nailbed.

My name is Adelaide Revere.

Welcome to Damascus Vesta.

We live here now, at the end of the Moira Valley Line.

THE END

Thank you for reading! Did you enjoy? Please add your review because nothing helps an author more and encourages readers to take a chance on a book than a review.

Don't miss more from J.L. Delavega at www.jldelavega.com

And find your next read, ABOVE THE FOLD, by Corrina Lawson. Turn the page for a sneak peek!

You can also sign up for the City Owl Press newsletter to receive notice of all book releases!

SNEAK PEEK OF ABOVE THE FOLD

BY CORRINA LAWSON

Trisha staggered to her motorcycle just as hangover dizziness hit full force. She dropped to one knee on the slimy blacktop of the narrow alley, clutching the soft leather of the bike's seat for balance. A deep breath brought a whiff of urine and wet rats into her nostrils.

The rising sun peeked over the far corner of the four-story brick monstrosity that held the punk club where she'd spent the night.

Best time to see the sunrise, when I'm ready for bed.

But the beeper in her jacket pocket vibrated. Her fingers fumbled over a wad of tissues, breath mints, quarters, and subway tokens before she finally clutched the beeper.

Her editor's number stared at her from the display.

Damn. Phone. Now. Back inside.

As she turned, the sunlight caught the tank of her restored Indian Chief, making the bike's Indian head logo seem like it was mocking her.

Her sunglasses cut the morning glare enough for her to stumble past the dumpster to the back door of the club from which she'd come. She slapped her hand against the bricks for balance, inadvertently placing her palm right in the middle of the "beware" in the "Beware Out-of-Towners" message spray-painted on the wall.

She pushed past through the creaky, crooked door into the club, where the smell of smoke washed over her. The darkness, such a contrast to the dawn, nearly blinded her. Oh, right. Sunglasses off.

"Dick!' she called.

"Jesus, Red, you don't have to shout," Dick answered from his post behind the bar. "Thought you'd gone. I'm just about to clear out the refuse."

Trisha's eyes adjusted to the light, seeing several people passed out on stage. They'd be in for a rude awakening. Dick wasn't gentle, she knew by experience.

She made the universal gesture for a phone. "Need to make a call. Now." She held up her beeper.

"Aren't we important this morning." But Dick slammed the club's phone on top of the bar.

"Hell, yeah, I'm important. The paper can't run without me," she shot back, sliding onto the stool. She could ask for water, but who knew what was swimming in it. "How about a Coke?"

Dick rolled up his shirtsleeves, dug into the ice, and tossed her the can he'd found. She caught it with one hand. Jolt. Perfect.

"Nice reflexes after all that tequila," Dick said.

"Thanks." She searched her back pants pocket and dropped a five on the bar. It stuck to something. Not her problem. Let Dick peel it off.

She cursed as it took forever to dial the old rotary phone.

"Connell," she announced as someone picked up.

"Trisha, sorry for taking up your day off—"

City Desk Editor Joe Wilson sounded crisp and businesslike and not the least bit sorry. An alcohol-induced migraine, centered just above her left eye, made it hard to focus on his words.

"—but I need you to get to City Hall in the next hour, to cover a press conference about the new zoning regulations."

"*Zoning regulations*?" It sounded worse when she repeated it. "Joe, I'm a crime reporter. Why am I covering zoning regulations? Put a stringer on it."

"Cardoza wants it covered, which means a stringer won't do, and Tony's in court all day. We need someone who can write something catchy, not boring, about this."

"Hell." Cardoza, the publisher of the *New York Herald*. Joe's boss.

Trisha cradled the phone in her ear and pulled out the little notebook and pencil she kept in the inside pocket of the black leather jacket. "Exact time. Which room at City Hall. Anything else you got."

Joe rattled off the information, adding the names of the deputy mayor holding the press conference. Behind her, she heard Dick hauling the remnants of his customers to their feet.

"Got it," she said. "Anything else?"

"Be aware of any undercurrents. Word is that this is just a money grab by developer friend of the deputy mayor. The rest of the reporters will ask polite questions. You won't."

A chance to harass a deputy mayor at City Hall? The assignment was looking up. Some water and aspirin, and she'd be able to focus.

"Oh, and be presentable, Trish. Cardoza is watching this story. He'll hear if you roll up to the press conference looking like a punk."

"He wants me to wear a dress, he can buy me a damn car. He wants me to get there on time, I need to use the Indian."

"Look half-businesslike, at least. Don't show up looking like one of the Ramones."

"The Slits are the female punk band." Trisha took inventory of her clothes. The blue jeans, faded T-shirt, leather jacket, and motorcycle boots weren't even half-businesslike. Not to mention the smell from the whiskey someone had spilled on her.

Dammit, this was supposed to be her day off.

"Sure. No problem."

"Every time you say that, there's a problem. You're not home, are you?" A long pause followed, broken by one of Joe's familiar long-suffering 'what-the-hell-are-you-doing-with-your-life' sighs. "Trisha, have you even been to bed?"

"I'll sleep when I'm dead."

"You know I've got no choice on this."

That was as close as Joe would get to an apology for putting her in a tough spot, "I know," she said. "I'll be there and get what you need."

She hung up, fished a couple aspirin out of her inside pocket, brushed off the lint, and washed them down with the Jolt. She pulled out the Celtic cross she wore around her neck and kissed it, wondering how the hell she'd get presentable in an hour. She'd never make it to Midtown, then crosstown to her place in Hell's Kitchen, and back to City Hall in time for the press conference.

She chugged the rest of the Jolt and dialed another number.

"Hey! Time's up," Dick called.

"Just a sec," she called, putting her back to him. Dick might have grabbed the phone out of her hand, but the kid stumbling out the front door threw up, drawing his attention.

David, be home, she thought. She was only five blocks from David's place near the Village.

He answered. *Score.*

"Hey, I need a favor. I—"

"Hey, Trish, not in position for favors today."

He shouted in Spanish. A horn sounded. Not his apartment. The call must have been forwarded to his car phone.

"What's wrong?" she asked.

"Ah, the damned museum exhibit. It's been a pain in the ass since day one. Now there's some minor deal about the alarm and Grayson's being fussy about it, so I got dragged out of bed to check it out."

"You sure everything's okay?"

Dick slopped a mop at the mess on the floor. She figured she had sixty seconds before he cut off her call.

"It's fine. Like I said, it's probably Grayson overreacting." David shouted again at the other drivers, this time in English. "Look, Trish, what did you want, anyway?"

"I need to get a change of clothes from your place. Is the coast clear?" David's fiancée wasn't her biggest fan.

The sound of squealing tires echoed in the background. "Yep, Darlene's at her mother's place this week, studying. Take whatever you need," he said.

"Thanks. Be careful out there, okay?"

"Always am, unlike you," he said. "Wait, Trish, you're not in trouble, are you?"

"Not yet. But it's early."

"You be careful then, too. Later."

She hung up, yelled thanks to Dick, received a grumble in response, and slipped out the back door again.

This could work. If her memory served, David had a blazer she could borrow that would be suitable over one of his T-shirts. Not strictly businesslike but, hey, *Miami Vice* style jackets with T-shirts were all the rage now.

She might even have time for a shower there.

Waitaminute.

She hadn't concentrated on what David said because she'd been worried about her own problems. But he'd said his boss rousted him out of bed to answer a possible alarm at the museum. David's security firm had installed a sophisticated system to protect a high-profile art exhibit at the Museum of Historic Arts. Several anonymous threats had been made against that exhibit, which contained artwork once lost in World War II. (Presumably, the museum had bought the art from Nazis or their heirs.)

An alarm might mean a break-in and that would equal a big story, especially given the Nazi connection. A story that would beat the hell out of some press conference about mind-numbing zoning regulations, even if the developers were paying off the deputy mayor.

Political corruption equaled business as usual.

Nazis and a museum art theft on the other hand? That was a juicy story. An above-the-fold headline story.

Option one: take the sure thing, file the required story, and get in good with Cardoza.

Option Two: Disobey a direct order on a hunch that, if it fizzled, would get her fired.

Her hand hovered over the scars carved into her midsection. Following the rules had never gained her a damn thing. She jerked the gloves out of her jacket and shoved her hands into them, using her boot heel to push the kickstand up.

A bald guy dressed in skinny black jeans and the remains of a T-shirt stumbled into the alley. His eyes widened.

"Well, hey, sweetheart," he drawled. "You are a damn fine sight this morning."

Skinhead. Thrash metal dude. The club had been full of them last night, even though the band had been pure three-cord punk. But hardcore fought to replace it. Gah. Another great scene lost.

"Buzz off," she said.

He stumbled closer, aiming to cut her off. "Aw, c'mon, I saw you in there, redhead, fooling around. Give us a kiss to celebrate the morning."

With a flick of her wrist, the switchblade appeared in her hand. Another flick, and the blade opened. "Get the fuck out of my way."

"Shit." He scrambled backwards. "Jesus, bitch," he said as he vanished around the corner.

Bitch is right, she thought, as she closed the switchblade and dumped it back into a pocket.

The Indian roared to life, echoing in the alley. Trisha burned rubber as she turned and accelerated onto the street.

⁕

Grayson slowed down to a brisk walk as he approached the entrance to the *Lost Treasures* exhibit. The click of his wingtips echoed around him, with the shadowed, silent faces in the hanging paintings the only witnesses to his concern.

He turned the corner and blinked at the change from the dim nightlights to the overhead fluorescents illuminating the exhibit's entrance.

Museum Security Chief Conrath stood by the door, his thumbs hooked in his belt and his feet in a wide, belligerent stance.

"I told you, nothing's wrong. You should have stayed home," he said.

If nothing was wrong, why was Conrath so defensive?

"Give me a status report."

"I don't report to you."

A familiar attitude. Conrath had been mulish from the start about working with a private security firm.

"For matters concerning this exhibit, yes, you do report to me," Grayson said.

For a moment, Conrath met his gaze. Then he dropped his stance and jabbed a thumb at the exhibit entrance. "Your alarm's got a glitch. But the door is locked tight. No one's gone in or out. We're secure."

"I'll check inside for myself, thank you," Grayson said.

Conrath stepped in front of him, blocking Grayson from the door. "It's not your problem."

"Exactly what are you afraid I'll find inside?" He kept an eye on Conrath's gun hand. This could be the man being difficult, as usual. Or it could be something far more sinister.

"Okay, fine, it's an employee problem, and I'd hoped to cover for her. I don't want to fire the girl."

"What did she do?" Grayson asked.

"Abandoned her shift," Conrath admitted. "But that's my problem."

"There's a guard *unaccounted* for?"

"I knew you'd view it that way. But she probably just took off without telling her supervisor. You know how college students are, especially girls."

None of this reassured him. "Which guard?" Grayson asked.

"Adrienne Katz."

"The criminology student?" She'd followed Grayson around, asking exactly the kinds of questions that a person who wanted a career in law enforcement should ask. "It's highly unlikely she'd leave her post voluntarily. For any reason."

"Girls are unpredictable and emotional." Conrath shrugged. "They often think what's a major crisis is only a minor one."

"You checked inside *Lost Treasures* to be sure she wasn't there?"

"I checked to make sure no one went in or out." Conrath glared. "No passcode has been used. I didn't go inside, and it wasn't worth calling the director about."

Entry required two keys plus a passcode to open the door to *Lost Treasures*. Grayson had all three, as did his partner, and his main assistant, David Velasquez. But only the director had all three on the museum side.

"With a guard missing, I should have been alerted instantly, not brought here by an alarm. We need to go inside the exhibit." Grayson suspected Conrath knew, deep down, that the problem was more than a missing guard and wanted to blame Grayson for whatever mess this turned into.

Or else Conrath was involved in something.

Grayson pulled out his keys, though he never took his eyes off Conrath. Most museum robberies were inside jobs.

There were no signs of tampering—either on the entry panel or the locks above and below the door—nor could he see any marks on the heavy metal of the door itself.

"Use your key. They need to be inserted simultaneously," Grayson said. He could do it himself, but then he wouldn't be able to watch the other man.

"Fine," Conrath snapped. "Let's get this over with and then I can get back to doing my job."

Grayson hated the idea of going inside with only Conrath as an unreliable back-up. David would be far better. Where the hell was his second?

As if on cue, David jogged into view around the corner, his sneakers squeaking as he skidded to a halt. A waist holster containing a Glock was strapped crookedly to his belt. Customary stubble decorated his chin, but the lack of a blazer pointed to hurry.

About time.

"Check your outer alarms again, Chief," Grayson said, dismissing the man. "David and I will go into the exhibit."

Conrath glared, deliberately let the key drop to the floor, and stomped off.

"What's his deal?" David pulled out his set of keys.

"The usual griping about outside contractors. At least, I hope that's all it is."

Grayson and David slid their keys in the twin locks and turned them simultaneously. The upper and lower deadbolts disengaged. Grayson punched in the passcode and drew his Beretta out of his shoulder holster, comforted by the familiar weight in his hand. "A guard is missing. The entire area must be secured. Take no chances."

"Yes, sir." David drew his Glock.

Grayson pushed open the door, gun and gaze sweeping from right to left.

On the far wall, the once pristine white paint was covered with black swastikas that resembled malevolent spiders crawling towards the ceiling. The five masterpieces by Cezanne were gone, their frames empty. A crumpled figure in a museum security uniform lay motionless on the floor below. The pieces of a crushed security radio decorated the floor near her.

"Fuck," David breathed out.

Oh, bloody hell, no. His English mother's favorite curse sounded in Grayson's mind.

He tapped David on the shoulder, silently asking for cover. David nodded, his face white. Grayson rushed to the downed guard.

His fingers sought the pulse at her throat, hoping beyond hope. But no breath, no pulse, nothing.

Grayson pushed Katz's hair away from the other side of her head. Half of her skull was smashed in. Pieces of white cranium mixed with bright red blood. A lumpy mess that must be part of her brain had leaked onto the black marble floor.

Bile rose in his throat. He swallowed, the acid burning his tongue.

"We need to secure the rest of the exhibit," he said through clenched teeth.

David glanced at the dead guard, swallowed hard, and nodded.

They moved in silence through the twists and turns of this wing of the museum, searching for anything out of order in the other six rooms. Nothing. The perpetrators were long gone, and oddly, they'd only taken five paintings.

Having secured the scene, they returned to Katz's body.

So young. Katz was only four years older than his own daughter. How had she gotten inside without keys or passcode? Who had relocked the main door? And how had the thieves gotten inside the exhibit without leaving any traces in the rest of the museum?

David holstered his weapon, knelt over the girl, murmured a blessing in Spanish, and made the signs of the cross. Grayson seconded the prayer. He'd made a mistake, somewhere… one that led to this woman's death. Her blood was quite literally on his hands.

He took a deep breath and smelled something odd and out-of-place. "Notice that?"

David sniffed. "Gasoline."

"That or something like it."

The odor originated at the base of the wall where the paintings had been.

"What does that mean?" David asked.

"I'm not sure yet. But we need to leave all this alone until the police arrive to process the crime scene."

"911?" David asked.

"No, you call 911 and it'll go out on the scanner. We'll have a media circus here." He stood. "I'm calling in Dorothy at Major Crimes. I'll use the phone at the front desk. You stay here." He closed his eyes for a second. "Watch over her."

"Of course." David glanced over at Katz and the wall full of the hateful Nazi symbols. "We need to get these assholes."

"Yes."

Not only had Grayson's security failed to protect the exhibit, it'd failed to protect an innocent young woman.

He'd get them, no matter what it took.

*

Don't stop now. Keep reading with your copy of ABOVE THE FOLD by City Owl Author, Corrina Lawson.

And sign up for J.L. Delavega's newsletter to get all the news, giveaways, excerpts, and more!

Find more from J. L. Delavega now at www.jldelavega.com

And then, discover ABOVE THE FOLD by City Owl Author, Corrina Lawson.

●

In 1980s New York City, a crime reporter with little to lose risks the only thing that matters to uncover the truth....

Trisha Connell's journalism reflects her punk rock lifestyle: relentless, confrontational, and bitingly honest. It's a style that scores front-page headlines but has her forever teetering on the verge of victory or disaster. Now one crime will forever change Trisha's life.

As she charges into the story of a sensational theft at an art museum, she discovers a murdered guard is someone she knew, a former foster kid who was adopted and supposed to be living a good life. To make it worse, the guard is suspected to be one of the thieves.

Determined to uncover the truth, Trisha bulls her way into the story, risking her life and career on what could be the story of the decade, if her editor doesn't fire her first. She finds an ally in Edmund Grayson, a security expert assigned to the museum, who's driven by his own guilt in failing to stop the murder.

Chasing the story will take Trisha from the punk clubs to the high society to the inner workings of newspapers of New York in the 1980s. It will take all her street skills to survive.

●

All reviews are **welcome** and **appreciated**. Please consider leaving one on your favorite social media and book buying sites.

Escape Your World. Get Lost in Ours! City Owl Press at www.cityowlpress.com.

ACKNOWLEDGMENTS

Thanks to the following: sisters, brothers, and friends, grandmothers and mothers, aunts and cousins, people I have loved, and those I always will.

Tee, it's been a pleasure to tell the Revere's story and grow as an author with your help. And thank you to the team at City Owl for the work put into these books.

My agent, Sarah, thanks for always being willing to help out and answer questions. Time to go write more books! Matt, even though you weren't involved in the writing of this final book, you're still the one who sold the series.

All my best book friends: Sarah my favorite Goblin, Kristin, LB, Dino Derek, Mykalee & Marla. Writing is a solitary pursuit, but you all make it less of a lonely road.

* Special thanks to the Situation Pannel for your dedicated work on the "Pants or No Pants" discourse. *

And one more bow to Olive for suggesting the glorious, savage ending of Kane and Millard. (I still wish I'd thought of it first). It's perfect. She also saved sweet Raleigh's life on a late night in August. Because of her he lives and has a future.

ABOUT THE AUTHOR

J.L. DELAVEGA is the award-winning author of feminist bloodbath THE REVERE TRILOGY.

Her work has been recognized for its unique blend of western gothic meets dark fantasy and horror. *Smoke and Other Storms* has been nominated for numerous awards and won the Reader's Favorite silver medal for western fiction (2024).

She lives in the Las Vegas desert and could say she makes all her own clothes but that would be a lie.

www.jldelavega.com

facebook.com/Ninjenaiyauthor

instagram.com/ninjenaiyauthor

threads.net/@ninjenaiyauthor

ABOUT THE PUBLISHER

City Owl Press is a cutting edge indie publishing company, bringing the world of romance and speculative fiction to discerning readers.

Escape Your World. Get Lost in Ours!

www.cityowlpress.com

facebook.com/CityOwlPress

x.com/cityowlpress

instagram.com/cityowlbooks

pinterest.com/cityowlpress

tiktok.com/@cityowlpress

www.ingramcontent.com/pod-product-compliance
Lightning Source LLC
Chambersburg PA
CBHW021844010726
47493CB00005B/1546